MIDNIGHT ROAD

"Old Trails was ugly of frame, face and temper. For the life of me, I couldn't understand how he could have sired Samal. Not that Sam didn't have a temper, too. She had a short fuse and could cuss a blue streak. Her tantrum storms were short-lived, usually, but they were entertaining while they lasted. The only thing wrong with her that I could see was that she turned into a creature of soft curves...."

So begins the story of 15-year-old Jeff Carr as he begins to grow up one Texas summer, and face some of the harsh truths around him. Everyone says he favors easy-going Kenty Hooker more than his own dad, Bant Carr, but folks always have to have something to talk about. Jeff's got other things on his mind—like Sam, who is turning into a woman in front of him; and her brother Coy, whose mean streak is suddenly getting a lot wider. And Fergus, the brother they don't talk about; the one who lives under the house to avoid the beatings of Coy and Old Trails. But while Jeff is making the Trails family his business, Bant is nursing a brooding pain that will soon explode into violence. That year, none of their lives will ever be the same.

JADA M. DAVIS BIBLIOGRAPHY

One for Hell (Gold Medal, 1952)
The Outraged Sect (Avon, 1956)
Midnight Road (Stark House, 2014)
So Curse the Day (unpublished, 1981)

Midnight Road

By Jada M. Davis

STARK
HOUSE

Stark House Press • Eureka California

MIDNIGHT ROAD

Published by Stark House Press
1315 H Street   ·
Eureka, CA 95501, USA
griffinskye3@sbcglobal.net
www.starkhousepress.com

ISBN: 1-933586-54-0
ISBN-13: 978-1-933586-54-0

Cover design and layout by Mark Shepard, www.SHEPGRAPHICS.COM
Proofreading by Rick Ollerman

The publisher would like to thank Mark and Jeff Davis for all their help in bringing their father's book into print, and for sharing their memories of growing up in Texas.

First Stark House Press Edition: February 2014

First Edition

Contents

Contents

MIDNIGHT ROAD:
THE QUIET NOIR OF JADA DAVIS

BY RICK OLLERMAN

West Texas is a vaguely defined semi-arid to arid land filled with small mountain ranges and rugged terrain. The annual rainfall is less here than in any other part of the state. Communities are mostly rural in nature and this was as true more than a century ago as it is today. In the early twentieth century, all these things had a much greater impact on the relatively poor residents of this hard and unforgiving land.

Jada Davis was born here in 1919, one of eleven brothers and sisters. The family had little money and as children, Davis and his siblings were sent out to pick cotton for whatever extra they could, but the family remained poor. When the Great Depression hit, Davis said it brought no measurable change to their lives: they were already that far down. If rain didn't fall, crops didn't grow, and the family struggled for food. It was a hardscrabble way of living with few ways out.

There weren't many escapes available to children like Davis, and he found relief in reading, whether it was old newspapers, catalogs, or magazines like *True Detective* and *Wild West Weekly*. Eventually a neighbor gave Davis a box of old books and it was like finding gold. He read those books over and over again, and they would come to inform his life. Davis began writing himself and sold his first story to *Liberty* magazine when he was just fifteen.

When World War II hit, Davis had already joined the Army but contracted tuberculosis and spent the fighting years in a hospital sanitarium. Afterwards, still wanting to contribute, he volunteered for medical radiation experiments. Although he remained healthy for many years afterwards, he would eventually die of lung cancer in 1996.

In his post-service life, Davis became an editor and a writer for newspapers back in the land where he came from, West Texas. Though he had submitted his first novel to Random House when he was just eighteen, and another while attending the University of Texas, it wasn't until 1952 when Fawcett Red Seal published *One for Hell*. This was followed by another paperback original, this time from Avon in 1956, called *The Outraged Sect*.

The books themselves could not be more different although both were based on an accumulation of Davis's real-life experiences as a West Texas newspaperman. *One for Hell* is as tough and noirish a story as you'll find, the tale of a drifter named Willa Ree. The book opens as Ree, a functioning so-

ciopath, is riding the rails with a man who tries to rob him. Ree drives him
off and offers to fight, but the other man backs down good-naturedly. They
get to talking amicably (as long as Ree promises not to throw him off the
train) and Ree tells him his name but the man pronounces it as "Willie." Ree
spells it out for him:

> W-I-L-L-A. The other man laughs and Ree slugs him, breaking his jaw.

This opening shows the dual sides of Willa Ree, a big, physical presence
with just enough smarts to look out for himself and just enough polish for
others to think they could use him to further their own ends. All of them
are wrong. Willa Ree falls into a situation where he can be of use to a power
broker of a rail-stop town, and each of them take advantage of the other in
a rising crescendo of violence and corruption. We know someone's going to
blink, something's going to crack, but Ree is resilient and rides out the crest
far longer than he ought, until his own amorality, strength and raw guts are
inevitably overwhelmed by forces maybe not much better than he is.

In contrast, *The Outraged Sect* is the story of a good man in a bad town, a
reporter sticking his neck out for peace and justice where it involves a group
of non-violent sectarians, a people just looking for a place to live in peace.
Rumors begin flying and soon the townspeople are all worked up in those
Cold War years about communists and being on the wrong side of patriot-
ism. One man, Book Morris, who run the local paper, tries to do what's right
not only for The Sect but also for the town of Oasis. But like Willa Ree in
One for Hell, where you have a bad man against a good town, *The Outraged
Sect* gives us the reverse. At some point, the sheriff calls Morris in for a meet-
ing:

> "Have a seat, Book."
> "I'll stand."
> [The sheriff] sat down and lit a cigarette. "Book, you're always fight-
> ing me these days. How come?"
> "I'm not fighting you, King. In a way, I'm fighting for you. I'm try-
> ing to stop you and the people of this town from making a bad mis-
> take. You're not being fair. You're throwing justice and decency out
> the window. Maybe you're doing what you think is right. I don't
> know. But I do know this. I'll be fighting you from here on in. I'll fight
> you any way I can. [...]"

They argue about corruption in the department and the situation is far
from defused.

> "You're getting in my way, Book. You've needled my department with
> those sly little articles, and I'm not too dumb to know when you're
> slanting things against me. You're in my way and I'm going to walk
> all over you."

"You'd better wear boots."

And the die is cast for the rest of the book and its final showdown. If *One for Hell* is Town vs. Man, then *The Outraged Sect* is Man vs. Town. Davis once said grocers had stacks of his books for sale with signs lettered, "Read about people you know."

Davis later turned down an offer to develop his writing career in New York and took a job with Southwestern Bell that offered much greater economic security. Although he ended up as a senior executive in public relations, Davis said he had hoped to retire early and resume the career he "should never have abandoned."

But he did keep writing, leaving us at least two unpublished manuscripts that may indeed be the pair he described as being better, in his opinion, to both of his published works. *So Curse the Day*, written in 1961, is the story of another drifter, a femme fatale, and the turmoil a determined and talented stranger can bring to a small town.

The other is *Midnight Road*.

There are stories in the deep rural areas of all parts of the country, every-day stories lost in the bigger events and happenings of their states, regions and countries. These stories are the small ones, the quiet ones that are loud in people's lives, tales of the events that shake and form an individual into who he or she is, or who they'll eventually turn out to be. Hard work and personal tragedy were no strangers to the people of the semi-frontier of West Texas in the late nineteen twenties, and here Davis gives us a deep look into the life of a young boy named Jeff Carr. He lives as an only child in a hand-built house on a farm in a valley, working side by side with a man he loves as a father but calls only Bant (short for "Bantrim"), and his mother, Pearl.

Davis gives us a glimpse at some of the many ways a rural fifteen year old can lose his innocence, while at the same time showing us the many ways adults can hide what they see before them. Davis's world in *Midnight Road* will touch you in the way old photographs call up sensations from your childhood past, with images familiar yet strange, happy and sometimes un-fulfilled, even some perhaps unremembered altogether. Good times and dark times side by side, joy and bitterness, recalled and forgotten.

This is a world where friends are friends but can still suffer a fight now and then; where neighbors may dislike each other but when one is in need, they get help without question–from everyone–and nothing is stronger than the bond between the people of the community when they absolutely have to have it. This leaves room for plenty of cracks, and it's usually in the context of grief. It's here that the action and beauty of *Midnight Road* takes place.

Murder, attempted murder, scandal, lynching, and sudden violence suffuse the fabric of Jeff Carr's story. There's a nobility to Jeff's youth and despite the disappointments, the pain of a difficult life and the loss of his first love, Davis has an ability to make us see and feel Depression-era West Texas through his character's eyes. He give us a book that goes far deeper than most paperback originals and resounds with the reader long after it's finished.

Midnight Road is a special book. As in *One for Hell* and *The Outraged Sect*, he writes from an autobiographical perspective at times, and some of the incidents that happen to Jeff Carr happened in a similar form to Jada Davis. His son, Mark, tells us that Davis and a friend once went exploring the tunnels of a sandstone hill one day after church. Wearing their Sunday-best, they found that when the tunnels got too narrow, their clothes would bunch up as they tried to back their way out, effectively trapping them. Forced to go forward into the unknown, they had little choice but to hope for wider spaces and eventual escape. It took hours to get free but Davis suffered nightmares over this well into his later years.

The Army experiments and years of smoking perhaps finally caught up to Jada Davis, the man named for a jazz song written in 1918 ("Ja-Da" by Bob Carleton) and popular for more than three decades. He passed away in 1996, not having actually retired early and returned full time to writing, that career he "should never have abandoned."

For now, though, he's left us with four books (one as yet unpublished) and all of them are facets of his literary vision, each contributing to the genre and reflecting his life in their own way. Davis didn't write multiple versions of the same book. No, he did something much better and much more difficult: he gave us books we could care about in different ways, though none so deeply or as affecting as *Midnight Road*. This is his quiet noir, his previously undiscovered masterpiece of rural Americana. Lost no more, you'll want to read the book more than once, and even if that's all you do, it won't be easily forgotten.

OCTOBER, 2013
LITTLETON, NH

Sources:
"A PQ Interview with: JADA DAVIS," by Bill Crider, *Paperback Quarterly*, *vol. 1, no. 2*, The Pecan Valley Press, Brownwood, Texas, Summer 1978

MIDNIGHT ROAD
By Jada M. Davis

...with apologies to those who live in the Big Bend and those
who visit there. I have taken some liberties with the terrain
and characteristics of that wide and beautiful country. I did so
because everything must happen somewhere. In fiction, the
everything doesn't always fit the somewhere.

CHAPTER ONE

Old Trails was ugly of frame, face and temper. For the life of me, I could-
n't understand how he could have sired Samal. Not that Sam didn't have a
temper, too. She had a short fuse and could cuss a blue streak. Her tantrum
storms were short-lived, usually, but they were entertaining while they
lasted. The only thing wrong with her that I could see was that she turned
into a creature of soft curves. Largish bumps appeared on her chest. It happened all of a sudden. One day she was skinny and bony and tough as nails
and, overnight, she grew tits. Her growing protuberances bothered me when
we wrestled and I found myself letting her pin my shoulders to the ground.
She was sixteen-going-on-seventeen and I was looking forward to sixteen.
Mama scolded us the last time we'd wrestled. I had let Sam throw me and
pin me, but she hadn't straddled to push my shoulders down with arm
strength. She'd lain atop me, prone, and her soft breasts had been hot as fire
on my chest.

"You're not children now," Mama said in her quiet voice. "It's time to stop
wrestling."

I'd seen Old Trails head across our valley toward the wild mountains on
the first day of May. He was followed by three pack burros, neck bells clanging. Those burros followed him like dogs. He didn't even look at us when
he passed our house, didn't tip his hat to Mama or speak to her and didn't
ask leave to cross our property. He just headed west across our valley. I knew
where he was headed, though, because he'd been making the trip for as long
as I could remember.

"I hope the old fool finds it," Mama said. "Samal is too smart for that pack
of animals she lives with. She needs to go off to college."

Old Trails was off on his search for the Lost Nigger Mine, which isn't a
mine at all. Legend has it that a bunch of cowboys had been gathering Long-
horns from the canyons and gullies of the Chisos Mountains and one of them
was black. He'd been told to scout atop the mesas and he had come back into
camp with his pockets full of big chunks of pure gold. It was just lying around
on top of the ground, he'd said. The cowboys tried to make him guide them
to the treasure and he refused. No matter, they told him. You were on a mesa
and we'll find it. They killed their golden goose before realizing there were
mesas and mesas in the Chisos.

Old Trails always returned from his futile prospecting trip on June 1, and
on that date I spent the morning scan
ning the valley through binoculars. I saw him and his burros at two o'clock

in the afternoon, tiny specks in the distance, and rode my paint pony out to meet him. He ignored me at first, but I fell in beside him and let the pony amble, rode beside him until we were almost to the house before I spoke.

"You didn't find it," I said.

"I wonder if your Mama would be of a mind to offer me a cup of coffee? I ran out two days ago and I'm about to have a fit."

"I'm sure she would, Mister Trails. We'll just go up on the porch and you can cool off."

"Where's Bant, boy?"

"He left yesterday for Fort Davis with forty yearlings and ten colts, Mister Trails."

"By hisself?"

"No, sir. With two wetbacks who were passing through and needed work."

We reached the corral and Old Trails opened the gate for his burros. They went straight to the grain trough and began licking its empty bottom. Old Trails headed for the house, went up the steps of the porch and seated himself in Bant's rocker just as Mama came out of the breezeway with coffee and cups.

"I saw you coming, Mister Trails," she said, her smile as welcoming as it would have been if she'd admired the old crank.

"Pearl," Old Trails grunted, not looking at Mama, just barely acknowledging her presence.

"How's Samal?" Mama asked. "We haven't seen her for a while."

"How would I know? I've been off prospecting a full month."

I cleared my throat, not sure the man would answer any questions I might ask. "Did you find the gold, Mister Trails?"

He looked at me as if I were some kind of curious insect, frowned, took out his pipe and took his time filling and tamping it. "That gold is there, boy. Somewhere on top of some mesa. I'll find it one of these days. You can bank on that. But, no. I found no gold. I found something else, though. In Dry Valley. Damndest things ever you seen."

I waited while he struck a match on the arm of Bant's rocker and sucked at his pipe.

"Have you ever been to Dry Valley, boy?"

"Yes, sir."

He puffed at his pipe and then pointed the stem at me. "Maybe you'd better keep what I'm going to tell you to yourself. People won't believe it and they're liable to think you're touched. Have you ever seen the spring at the north end of that valley? Up in a box canyon?"

"Yes, sir. I have."

"Do you know what I saw at that spring? Just last night and again this morning early?"

"Gold?"

Old Trails snorted. "No. Not gold. Let me tell you what I saw. I made camp there last night under the overhang about twenty yards from the spring pool. Well, sir, and may I be struck dead if I'm not telling the truth, two animals came to drink. Same thing happened again this morning. You wouldn't believe what I saw."

"Antelope," I said.

"Two animals drank at that pool, boy. They stood side by side like brothers and they left together. Just like brothers. Not antelope. A camel and a bull buffalo."

I stared at the old man and then looked at Mama. She smiled, arched her eyebrows, wrinkled her nose and shrugged her shoulders.

"You're kidding me, Mister Trails," I said.

"No, boy. I'm not. People can say a lot of things about me... and doubtless do. But nobody will say I lie. I saw a camel and a buffalo bull. Now, I'll admit that's the first camel I've ever seen, but I've seen pictures and I can't be wrong. It had a hump on its back and a long neck. A buffalo bull was with him. Now, tell me this, boy. What is a camel doing in that valley and how did it get there? For that matter, where in tarnation did a buffalo bull come from? Tell me that."

"Camels come from Arabia."

"I don't know where that is, but I know it's across the ocean. Don't tell me that animal could swim that far. Now, first I thought to kill the buffalo, but he was a grizzled old fellow and his meat would have been like shoe leather."

"I'd sure like to see that camel."

"Well, the only way out of that valley is the pass that leads from this one. That means the animals got there by crossing this valley. More than likely. If they come out, they'll have to come through here."

"I've heard something about camels in this country," Mama said, "but for the life of me I can't remember what."

"Buffalo have been gone for a long time," Old Trails said. "How that bull got there I don't know. As for the camel, I wouldn't believe anybody who said they'd seen it. I guess I couldn't fault anybody for not believing me."

"I believe you," I said. "I believe you and I'm going in there to see for myself."

Old Trails finished his coffee, went to the edge of the porch and tapped his pipe against a post to empty it. "Good coffee, Pearl. I'm obliged."

"You're quite welcome, Mister Trails. Tell Samal we miss her."

We watched the old man gather his burros and leave, watched him walk east to the gap in the mountains, watched until he and his burros were specks in the distance.

"Do you really believe him?" Mama asked.

"I don't think he'd make up a story like that."

"Samal will know whether there've been camels in this country. She's read every book in the whole county."

I saddled Bant's riding mare, a Morgan he prized, and rode out to check the cattle. We had two thousand acres in our valley and one mouthful of our grass was better for a cow or horse than ten mouthfuls of lush grass in other parts of the state. Bant usually ran a hundred head of cows and sold off the yearlings every year. His horse herd was his joy, though, and he vowed that some day he'd raise nothing but horses. He had ten Morgan mares and a stallion he swore was pure Arabian. He knew, he said, because Arabian horses have spinal columns that are one bone shorter than those of other horses. He always had buyers for his colts. They were easily trained as cutting horses, were sure footed and had blinding speed for short distances.

The cattle were grazing along the banks of the spring-fed stream and the horses were shading beneath cottonwoods and willows. The sun had already dipped behind the mountains, but I rode on up to the northern end of the valley to look at the hundred acres planted to maize and alfalfa. It was fenced, as was our shinnery land. Spring rains had been unusually heavy and prospects were good for a bumper crop. I started for the house, then stopped and dismounted to look at our valley.

The elevation on the valley floor was about four thousand feet, but pinnacles surrounding it were a mile or more above sea level. It was red rock country, with the reds of the peaks stained here and there by ancient lava flow. I could see, on the upper slopes, stands of piñon pine, alligator junipers, oaks and maples. Higher up were ponderosa, limber pine and quaking aspens. One day, I thought, I'd have to leave the valley for college. Mama wanted me to go, but I wondered whether I could tear myself away from this place.

I was tempted to ride to the south end of the valley to the shinnery, twenty acres of sandy loam in unlikely country for no reason at all. We had cleared it of most of its oaks and planted watermelons, cantaloupes, black-eyed peas, squash and cucumbers and just about every vegetable known. Peach trees thrived, as did apples and pears. It was getting late, though, and I decided to wait until morning.

It was dusk when I reached the house and Mama had done the milking. I threw out hay for the cows and any horses that might wander up to the corral, fed the pigs, started for the house and stopped to listen to cowbells.

"Jeff," Mama called from the front porch. "Could that be Bant coming?"

"He couldn't be back this soon. It must be cows on the loose."

I went on up to the house and sat on the steps while the clanging of bells became louder, saw then in the gathering dusk a rider on a horse and two pack burros.

"Hey, Jeff!" It was Samal's voice. "Hello the house!"

"Hey, yourself," I called back. "Are you going to look for the Lost Nigger Mine?"

"I'm going to catch a camel and a buffalo and start my own circus. Do you want to come along?"

"Well, somebody'll have to take care of you."

She rode on up to the porch and slid to the ground, went straight to Mama for a hug and kiss. She had ridden that damned stallion, Rancor, the meanest animal that ever lived to draw breath. He hated everyone, almost. He loved Sam. I think he must have hated me more than he hated Old Trails and he tried to kick or bite Old Trails every chance he got. He must have been sixteen hands tall and was a skewbald with white and brown spots. He had the wildest eyes I've ever seen on a horse and he'd bite, kick, tromp and stomp and throw a hissy fit if anyone but Samal tried to mount. Most people thought he was the best cutting and roping horse in the country, but that couldn't be proved because nobody had ever seen him work with anyone except Samal on his back.

"Jeff," Sam said, "will you take Rancor to the stable and give him some grain? Hay will be fine for the burros."

"I'll take the packs off the burros and give them some hay. I'll lead Rancor to the corral and unsaddle him, but I'm not about to lead him into that stable."

I knew what would happen with Rancor. The brute would let me lead him into the stall and then he'd pin me. He'd do it very slowly, as if by accident, moving in and pinning me just enough to trap me and then, little by little, leaning more and more of his weight against me.

"Take them on down, then," Sam said. "I'll be along in a minute or two."

I took the packs off Betsy and Boo, placed them on the porch while Sam and Mama made woman talk. I led Rancor on down to the corral and the burros followed. Rancor stood still while I took the saddle and blanket off him, patient as always when something was coming *off*, and then I decided, what the heck, I'll go ahead and tuck him in. Before I unshucked his bridle, though, I poured a measure of oats into the feed bin at the back of the stable and led Rancor inside. He was nosing the grain when I slipped the bridle off and sidled out, back to the wall. The ornery critter moved against me, not hard, and I stood still. He was more interested in oats than crushed human and I was able to get out without getting mashed or kicked.

Mama and Sam had gone inside and I went on in. Mama was in the kitchen and I could smell venison steaks frying, coffee perking, biscuits baking. Sam was at the bookshelf, the first place she always visited at our house.

"Do you ever read Shakespeare?" she asked when she heard me enter.

"Sure."

"Do you think I could take this one with me? I can read while I ride."

"Take it. Can you read Latin?"

"No, and don't tell me. You can."

She was standing with her back to me and, as ever, was dressed like a boy. Her pants, tight over rounded buttocks that I'd never thought interesting until now, must have been hand-me-downs from her brother, Coy. She turned to face me and my eyes were riveted to her chest. Her tits had grown in the two months since last I'd seen her and they pushed at the fabric of her shirt as if seeking escape. I'd never seen a woman's tits; not bare, and I longed to see Sam's.

"Hey," she whispered, waving her hands in front of my face and snapping her fingers. "Look at me. I'm Samal. Remember me?"

"You've grown."

"You noticed. What fascinated you?"

"You're pretty."

She was smooth and brown as a honey nut. Her lips were full and her nose, just long enough not to be snub, called attention to high cheek bones. Her eyes were more blue than blue and her hair, glossy brown and long, was coiled in one big pig-tail that fell from the left side of her head and over her shoulder.

"You like?" she teased.

"I like."

"I think you've reached manhood, Jeff. Are you going with me to see the camel and buffalo? I've packed everything we'll need."

"I'm going."

"Do you know where the camel came from?"

"I'm not ignorant. Camels live in Arabia. Obviously, this one must have escaped from a circus."

"No," Sam said. "He's wild."

"Mama said she remembered something about camels in this country, but she can't remember what she heard."

"Well," Samal said in the school-teacherish voice that always irked me, "Jefferson Davis brought some over when he was Secretary of War. From Arabia. Arabian camels have one hump. There are camels called dromedaries that have two, but they come from North Central Asia. They're really Bactrian camels."

"Thank you very much."

"Old Jeff Davis thought camels would be just great for the western desert, so he brought fifty or sixty over before the War Between the States. He brought some of their keepers to teach our soldiers how to manage them, but the project didn't work out. The camels were turned loose and ran wild."

"Wait a minute," I said. "How long do camels live?"

She wrinkled her forehead and squinched her nose. "About thirty or forty years."

"And when did Jeff Davis bring them over?"

"In eighteen-fifty-six."

"Seventy-four years ago. Our camel would have been three or four or five years old when he got here, so he'd be close to eighty years old."

"There are bull camels and cow camels, Jeff. Cow camels have babies after certain acts, but you probably don't know much about that. Now, I read that camels were seen ten or fifteen years ago in Arizona and New Mexico. That means they were born in this country. This camel... *our* camel... could be a son or grandson of the originals."

"Well, no matter. I want to see a camel. As far as that goes, I want to see a buffalo. The two are together, so they probably escaped from a circus at the same time."

"I don't believe it. There could be remnants of buffalo herds running wild. I read that a man named Hornaday set up preserves in several places, with government help. Our buffalo must have wandered off from one of those herds."

She proceeded to tell me more about camels and buffalo and bison than I needed to know and I was saved from her lecture when Mama called us to supper. We ate and Sam helped me with the dishes while Mama made hot chocolate for dessert. We took our cups to the front porch and sat listening to the night sounds. Mama went to bed early, but Sam and I began "remembering when." As usual, our remembering centered on the time my Uncle Lafe, Mama's brother, left his hardware store in Victoria for hired help to run while he took Sam and me on a trip through the Davis Mountains and the Big Bend. That was when I was ten. We had four pack burros for our three-week trip through the Davis Mountains and then we brought them home and rested three days before going to Terlingua. We rafted on the Rio Grande, took pack mules and explored mountains and canyons, saw the Capote waterfall and its snails, the largest in the world. We saw Bluebonnets as tall as I was, saw giant daggers and springs of hot mineral water. The country was a geological confusion, desert and rivers and springs, chunks of sunken mountains and massive peaks, dry-bed lakes and beds of volcanic lava, cuestas, playas, vegans and arroyos. We saw Mexican buckweed, madrone trees and catclaw mimosa. We saw houses with ceilings made of carrizo grass.

"Remember the Carmen Mountains?" Sam asked, and I remembered those mountains that lie in Mexico, stairsteps with sheer faces of limestone and dark volcanic debris, stains on the limestone at the feet of cliffs that formed precise patterns of white and dark bands. We saw the sun strike those cliffs full-face just before sunset and saw the colors change to burning orange on the limestone palletes. The colors changed to smears of red before twilight and then turned to purple when the sun sank below the peaks of the Chisos. We saw the same cliffs on a morning when summer clouds moved in and marveled at the purple shades of the bluffs. We wanted to go on down to Monterrey to see the Horseshoe Falls, but we'd been gone too long, Uncle Lafe told us, and he was sorry. We'd have to go home without seeing the pocket of tropics just a hundred miles from where we were standing, tropics with palm trees and exotic plants we couldn't dream of. So we'd gone home, the memory of what we'd seen and where we'd been etched forever on our minds, there for the seeing again when Sam and I met to call forth the pictures and colors and feelings.

I went to bed at midnight, but Sam stayed up to read. Still, she was up and calling me at six, ready to pack the animals and go, but Mama said I couldn't leave until I'd turned the watermelon and cantaloupe vines. Sam offered to help and we saddled up. I wanted to take one of the Morgan mares, but Mama warned against it. There was nothing to do but saddle my paint, just a pony suitable for a child. Sam didn't tease me. She'd been riding that outlaw, Rancor, for two years while I rode a pony and I wished Bant would let me have a real horse. We rode down to the shinnery to turn the vines. That meant we'd take the runners of the vines and move them up to the top of the mounded rows on which they grew so we could plow between rows and take wagons in for loading when the melons ripened. We only had six rows of watermelons and three of cantaloupes and the rows weren't long. We finished in a couple of hours, fretting all the while, anxious to be on our way.

Mama had packed a lunch and we headed west across our valley, the fringing mountains red in the distance, the air fresh and almost cool. Our horses, even mine, wanted to run, but the docile burros were plodders and we kept our mounts reined in. We reached the pass leading to Dry Valley, though "pass" meant only that a traveler could get from one valley to another if he was willing to climb, walk and lead his animals. It was a gap in the mountains, a high gap, stone-littered and boulder-strewn. We led our horses over the rocks and shale, around boulders, clattering along in our boots and leading horses that stepped hesitantly, fearfully. The burros followed, surefooted as mountain sheep. We were all strung out. I led the way because Rancor showed signs of balking. It took an hour to reach the top of the gap and we stopped to rest.

I don't know why we called Dry Valley dry. It wasn't as well watered as ours, but the average rainfall in the Davis Mountains is eighteen to nineteen inches a year and Dry Valley received at least that much. Our valley, for some reason that had to do with prevailing winds and fringing mountains not high enough to shield off incoming moisture, usually got twenty-three to twenty-five inches of rain each year. That made a difference. Still, Dry Valley was called Dry Valley and I think it was because the soil was poor and the valley floor was rock-littered. It had a desert-like appearance.

We sat on a boulder and took turns using the binoculars. "I don't see a camel or buffalo," I said.

"They're there. They could be up in the box canyon."

"Maybe they're not."

"You think Pa lied to us."

"I'm not saying any such thing. They could have gone someplace else."

"Well, they'd have gone into your valley and we didn't see them They're down there. Probably in some arroyo. You'll see."

"Have it your way."

It took another hour to reach the valley floor and another thirty minutes to get to the box canyon at the northern end. The rock cliffs of the canyon were sheer, maybe eight-hundred feet high, and the canyon was narrow and shadowed. A spring bubbled out of the rock near the base of the northern cliff that stoppered the canyon. It bubbled out of a fissure some ten-feet above my head and trickled down the rock face into a pool about ten-feet wide and twenty-feet long. The water didn't go anywhere, didn't flow out of the pool, and Sam said the soil at this point was porous.

We found camel tracks and buffalo tracks. At least, they weren't burro tracks or deer tracks, antelope tracks or tracks of cattle.

Sam crowed triumphantly. "See? What did I tell you? They must come up for water every evening."

"What are we going to do with them? Just look at them and let them go?"

"We could herd them back into your valley. Your crops are fenced and they couldn't hurt anything."

"I don't know what Bant would say. Besides, I doubt that we could herd a wild buffalo and camel."

We let our animals drink their fill, unsaddled the horses and lifted the packs from the burros. We hobbled the horses so they couldn't get far, but let Betsy and Boo run free. They'd come to water in the morning, we knew. We took the gear to the overhang under the eastern cliff, stooping to get inside. There was a sand floor and someone had set a circle of rocks for a campfire.

"Let's go get some firewood now and then go swimming," Sam said.

We took some heavy cord and the hatchet and went to a stand of straggly mesquite we'd spotted about a half mile to the west of the box canyon. There were lots of dead branches and we made two bundles to carry. Back in our camp, Samal unpacked a skillet, a pan, the coffee pot and some cans of beans, cans of corn and some bacon. She unrolled the blankets, four of them.

"Two blankets each won't be enough, Sam," I complained. "I could have brought more. It'll get cold tonight."

"We'll snuggle," she said. "One blanket on the ground and three for cover. We'll be warm. Do you want to go for a swim?"

I'd been afraid she'd changed her mind. In truth, all the way to the mesquite clump and back again I had imagined how Sam would look in the bare. The thought had made my manhood stand straight up and I think she must have noticed. Now she had mentioned swimming again and old Johnny Pecker stood at attention again.

"We might as well cool off," I said.

She sat down and pulled off her boots and socks. I did the same and was about to unbutton my shirt when she headed for the pool, at a run, fully clothed, and dived in a belly-busting lunge. There was nothing for me to do but do the same. I was disappointed.

It turned out better than I thought it would.

Sam's shirt, when wet, moulded her tits and became almost transparent. It was almost as good as seeing her bare. Her pants, I saw when she got out on the bank to jump in again, clung to her legs and thighs and buttocks and stretched tightly between her legs to reveal some sort of cleavage. I stole a few feels, too, as if by accident. Sam knew I was groping on purpose, but didn't seem to mind. In fact, she seemed amused.

"Jeff," she said, "would you if you could?"

"Could what?"

"Could you if you would?"

"Would what?"

The water was cold and we didn't stay in long. Sam got out first and ran to the overhang. Now, I thought. Now's the time. I'll see her buck naked because she's cold in those, wet clothes and she'll strip.

She fooled me. She shucked her pants off without bending once and her shirt-tail covered her buttocks, just barely, and barely covered what it was I couldn't imagine between her legs. She wrung water from her pants and spread them over a rock, Put a blanket around her shoulders and took the shirt off underneath. I climbed out of the water, my manhood pushing hard against my pants, straining hard, and walked up the slope to join her.

"Well," she said, eyeing me without an ounce of shame. "I think you would if you could and could if you would."

"You ought to be ashamed of yourself, Samal."

"I don't know why. I just mentioned something as natural as breathing."

"Maybe you've had practice."

"You'll get your ears boxed if you're not careful. I'll have you know I'm a virgin."

"Then how come you know so much?"

"Women are just naturally more knowledgeable than men. They know they're built to bear children and they get curious at an early age. I think I might need some practice, though and you're just the right age. Size, too, for that matter."

"You talk like a hussy."

"You wouldn't know a hussy if you met one on the street. I'll bet you don't even know what the word means."

"A hussy is a woman with a bad reputation."

"Maybe. But not necessarily. It can also mean a girl who is pert or forward. That's what I am. Pert *and* forward."

"Well," I said, "we'd better get a fire going and dry our clothes."

Sam did most of the fire-making because, somehow, she could move around, bend and stoop without allowing her blanket to gape open or fall from her shoulders. She had the decency to turn her back while I undressed and draped a blanket around my shoulders, but I stepped on mine when I bent for wood and the damned thing came clean off. You would have thought she had just caught a glimpse of a funny freak in a circus side-show, she laughed so hard. We opened some beans and Sam fried bacon. She dropped in some sliced biscuits she'd brought from home and let them sizzle in the grease. She put the coffee pot on the embers and we drank from tin cups while darkness gathered.

"I'm sleepy," I said.

Sam laughed.

"What's so funny about that? I'm tired and I'm sleepy. That's not so unusual."

"I never knew you went to bed so early," she said. "I'll bet you drop right off to sleep."

"I probably will."

"Piffle."

"What does that mean?"

"Piffle means nonsense."

"You're always showing off, Sam. I read as much as you do. Piffle is derived from the words piddle and trifle. I'll bet you didn't know that."

"I still say you're not tired. You're just horny."

"Horny?"

"You're such an innocent, Jeff. Horny means that a certain part of your body, which I won't bother to identify, is as hard as a horn."

"You're vulgar, Sam."

She laughed and began spreading blankets on the sandy floor. "It'll be cold tonight, like you said. We'll have to snuggle. Unless you think you'll get too horny."

The canyon was as dark as the depths of a cavern before I joined Sam beneath the blankets. I sat in stubborn silence before the dying embers of the fire until I thought she might be asleep. She wasn't. She giggled when I crawled under the covers and I stayed as far away from her as I could.

"Are you pouting because I teased you?" she asked.

"I'm not pouting. Just thinking."

"I'll bet you're thinking."

"Well, I am. I was wondering how that camel and buffalo found this valley and where they came from."

Our bodies weren't touching, but I could feel her presence. I could feel her warm body without really feeling it. My chest was tight and I fought to breathe normally, tried not to gasp. I felt her then, really felt her. She had moved to me, moved until her body touched my body and her flesh burned mine. I felt her hand, light as down, on my stomach, felt it move up to my chest, down to the stomach, down and still down. Her fingers just stirred my pubic hairs, just touched my manhood, and then her hand was on my thigh, one thigh and then the other and moving up again past my manhood, just flick-flicking it with the barest of touches. She brushed my pubic hair, gently pulled pubic hairs, and then I turned to my side and cupped her breasts, allowed my left hand to explore her smooth back and rounded buttocks. Her hand found my manhood and she lifted her body, allowed her weight to rest atop me, took my face in both hands and kissed me, opened her mouth, loved my mouth with her tongue and, without warning, I exploded.

Samal didn't laugh. She held me to her, cradled my head to her shoulder and kissed me.

"It'll be better next time," she promised.

"Will there be a next time?"

"You'd better believe it, love. I'm a woman grown and I ache for something I've never had. Sleep and gather your strength. Believe me, you're going to need it."

We slept warm and close and I awoke to dim gray darkness, lay with Sam's body cradled to mine, lay with her buttocks nested in the lower curve of my body, lay with her back warm against my chest. She must have been awake before me because she turned over to face me. We made love, gentle love, and slept again. I awoke a second time when she shook me gently and whispered in my ear.

"Shhhhh… shhhhhh… shhhhhh… they're at the pond, Jeff. Both of them."

The camel and buffalo were drinking with our horses and burros. We watched while they drank their fill, crouched on our knees at overhang's rim and watched until they turned to face us. They seemed as curious about us as we were about them and seemed unafraid.

"They've never seen people," Samal said.

"You can't know that. Maybe they've seen thousands of people when they were with a circus or wild west show."

"They're wild things, Jeff. They're not afraid because they don't realize they should be."

"Well," I said, standing up. "We've seen them. What do we do now?"

"Let's herd them to your valley."

"What would I do with a camel and a buffalo?"

"Nothing. That's just the point. They'd have plenty of grass and water and they could live out their lives in peace."

"Bant might not want them."

"There's no reason he shouldn't."

"There's no reason he should. Why don't we herd them to your place? Do you think Old Trails would like that?"

"My pa would take them in, but we couldn't herd them that far. Let's take them to your valley and if Bant objects, we'll herd them back here."

"Let's do it, then," I said.

We packed the burros while the camel and buffalo watched, saddled the horses and began herding our strange, wild animals across the valley floor. We didn't push them hard and they ambled along as if accustomed to being driven. Things were different when we reached the pass. The animals had been docile on level ground, but balked when we began to climb. We crowded them and they acted in concert. The camel went right and the buffalo went left, circled behind us and stood watching. Three times we went back for them and three times they repeated their flanking maneuvers. When we went back the fourth time, they galloped awkwardly across the valley floor.

"They like it here," Samal said. "We'll leave them."

"Fat chance of doing anything else. It's just as well. I don't think Bant would allow them in our valley."

"We saw them, Jeff. That's the main thing. The trip was worth it."

"In more ways than one," I said, and Samal had the grace to blush.

We had dismounted to watch our wild things gallumph their way to freedom and were just starting to mount up again when the Indians, or whatever they were, came up out of a dry arroyo in the path of the fleeing animals.

"Yaqui," I breathed.

"Or Apache," Samal said. "They could be Apache."

"Maybe just ladrones out of Mexico, somewhere deep in the Mexican mountains."

There were five of them and two had rifles. Only one was mounted and he wore a top hat and a frock coat. His horse was shaggy, a mustang. The four on foot had long black hair and wore breech-clouts. That's all. Just breech-clouts.

"They wouldn't shoot our animals," Samal said.

"They sure as heck will."

"We've got to stop them."

"I don't know how. We could ride toward them and whoop and yell, but that could get us shot."

The Indians killed the buffalo first. The two with rifles flanked it, shot it, and the magnificent beast went to his foreleg knees, just sank, and then its huge head drooped and it rolled over on its side. The camel was easy prey. Unafraid, still curious in its innocence, it turned back to sniff at its dead companion and was shot.

"The bastards," Samal said.

"Maybe they're hungry."

"I hope they choke. I wish I had a rifle."

"We'd better get out of here," I said. "There's nothing we can do."

We mounted and started up over the pass, but we'd been seen. The mounted Indian galloped toward us while his four companions began butchering their kills. I did the only thing I knew to do. I wheeled my mount and headed for the approaching rider. Samal yelled at me to come back, but I kept going. The Indian wheeled his horse and went at a trot back to his kill. I watched him for a minute and returned to Samal and our pack train.

Samal retreated into one of her rare, black and silent moods. I let her be. We climbed up and over the pass and reached our valley before she said a word. Her mood changed completely and she fantasized that we'd get our rifles and track down the marauders who'd shot our buffalo and camel, our pitiful wild beasts.

"We'll shoot those bastards like the dogs they are," she said.

"We'll have to find them first."

"That will be easy. They have one horse and they'll load the poor thing with camel and buffalo meat. They can't go over the mountains with a load like that. They'll have to wind around and find the passes. We can circle around the mountains and be waiting for them at the river."

"Bant would never let me go and I doubt that Old Trails would let you go."

"We can tell them we're going on a hunting trip."

"No way," I said. "Bant will come back from Fort Davis with a million things for me to do."

"I'd like to get a shot at those Mescaleros, Jeff. Wouldn't you?"

"Now they're Mescaleros."

"Apaches, Yaquis, Mescaleros, whatever. It doesn't matter a whit. They're still animals."

"Well, maybe they needed meat. They probably came from some poor Mexican village in the mountains and their people could be starving. Besides, it's not practical. Bant would never let me go."

She grinned at me. "You're a man now, Jeff. You've proved that. We could go without permission."

"I'm still fifteen."

"A big fifteen," and she grinned again, "in more ways than one."

"You're terrible, Sam."

"You're old enough to make a baby."

I allowed her words to float between us, felt a chill, felt my mouth go dry. "I hadn't thought of that," I said.

"I had. A woman has to think of such things. Fortunately, I thought of it before we did anything. You needn't worry. I've listened to the married women and I've studied about rhythms and cycles and all that stuff. I won't have a baby this time."

"You can't be sure."

"Well, if I'm pregnant, we'll get married. Would you like that?"

"I don't know. I hadn't thought about it. I don't even know whether they'd let me."

"They? You mean Bant and Pearl?"

"I mean the law."

"Maybe they wouldn't. Then, again, maybe they would. Tell me something, Jeff. I've been curious and I've heard people talk about it. Why do you always say Bant this and Bant that instead of Papa this and Papa that? You never say Pa or Papa. It's always Bant."

It was something I'd not thought about for years. "Bant won't let me. Even when I was young, just a baby, he wouldn't let me. He spanked me once for calling him Papa."

"Why won't he let you, do you think?"

"I don't know. Just his nature, I suppose."

"Have you ever thought he might not be your father?"

"Watch it."

"Don't get mad."

"Why wouldn't I get mad? You're hinting that I'm a bastard."

"That's just a word and it doesn't mean anything to me." She reined in and dismounted, but I kept to my saddle and looked down at her.

"Did you know Kenty Hooker has come back to his home place?" she asked. "Well, he has and he's as rich as Jay Gould. He spent a night with us last week and, Jeff, he's the most handsome man I've ever seen."

"He's old enough to be your father."

"And yours."

"I thought he sold Hooker Valley to some English Earl or Duke or something years ago."

"He did. He sold it when his folks died. Sold it for nearly nothing, he said, and started drifting. He was at Ranger and Desdamona during their big oil booms and made some money, but he really struck it rich in Wichita County. He bought the home place back from the Englishman and there's a crew of carpenters and stone masons out there now. They're working full time on a house and barns and such. He plans to raise fine horses and fine cattle."

"I've heard stories about him all my life. He was wild."

"He and Bant were close friends and rivals for your mother's hand."

"I heard."

"You look just like him."

"We'd better get on to the house," I said.

"No, wait a minute," and she reached up to grab my hand. "You can get mad if you want, but I'm going to tell you something you'll be hearing from others. People are talking. At least those who've seen Kenty since he came home are talking. With him gone all those years, they just saw you grow up and didn't think anything about what you looked like. They didn't realize you're Kenty's spitting image until he came back."

"I favor Mama."

"Some. You do. But you look just like Kenty."

"Does Mama know he's back?"

"I didn't tell her."

"Well, don't tell her," and I pulled my hand from hers and rode on toward the house. I looked back once and saw that she was following me and the burros following her. I rode into the corral and unsaddled, hoping Sam would go on home without stopping. She wasn't about to do that. She rode Rancor through the corral gate, slid off and began to unsaddle.

"You can help with the burros," she said. "It's too late to head for home and I'm going to spend the night. You needn't be mad at me, either. I wouldn't hurt you for the world and you know that. We're friends." She turned to face me and smiled. "How could we get to be better friends?"

"I don't mind about me, Sam. Bant's just a man I live with, but look at what it makes Mama."

"Your mother is the best and smartest woman I know. So what if she got pregnant by Kenty and married Bant when Kenty ran out on her? Would that make her bad? Do you think she's the only woman forced to find a husband in a hurry? Would I be bad if you made me pregnant? I made love with you and I don't think I'm bad."

"Mama's not bad and neither are you. I don't know, Sam. Maybe it isn't true. Just because I resemble Kenty Hooker... well that doesn't make it true."

"I knew you'd hear the gossip pretty soon and I just thought you should hear it from a friend." Sam's voice was husky. "You're not mad?"

"I'm not mad. I've heard it before. I don't know what I am, but I'm not mad."
We fed the animals and went on up to the house. Mama met us on the porch with the coffee pot and cups and we sat in the cool shade until it was time to do the chores. Mama gently scotched Sam's notion to go hunt the men who'd shot our animals and started talking to her about getting Old Trails to send her away to college. Sam offered to help with the chores, but I told her I could handle things and went on down to milk the cow and put out feed for the livestock coming up from the pastures. The sun was down behind the mountains by the time I'd finished and I was half-way between barn and house when I heard a car's motor. The sound got louder and then I saw headlights. A Model T pulled into our front yard and Bant stepped out.

"Did you turn the melon vines?" were his first words.

"Yessir."

He lifted his saddle from the back seat and unstrapped his bedroll.

"Take the saddle to the barn," he said.

"Did you buy the car?"

"I didn't steal it," he said, and went on into the house.

Bant, I knew, had some liquor in him. He was a quiet man. I will always remember him as a quiet, gray man. His hair had been gray all my life, wavy and gray. His eyes were gray and, for some reason he always wore gray shirts and gray pants. He was a handsome man, wide of shoulder and trim of hip, with a straight nose, high cheekbones, a wide and generous mouth. By nature, I think in looking back, he was a kindly man. There were times when his love showed. Rare times, I'll admit, but times. There were times when he'd become down-right talkative with me. He'd tell me about his plans for the valley and things I should do when he was dead and gone and the valley would be mine. At other times, too, it was possible to read the puzzled hurt in his eyes when he looked at me. He was soft-spoken and seldom curt, but given to curtness when drinking or when one of his black moods took him. I avoided him as much as possible on the rare occasions he brought a bottle home or when one of his moods hit.

I took the saddle to the barn and went on back up to the house. Bant's mood had changed as it often did in Samal's presence. He liked her, liked to talk with her, liked to tease her. She was telling him about the camel and buffalo and he agreed that the animals' killers should be shot like dogs.

"I wish I'd seen them," he said. "I wish you'd been able to bring them to our valley. They were the last of their kinds in the wild, I'll wager."

He became silent after supper and I went out to the porch to sit. Sam took a book to bed in the spare bedroom and Mama sat with Bant in the living room. For a while I could hear only the murmur of their voices, but once Bant spoke loudly.

"I thought I was really something in those days," he said. "There I was, bragging to my friends about my new son and fool enough to say there wasn't one of them man enough to make a baby in seven months. That's when Adrian Pride said what he did. Do you know what he said, Pearl?"

Mama's murmured reply was too low to hear, but I knew she was saying what I'd heard her say a hundred times in my life. "You've told me time and time again, Bant."

"I'll tell you what he said," Bant's voice was loud and rough. "He said I was quite a man, quite a man. Not just any man could make a baby in seven months and he was willing to bet his ranch against mine that I couldn't do it again."

Mama must have left the room, but I could hear Bant's rocker screeeeeeking for an hour before he blew out the light and went to bed. I sat where I was and made up my mind to leave the valley when I was eighteen, college or no college. Kenty Hooker, I thought. All my life I've heard Kenty Hooker, Kenty Hooker, Kenty Hooker. What would I do when I met him at last? What would I say? Hello, Papa. Glad to meet you?

In the morning, Sam was gone. I had no idea how much I would be missing her.

CHAPTER TWO

I remember the first time I saw Kenty Hooker. I had gone down to the shin-nery for a ripe melon and I wasn't looking for just any melon. The one I wanted had to be almost blue, with little golden flecks on its skin. We'd had one vine of them the year before and the melon meat was orange, sweeter than sugar. Bant said it was a new melon, a cross between yellows and reds, a hybrid, and we saved the seed from every single one we ate that summer.

"We'll call it Pearl's Pride," Bant announced, and we'd planted a full row.

It was mid-July and I was barefooted. The sand was hot and I was forced to run between the rows, ran fast enough to kick up puffs of dust periods where bare feet landed. After a while I spotted the melon I wanted, plucked it, hoisted it to my shoulder and trotted to the orchard to flop full length in the shade of a peach tree. A bumblebee came dragging his way through the heavy air, just skimming the ground, passed me by and left his buzz behind for a fraction of an instant. Somewhere a bird chirped, but only once, as though the chirp was not intended and not in tune with the stillness of the day.

There was no breath of air, though leaves trembled and sighed and rus-tled and whispered. A buzzard wheeled and circled over the valley, went up slowly and came down fast and wheeled around and around, slowly wheeled and circled. Once it dipped down toward my tree and shade place to examine the slight movement it glimpsed, but then it floated up and back to almost out of sight on unmoving wings. It climbed and circled higher and wider, still higher and wider, became smaller and smaller in the sky and finally climbed and circled into nothingness. I ate the heart from my melon and turned the rinds upside-down, sat with my back against the bole of the tree and watched the sun sink behind the distant peaks. Shadows came to our valley, though two hours must pass before real sundown. An insect disturbed the stillness with a sharp rattle and others rattled tentatively, formed a cho-rus and filled the air with strident shrillings. A wagon moved in the far dis-tance and the creak of harness and skreek of chains seemed a stone's throw away. A dog barked somewhere and somewhere a man called.

Bant.

I went at a trot to the house, stopped at the woodpile for an arm-load of kindling, dumped it in the box on the back porch and went on into the house. Mama was bustling about the kitchen.

"We have company," she said, and there was no need to say more.

Kenty Hooker was sitting in a cane-bottomed chair in the living room, the chair tilted back against the wall beside the fireplace, and he was tuning Bant's fiddle. Bant sat in the rocker by the window. The room was warmed with the soft glow of light from the kerosene lamp and by Kenty Hooker's smile. He stood to shake hands, grasped my hand with both of his, looked at me and winked, let go of my hand and reached out to hug me to him. He was Bant's size. His black hair had fallen down over his forehead, almost to his eyes, and his face was a dreamer's face. I don't know why I decided that, but that was what I thought. His eyes were brown like mine, his nose slightly beaked like mine, his lips full and generous like mine, his skin nut-brown like mine.

"Jeff, meet Kenty Hooker," Bant said.

"I've brought you something," Kenty said. "Go take a look in the corral."

Bant stood. "I'll tend to the stock," he said, and his voice sounded strained.

I went down to the corral with Bant. He walked ahead of me and began putting out grain and hay while I stood at the gate and stared at two strange horses, a stallion and a colt. Appaloosas. I'd never seen such horses. The stallion had leopard spots, white rimmed eyes, and closer examination proved he had the classic black and white stripes on his hooves. The colt, about a year old, I judged, was his twin.

Bant came out of the barn. "That's a fine filly."

"I thought it was a stallion."

"You're lucky it's a filly. We can't have two stallions on the place."

Kenty Hooker came down to the barn and told me about the Appaloosa, how the breed had been originated by the Nez Perce Indians, how prized they were.

"The Spanish probably brought them over," Kenty said, "but the Nez Perce bred them. The word, Appaloosa, comes from the word Palouse, but I don't know what that means. The Nez Perce just called it the Raindrop horse."

"She's beautiful."

"She's tame as a baby and ready to ride. Bant might try breeding her to that Arabian stallion when her time comes. That get should be interesting."

His stallion followed him into a stable and began eating its grain. I just placed my hand on the filly's neck and led her to a stall, fed her and patted her, ran my hands over her entire body.

"I'll name her Raindrop," I told Kenty.

We went on back up to the house for supper and Kenty told us what he had planned for Hooker Valley, about his days in the oil fields, and after supper he played the fiddle for us. It was music I'd never heard before and Mama told me later he'd played concertos by Bach. He left about nine, saddled up and left. Bant tried to get him to spend the night, but Kenty said he expected new workmen at his place come morning and he had to be there to direct their work. I watched him ride out into the darkness and heard him call back to me.

"Jeff, you ride over to see me when you get the time. I'll show you some more horses."

"I'll do that, Mister Hooker," I yelled. "Thank you for Raindrop."

His laughter floated back. "Mister Hooker was my father," he called. "My name is Kenty."

I could hear Bant clumping around the house long after I'd gone to bed and once I slipped down the hall and peeked into the kitchen. He was drinking from a brown bottle. Mama kept calling him to bed, but he just sat at the kitchen table and drank from that bottle. After a while Mama went to him and they talked in low voices for a long while. Once he cried out as if in pain.

"Why did he have to come back?" he asked.

They talked far into the night. More than once I dozed off, only to awaken to hear their voices in the kitchen.

"There'll be talk again," Bant said. "Pearl, I don't think I can stand it!"

When morning came I asked Mama flat out what Bant couldn't stand. She was making biscuits, her arms white with flour up to the elbow. She turned around, laughing, and made a playful swing at my face. She was pretty then and that's how I picture her in my mind's eye. Later, at the trial, she was wan and worn, but on this day she was pretty. Her hair was black as pitch and long. Her face was young, the eyes soft blue. I remember how Bant once held his hands at her waist, almost encircled her waist with his hands. She seemed long and tall on that morning I remember, but later I saw that the top of her head didn't come up as far as Kenty's chin.

"You had a dream," she told me. "Bant can stand anything. Besides, there's nothing for him to stand. Now, go wash up and call him to breakfast."

I went down to the corral where Bant was forking hay to the cows and Raindrop followed me around like a dog. Bant looked at her teeth and said she was two years old.

"She'll be three in January," he said. "All purebred horses have birthdays on the first of January, no matter when they were born. This one probably is about fourteen months old, but she'll be counted as a two-year old. Still, she's just a baby, so be easy with her. Don't break her down. In human age, she'd be about four years old, so remember that."

"When will she be grown?"

"She'll be fully grown when she's five, but she can be bred when she's three. You can ride her, but don't ride her hard."

We went in to breakfast and Bant told me to take the wagon and bring all the ripe melons to the house for the cows and pigs.

"Save out three or four for us," he said, "and bust the rest for the animals.

Don't worry. There'll be plenty and more than plenty for the rest of the season."

The job took two hours and seemed like all day. I could hardly wait to put a saddle on Raindrop. Whether she'd throw me, I didn't know. Kenty said she was tame, but he hadn't said she'd been broken. I needn't have worried. She stood unmoving when I saddled her, stood still as stone when I mounted, and then obeyed my every command. Someone had done a good job. I allowed her to gallop, but not for long, and she was anxious to run. She'd be fast. I knew that. You can tell by the way a horse moves.

The days passed slowly and I thought more than once about riding over to Hooker Valley. Every time I planned it, Bant seemed to sense it and outlined chores that needed doing. I thought of asking his permission to go, but realized that might throw him into another one of his black moods. We finally had a good rain and it turned off cool. It rained all night and all the next morning. The sun came out to sparkle the valley in the afternoon and, since it was too wet to work in the fields, I had no chores to do until evening. I rode Raindrop into the foothills and didn't get back to the house until the sun had dipped behind the mountains. Kenty Hooker drove the most beautiful automobile I'd ever seen into our yard just as I'd headed from the corral to the house. It was a Lincoln, red with black trim, and our Model -T looked drab beside it.

"How's my boy?" was his greeting, and I didn't know how to take it. I ducked my head and mumbled like a child and he changed the subject quickly. "How's our Raindrop horse? Do you like her? Did Bant mind that I gave her to you?"

"She's fine," I said. "Gentle as a kitten. Bant says she's just a baby and that I should ride her easy. No, sir, he didn't seem to mind."

"I'm glad. Now, listen, son, let's form a conspiracy. On the way over here I got a hankering for ice cream. Ice cream from a home freezer. To tell you the truth, I can't remember when I've had such a craving. I'll bet I haven't eaten home-made ice cream since I was just a boy."

"Maybe we could make some."

"Well, here's our conspiracy. After a while, say in an hour, you could say something about how good some ice cream would be. I'll say that sounds like a heck of a good idea and your mother will be too polite to say no."

We went on to the house and Mama and Bant came out to the porch. Bant seemed cordial, seemed glad to see Kenty, went out to admire the new Lincoln and didn't seem in the least envious.

"I ordered it special," Kenty said. "The seats are made of leather and the dashboard is teak. It drives real well."

"It must have cost a fortune," Bant said.

"I'm a lucky man," was Kenty's reply. "I have more money than is really decent. In fact, Bant, I was thinking on the way over here that you could make your valley pay twice as much if you had a boost. I'd be more than happy to provide that boost."

"I've always made my own way and I always will," Bant said.

"You're my best friend, Bant. I hope I haven't offended you."

"No offense taken."

We sat on the porch for nearly an hour while Kenty and Bant remembered things they'd done together as boys and young men. Kenty winked at me during a lull in the conversation and I said it sure would be fine to have some good home-made ice cream.

"Now you're talking, Jeff!" Kenty said. "Some ice cream is just what we need. I can't remember the last time I had home-made ice cream."

Mama wasn't fooled and I knew it. Her eyes twinkled.

"Some ice cream would hit the spot," Bant said, rising to the bait.

We went to town in Kenty's car and Bant drove. Kenty promised to teach me to drive and Bant said it would be best if I learned to drive the Model T first. We got a block of ice in a gunny sack and, once home, Kenty clubbed it with the flat of an axe, broke it into small chunks. By the time he'd finished, Mama had the ice cream mixed. We prepared the freezer, using plenty of salt, and I sat on it while Kenty turned the handle. Mama went back into the house and busied herself in the kitchen. Bant moseyed down to the corral.

"You know," Kenty said, "there ought to be an easier way to make ice cream. This business of turning the handle gets boresome."

"This is the only way."

"I don't know about that."

"What other way is there?"

"There ought to be a mechanical way."

He turned for a while but his heart wasn't in it and his mind wasn't on it.

"Get the jack for the Model T, Jeff," he said.

I got the jack and Kenty jacked up the right rear wheel of the Model T. He whistled cheerily while he worked, sent me to get some baling wire, pushed the ice cream freezer over beside the car and tied its handle to the lifted wheel.

"All right, Jeff," he said. "You sit on the freezer and you'll see the marvelous Hooker Automatic Ice Cream Freezer on its maiden voyage."

He started the motor while I sat on the freezer and the wheel started turning and I wasn't sitting on the freezer and the freezer bucket was spinning with the wheel. Milk splattered over me and over the side of the car and on the ground. Kenty cut the motor and stepped out of the car to eye the freezer and the spilled milk.

"There goes our ice cream," he mourned. "It seemed like such a good idea."

"The fellow who said you shouldn't cry over spilled milk didn't know it was supposed to turn into ice cream," I said.

Bant walked up and surveyed the damage. "It looks like one of the famous Kenty Hooker inventions."

"It should have worked," Kenty said.

"It might have if you could have slowed down the car wheel."

Bant went up on the porch and watched while Kenty and I wiped the milk off the Model T. Mama came to the door and we faced her shame-facedly. She frowned for a moment and then laughter drove the frown away.

"I'll vow, Kenty Hooker," she said. "You'll never grow up. You haven't changed a bit."

"I'll never change, Pearl," he said. "You know that. When I like something or somebody, the like is for always. Things are just the same for me, always, and always will be."

Mama's eyes dropped. "People should change. I guess people should make themselves change."

I happened to glance at Bant, saw the black, frozen look on his face and looked away. Bant stood up, literally throwing his chair back, and stalked into the house.

"Well," Kenty said, "there's no ice cream to keep me around here. I'll be going now."

"Supper's almost ready," Mama said.

"Another time, Pearl. I'm sorry about the ice cream."

Bant didn't hit the bottle that night, but his mood was stormy and I gave him a wide berth. I brooded about Kenty's words for days, couldn't understand why he'd flaunted his obvious feelings about Mama in Bant's face. He surely knew Bant's suspicions, surely knew about the gossip sweeping Fort Davis County. I made up my mind that I wouldn't visit Hooker Valley and hoped Kenty would stay away from us. He didn't. One Saturday afternoon Bant went into town and I rode Raindrop out across the valley. I had planned to go swimming, but changed my mind and rode back to the house. Bant's car was in the yard and I heard Mama's laughter when I stepped up on the porch, heard Kenty murmur something, stood where I was and felt a wrongness about them being together with Bant gone. I went on inside and they weren't even sitting close together. Still, I had the feeling they'd moved as I'd entered. I could have been wrong.

They seemed to have their private jokes, Mama and Kenty, and more than once one of them said things that caused Bant to stiffen-and go cold and distant. Always, when this happened, Kenty would leave almost at once. And, always, later, Bant would drink from his bottle and say strange things, accusing things, to Mama. He never accused her of anything in my presence, but the words would come after I'd left the room. They were bad days and all joy left our house. I'd distract myself by thinking of the night Samal and I had spent in that box canyon. Most of those times I'd plain ache for her but it wouldn't last long. Night after night I'd lie awake listening to Bant's footsteps clumping in the kitchen and I'd know that strange, lost look would be on his face and in his eyes.

I remember little things along with the big things, and maybe that's because some of the little things built up to bigger things later. The pump I remember, Kenty Hooker's Remarkable Mechanical Pump.

We had two wells, a windmill for one and a hand pump for the other. The well with the hand pump had been sunk first. We used it for years, but seldom used it after Bant had a new well dug and a windmill installed. The windmill sucker rod broke one day and we were forced to pump water by hand for a week. I was pumping water for the cows and it was heavy work. Kenty drove up and came down to observe, finally caught hold of the long bar that served for the handle and we pumped until the water trough was half filled.

"Do you have to do this every day?"

"Just about."

"When will the windmill be fixed?"

"I don't know. A part had to be ordered."

"There's a stream down in the valley."

"Some of the cattle and horses come up here at night and need water."

"Well, there ought to be an easier way."

"A mechanical way? Are you going to tie the pump handle to the back wheel of the Model T?"

"Not this time, funny fellow," he said. "Here, you just follow me. We'll see what we can do."

I followed him to the tool shed and watched while he rummaged among tools and scraps of metal. Now and then he'd find a rod or flat piece of iron or bolt that seemed to please him. Finally, he gathered up the things he'd found and headed for the pump. He sent me back for a brace-and-bit and a saw, called for a barrel, helped me find a pine board long enough to serve for a see-saw, and went to work. After an hour he stepped back, satisfied.

"There it is, Jeff," he said. "The Hooker Automatic Pump. Kenty Hooker's Remarkable Mechanical Pump. It isn't entirely automatic."

"How does it work?"

"You can see how it works. The see-saw is connected to the sucker rod, just like the handle. Just see-saw and the water will flow."

Neither of us had heard or seen Bant and we jumped when he laughed.

"Who'll be on the other end of the see-saw?" he asked. "Jeff can't see-saw by himself."

"I hadn't thought of that," Kenty admitted.

"I'm too heavy for him," Bant said. "His mother's too busy."

Kenty snapped his fingers and headed for the barn. He returned two minutes later with a gunny sack and a shovel, filled the sack with sand, tied the open end tightly with wire and lashed the sack to one end of the see-saw.

"This sack can be the boy's partner," Kenty said. "All he has to do is kick against the ground when his end is down."

"You fooled me, Kenty," Bant said. "I thought you and Pearl would want to be see-saw partners."

Kenty didn't say a word, didn't act like he'd heard, but I felt uneasy and guilty for Kenty and Mama, as if Bant had aimed his words at me and I was somehow at fault. I got on the see-saw and pumped a little water. It was more trouble than pumping by hand, but I didn't tell Kenty. Kenty watched a few minutes, said he'd see us later and walked to his car. I went on see-sawing while Bant watched Kenty drive away.

"That's enough water, boy," he said. "The windmill will be fixed tomorrow."

The summer ran its course and we had an early fall. Time had passed, but it had been a slow-flowing stream that was never ending and not all the days were bad or sad. I savored the fragments of a teen-age fantasy world halfway between the poles of imagination and reality. I missed Samal and wondered if we'd ever be together again. Sunshine was golden and I tasted with my eyes the shades of green that grownups can't see. I counted dust motes floating in the shafts of sunlight lancing through a window in late afternoon. I saw the down on chicks as separate strands of silken color and the feathers of bantams as fans of varied hues. The water of our stream sparkled. Turtle heads were alligator snouts and crawdads were lobsters from the sea. The warm sun bathed me and the winds caressed me and dust was a friendly thing.

Kenty kept coming back to our house and I kept telling myself it was because of me or because he truly liked Bant and was trying to reach out to a family that was close to him. He became my friend and, though I fought against it, thought of him as my father. There was a bond between us and both of us felt it. We could walk together without speaking and our minds and thoughts reached out and became one and the same.

Bant changed. He changed so slowly that it seemed a natural thing. He became more moody, retreated deeper and deeper inside himself, and more and more he drank from his brown bottle. Now and again I watched him as he watched Mama, and the way he looked at her left me cold and frightened. He had a way of looking at me, too. He looked at me as at a stranger. The wall between us, almost surmountable at first, became a high and solid bar-

rier. I think he felt it and tried to tear it down. He seemed to grope for a closeness we never had, tried to find his way over the wall, but he'd never been
able to do it when it was low enough to step over and certainly couldn't jump
it when it grew higher than I could reach. I tried to help him and didn't
know how, couldn't help him because of my own shyness and the cold stillness that left me mute and distant.

Once, near summer's end, I read late in the living room and Bant told me
to go to bed. I didn't move fast enough to suit him and he slapped me. It was-
n't a hard slap and hardly hurt at all, but he'd never slapped me before. He'd
spanked me a time or two when I was a child, but he'd never slapped me. I
went to my room without saying a word. Tears stung, but I was too old to
cry. I lay in darkness for a long while, heard the door open, heard tip-toed
footsteps, felt the side of my bed sag, felt Bant's big hand smooth my hair
gently as a feather, and then he was gone. Kenty stayed away for several days
and Bant was able to chip away at the barrier between us. They weren't big
chips. That wasn't Bant's way. His chipping was done with the tone of his
voice, his forcing of simple statements that he ordinarily wouldn't have made.
Just little things I noticed. He laughed and smiled occasionally and I began
to hope Kenty would stay away forever. Still, it didn't last. Bant retreated inside himself again and drank again from his bottle late into the nights. I began to realize I'd had my childhood dreams and had seen the world and those
I loved in bright colors, light colors. I had walked a golden thread across a
bridge of days, across a moat of time, and now I'd reached the other side. The
enmity between Bant and Kenty had begun as a slashing cut, but now it was
festering and there was to be no healing. A sore inside Bant was sending ten-
tacles of hate to poison his mind and body.

Kenty came back to our house eight days after the see-saw incident, but
he stayed in the yard and asked if Bant was home. When I told him Bant
had gone into town he told me that Loren Starr had robbed a bank and killed
a policeman.

"His trial is today," he said. "I'm going. I'll bet Bant will be there. Do you
want to go?"

Loren Starr was sentenced to death and I was stunned, but that was the
beginning of my awareness of the world beyond the valley. Jess Blackwell
killed his father-in-law and Kenty took me to that trial, too. On the way
home he told me Jess went free because he had money. I began reading about
Senators and Congressmen, at least about those from my world, and I worried about President Wilson's health. He'd suffered a stroke in Pueblo, Col-
orado, the year before and I was afraid he wouldn't be strong enough to continue his battle for the League of Nations.

Kenty came to the house late in an afternoon, his spotted hound, Bayard,
sitting in the front seat beside him. "Did you ever see a coon, Jeff?" he called.

"Lots of times."

"Did you ever catch one?"

"I can't say that I have."

"Well, they should be swarming in the Narrows and I think it's time to catch one. We'll talk Bant into going along."

Bant came walking from the house, milk buckets in hand. "Do your chores, Jeff," he said.

Kenty helped with the chores. He chopped wood and helped feed the stock. We gathered eggs and he kept telling me about times when he and Bant roamed The Narrows with their dogs.

"Sometimes we went hunting with the men, Jeff," he said, "and our dad-dys let us run with the pack. I had the best nose of the lot. Bant had a pretty good nose, but not as good as mine. I've lost my sense of smell, of course, but that happens to old dogs and old men. But, as a kid, Jeff, I could tree pos-sums or lead the pack after a coon or fox. If I'd been born a dog, I would have been better than old Bayard. I stopped running with the pack, though, the night I took out after the biggest boar coon that's ever been seen in these parts. That coon went into the water and I didn't know any better than to go in after him. The water was icy cold and deep and swift. I swam out and grabbed that coon by an ear and he grabbed me and took me under. I'm telling you, son; he would have drowned me if Bayard's great grand-pappy hadn't jumped in to help. You ask Bant if it isn't true."

Bant hooted and I laughed. He squinted at the sun, just dipping behind the mountains. "It'll be a good night for possums and coon. There'll be a nip in the air tonight."

Mama dished up ham and sweet potatoes for supper and Kenty urged me to eat heartily. "Get a good coat," he warned. "We'll build a fire, but we won't be sitting beside it all night."

I was ready to go, but Bant and Kenty seemed to be in no hurry. Bant smoked his pipe and Kenty rolled a cigarette while Mama made cold meat sandwiches and wrapped them in brown paper. Finally, at dusk, Kenty said we should be on our way. I sat in the back seat of Kenty's car with Bayard and listened to the two men in the front seat laugh and talk as if there were no differences at all between them. It was dim dark when we left the house and the night air was crisp. We drove on a gravel road for several miles before turning off on a deep-rutted road that led to the Narrows. The head-lights cut a dim swath in the darkness. I shivered and huddled close to Ba-yard until Kenty stopped the car and flicked off his lights.

"This is the end of the ride, Jeff," he said. "We walk from here."

We walked into an eerie place, a dark shadowed place, a place where grew giant oaks beside massive rocks that were more felt than seen. We followed the course of a ravine and walked by feel. When we talked, echoes came bouncing back.

"There's a little valley beyond," Kenty said. "That's where we'll hunt. First, though, we'll meet up with some other people."

"How do you know where they'll be?"

"There's a cave up ahead. We call it the Needle's Eye. Hunters meet there to build their fires."

I tagged along behind, stumbled along, kept close up. After a long while I sensed the ravine had narrowed. It was darker, if possible, so dark that I was forced to follow Bant and Kenty by the sounds they made. And then, quite suddenly, I was alone.

"I can't see you," I called, stood still and waited.

"Hey!" I yelled.

My echo mocked me.

It was quiet, dead still quiet, but Bayard padded up behind me and nuzzled my leg. I stooped and caught hold of his ruff. He stepped ahead and led me straight toward the looming blackness deeper than blackness, a solid rock wall.

"He's found us," Kenty's voice came from somewhere in the darkness.

"Where are you?" I asked.

Kenty struck a match. By the light of its flickering flame I could see a group of men, Kenty and Bant, John Parl and Jack Medfort. We were in a cave, a crack in the solid rock wall, and within moments Kenty had stuck match to kindling. A fire blazed and I could see the men squatting on their heels. The story swapping went on for an hour, until the fire had burned down to glowing embers, and then Kenty said it was time to hunt. He took the coffee pot outside and returned with water, threw in coffee grounds and crumbled egg shells, raked embers to one side and placed the pot on it.

It was a good hunt, though possums were not as plentiful as we had hoped. We caught six and Bayard treed two coons. I shook two possums from trees by myself, but the coons were allowed to go unmolested.

"They're no good to eat and their hides wouldn't bring fifty-cents apiece," Kenty said.

My legs were trembly and my eyelids were heavy when we headed back to the cave. Kenty threw wood on the embers and we warmed ourselves before a raging fire. Kenty brought tin cups from a shelf of rock and Kenty served the coffee. I sat, half asleep, munching a meat sandwich and drinking the steaming brew. The talk turned to hunting and dogs. Old Bayard's ancestry was tracked back to Old Blue, the king of dogs if the stories I heard that night were true. I only spoke once to ask where Bayard and his line had been while he was away for all those years.

"Eben Grant kept Bayard's pappy until he died," Kenty said. "He bred several bitches, but kept only the finest of the line. Bayard is ten years old now and I'm hunting for a fine bitch so the line can go on."

I nodded before the fire while the men talked. Words had lost all meaning to me. I knew the talk was still of dogs, but what was said floated around past my hearing. Only the tone of Jack Medfort's voice aroused me.

"You can say what you want," he was saying. "You'll never make me believe Bayard's sire was Bull Durham. The Durham had a long nose and Bayard's nose is more square. The Durham was a dun, but Bayard is gray with brown spots. The Durham had a little old crook in his tail and Bayard's tail is straight. If you'll just try, you'll remember that Bayard's mother was more like Bull Durham than Bull Durham himself. No, boys, Bayard is a bastard, sure as you're born."

I came wide awake and saw at once that Kenty was angry. "Eben Grant saw to the breeding," Kenty said. "Bayard is a true son of Bull Durham and that's all there is to it. Just because he doesn't favor his sire doesn't prove a thing. Maybe he favors some of his ancestors. If Pa was alive, he could tell. But I'm convinced Bayard is the son of Bull Durham."

"He hunts like Bull Durham," Bant said. "He ought to be hunting something better than possums and coons, though. He's too good a dog for trash hunting."

"He's smart, Bant," Kenty said. "Possum and coon hunting won't hurt him a bit. Oh, I'm with you on one thing. I'd love to sit by a fire and hear him baying after a fox. Still and all, though, Bull Durham hunted possum and coon in his time and it didn't bother him a bit. Besides, Bayard is ten years old. He won't have many hunting days left."

"He's a bastard," Jack Medfort said. "Now, I'm not saying he's not a good dog. He's got enough good traits from his mama to make him a first class dog. But he's not the dog Bull Durham was."

"I side with Kenty," Bant said. "In the first place, the breeding was supervised and certified. Eben Grant was careful with his dogs and his word is his bond. He didn't leave a bitch running around in heat. He tended to her mating. He wanted a last batch of puppies from Bull Durham and he got them. Bayard was the pick of the litter."

"Lot's of she animals run loose in heat and their masters don't know about it," Jack Medfort said. "I've heard tell of a few respectable married women whose offspring turned out to be bastards."

"I wouldn't call the mothers of bastards respectable," John Parl said.

"About Bayard," Kenty said, a little desperately, it seemed to me. "His mama was a bitch, but Bayard's no bastard."

"Yes sir," Jack Medfort said in a musing tone. "Some women, well regarded women, mind you, sometimes go astray. Why, you'd be surprised to know about some of the women in this very community."

I sat staring at Jack Medfort's face, at the sly smile, the slack lips, the weasel

eyes. He was baiting and I knew it, and I was sure I knew the victim he
wanted to sting.

"Let's cut out this talk," Kenty said. "It's dangerous and wrong."

"What's the matter, Kenty?" Jack gibed. "You act kind of nervous."

"I'm not nervous, Jack. I just don't like this kind of talk."

"No names have been mentioned. Anyway, you're a bachelor. You've got
no wife to worry about."

"Keep them pregnant in the summer and barefoot in the winter," John Parl
said, and laughed silently, shoulders shaking. "That's my motto."

"Take old Kenty, here," Jack Medfort said. "I'll bet he's afraid to throw a rock
for fear of hitting one of his kids. He ever throw a rock at you, boy?" and he
turned to face me.

"You've gone too far, Jack," Kenty said. "I'd advise you to back off now. I said
now."

"I'm not the kind to back off."

Bant stood before Jack Medfort, looking down at him. "What are you trying to say, Jack? Spell out what you're trying to say."

"Aw, he just likes to hear the sound of his own voice, Bant," Kenty said.
"Jack's not happy unless he's nasty talking somebody."

Jack Medfort stood, stretched, yawned. "I guess it's time to go home. My
old woman will be in bed waiting for me. I can depend on that."

"Let's all have another cup of coffee and go home," John Parl said. "Let's
stop the foolish talk and just have a cup of coffee and go on home."

"No," Bant said. "I want Jack to explain himself. I don't think he's crazy
enough to be saying what it sounds like he's saying. So, all right, Jack. You've
hinted at things but you haven't spelled it out. Let's hear exactly what's on
your mind."

"I haven't hinted at anything," Jack Medfort said. "I was just talking to pass
the time. That's all. Just talking."

"Talking through your hat," Kenty said. "You're going to be in a pack of
trouble one of these days, Jack."

Jack Medfort shrugged. "Let's go home, men. You, too, boy. You are Bant's
boy, aren't you?"

Bant hit him, hit him on the mouth. I heard the crunch, saw the blood on
his chin, saw his knees crumple and his eyes glaze. He went to his knees,
lowered his head and stayed there.

"Let's go home," Bant said, and walked out into the darkness.

Kenty took the coffee pot off the embers and tossed its contents on the
ground. He placed it and the tin cups on the rock ledge and we found our
way back to the car. Bant was waiting for us and we started for home. We
were half-way there before a word was said.

"You shouldn't have hit him," Kenty said.

"He had it coming."

"It'll start talk."

"The talk has started. The fact is, it never stopped."

"I'm sorry," Kenty said.

CHAPTER THREE

September brought golden sun-filtered days and crisp-chill nights. Bant seemed to have found some relief from his encounter with Jack Medfort and, for days and nights, didn't drink from his brown bottle. He didn't have much to say, but that wasn't unusual. What was unusual was that he wasn't short and curt with me. He seemed more at ease with Mama and seemed to welcome Kenty's visits. Kenty came often and sat until bedtime, sat with us before the fire, played Bant's fiddle, told stories about the oil fields, told us about the progress made on his house and out-buildings and urged us to come over for a look. Once he brought up the subject of our valley and what it could become, again offered to put up the money for its betterment and appealed to Mama to make Bant accept.

"You're my family," he said. "I have enough money to make me ashamed and I'd like to see it put to good use. You can pay me back in ten years if you want."

"We're doing just fine," Bant said. "We have everything we need and we're doing better all the time."

"We need new corrals and a new barn," Mama said. "You're having to stack hay in the fields and you're adding cattle and horses every year. Jeff will be going to college one of these days and you'll need help to handle things. You'll need help to handle things and I won't have your wetbacks in the house. You'll have to build a bunkhouse."

"Just a shack," Bant said. "I can throw that up by myself."

"College for Jeff will be expensive."

"I've planned for that, Pearl. We'll have the money when the time comes. As far as that goes, Jeff has one more year at Rock Creek School and then he'll have to go to Fort Davis one year. I've planned for that, too. He'll board in town and I'll bring him home on the weekends."

That was the first time I'd heard Bant speak of my future. Mama had mentioned it often enough, but Bant never had. I'd worried about high school. Rock Creek was a four-room school three miles distant and I'd always ridden my pony, but it was fifteen miles to Fort Davis, too far to ride a horse.

Mama and Kenty dropped the subject, but later I asked Mama why Bant was unwilling to borrow money from Kenty.

"Pride, I suppose."

"He's borrowed money from the bank," I said. "What's the difference?"

"They're like brothers in some ways," she said, "but they've always been... rivals. We can forget it, Jeff. Bant will never take money from Kenty."

I thought about the Narrows and decided to explore it, but decided not to tell Mama and Bant. It was a wild place, full of rattlers, and they'd tell me not to go or worry if I did. I thought of saying I wanted to visit Samal, but Bant despised Old Trails and would tell me I couldn't go. Finally, on a Saturday, Bant and Mama decided to go into Fort Davis. I told them I was feeling puny and would stay home. The moment they were out of sight I saddled Rainbow and was on my way.

I found the place Kenty had parked his car the night we'd gone hunting and I tethered Raindrop to a tree there.

I went to the Needle's Eye first and then followed the stream we call the Torrent up the narrow canyon that gave the Narrows its name. The stream wasn't more than ten feet wide at its widest point and it was wicked. It boiled and burbled and whirled and sucked. Only strong swimmers ever breasted it, I'd been told. I was just about to turn back when I heard whoops and yells up ahead. I climbed ten feet up the canyon wall for a look and saw the whoopers. There were six of them, counting the skinny little kid. Coy Trails I recognized at once, Samal's brother, so the little one had to be Festal. The other four were the Fancher boys. Their names were Pratt, Neyland, Delly and Forbis from Crandall's Cove. They were all buck naked and five of them were in the water, but one by one they'd come out to the bank and try to get the little one to jump in.

I'd seen Coy before, in town, but hadn't paid him much attention. The scandal of the county, he'd been a football hero in high school. People said he was smart as a whip, but just plain sorry. He was accused of robbing three or four stores and stealing chickens. He and the Fancher boys were at least twenty years old and all were big. Coy came out of the water and squatted in front of Festal and I had a chance to see him up close. He was a handsome man, I had to admit that, and there was something special about him. It was the way he held his head, partly, but it was more than that. It was the way he held his body, if there is a way to hold a body, and the way he moved. He moved and acted like he was a king and knew it and expected everyone else to know it and respect him.

The Fancher boys began to yell at Festal, began to splash water at him, and the tone of their yells became threatening. They must have tired of yelling threats and dares, finally, because they came out of the water and surrounded the poor kid. Coy shook his finger in the little boy's face, but I couldn't hear what he said. Festal was stubborn, or just plain scared. He shook his head from side to side, backed off when crowded, and I wanted him to run. Coy struck a commanding pose and pointed at the water.

They'll throw him in, I decided. Sure as shooting they'll get tired of his stubbornness and lose their tempers and throw him in.

I looked at the fast moving, boiling Torrent and wondered how long Festal could last in such water. Not long. Just as I'd feared, Coy and the Fanchers decided they'd had enough. They moved in toward him and Festal backed away, but I knew they'd catch him. I stood on top of a boulder and threw a rock the size of my fist as far as I could throw it. The thing hit the water's edge and made a splash I could see, but those big boys were too busy trying to corner the little fellow to notice. I yelled, but the wind blew my hollering back down my throat. I jumped up and down and waved my arms and screeched, but the boys had their backs to me and didn't hear. Festal was all hunkered up and too busy backing away from the four crazies to pay attention to some idiot who should have been minding his own business instead of dancing atop a canyon wall that was higher than a lot of buildings.

They caught the kid just as I started climbing down. I had realized I couldn't do any good from a distance, so I began picking my way down the canyon wall. I slid and scrambled and scrabbled for hand holds, stuck my toes in cracks too small for anything but toenails, found hand holes in fissures that weren't there and slide-burned my way over humps that should have stopped me. Because the Good Lord looks after some fools, I made it to the bottom.

Wrath was a fearsome thing inside me and I feared for the physical safety of those fools once I got my hands on them. Rage and righteousness gave me the strength of ten and I figured on wringing Trails' necks as easily as Mama wrung chickens' necks.

They saw me coming. They had the little fellow spread-eagled in the air, swung him back and forth in a one-for-the-money-two-for-the-show cadence. They paid me no attention at all, even though I was screaming at the top of my lungs. They let little old Festal go before I could reach him. I could see him sailing in slow motion, sprawled out in the air, arms out and legs out, head up and neck stretched, mouth wide open and screaming soundlessly, eyes wide and starey. He seemed to hang in mid-air and he saw me, begged me with his big scared eyes, and then he dropped like a rock and splashed the water and was gone.

I pulled off my boots, standing and hopping around to do it, shook my fists at the new enemies and told them I was going to kill them, and then I dived into the Torrent. The water was icy cold and the shock of it drove air from my lungs. The water plucked at me and sucked at me and sent me skirling. I turned a few flips under water, hit bottom a time or two, rolled over and over and then righted myself and started swimming around and grabbling around with my hands. Something sucked me under and I reached air just before my lungs burst. Just then it was every dog for himself and Festal Trails was the least of my worries. Rage returned only after I managed to suck in enough air to live. I swam against the current, worked just hard enough to hold my own, looked for the kid and decided he was gone.

Four big boys were standing on the banks of the Torrent watching me. They seemed mildly curious. Coy was smoking a cigarette. He took a deep drag and passed the butt to one of his brothers.

"Come help," I yelled. "Don't you know you've drowned that boy?"

"Aw, he won't drown," Coy answered. "He'll come up swimming like a tadpole in a minute. You'd better get out of there, though, if you don't want to drown."

I had found shallow water and stood with legs braced against the current. "Just remember I saw you throw him in. If he drowns, I'll have the sheriff on you."

"He won't drown," Coy said. He had a pleasant voice, a sort of laughing voice. "If he does drown, you might drown, too. Ever think of that?"

I knew a threat when I heard one, but Coy Trails made his threat as nice and pretty as I've ever heard one. I stood there, miserable and cold and uncertain.

There was no future in waiting for Festal to surface again, so I went under. I stayed under, fighting the current, being tumbled by the current, as long as I could. I kept hitting bottom, kept being scraped along the bottom. The water roiled me around and I knew I wasn't accomplishing a thing. Down there under the water I felt as futile as a fish in the middle of forty acres of plowed ground. Finally, with my strength going fast, I knew I'd have to give it up.

The four had finished their cigarette and one of them, Forbis, flicked the short butt at me. The thing landed in the water not two inches from my nose.

"You murdering son of a bitch," I said.

"I reckon we'd better find Festal," Coy said.

"He don't seem in no hurry to come up for air," Neyland said.

Two of them, Pratt and Delly, walked down stream and waded in.

"He's not down there," Coy called. "Let's look in front of that big rock."

"I figure he's way down stream," Delly said.

"I say he ain't," Coy yelled. "He went limp and settled to the bottom. He's probably caught up against that rock. I'll look there and you all wait until I come up. If I don't find him, we'll spread out and look."

Coy dived in, knifed into the water, came up and treaded water, went under again and came up beside the huge rock with Festal in his arms. He swam at an angle upstream and shoreward, swam easily with one arm, cradled Festal easily with his left arm and went ashore near me. I followed him out and stood shaking with rage and cold.

"You waited too long," I said. "He's dead. I'm going to get the sheriff and see you hang, all of you. I'm going to watch them build a scaffold and then I'll watch while they hang every living mother's son of you."

"You talk too damned much," Coy Trails said. "If I was you I'd haul ass for home. If this boy is dead I'm going to hold your head under water until you stop breathing. That way, see, we won't have to worry about the sheriff."

He bent over Festal for a second or two and then went over and picked up his shirt. I thought he was going to spread it over the boy to keep him warm, but he got a sack of Bull Durham and some matches from the pocket and dropped the shirt.

"Samal's gonna raise hell," that fool Pratt said. "We shoulda dragged him out sooner."

I knelt beside the boy and rolled him over on his stomach. He was cold, cold, and his skin was tinged with blue. I turned his head to one side and started trying to prize his mouth open. His jaw seemed locked. I parted his lips and saw his teeth gritted.

Something snapped inside me.

There was a fist-sized rock beside Festal's head and I hefted it. Everything was red. The green trees were red and the sky was red. I lifted that rock and I screamed. I guess I frothed at the mouth. I threw the rock at Coy and I don't see how I could have missed. I missed. Coy didn't change expression, just went right on rolling his cigarette.

"Get his mouth open for me," I said. "You're the strongest," and I knocked the cigarette makings out of his hands.

"You're a spunky little bastard," he said.

He knelt beside Festal and, easy as pie, opened the locked jaws. He backed off then and I reached inside the boy's mouth and hooked a finger behind his curled tongue and pulled it straight. I straddled him and started pumping against his back. I didn't have much idea about what I was doing, but water gushed out of his mouth and he made a gagging, choking sound. I began to pump, timed the pumping against my own breathing, pressed down and let go fast, pressed down and let go fast and kept it up until I thought my arms would drop off. Coy pushed me aside, then, and he turned Festal over on his back and began pumping against his chest, did it with easy rhythm, and I could tell he was doing some good. It wasn't long before Festal was breathing easy. He coughed and then he vomited and then he was a lot better and in no time at all he was sitting up.

He wasn't a bad looking boy. I guessed he was about twelve or so. Cut his hair and he'd look like any other kid, provided he had on some clothes. Naked, he'd always be different because there were scars all over his body. There were welts and cuts and stripes on his legs and buttocks and back, and he'd been whipped so many times that scars had formed on top of scars. There was a scared look in his eyes, too, the kind of look you see in the eyes of a dog that has been kicked and whipped when he hasn't done anything he knows of to warrant kicking and whipping.

"They nearly killed you this time, Festal," I said.

He hung his head and didn't say anything.

"Maybe next time you'll come on in the water when we tell you," Coy said.
"We was just going to teach you to swim."

"Leave him alone," I said. "You've done enough for one day."

Coy grinned at me. "You're mighty biggity for a kid. You ain't big enough
to be so uppity. I've put up with you this long because you've got spunk, but
don't push your luck, kid, or I may send you home without the family jewels."

"I don't have any jewels."

"I'm talking about your balls, kid. I may kick them off or I may cut them
off."

"I'm not afraid of you, Coy Trails. Or your fool friends. I already know
you're trash. Animals wouldn't treat their own the way you've treated Festal. Look at all those scars."

"Pa did that," Coy said. "He hates the little bastard."

"Why?"

"Because he's a bastard."

Coy Trails lifted his eyebrow and it made him look wicked. It's a funny
thing, but he didn't look wicked until he lifted that eyebrow. The fact was
that he was handsome. He was tall and he had broad shoulders, like I said,
and his waist was narrow and his muscles were smooth and ropey. His neck
was thick, but long enough. He had blue eyes, the clearest and bluest eyes
you'd ever hope to see on a man. His hair was coal black, the eyebrows black
and heavy. His forehead was broad and his nose straight and true. His mouth
was wide and it was a good thing for him because his lips were softer and
redder and fuller than a man's lips should be.

"Who gave you the idea I was so mean?" Coy asked. "Was it Samal?"

"It was everybody in the county."

I shouldn't have said that. Coy moved so fast that I had no time to duck
or even flinch. He swung his right hand and there was a clopping sound and
the next thing I knew I was flat on the ground with blood flowing from my
nose.

"You can tell everybody in the county that I did that. And from now on,
boy, you watch your tongue."

"You'll be sorry you did that," I said. "I'm still not afraid of you. Don't think
I am just because I don't get up and fight. I'll bide my time."

He reached down and helped me to my feet. "Strip off them clothes and
we'll wring them out for you. While we're doing this, wash the blood off
with cold water. It'll stop the bleeding. I didn't hit you hard. Don't forget your
boots."

I stripped and bathed my nose and face while Coy wrung water from my clothing. I dressed, then, and hobbled away. I looked back once, but there wasn't a soul in sight. I went on back to Raindrop and rode home, rode into the yard and saw I'd arrived ahead of Mama and Bant. I unsaddled, went inside to change clothes, hung my wet things on the line in the back yard and started doing my chores.

There were a thousand stories about Old Trails and Coy, but I don't know how many of them were true. A favorite story, often told, was about Coy's initiation into the chicken stealing business. As a teen-aged football hero, he was popular with the town girls. The trouble was, he had no money for dating and decided to steal chickens and sell them. He tried once and failed because the chickens made so much noise he was forced to run. To learn the trade, he went to the county expert, Cletus Fancher.

"I'll tell you what, boy," Cletus is said to have told Coy. "You bring me one shoat Old Trails is raising for meat and I'll make you the second best chicken thief in the county."

Coy stole the pig while Old Trails was away and took it over mountains and down mountains to Cletus Fancher. That night, they selected the hen house of Olin Telford for their first raid. Cletus took the first three and shoved them into a tow-sack and then it was Coy's turn. The hens on the roosts raised a ruckus, flapping and cackling and squawking, and Olin Telford caught Coy and Cletus red-handed.

"I swear, Coy," Cletus said as Olin held them in place with a shotgun. "If I told you once I told you a hundred times. You're supposed to slide your hand under the roosting fowl and just let it step into your hand. Don't never just grab a chicken, boy! Let this be a lesson to you!"

They say Olin Telford knocked Cletus down with the butt of his shotgun, but then he took a fit of laughing and let the two go free.

"Hey, Cletus!" Olin Telford yelled into the darkness. "It's bad enough to be a chicken thief your ownself, but you'll never teach that boy your technique. Good chicken thieves are born, not made!"

"You mind your own business," Cletus yelled back.

"I'll do that if you'll let the boy practice on your chickens and not mine!"

Old Trails lived on a mesa too small for running more than twenty head of cattle, but the soil was rich and well watered. It was said that he'd made money in years when others' crops had failed and that he had every dime he'd ever made hidden in crocks buried somewhere. I heard that story often and wondered if Coy had dug holes all over the place hunting the treasure. It was a strange family. Samal I knew and loved. She was smart, too. Coy, though, seemed bent on a life of crime. He was suspected of having robbed the bank at Presidio. When four masked men robbed stores in Fort Davis, people said the robbers were Coy and three of the Fancher boys. It was said, too, that Old Trails and Coy had a still in the Narrows that turned out the best corn whiskey in the state. People could drink it without fear of going blind, it was said. Old Trails, they said, did not allow old batteries or dead rattle snakes to ferment along with his liquor.

It was Festal who interested me. If all the stories I'd heard were true, the old man and Coy hated him like poison. I'd never laid eyes on him until that Saturday when he'd nearly drowned, though Samal talked about him affectionately and I felt that I knew him. Now, the very next day, in church I heard people talking about Festal and the way his pa and his own brother treated him. One woman told Mama that Old Trails had whipped him and tied him, suspended by his feet, from an oak tree limb.

"He was unconscious for more than a day," the woman said.

Another woman said he had been buried in a hole, with just his head sticking out, and had been left there for almost half a day, the hot sun beating down on him, before Samal found him.

"We should have the sheriff on them," Mama said. "I know Samal is a good girl and I know she'd like all that cruelty to stop. I'll wager she would testify against that old reptile and his boys."

"It's family business," Bant said, "and not ours."

Kenty visited us that Sunday afternoon and I told him what the Trails boys had done. He said it was too bad and that Samal shouldn't have to live with such trash.

"She wants to take a room in Fort Davis and finish high school," I said. "She wants to go to college after that."

"She'll have her chance," Kenty promised. "I'll see to it."

"But what about Festal? Why do they treat him like they do?"

"I don't know for sure. Some folks say he's not really a Trails."

"He looks a lot like the others."

"I know. I visited them soon after I got back. The gossipers say he's Coy's son, but that can't be true. Coy is no more than about twenty-one or twenty-two and the boy is about twelve."

"I'm going to find out more about him," I said.

"Don't fool around with those people, Jeff. Don't go near the Trails place. Those people are bad."

I didn't heed his advice. Two days later, at breakfast, I asked Bant and Mama if I could ride over to Hooker Valley. Bant acted like he hadn't heard, just went on eating, but Mama said it would be all right unless Bant had some chores for me. Bant still acted like he hadn't heard anything, so I asked him point blank if it was all right with him.

"Go ahead," he said. "Tell Kenty to drop over before Saturday. The Winchester people are sending their best rifleman into Fort Davis to challenge all comers. There's a hundred dollar prize to the man that can beat him."

"Are you going to try?" I asked.

"You'd better believe it."

I saddled Raindrop and headed out on what I considered to be about my last outing before the start of school. Kenty's valley was between our place and the Narrows and it took an hour to get there. I hadn't seen the valley in years, but now in the last days of summer, it was beautiful. I stopped on a crest to look. The valley, like ours, was lush blue-green, even this late in the year, surrounded by red-tinged mountains, studded here and there by groves of trees, laced by a spring creek graced by willows.

I gasped at sight of the house and the number of outbuildings, all red tiled, all made of native stone. There was a bunkhouse, large enough by my guess to house a dozen men, a cookhouse between the bunkhouse and the main house, connected to it by a covered walk-way, one large barn for the storage of hay and grain, another for the storage of equipment, one for cows and a stable large enough for twenty horses. There were corrals for penning, corrals for training of horses, loading chutes and what I took to be a quarter-mile running track. I saw it all, saw no person, entered the house and wandered through rooms freshly painted, freshly paneled, marveled at the workmanship and wondered why one lone man would need such a house. The hearth before the fireplace in the living room, the hearth alone, was half as large as our entire living room. There were fireplaces in bedrooms, in the dining room, and even in the kitchen.

The day stretched before me and I was reluctant to ride home, felt vaguely dissatisfied with myself, found myself dreading the start of school and wondered why I didn't look forward to it as I always had. The late days of summer, I decided, are the best of all in some ways and in other ways the worst. They are golden days made for dreaming and planning and some day I'm going to amount to something days, but they are the bitter sweet days, too. Especially, I've found, in looking back, if one is a teenager who has for the first time in his life looked deep inside himself to discover that he is nothing special. I found, on that day, that my thoughts had never been as deep as I had imagined, had never been different from the thoughts of millions of others. I didn't like my feelings that day and found myself wondering if they'd been caused by the sight of Hooker Valley and the grand place Kenty had built for himself.

I mounted Raindrop and headed for the Narrows, tied him in the shade of a tree and went down that narrow canyon, paused to throw rocks into the Torrent, dropped in sticks to race in the water and watched them bobbing and weaving and riding crests and skittering like small boats in the swift current. I paid little attention to my surroundings until shadows fell about me thick and cool and heavy. I looked up, then, and knew I had wandered past the Needle's Eye to a place called the Gorge. It was a wildsome place, quiet except for the swifting gurgle of the Torrent, shut off from the sun and barren as a rocky desert, a canyon place, narrowed to a small gap at the topmost crest of the cliffs, wider at the base and narrow at the top so that when you looked up, you saw an almost-ceiling of rock above.

The Torrent, farther on, widened and quieted a bit, ran quieter and deeper, and the water was green and white-froth flaked. There were sandy beaches and flat, white stones. All in all, except for the lonesomeness and wildsomeness, it was as pretty a place as I'd ever seen.

I sat down and leaned against a rock. The coolness was refreshing and I felt my muscles go limp, felt my eyelids grow heavy. The water sound was soothing and deep sleep slipped up on me. I don't know how long I slept because the canyon blocked out the sun, but I knew what I'd heard to rouse me. A girl was singing and I recognized Samal's voice. I started to stand up, but then my eye caught a flash of white and the singing was stilled and I heard water splash. It was quiet for a moment and then she laughed.

"Here I come with both eyes open," a man called. Kenty Hooker.

He stood on a rock thrust out over the Torrent and he was as naked as a jaybird. For a count of three he stood there, swung his arms, and his body lifted to tip-toe. Like a bird in flight, he arched into the air, flew cleanly, swiftly, and there was scarcely a splash, scarcely a ripple, when he hit water. He went under and stayed under. For a while I thought he might have hit a rock under water, thought maybe he was dead or unconscious, that his body would be taken away by the current.

Samal didn't act scared. She swam over to a flat rock and I watched her climb out to stand in nakedness. I watched and didn't breathe. She was golden honey white, rounded and curved in wicked pleasant soft round curves and I sucked in breath, sucked in air and trembled.

Kenty broke water, went to his back and floated, filled his eyes with the sight of beauty naked and unashamed.

I crept closer.

This is no place to be, I told myself, and crept closer.

"You go along home, Samal," Kenty said. "You go on along home now, like a good girl. I don't want to hurt you, honey, but I'm just a man and might not be able to help myself if you keep standing there like that. It's just about more than a natural man can bear."

Samal laughed. It wasn't innocent laughter or teasing laughter, just amused laughter. She laughed and dived into the Torrent and Kenty swam away from her. He swam across the stream, climbed the rocks and disappeared. He was gone a couple of minutes or so and then he returned to stand again on the high rock. He was dressed and he stood up there to look down at Sam.

"We won't meet here again, Sam," he said. "You hear me, honey? We must-n't."

Sam swam close to the rock and looked up at him. "Are you still in love with Pearl?"

"Why do you ask that?"

"Well, are you?"

Kenty stared down at her for a long moment. "That's not a fair question, Sam. But, since you've asked it, I'll answer. I guess a man always loves the first girl he ever loved, but it's not the kind of love you're thinking about. Pearl is the finest woman I know, always was and always will be. Bant is my closest friend. He's like a brother to me. Besides... there's Jeff. I want to help him over the humps."

"Do you want to know something, Kenty?"

"Tell me."

"I'm going to marry you one of these days."

Kenty grinned, shook his head, turned and was gone. Samal swam across the pool to a flat rock and I watched her lie there, watched her until she stood up and dressed. My manhood was erect, swollen, and my mouth was dry as cotton. She slipped into her dress, wriggled a little, and then walked toward me. She walked toward me and I ducked. If she saw me, she gave no sign. I ducked behind rocks and behind trees, and then when I was safely out of sight I ran for a hundred yards down-stream. I sat on a rock and waited.

"What are you doing here?" she asked when she came up to me.

"Nothing," I muttered.

She smiled, all innocence. "Did you see me in swimming?"

I hesitated, and then decided to be truthful. "Yes."

"Really?"

"Yes."

"Did you get an eye full?"

"Yes."

"You're wicked," she chided, and smiled.

"Can we do it again?"

"Right now?"

"Yes."

"No. You've had your treat and I had mine. I'll save myself for my husband. I'm not a loose woman, Jeff."

"I never thought you were."

"It was fun, though, wasn't it?"

"Come on, Sam. Just one more time."

"I'm sorry, Jeff, I really am. But, no. My mind's made up. I'll be getting married one of these days and from now on I'll save myself. Do you want to come to my house with me? We still have some late melons."

"Kenty said he'd send you into Fort Davis to finish school. Are you going?"

"He offered," she said, "but I'm not going. Festal needs me and, besides, I've decided I don't want to finish."

"You always wanted to go to college."

"I'm going to marry Kenty Hooker, Jeff. I told him. You must have heard."

"He's old enough to be your father."

"That doesn't mean a thing. Come on, we'll go to my house."

"I left Raindrop tied to a tree."

"He'll be all right. It isn't far and you can get him later."

"Maybe I'd better not."

"Don't worry about Coy and my pa. I can handle them. Festal told me how you helped him and I'll always love you for that."

"Why don't you get the sheriff to arrest Old Trails and Coy? Festal has sores all over his body."

"He hasn't been whipped for more than a year now," Sam said. "I peppered Pa and Coy with buckshot the last time they whipped him." She laughed. "It took an hour to pick the shot out of their asses. I told them I'd blow their heads off the next time and they believed me."

"Did you mean it?"

"You'd better believe it. They did."

"Why do they treat him like that?"

"You've heard the gossip. Don't tell me you haven't. My mother ran off just after Festal was born. He was a weak baby, real sickly, and he's not right until this day. There are times when he's as bright as a new penny and other times when he won't talk at all. There are times when what he says doesn't make sense. His words will jumble and he'll say things like 'I'm trying to as the white horse clouds rosy white talk as far as you Babel Tower twice.' It's weird, Jeff, but it doesn't bother me. I know he's bright. There's just something that goes loose at times. I was teaching him his lessons not long ago and he wrote 'What's wrong with me?'"

I followed her up the Narrows to a place where the canyon walls were sloped and we climbed the north one, came out on a mesa, though it wasn't as flat as mesas generally are. It was rocky, with some stunted trees. I walked in dread of Coy Trails and his old man, but followed Sam through a stand of oaks to a trail. It wasn't a road and it wasn't a lane, more trail than either, but not a trail. It wound around and almost curved back on itself. The ruts were deep where the topsoil had washed away, but the bottoms of the ruts were solid rock.

Rocks lined the trail, and that was a peculiar thing. Some of them were as large as wagons and a few were as big as houses, but the peculiar thing was that they lined the trail. I wondered why the trail hadn't been made out on flat ground.

The Trails house surprised me. It was a big house, bigger than ours, and solid and substantial. It was set at the edge of a bluff that led to a small valley, but it was a part of this high landscape and not a thing separate. It was made of log, mostly, but there were frame wings and wings made of rock. The roof wasn't flat, but it wasn't steep and pitched, and the shingles were weathered gray like the rocks on the mesa. The porch was long and wide and covered, shaded by vines. Flowers grew in the yard, grew in patches here and there all around the house, and cobbled walks led from the ends of the porch to outbuildings. Samal ran ahead of me and I stood looking the place over.

"Someone has been telling lies," I muttered aloud. "Old Trails couldn't be all bad if he built a house like that."

"You're crazier'n hell," someone said. "His pa built this place."

I stared at the biggest rock beside the trail and couldn't see anything but rock until the business end of a rifle nudged around the corner and sunlight glinted on polished metal. "All right, Festal Trails," I said. "Don't point that thing at me. I proved I was your friend when they threw you in the Torrent."

"I ain't got ary friend in the world but for Sam. Everybody hates me and some day I'm gonna shoot every living soul that walks and breathes. Except for Sam and me. What's your name?"

"Jeff Carr. You don't hate me and you won't shoot me because I'm your friend. Do you remember that I helped you?"

"I remember."

"Tell me something, Festal Trails. Why do you stay around people who whip you and throw you in the Torrent and hang you by the hands or feet from a tree and bury you in a hole? Why haven't you run away?"

"Hell, boy, where would I go? How would I live? I get funny spells now and again. Besides, they'd catch me before I could get out of the county."

"Well, Sam says things are getting better for you."

"Some. She shot Coy and Pa in the ass. What are you doing here? Don't you know better'n to come up here? Pa don't allow no kids to come up here."

"Samal brought me."

"Well, you ain't to the house yet. If I was you, I'd turn around and go back to where I came from."

"Come on out from behind that rock," I said. "I'm not going to hurt you, for goodnes sakes."

"I'm not afraid of you," Festal said. "I just don't feel like coming out."

"Aw, come on out."

"You go on along back home."

"Look, Sam's your sister and the best friend you have. She's my best friend, too, and she wanted me here. I want to be your friend, so come on out here where I can see you." I had half a mind to stop the yammering and arguing and go on home like he said.

He came around the rock and the minute I saw him I knew why he had-n't wanted me to see him. He wore overalls with galluses, but no shirt. His shoulders were cut and striped with new wounds cut across old scars and I knew his back would be cut and slashed as bad or worse.

"Who did it?"

"Coy. He's a mean sonuvabitch."

"Did Old Trails see it?"

"He egged it on."

"When did it happen?"

"This morning. Coy whipped me because I spilled a bucket of milk."

"And your pa egged him on?"

He was puzzled. "Pa's the one that whipped me. Grandpa egged him on."

"Coy is your pa?"

"That's what Grandpa says."

"What does Coy say?"

"He says it ain't so. Says he's my brother and Grandpa is my pa. Coy says if he was my pa, then my Grandma would be my ma and that it ain't true. Hell, I don't know."

"Who is your mother if your grandmother isn't, like Coy says?"

"Wouldn't you like to know?"

"Come on, Festal. Who is your mother?"

"Grandpa says Sam is, but Sam says that's a cruel lie."

"What does Coy say about that?"

"He says he's done a lot of bad things, but that he has never fucked his own sister."

"Well, you believe Sam and Coy. They're telling the truth. Old Trails is your father and your mother ran away from him just after you were born. Come on. Let's go show Samal what Coy did to you."

"I wish I had a real mother and a pa that liked me," Festal said. "Coy tells me that Samal is my mother and Grandpa is my pa. Sometimes I call Coy my pa and that makes him mad. Real mad. He slaps the shit out of me. Some-times I call Grandpa my pa and that makes him mad. I don't get mad at Sam very much, but when I do, I call her Ma. She just laughs. She don't get mad and slap me. It's a real mess."

"Look, Festal. Sam isn't old enough to be your mother. You must be about twelve. She was a child when you were born. You could have figured that out. As far as that goes, Coy wouldn't have been old enough to make a baby. They'd have been too young to do that."

"You don't know. You wasn't there."

Festal shouldered his rifle and squinted at the sun. He looked me up and down and then walked around me. I felt like a prize pig at a county fair.

"Do you ever get whipped?" he asked me.

"Not to speak of."

"That's good."

He started across the yard to the house and, though he didn't ask me to follow, he didn't tell me to go on home as he'd done before. He walked maybe fifty steps before he stopped.

"I don't know that you should come in the house, Jeff Carr. I don't know how Pa would take it."

"Do you mean Coy or Old Trails."

"Hell, don't start that again," the boy said, grinning a little. "The next thing I know you'll be saying if my own pa is my grandpa, then that makes me my own pa's brother. Then, if my brother is also Pa... oh, to hell with it."

"Well, they can't do more than shoot me or order me off the place," I said. "Besides, they won't try anything with Sam around."

"That's what you think."

We walked a few steps and I skipped ahead of Festal, headed him off, stood in front of him and made him stop.

"Did they really hang you by the toes or thumbs?"

"Naw."

"By the hands or feet?"

"They hung me by the wrists. I didn't go unconscious, either. I was still hollering when they cut me down."

"How long did they leave you hanging?"

"I don't know. Half an hour. Maybe half a day. It seemed like a week."

"Where was Sam when it happened?"

"Off somewhere. They wouldn't do a thing like that when she's around. It wasn't so bad. The whippings are worse. But you wait and see. One of these days I'll take a shotgun and blow their fucking heads off. Maybe Sam will beat me to it."

He walked around me and I followed him up on the porch before the dread hit me. My knees became weak and I could feel the flesh on my thighs tremble. I don't know why. I really didn't think Coy or Old Trails or the Fancher boys would bother me when Sam was around, but fear hit me just the same. I wanted to go home. I lifted my arm and let my hand almost touch Festal's shoulder. I thought of telling him I'd just remembered that Bant had told me to clean the chicken pen before dusk or that I'd forgotten to give the pigs water or something like that. I let my hand fall. My feet were braver than the rest of me and we walked to the end of the porch and around its corner to a second side. There was an old woman, black and old, incredibly old, wrinkled, dried up and withered to skin and bones old. Her hair was white, kinky curled and white, but her eyes were black buttons, shiny and bright, alert with the light of intelligence. She was in a rocker, rocking back and forth, back and forth, and she was shelling peas.

"That's Emma," Festal said.

"Who is Emma?"

Festal frowned. "Just Emma. She's always been here."

"Maybe she's your mother," I said, not thinking, and then wished I could bite my tongue off.

"Maybe so," Festal said. He sniggered. "Maybe so. Only my hair's not kinky."

The porch was shadowed. Inside the house someone was playing the organ. It wasn't a hymnal and whoever it was could really play that thing. There were odors of food, delightful odors, and all in all it wasn't the sort of house I had expected the Trails bunch to live in.

"Who's that?" the black woman asked, pointing at me.

"This is Jeff Carr," Festal said. "He's come to see me."

"You know your pa don't allow no kids up here," she said. "Mister Carr, I'd run along home if I was you."

"I told him," Festal said.

"Did you come with Samal?" the old woman asked.

"Yes, ma'am."

"Well, Mister Carr, this boy's pa and brother can get awful mean when they gets mad. You'd be a lot better off was you to run along home."

"I've come visiting," I said.

The old woman bent to her peas. "I warned you."

"We'd better go to my place," Festal said. "Nobody'll bother us there. Listen, Jeff Carr, don't you say nothing to Sam about that whipping I got this morning. I'll let her know after supper."

"I think she ought to be told now."

"She'll know soon enough. She'll see the cuts and welts and then she'll scare the shit out of them buggers. I don't want to start anything while you're here. Come on."

He went down the steps and dropped to his knees, scooted out of sight beneath the house by the time I had reached the ground. The house was built on stone piers and there was plenty of head room. It was clean under there, and cool, but I had to take it slow until my eyes became accustomed to the shadows. The first thing I noticed was Festal's machinery, and that was a sight.

There must have been a thousand spools under there, all sizes, wooden thread spools, and all were interconnected with twine string. The spools were attached to the floor beams and were used as pulleys and cogs, and the string was like a spider web that ran over pulleys and under pulleys from joist to joist. Festal had built little hoists and slings and such, and when he pulled a master string the whole thing worked. He had made gears out of some of the spools and was able to lift things you wouldn't think could be lifted without the string breaking.

"You got any spools at your house?" he asked.

"I can save them for you."

"I'd be thankful. It gets lonesome under here when I have to stay hid out a spell, so I haul things around, all under the house, with them spools and the little hoists. It makes the time pass."

There was a sunken room at the middle of the house, a cellar room, its walls reaching out of the hole and hitting the house flooring. There were some small windows in the space between the floor of the house and the ground and Festal went in and out through one of the windows.

"There used to be a stairway from the house to the room," Festal said, "but it was boarded up long ago. I'm glad, 'cause they seldom bother to look for me there. They're too big to get through the windows and they'd have to tear up the floor to get to me."

We went into the room. It wasn't large, not more than eight by eight, but Festal had fixed it up nice. He had a cot and some boxes for tables and chairs, and he had pictures cut out of magazines. Somewhere, he'd found an old kerosene stove and he had pots and pans for cooking and some dishes.

"I've got a goodly supply of vittles, too," he said. "I reckon I could stay down here a month if I had to. I guess I'd get pretty tired of red beans and butter beans, but I could do it."

"Do they lay for you when you come out?"

"Sometimes. Once the old man climbed under here with a long fishing pole and jabbed at me through the window."

"What did you do?"

"Told him to get the hell out and leave me alone or I'd burn the house down. I'd a done it, too. He knowed that."

"Where is Old Trails now?"

"In the house, most likely."

"Let's go see him."

"Coy or some of the others could be there."

"I'm not afraid of them."

"All right by me, but you're a glutton for punishment."

"Samal is there," I said. "They won't bother me."

"You can't never tell what they might do, Jeff Carr."

"You've sure got a crazy family."

"Don't say that." His lower lip stuck out and he squinched his eyes. So help me, he doubled his fists and I thought he was going to swat me.

"For crying out loud, Festal. You don't mean you'd take up for them?"

"I'm a Trails."

"So what?"

"So I'm a Trails I stick up for my own kin!"

"You're touched," I said.

His mood changed instantly. "Come on and we'll go up there. I pretend I am sometimes, but I'm not."

Festal went out through the window of the sunken room and I followed, crawled behind him to the edge of the porch. The old black woman was still rocking in her chair, the peas for shelling forgotten in her lap. If she saw us, she gave no sign and we walked across the porch to the front door. Inside, the floor was of polished pine, worn smooth by generations of scraping feet. The wall of the house on this side was formed of logs, chinked, and the wood was sound. The outside door was massive, hand-carved, and led into a hallway. Festal led me to a second door and started to open the knob, but the knob turned before he could twist it. The door opened to the inside and we stood facing Old Trails. Festal cringed like a whipped dog and stepped back to stand behind me.

The old man was old, bad-smelling old, and again I wondered how he could have fathered Samal or, for that matter, either of the boys. His skin was like dried leather, but smooth as leather. He had no wrinkles except those spread like cobwebs from the corners of his eyes. His eyebrows were long and white, shaggy, and the eyes were deep-sunk. They should have been small to fit the rest of his face, but they were large and clear and blue. Strangely, they twinkled and made him look kindly. His nose was long, thin, straight, and his lips were colorless.

"What brings you here, boy?"

"I came with Samal."

"She knows better than that."

The old man blocked the doorway. "You must be meaner than Old Scratch," I said, ashamed of the tremor in my voice. "You've whipped Festal like a dog and you've got to be too mean to live. Does it give you pleasure to whip him or see him whipped?"

Those blue eyes of his went right on twinkling. He scowled at me, but those eyes went right on twinkling.

"I'd say you don't have a great deal of common sense," he said. "Maybe it's guts you've got, but I wouldn't give many pennies for your common sense."

"You're trash," I said, all fear gone. "Nobody but trash would treat company the way you're treating me."

"Young feller," he said, "my pappy could trace his blood back to England. That's more than you can say because you don't know whose blood to trace."

"That wouldn't make your blood good, Mister Trails. Your pappy probably traced his blood back to English trash."

You'd have thought I'd said something funny. The old man threw back his head and laughed, leaned against the door jamb and laughed until tears rolled down his cheeks. He shook himself, then, shook laughter from himself as a dog shakes water. He reached out and caught my left arm, dug his fingers in, and I felt the brutal strength flowing to that hand from his wizened body.

"Well, now," he said. "You've got more guts than sense, but you're welcome to my home. Come on in the house. I'd be proud to have you come inside."

He turned and I followed, sensed Festal following me, felt some part of his fear jumping the gap between us. We entered a large room, dark and large. The walls were of paneled oak and there was just enough light from one lamp on a table to reveal mounted heads of deer and antelope, framed pictures, massive furniture. My feet explored the depths of a carpet. I marveled at the quiet feel of richness, the soft smell of substance, the quiet sense of gentility.

Samal was sitting on a stool before an organ, smiling at me.

"I was just coming to look for you, Jeff," she said. "I see Festal found you."

Festal was still hanging behind me and Samal stood, took a step forward, frowned and looked at Old Trails.

"Festal," she said. "Are you all right? Come over here to the lamp and let me look at you."

Festal walked forward, shuffled with head down, and Sam ran her fingers over the wounds on his shoulders and back. It was Old Trails' time to cringe then and I saw that he dreaded Sam's wrath.

"Come on out to the kitchen," she ordered Festal in a quiet voice. "I'll doctor you."

Festal followed Sam and I stood in the middle of the floor wondering what had possessed me to follow Sam into such a crazy mess.

"Well," Old Trails said. "You wanted to visit, so visit." He nodded at a rocker and I sat.

"I didn't whup the boy," he said.

"You watched."

"That's not the same thing. The boy needed it."

"People have talked about having the sheriff on you," I said, "but most of them don't have the nerve to do it. I'll do it myself."

"It's none of the sheriff's business. It's a family matter."

"Just the same, I'll do it."

"The boy has no feelings," he said. "He's just like an animal."

"He does have feelings. He hurts inside as much as he does on the outside. You wouldn't treat an animal like you treat him."

"You'd be smart to mind your own business."

We sat in uneasy silence until Sam returned to the room with Festal behind her. They walked across the room and went out through another door. The old man cleared his throat.

"She's mad," he said. "She gets awfully quiet when she's mad. I didn't whup the boy, though. Coy done it."

"You could have stopped it."

"It was none of my business. None of yours, either."

Sam returned, opened a door quietly and stood framed. She had a shotgun.

"Jeff," she said. "I'm sorry, but you'd better leave."

"All right," I said, and at the door to the hallway I paused and said, "I hope you change your mind about finishing school, Sam. Kenty will see to your board and lodging in town."

"I'll think about it." Her eyes were pinned on Old Trails and the man sat frozen in his chair.

I went out, crossed the porch, walked across the yard and had just reached the trees when Old Trails came slamming out. He went across the yard at a run and Samal reached the porch just as he reached the shelter of the big boulders. She fired in the old man's general direction, but I knew she'd missed.

"I didn't do it, Sam!" the old man yelled. "I told you Coy was the one, dammit! Now you put that gun down and listen to reason."

"I'll see to Coy when he gets home," Sam called, "but don't you come back to this house if you don't want to get shot."

I headed for the trail to the Narrows and had gone a hundred yards when Old Trails stepped out from behind a rock.

"Ain't she a scooter?" he asked. "Did you ever see anybody with that much spunk?"

"She wouldn't be amiss to shoot you, Mister Trails," I said, "but she might not be the one you should worry about. I think Festal will shoot you one of these days."

"Mind your own business," the old man said.

I went on back to the place where I'd left Raindrop and started home, remembered I had been told to tell Kenty about the shooting match and headed toward Hooker Valley. His car was in the front yard and I found him on the back porch.

"Do you know what I forgot?" was his greeting. "I forgot to build a place for my car. Do you know what I was just thinking? I think I'll build a rock road from the front around here to the back and build a storage room for the car back here. I'll even have a door leading into the house. Won't that be something?"

"I never heard of one like that."

"Big mansions have them back east, though most of them were stables, I guess. Where've you been, Jeff?"

I told him about my visit to the Trails place and what had happened. He listened without interrupting and then advised me to stay away from there.

"We need to get Samal away from that bunch," he said. "One of these days she'll shoot the old man or Coy, or both. I don't know what to do about Festal, though."

"Somebody should do something," I said.

CHAPTER FOUR

Kenty came at noon on Friday to practice for the shooting match.

"Have you ever shot at glass balls in the air, Bant?"

"Pebbles. Never glass balls."

"The same with me. I don't even know the rules, but I understand that each shooter can select somebody to toss the balls in the air for him. Jim Nabors said he saw a match in San Antonio once and the balls had to be tossed at least twenty feet into the air."

"Can we use our own rifles?"

"Nope. We'll have to use Winchesters."

"I don't have a Winchester."

"You do now," and Kenty caught Bant by the arm to steer him to his car. "I brought you a Christmas present a little early."

He opened a rear door, reached in and lifted out two rifles. "These are Winchester automatics."

"My Remington is an automatic."

"I know, but the Winchester people are sponsoring the match and the rules say we have to use Winchester rifles. It makes sense when you think about it. This is for advertising and they wouldn't want a Remington to win the match."

"Seems to me they don't have much confidence in their product. Besides, not that many people own Winchesters."

"They'll loan Winchesters to anybody who files, but I figured we needed our own rifles for a little practice."

"How much is the filing fee?"

"Five dollars," Kenty said. "I filed for both of us."

"You didn't take me to raise. I can pay my own filing fee and buy my own rifle."

"You can give me five dollars for the fee, but the rifle is a present from me to you. Don't spoil my pleasure, Bant."

Bant hefted the rifle for balance, put it to his shoulder and sighted. "We'll have to adjust the sights, more than likely."

"I did that at the store. Jim Nabors has a range in back of his place and he helped me."

"I don't feel right about taking it, Kenty Hooker. Did you bring cartridges?"

"Boxes and boxes."

"How much do I owe you? All told?"

"Five dollars for the filing fee."

"I mean how much in all?"

"Listen, Bant," Kenty said. "I've put my feet under your table these past weeks more often than Jeff has. Now, can't you let me do one little thing without making a stink? Just this one time?"

Bant grunted and reached for his pocket purse. "Here's five dollars for the filing fee and thank you for the rifle."

Kenty confessed he didn't know how large the glass balls would be and we gathered pebbles about the size of the end of a man's thumb, filled a small bucket.

"These are probably smaller than the balls will be," Kenty said, "but that will be to our advantage if we practice on these."

"Are the balls colored?" Bant wanted to know.

"That I do know," Kenty said. "They'll be clear glass."

"Are they like marbles? Or made special?"

Kenty said he didn't know.

"How many shots will we get?"

Kenty confessed he didn't know.

"You don't know much about shooting matches, do you?"

"Just enough to beat you tomorrow," Kenty promised.

"We'll see about that. Well, old son, I never saw a shooting match, but this much I do know. You don't shoot while the target is on the way up and you don't wait until it starts falling. The trick is to catch it at the top of its movement. Everything that goes up has to stop somewhere, just before it starts down. That's the time to shoot."

"Sounds reasonable."

The men loaded their rifles, five shells each, and took positions with the sun at their backs. I stood between them, but only after they'd argued about my positioning.

"I'll swear, Kenty," Bant grumbled, "I don't see why you didn't learn more about the rules."

"You were in town first," Kenty said. "Why didn't you find out?"

"I asked around."

"Well, so did I," Kenty said. "The Winchester man hadn't come to town yet and nobody seemed to know much about the details. Jim Nabors was registering people that wanted to shoot and said the match will be held on his place east of town at nine o'clock in the morning."

"How many people had he registered?"

"Twenty."

"There'll be more, then. There are some good shooters in the county. Will the Winchester man shoot?"

"That he will. His name is Will Rutledge and they say he traveled with Buffalo Bill's Wild West Circus for a year. He shot against Annie Oakley and Bill."

"Who won?"

"They say that he beat Bill, but Annie Oakley beat him."

"All right," Bant said. "Toss a pebble, Jeff."

My first throw was too low and my second too high, but then I found a rhythm and Bant got a hit on his first shot. Kenty got his first and I continued throwing until my bucket was empty. The shooting was almost even. Bant hit forty-eight of fifty-two and Kenty hit forty-seven.

"Glass balls will be easier to see," Kenty reasoned. "Especially if the balls are clear glass. It's hard to judge when these rocks reach the top of their climb."

Kenty ate supper with us, but left early after cautioning us to be ready to leave for town at seven the next morning.

"You come at six o'clock," Mama told him. "I'll have breakfast on the table."

"Are you going with us, Pearl?"

"I wouldn't miss it."

I was up the next morning long before light, long before Bant and Mama, and tended to chores. I even did the milking. Mama was in high good spirits and hummed and sang while cooking breakfast. Bant, though, was nervous as a cat.

"Hope this weather holds," he said after his third trip to the yard. "It'll be hard to see the targets if it's overcast."

"There's not a cloud in the sky," Mama reassured him. "Clouds can come up fast in this country. Where's Kenty? He ought to be here by now."

"It's not six o'clock yet."

Kenty drove into the yard not a minute later, just bubbling, happy as a cow in corn. I went out to greet him and he wrestled me to the ground, sat on me and mussed my hair, stood then and lifted me to my feet.

"I thought I'd do that while I still can," he said. "I'm willing to bet I won't be able to do it three years from now. I swear to you, boy, you're going to be a man to make me proud. Brains and brawn. That's what you'll have," and he kept his arm around me and walked me into the house. "Tell you what I'll do," he said. "I'll buy you a new Winchester and pay your filing fee if you'll shoot in the match. What do you say?"

"I haven't shot enough, Kenty. I probably couldn't hit the side of a barn from the inside."

"Well, we'll have to see about getting you a rifle, just the same. Every man ought to know how to shoot."

We went on in to breakfast and, at seven o'clock on the dot, were on our way. Mama sat in back with me. Bant and Kenty sat in the front seat and bantered each other all the way, bragged about their marksmanship and how one was going to humiliate the other. Mama looked pleased and happy and I could tell she thought the strain between the two men had been eased.

The shooting match site was like a carnival. At least two hundred people had gathered in a meadow on Jim Nabors' ranch and were milling about. I counted ten automobiles, all shiny black, and there must have been thirty or forty wagons. Teams of horses and mules had been tethered under trees and open-sided tents had been set up in the open. There was a tent for lemonade, one for barbecue and beans, another with long trestle tables and benches where, for ten-cents a family, diners could sit to eat. A traveling medicine man was selling snake oil, only twenty-five cents a bottle, just two-bits for an elixir that would cure everything from hang-nail to consumption. Jim Nabors had a tent for his rifles and pistols, for ammunition and for glass balls just like those to be used in the competition. I went with Kenty and Bant to examine the balls and they were larger than marbles, maybe twice as large, and the glass was clear.

There was a bluff backing the meadow, to the west, and an area had been roped off. Only shooters and glass ball throwers would be allowed beyond the ropes, we were told. Shooters could stand with the sun at their backs. I was allowed to toss ten of the balls for practice, but Kenty and Bant were not allowed to shoot until the competition had been called. Still, they were gleeful.

"It's going to be a snap," Kenty chortled. "The balls will be easier to see than pebbles. The sunlight will make them glint and we can tell when they reach the top of the climb."

"They might just as well give me the prize money now," Bant said. "I couldn't miss if I wanted to."

"Well, now, gentlemen," a deep voice said. "I admire confidence in a man."

We turned to face just about the biggest man I'd ever seen. "I'm Will Rutledge and I represent Winchester," he said. "I'll be shooting against you and I'm not willing to concede. If it's all the same to you, we'll go ahead and shoot just for the fun of the thing."

He didn't look like a shooter and he didn't look like a man who'd traveled with Buffalo Bill. He was on up in years, but he was well preserved, solid as rock. He wasn't just tall, either. He was big all over. His neck looked like it would fit a bull and his shoulders were twice as wide as Kenty's or Bant's. His face was unlined and his long hair, white as snow and wavy, almost touched the shoulders. He had shaggy white eyebrows, a brown handle-bar mustache, and he wore a gray business suit with blue stripes.

"Have you tried your rifles?" he asked.

"We have, sir," Kenty said, stepping forward to shake hands. "I'm Kenty Hooker and this is Bant Carr. This young man is Bant's son, Jeff. We've heard about you, Mister Rutledge, and we know you'll be hard to beat. Bant and

I will try to give you a run for the money."

The shooting started at nine o'clock on the dot and thirty men took their places.

"Gentlemen," Jim Nabors called. "Your attention, please." He cleared his throat. "I don't have to tell you that safety is the most important consideration. Some of you are using the new Winchester and may not be familiar with it. You've used guns all your lives and you know as well as I do that an empty gun is a dangerous gun. Handle your rifles with the greatest of care.

"Now, we have some rules. There are thirty of you and I know you don't want to be here all day. Here is how we will proceed.

"First. Every man has to have his own thrower. I notice some of you are doubling up with just one thrower between you. There are plenty of boys and men who will volunteer to throw.

"Second. We'll start on my left. The first man over there is Bentley Coggins. I'll stand behind him in the preliminary match, which is an elimination contest. When I go over to stand behind Bentley, his thrower will toss a ball into the air and Bentley will fire. Remember this, too. If any man fails to fire—and this rule stands even if the ball is thrown too low or too high, or if the shooter fails to fire for any reason—I'll give that man a miss."

There was a rumble of muttered voices and Jim Nabors raised both hands.

"That's the rule, gentlemen, and you'll have to live with it. You can see that the thrower is just as important as the shooter. Well, almost as important.

"When Bentley has fired at his first ball, I'll step over behind the man on his right, which is Bant Carr. His thrower will throw his ball immediately, and I'll step over behind the next man, Kenty Hooker. I'll continue in that fashion until all of you have taken a first shot. We will then start at the extreme right and continue the shooting as I move from man to man toward the left.

"Does everyone understand? Good. You will have ten shots in this preliminary match and we'll separate the men from the boys. Any man who misses two of ten will be eliminated. I suppose I've hunted with about every man Jack of you, except for Will Rutledge, and I reckon that more than half of you can go home early or stay as spectators."

There were scattered boos from the shooters and someone yelled, "What about Will Rutledge? Don't he have to take these same ten shots?"

"I'm glad you asked that question," Jim Nabors said. "Will Rutledge is shooter thirty-one and he will take his ten shots. However, gentlemen, he has volunteered to take his shots rapid-fire. His thrower is none other but the champion glass ball thrower in the United States and Canada, yours truly, me. After those rapid-fire shots, Will Rutledge promises to show you how it's done. His thrower for the rest of the competition will be Bill Monday.

Mister Rutledge, will you step over here to the center where everybody can see?"

Will Rutledge took his place and Jim Nabors took a place about ten steps in front of him and slightly to the shooter's left.

"We need another thrower for Kenty," I said to Bant.

"Don't worry about me," Kenty said. "Pearl can throw for me."

Bant frowned. "That's hardly fitting."

Mama left a group of women when Kenty beckoned and came over to stand beside him. I saw Bant go stiff and still.

Will Rutledge was a showman. That, considering his profession, wasn't surprising. He lifted his rifle, lowered it, and went forward to move Jim Nabors a foot to the left. He checked his rifle again, fingered a glass ball and held it up to the light. He squinted at the sun and said something to Jim Nabors. Turning to the other shooters, he held a hand up with five fingers spread, pumped his right arm five times and made a horizontal sweeping motion with his hand, palms down.

What happened next was a surprise and it was evident, at least to me, that the men had done some practicing. Jim Nabors threw five balls into the air, all together, and threw them high, almost out of sight. Will Rutledge fired five times, levered that rifle faster than seemed possible, and five glass balls were shattered. There wasn't a sound from the crowd until Kenty laughed and said, "He's trying to discourage the rest of us."

Will Rutledge reloaded and took his next five shots in singles. He didn't seem to take aim. Jim Nabors would toss a ball and Will Rutledge would raise a rifle, casually, and the ball would disappear.

"Amazing," Kenty said.

Jim Nabors went back to his stump. "Ladies and gentlemen, I think you will agree that Will Rutledge has qualified. Now, if any of you shooters want to have five balls tossed up at the same time, please step forward."

"I've a notion to try it," Bant said.

"Don't get suckered in," Kenty warned. "There's prize money at stake."

Bant and Kenty qualified with nine hits each and the first round of shooting didn't take long. Sixteen shooters missed their first two shots and were eliminated. Four were eliminated after six shots and two after eight. That left nine shooters, including Will Rutledge. The professional's new thrower, Bill Monday, was as good as Jim Nabors and, this time, Will took all his shots rapid-fire, five at a time. Then, after the eight remaining shooters had finished their second ten shots, only five shooters were left: Bant, with nine hits, Kenty with five hits, Tom Dublin with eight, Coy Trails with nine, and Will Rutledge with ten.

"Ladies and gentlemen," Jim Nabors announced, "the going gets rough right now. Five shooters will shoot continuously, one at a time, until there's a miss.

Will Rutledge will shoot first, if that's what you want. It's up to the shooters."

"Let him shoot first," Coy Trails yelled.

"I second that," Kenty called.

"I third it," Bant said.

"Any objections?" Jim Nabors asked. The shooters were silent.

"Very well then," Jim said. "The boys have been eliminated and the competition among men begins. Mister Rutledge, take your position."

I thought Will Rutledge would fire all day. He took his time between shots and aimed carefully, waited until the glass balls paused at the top of their flights just before starting down. On shot seventy-three he almost missed. His bullet just nudged the ball and sent it flying, but it was a hit. At shot eighty-seven his rifle misfired. A miss.

"Lucky for us," Bant murmured.

It was Bant's turn and I was tense. Bant complained after each shot that I had tossed too high or too low, too far to the right or too far to the left. After one shot he stormed at me so loudly that Kenty took my part.

"You're making him nervous, Bant. Calm down. He's doing fine. Just concentrate on your shooting and stop fussing at the boy."

"Mind your own business," Bant said. Kenty shrugged.

Samal had replaced Mama as Kenty's ball tosser because, I decided, Mama had sensed Bant's resentment. I wished she had substituted for me. Bant almost missed at forty-nine because he waited too long to shoot, but he managed to nick the ball. I tossed a bad one at seventy-three and another at eighty-four, but he managed hits and only glared at me. He missed at ninety-two because I threw the ball too far to the left.

"You did that on purpose," he gritted at me. "You could do better than that with your left hand."

"I'm sorry," I said.

Sam was a natural tosser. Her nerves were better than mine. She made a few bad tosses, but Kenty hit and only smiled at her and told her not to worry. Kenty was cool and relaxed. I knew he didn't need the money and was shooting just for the fun. His pride wasn't involved, as was Bant's. He knocked ninety-six balls out of the air before he missed.

Tom Durbin missed on his twentieth shot, but Coy Trails hit ninety before he missed. Kenty was the winner.

"I'm sorry, Bant," Kenty said. "You're a better shot, but you had bad luck."

"The boy wanted you to win."

"You waited too long to shoot. That's all. He was under a lot of pressure."

"Blood is thicker than water," Bant said, and walked away.

CHAPTER FIVE

Harvest time was a dying time and we were busy with the threshing and picking and storing. The days were warm, still, mellow warm and not hot, and the hint of crispness not yet felt but almost felt. The nights were cool, almost cold. Coyotes howled in the hills. Dogs bayed on the trail of coons and hunting horns sounded like wailing moans of the lost.

Bant went with me one night to the peanut stack in the fields. The threshing crew had come and gone, but there had been no daylight time left for hauling the sacks of nuts to the barn. My mouth watered for parched nuts and I suppose Bant had the same yearning, for usually he would not have strayed from the fire. Bant opened a sack and I filled my pan, but he stood looking at the moon.

"This is a funny time of the year, Jeff, but I think like it better than winter or summer or spring. Growing things are dying and I guess it's a time to remind us that we're just little mortal things with little time to live. It's a good time, though. It gives us a chance to stop and look back before looking ahead. Growing things die slow, but I'd rather die fast. I wouldn't want to linger around and think of all the messes I've left behind. You've seen a dog relieve his bowels, boy. Have you noticed how he turns to look at death that came out of his body? Well, at least a dog knows enough to scratch dirt over his dung. A man, now, will turn and look at his dung and feel proud if the hill of it is large and firm and curled. He doesn't see death, you see. He sees something born of him instead of filth and decay that was a part of dying from the day he drew his first breath. I'll tell you, boy. Look and smell and enjoy the season. Try to live your life so you won't worry about the messes you left behind and didn't cover up."

I think it was the longest speech he'd ever made in my presence. I certainly never heard him string together that many words in all the days that followed.

We went on to the house and I was weighted with a sadness I couldn't shake. What Bant said settled over me like a shroud. Still, the bright lamplight and the small fire in the fireplace cheered me. Mama, rocking and knitting, cheered me. We parched the nuts and then fell to playing hully-gully. Mama won all my peanuts and then broke Bant. She couldn't have been prouder and her laughter chased away the shreds of my gloom. We went to bed in laughter and gladness, and that was the last gladness in that house for a small eternity.

I don't know what time it was when I heard Bant stalking around the house. I slid out of bed and found my pants, but Mama wasn't in the living room and I found Bant on the front porch.

"Bant?"

"Shh."

"What is it?" A whisper.

"Somebody's at the chickens," he whispered in reply. "Stay in the house. Don't show a light."

I went to the front door and stood there shivering while he stalked across the yard to the chicken house. I remember thinking he was a good target in the moonlight and remember, too, snuffling back a giggle because he was wearing longhandles and shoes and nothing else.

"Stand where you are!" Bant shouted. "Don't make a move or I'll shoot!"

Chickens cackled and the flutter of their wings told me for sure there was someone inside. A hand touched my shoulder and I jumped, but it was Mama.

"What is it?" she asked. "What is Bant doing? Bant, come back! Do you hear me? You'll get yourself killed out there!"

Bant was stalking the chicken house, the shotgun at the ready.

"You, Coy Trails!" he called. "You come out of there with your hands up!"

There was a blasting roar, a spurt of flame from the door of the chicken house, and a man running through the moonlight and away. Bant bent over, doubled over, and staggered around in a circle. Mama screamed and I yelled, but I came to my senses first and ran across the yard to Bant.

He was groaning, staggering around, all bent over and groaning. He had dropped his gun. I caught his arm and led him to the house and up on the porch, and then Mama took his other arm and we guided him into the living room.

"Strike a light," Bant said. "I'm not hurt bad. He was using light shot and it scattered, but I must have a hundred pellets in my arms and shoulders and chest. I'm just thankful he didn't get me in the face and eyes."

"Sit down," Mama said. "Jeff, light the lamp. Here, Bant, back up to the chair and sit down... back a little... that's it... all right, now, lie back... no, that won't do, Bant. You'll have to lie back." I had the lamp lighted and Mama told me to get Bant's longjohns off while she boiled water and found bandages. She kept changing her mind and talking. "Throw wood on the fire, Jeff. Build it up. Put a kettle on the boil as soon as you can. Use kerosene on the wood if you need to. We need hot water in a hurry. Bant, hold your arms up. You're bleeding like a stuck pig. I told you to come back to the house. You had no business out there. You could have fired your gun in the air and he would have scuttled away from there. Trying to show how brave you are. Hold your legs out straight. Here, Jeff, help me. You take that leg and I'll take this and we'll strip him together. Oh, pshaw! Take his shoes off first. Now... pull together. All right, Bant, just lie back. Lift yourself a little... that's it. You're covered with blood and it'll take a mite of digging to get the shot out. Maybe I'd best send Jeff for the doctor."

"That's twenty miles round trip and I can't lie here and bleed."

Mama ran across the room to the clothes press and hurried back with a towel. She swabbed Bant's body, made me hold the lamp close, and stooped to peer at the wounds.

"Some of these are deep, Bant. I doubt I'd ever get them out. Maybe Kenty could go for the doctor."

"Kenty went to Anson to look at some horses," Bant said. "We'll have to send for Old Trails."

Mama sucked in her breath. "Bant!"

"I mean it, Pearl. I need help and I need it soon. I don't want to lie here and bleed to death. Jeff, saddle your horse and don't waste any time. Tell Old Trails I need help because his chicken stealing son shot me."

"He won't come," Mama said. "We'll be wasting time."

"He'll come. Meanwhile, bathe those wounds with alcohol and rub on some thick salve to stop the bleeding. You can be getting the shot that's just under the skin. Hurry, Jeff. Pearl, don't you dare use cobwebs to stop the bleeding. Do as I told you."

I slipped on my boots while Mama washed blood and I could see from across the room that fresh blood spurted from scores of tiny punctures. I ran out of the house, ran to the barn, scooped a bridle off its peg in the stall and felt my way in deep shadow under the shed roof. I hugged the wall lest a startled horse lashed out with its hooves, spoke aloud to calm Rainbow, felt my way with gentle hands along her side, along her neck, and encircled her neck with my arm. She took the bit without protest and two minutes later I was out the gate and galloping. I didn't pick the easiest way, but the shortest. More than once Rainbow had to clamber over rocks and across gullies. We skirted the Narrows and I dismounted to lead the mare up the steep hill to the mesa. Once there, it was a short run to the Trails house and I hallooed the house from a hundred yards away.

"Stop right there," someone said from the shadows.

"Who is it?"

"Coy Trails. You're the Carr kid. What are you doing here?"

"Bant was shot," I said. "He's hurt bad. I want your pa to go help him."

Coy stepped from behind a huge rock and moonlight glinted on metal.

"Is that the shotgun you used on Bant?"

"Stop being a fool, kid. You'll get yourself hurt one of these days."

"I'm going to get Old Trails," I said. "Don't shoot me in the back."

I dug my heels into Rainbow's flanks and almost lost my seat as she plunged. I dismounted in the yard and called for Old Trails at the top of my voice. I shouted twice, but my voice seemed thin and weak in the night.

"What is it, Jeff?"

It was Samal's voice and I peered through the shadows until I saw her leaning against the wall of the porch.

"Bant's hurt, Sam. He needs help. Someone was stealing chickens and Bant went out there and was shot."

Samal walked toward me and I could barely see the outline of her body until she walked out of the shadows. I saw her nakedness then.

"Bant said Old Trails would help him," I said.

"I'll call him," she said, and disappeared.

I heard a door slam inside the house, heard the mutter of voices, heard footsteps and the grumbling threat of Old Trails' voice as he neared the doorway.

"What is it?" he asked, looming up before me. "What's this about Bant being shot?"

"He's full of buckshot, Mister Trails, and he's bleeding something awful. I wanted to go for the doctor but he said he'd bleed to death before I could make it."

"So he sent for me, did he?"

"Yes, sir."

"He's too good to neighbor with me, but let him get in trouble and he asks for me."

He sat on the steps and I saw he had his boots in his hands. "The man treats me like I'm trash," he complained as he pulled on his boots. "But just let him get in trouble and I'm the first one he calls for."

"Well, look, sir, I'm not begging you. I can get those buckshot out."

"Them's mighty brave words," the old man grunted, "but you're not peppered with birdshot. Don't you think Bant had to swallow his pride before he sent for me? Do you think that was easy for him to do? Not on your sweet ass! It was like swallowing bitter gall!"

"I guess it was."

"All right," he sighed righteously. "Let's go. I'll go pick the buckshot out of his carcass. You wait here, though, while I get my special salve."

He went inside the house and before he returned Coy came into the front yard leading a horse. I mounted Rainbow and waited impatiently.

"You can go ahead," Coy said. "The old man'll run off and leave you anyway."

"He won't run ahead of Rainbow."

"Maybe not in a year from now, but your Rainbow is just a filly, not full growed. You'll see."

The old man stamped across the porch and down the steps, swung into the saddle and set off at a dead run. I dug my heels deep and Rainbow ran recklessly, ducked her head and strained for speed. I didn't catch one glimpse of the old man until I pulled into our front yard. It didn't take more than twenty minutes for the removal of the deepest shots from Bant's body. In another ten minutes Old Trails was finished with the shallow wounds and the smearing of his special salve. He had Mama tear a sheet into strips and did a neat job of bandaging. He accepted a cup of coffee and sat on the raised hearth to stare at Bant.

"I want to thank you for helping me," Bant said.

"I'd do as much for a sick pig."

"I know," Bant chuckled. "That's why I had the nerve to send for you."

"How did it happen?"

"Somebody, Coy, I think, was in my hen house. I didn't get a good look at him, so I can't prove anything and won't try. You'd better warn Coy, though. He'd better stay off my property. I'll shoot first next time and there won't be any warning."

Old Trails was so mad he couldn't speak. He stood and glared, trembled and glared, worked his lips and breathed heavily and snorted and glared. He started for the door and paused with his hand on the knob.

"You've the same as declared war on me and mine, Bant Carr! You've played the string out this time!" He pointed a trembling finger at me. "Don't come on my place again, young man! You're lusting for my daughter and she's too old and smart for you!"

Bant didn't do much around the place for a couple of weeks, but then seemed normal and acted normal. He still drank from his brown bottle in the late night and didn't have much to say to me. Still, he wasn't unfriendly; just short and curt. We went to church at Piper's Creek on the third Sunday. Our church house is right on the banks of the creek, shaded by giant pecans. The ground is as flat as a table top and as smooth. The sand is hard packed and free of grass. In the winter, the trees knock off the wind. In summer, it is always cool and pleasant. People come from miles around, in cars and wagons, and stay all day. There's Sunday School and church in the morning, dinner on the ground if it's summer, and singing in the afternoon. In the winter, some people go home for the noon meal and a nap, then return in mid-afternoon for the singing. When it's warm, people eat and rest under the trees or gather in groups to exchange news and gossip.

Samal's class must have recessed early because I saw her and Nancy Freeman and Sarah Turner and Janice Magness over by the cemetery fence looking at gravestones. I thought I'd go over and kill time until services started, but then I saw a gang of the older boys come up the bank from the creek. Coy was in the group and I wondered what brought him to church until I reasoned he'd come just to see the girls. Jeff Porten was with him, and so were Bert Parker and Chuck Rush and two others I knew but couldn't name. They saw the girls and headed for them, so I slowed my pace and let them get ahead of me.

I was actually embarrassed for those young men and women. Even Coy Trails acted the fool. He strutted around like a rooster, his chest stuck out and his legs stiff. Jeff Porten was the only one who acted naturally. The girls were just as silly as most of the boys. They hid their faces and turned away from the boys to giggle insanely, or so it seemed to me. The boys hit each other in the stomach, swapped blows on the shoulders, horsed around and showed off like a bunch of kids.

I don't know where Kenty came from. All of a sudden he was there. He said hello to me and then talked with the girls, except for Samal whom he ignored. Coy didn't like it. He motioned to one of his cronies and winked, then walked to stand in front of Kenty. The other boy went behind Kenty and dropped to hands and knees. Coy pushed Kenty hard and Kenty went sprawling back over the boy behind him. He landed on the back of his shoulders and head.

Coy was bigger than Kenty, heavier and taller. Kenty wasn't a small man, but Coy outweighed him by twenty pounds or more. His shoulders were wider and his hands, wrists and arms were bigger. He was just bigger big-boned.

I don't know how people on the church grounds knew a fight was starting, but they gathered quickly. Kenty came to his feet in one flowing motion and the look on his face should have made Coy want to apologize. Kenty was a fighting machine. I don't know where he learned to box, but his skill made him Coy's equal and a bit more. Coy couldn't really hit him a solid blow and Kenty's fists found their targets with splat-splatting speed. Coy was cut and bleeding in the first few seconds. After that it was just a question of how long Kenty could keep Coy from landing a lucky punch and how long Coy could take the punishment.

The girls were screaming and crying and raising a ruckus, except for Samal. That girl watched with a curious little smile on her face. The fight ended when the preacher came out of the church house. Men and women remembered where they were and several men separated the fighters. Coy was breathing hard and his chest pumped in and out like a bellows. His nose was bleeding and his mouth was bleeding. He had a cut over his right eye, cuts on both cheeks, a gash on his left ear, and big blue knots all over his face. Kenty wasn't marked. His hair was hardly mussed.

"I'll get you later," Coy growled, and Preacher Simms shook a finger under his nose and told him he shouldn't seek vengeance.

"Whenever you're ready," Kenty replied.

"I'll meet you at the deep swimming hole just down the creek a ways."

"When?"

"Right now."

"I can't meet you right now, Coy. I'm going to church with Samal."

The fight almost started again. Coy started for Kenty and the preacher stepped in his way and was almost dropped flat for his pains. Bant walked up, then, and moved in front of Coy. He kept moving and forced Coy to step back. Coy doubled his fists and crouched, but Bant didn't flinch.

"This is a church yard, Coy," Bant said. "You'll have to do your brawling some place else."

"I'll do that."

Coy walked toward a stand of pecans where most of the horses were tied, mounted his bay mare and galloped away. Slowly, almost reluctantly, the crowd broke and followed the preacher to the church. Kenty walked with Samal, sat with her near the front, sat stiff and still and kept his eyes on the preacher. Sam's color was high, though, and I saw her steal glances at Kenty.

Kenty and Samal went home with us for Sunday dinner and then went for a ride in the afternoon. Bant and Mama decided to nap and skip the afternoon singing. The day was too pretty for naps and I asked Bant if I could use his single-shot .22 rifle. I thought he'd say no, but he surprised me with a yes.

I'd had a shot at a squirrel and missed. The gun was pulling high and I decided to test it on a target. I shot twice at a knot in an oak tree and was ready for a third when I saw a flash of red through the trees. I stooped and peered, moving my head from side to side, but didn't see anything. I fired at the knot again, adjusted the sights, and then hit the target in the center.

"That's a pretty gun."

I jumped, startled, and Festal Trails laughed. He was behind a tree to my left, with only his head showing.

"What are you doing out here, Festal?"

"Just fooling around."

"How's your pa?"

I could have bitten my tongue as soon as I'd said it, but it didn't seem to bother Festal.

"Maddern'n hell," he said.

"How've they been treating you?"

"Depends on if they catch me. I stay out of the way most of the time."

"You have to eat."

"Yeah, but I roast squirrels in the woods and steal ham from the smokehouse. I slip into the kitchen at night and Samal slips stuff to me."

"That's a bad way to live."

"Well," he said, and grinned ruefully. "It's better'n being dead, I reckon. I know what you think, though. You think I'm like all the rest of them except Sam. You think I'm low-down and common and ignorant and mean."

"I don't think any of that."

He started walking away. I hurried after him and he quickened his pace. "Wait, Festal. Don't go. Stay and talk a while."

"You come hunting again," he called. "You just come hunting again and I'll follow the sound of your gun."

I let him go and walked out of the woods. I crossed a clearing, crossed a fence into our field and started toward the house. I was half way across the field when I saw Bant leave the house and head for the barn. I saw something else, too. I saw a man peer around the corner of the barn and duck out of sight. I started running, started yelling at the top of my lungs, but the distance was too great and Bant didn't hear me. I saved my breath and ran faster, but Bant had gone through the door of the barn when I reached the home meadow. I yelled again and Mama heard me. She opened the front door and stepped out on the porch, but I ran past her to the barn.

It was dark inside the barn and I had to stop and peer. At first I didn't see anyone, and then my eyes adjusted to the darkness and I saw Bant, Coy, and Old Trails. Bant was backed against the wall and Coy and his pa had their backs to me. I stood still, saw Bant glance at me and look away, and then I went forward on tip-toe.

"You're wrong, both of you," Bant was saying. "I know you have a still, but I don't know where it is. I wouldn't tell anyone if I did know. The fact is, I get your red-eye from Bert Shaeffer."

"You told the sheriff," Coy said. "You told him where to find it. I saw you not more than a hundred yards from it just before the sheriff came."

"When was that?"

"Yesterday," Coy said.

"I was hunting yesterday. Maybe I passed near your still. Thunderation, man! People hunt in the Narrows all the times How could they not pass by your still if it's there?"

"That's not good enough," Old Trails said. "Do you know what this has cost me, Bant? The equipment costs aplenty and it's hard to find. I'll have to go to court and pay a fine. I'll lose all the business I would have had until things get going again. The sheriff and his men poured my mash out on the ground and impounded fifty gallons of prime whiskey. It's a good thing I had my aged stuff hid where they couldn't find it."

"Neither one of you believes I informed on you," Bant said. "I don't know what's behind this, but I'll bet you're here because I had Kenty and Samal over here for dinner today."

"We'll take care of Kenty Hooker in our own time," Old Trails said. "Right now we're going to teach you to mind your own business."

"I wouldn't try it," I spoke up. "I've got a rifle aimed at your backs."

They ignored me.

"You'd better get out of here," Bant warned. "You've threatened me on my own place and that's enough to put you behind bars. I don't want trouble, but..." and he hit Coy in mid-sentence.

It would be more accurate to say he clubbed Coy. He used clubbed hands to smash Coy between the eyes and Coy went down without making a sound. He just folded and sank like a pole-axed steer. Bant turned on Old Trails.

"Take your whelp and get him out of here. Drag him out of this barn and douse him with cold water."

Old Trails held up both hands in a gesture of appeasement and said, "Take it easy, take it easy, Bant, I'll do just what you say, I'll go, I'll go, just don't let your young tiger pull the trigger on that wicked looking rifle." With that he reached down and grabbed Coy's shirt collar and dragged him out of the barn. He went to the well and drew a bucket of water, splashed it all over Coy and slapped him until consciousness returned. He was good enough to let Coy lean on him as they walked away.

Kenty and Samal returned just a little before sunset and stayed for supper. Bant was sullen quiet. He ate very little, talking not at all and only grunting when spoken to. He went out on the porch and called Kenty to step down to the barn with him for a "little talk." They were gone a long while and Kenty returned alone to tell Sam it was time to go.

"Just give me a few minutes," Sam said. "Pearl is giving me a new recipe."

Bant came in, went to the kitchen, and Kenty followed him. I went as far as the kitchen door and stood to listen, out of sight.

"You watch that Coy Trails," Bant said. "He's as dangerous as a snake. He'll strike when you least expect it."

"It would be my own fault if I let him hurt me, Bant. I don't know why he jumped me at church. He knew I could whip him. I fooled everybody else, but Coy knew all along I could whip him."

"Well, you sure fooled me. I thought Coy would knock your head off. Just the same, you watch him. His pride has been hurt. You whipped him in public and you're courting his sister."

"There's no harm in courting his sister."

"Well, go ahead and court her," Bant said. "You need your own woman."

Kenty just walked out of the kitchen and hurried Samal to the car. I watched them drive away, went straight to my room and went to bed. Once during the night I was awakened by the wind moaning around the corners of the house. It had turned cold and the wind told me a fresh norther had blown in. Half asleep, I listened to the wind and a tree branch scraping the shingles of the roof and the comfortable sound of a banging shutter that Bant swore every morning he would fix. The lonesome sounds of beams and boards creaking lulled me back to sleep again.

Some sound brought me out of sleep again and this time I knew I hadn't just drifted out of sleep because of familiar sounds. I lay pondering what I'd heard and couldn't identify it. Finally, with dread of the cold, I threw the covers back with the thought of investigating. The floor felt like ice to my feet and I snuggled back into my warm spot and pulled the covers to my ears. The sound came again, a scratching sound, a scraping sound. I don't know how I knew, but I knew there was some weak person or thing at the front door.

I didn't waste time. I jumped out of bed and groped my way through darkness to the living room. I was shivering in fits and starts and wondered how it could get so cold so quickly inside a tight house. A few embers glowed in the fireplace and gave enough light for me to cross to the door. I unlocked it, threw it open, staggered back as a blast of cold air beat against me, then forced myself to step forward. I couldn't see a thing. It was dark as pitch. The wind was a wildsome thing, a frenzied thing fringed with ice. I took another step and stumbled over a body.

Kenty was lying there. I knew it even as I knelt and ran my hands over his body to his face. I yelled for Bant and yelled again, but I was wasting my breath and knew it. The wind caught my yells and blew them away.

It wouldn't have been too difficult to drag Kenty inside the house if he hadn't been lying cross-wise to the door. I had to maneuver him around before I could drag him through. Once I had him turned in the right direction, it took only seconds to drag him inside. I closed the door, leaning hard to force it shut against the wind, and then went to the fireplace to fumble on the mantelpiece for matches. There was a lamp on the mantel and I lighted it, hurried to a table and lighted the big lamp there, then started piling kindling on the live coals in the fireplace. I let the kindling flare before piling on wood, fanned the flames, then pulled Kenty close. I didn't take time to examine him, though I could see crusted blood covering his face and matting his hair. The important thing was to warm him and I went to my room for all the quilts and a pillow. I covered him, lifted his head and slid the pillow under before going to get Bant.

Bant was a light sleeper and he sat up in bed the instant I opened the door. "What is it, Jeff?"

"It's Kenty. He's hurt bad and frozen stiff. I've got him in the living room."

Bant took just enough time to shake Mama and then he shucked out of bed, stepped into his shoes and pulled on his pants while he was walking toward the living room. He threw the covers off Kenty and took one look before yelling for Mama to hurry.

Mama put water on to boil while Bant and I rubbed Kenty's hands and feet. Bant took his pulse and said it was too weak, too shallow, dangerous. There was a head wound, but it wasn't a bad one. Bant guessed Kenty had been knocked unconscious and left to freeze to death.

"There's something else wrong," Bant muttered after a while. "He's thawing out and still his pulse is shallow. We'll have to undress him and see if he's hurt some other place. I'll have to get a doctor if he doesn't come around soon. He'll die on us if we're not careful."

I pulled the covers back and Bant started unbuttoning Kenty's shirt.

"Look," Mama said, pointing. "He's blood all over."

I saw it then, saw the blood frozen hard and dark and slick on Kenty's pants. Bant saw it and told Mama not to look. He unbuckled Kenty's belt, unbuttoned the pants, and I helped pull his pants down and off.

"They tried to castrate him," Bant said. "He lost a lot of blood, but he's not bleeding now. I'll get the doctor. You two keep him warm while I'm gone."

"Did they...?" Mama asked.

"No," Bant said. "He'll live to sire more bastards."

CHAPTER SIX

"My car will never start," Bant said. "I'll have to ride the mare."

"Kenty's car may be close by," I said. "He couldn't have crawled far."

"No telling where his car is. But... you run out for a half mile or so and see if you can find it. Hurry now. I'll be dressed and ready to take your mare, but he'll probably die before I get to town."

I started down the lane to the road at a fast trot, turned left where the road forked and ran another half-mile. I took the left fork because it would have come within a mile of the Trails place and Kenty would have walked Sam that last mile. I found the car within another two minutes and it was in the ditch. Kenty must have tried to get it out and someone must have jumped him while he was trying.

The car didn't want to start. I set the gas and spark levers, choked it, and twisted the handle until I was exhausted. It coughed at long last and gave me hope. Still, I was about to give up trying when the motor started. Even then, I was lucky to get it out of the ditch. I backed and filled, backed and filled, inched almost up to the level road and sank back again. I tried again and would have made it if the motor hadn't stalled. I had to crank again, back for a running start, and this time made it. The car rocked and slid, but it finally put its parts together and shuddered its way into the road. I drove slowly home and met Bant coming out of the gate on the mare. He dismounted without a word, got in behind the wheel and handed the reins to me. I put the mare back in her stall and went back into the house. Kenty was still asleep, his breathing ragged and raspy and his pulse shallow.

Bant made it back in two hours and the doctor was following him. Mama was sent from the room while the doctor examined Kenty. He said that the sonofabitch that did this ought to be burned alive and that we'd better be prepared to have a dead man on our hands. He said Kenty probably would develop pneumonia on top of everything else and he doubted there was a doctor in the entire whole United States of America who could save him then. He said he'd seen hogs butchered with a dull knife that was an example of a surgeon's art compared to what they did to this man. If he doesn't get blood poisoning or pneumonia, he said, Kenty would be fine because the stupid butcher must have chickened out or was scared off before he could destroy Kenty's manhood.

Mama came back into the room after the doctor finished his doctoring and bandaging. She made coffee and we all drank it at the kitchen table. Mama had been crying and the doctor said things like what had happened to Kenty could cause a woman to go into shock and that she should dissolve this little packet of powder in water and drink it down so she could sleep.

"Jeff," Bant said, "I want you to take the mare and ride over to the Trails place again. Tell Old Trails that somebody hurt Kenty bad. See if Samal is all right. The girl can take care of herself and probably walked on home, but I can't believe for the life of me that she'd leave Kenty when he was hurt. Unless she thought he was dead and knew who did this. On the other hand, she wouldn't have stood by and allowed this thing to happen without putting up a fight. She might be hurt."

"Well," I said, "the car was in the ditch with its front toward the road. Kenty might have taken Samal home and headed back this way."

"Not necessarily. Kenty would have gone to his place. No reason for him to come back here. My guess is that Coy Trails, or somebody, jumped him way up the road and then brought the car back this way to ditch it. You go, like I said. We've got to know if Samal is all right."

I gulped my coffee, got my heavy coat and cap and gloves and went outside. The wind nearly took the door off the hinges when I opened it. I might as well have been naked for all the good my clothing did me. There seemed to be nothing but a barbed wire fence between us and the North Pole, the way it felt. My face was numb and my ears stung and ached before I reached the barn and the cold made me so stiff I walked like an old man. The mare was skittish, dreading the cold, and I had a hard time getting her to take the bit. She pulled back when I led her out and bucked a little when I mounted. Once in a gallop, though, she warmed up and steadied down. I leaned forward, wrapped my arms around her neck and buried my face in her mane.

I took a different route to the Trails place than I had taken before. I crossed an open field and opened a wire gate that gave me entry to Trails land, took a lane that led through thick woods and brush, wound uphill to the mesa, and the wind wasn't as strong. I rode at the gallop, neared the house, picked my way around the huge rocks, dismounted and tied the horse to a tree. Old Trails must have heard me coming, though the shrieking wind made that unlikely. He had probably come out to the porch to take a leak.

"Well, boy," he said. "You must be a mite cold."

"Yes, sir."

"Bant hurt again, is he?"

"No, sir. It's Kenty. He's hurt bad."

I followed the old man inside and joined Samal at the fireplace.

"It's Kenty," she said.

"He's hurt, Sam."

"Tell me about it."

"Somebody cut him. Like you would castrate a pig."

Sam began to cry. She held both hands in front of her face and cried and the old man went to the fireplace and kicked at a half-burned backlog. I waited until Sam turned to me, and she sat down in a rocking chair and made me take a chair by the hearth.

"Was Kenty's manhood taken?"

"No. The doctor said he'll be all right on that score."

"Tell us what you know."

"Well, some time in the night I woke up and heard the wind and I lay there listening for something else I'd heard or thought I'd heard. It was a scratching sound at the front door and it came again. I don't know how I knew, but I knew it was Kenty. I went to the door and opened it and half stumbled over him. I got him inside and we got him warm and Bant went for the doctor."

Sam was white of face. "You said they tried to cut him, but his manhood wasn't taken?"

"The doctor says he'll be all right if he doesn't take pneumonia. No, Sam. He's still a man. Bant says he'll live to sire more... children."

Old Trails laughed. It was an ugly laugh and I glared at him. "Why would anybody do a thing like that?" he asked. "Who would do a thing like that?"

"Well, Mister Trails, Bant thinks it was Coy because Coy and Kenty had a fight."

"Coy wouldn't do that!" the old man shouted at me. "I didn't bring Coy up to do things like that!"

"Where was Kenty's car?" Sam asked.

"About a mile from our place. That means that somebody knocked Kenty unconscious and drove him back to where I found the car. He'd been hit on the head and was still unconscious when I started over here."

"Kenty stopped on the road and wanted to walk me on home, but we both smelled the norther coming and I finally persuaded him to let me find my own way. We'll go to him now, Jeff."

"There's nothing you can do."

"I guess not, but I want to be there. You go on ahead and tell Kenty and Pearl I'll be there as soon as I clear up some unfinished business with Coy."

It had come on to snow, though the flakes were scattered by the strong wind, and I knew the ground wouldn't be covered deep. I gave the mare her head and let her run. I saw the blurry shapes of cattle walking with the wind hunting shelter, and passed a small herd of goats in a gully out of the wind. I saw the lamplight from the living room window and the window in the spare bedroom and hoped Kenty was better. I wanted to go inside at once, but stabled the mare and picked up a backlog for the fire before entering the house. Mama fixed me a meal of fried ham and eggs and biscuits and sat down to drink a cup of coffee while I ate.

"Kenty's asleep now," Mama said. "His breathing is nice and easy. I think he'll wake up with a clear head."

"Where's Bant?"

"He went for the sheriff. That means bad trouble, son. I wish Kenty had never come back. I wish he'd go away again. I wish Bant would stop drinking. I wish..." and then she smiled. "Well, if wishes were horses, we'd have horses to ride."

I heard the motor of a Model T and Mama said, "That'll be Bant."

We heard Bant's footsteps on the front porch and he came stamping in. He went straight to the fire and held his hands out to it, shucked off his coat and hat and turned his wind-red face to us.

"The sheriff went on over to talk to Coy, Pearl. I guess Coy and Old Trails will be madder'n the devil at me, but don't worry. I'll not brook any foolishness. A man was hurt and I had no choice but report it."

"Did you tell him Coy did it?"

"I didn't need to tell him. He knew all about the fight at the church and said he'd have to question Coy."

"We're going to have another killing on our hands," Mama said. "Kenty will go looking for Coy as soon as he's able."

"Well, it'll be Coy's funeral," Bant said. He kicked at the fire logs. "It may be that Coy and Old Trails teamed up to do it. That old man is good with a knife. At least he was when he was younger. They say he came from Kansas and rode with Quantrell. I never saw him knife anybody, but he was a fool for dancing, even after he married and had kids. He'd go to a dance and some young buck would rile him and the first thing you'd know there'd be a knife fight in the front yard. He could use a knife or throw it. Still, when you stop to think about it, he wouldn't have stopped a castration job without finishing it up. The truth is, too, that I don't want the old man to get in bad trouble. I can't like him, but he's too old for a jail term."

Mama and Bant looked in on Kenty and then went to bed. I sat at the kitchen table until first light and then did the chores. Mama and Bant would sleep three or four hours, I figured, and I meant to go see Festal. Something told me he needed me, that he was in bad trouble, and I thought I could go to him and get home again before anyone in the house awakened. I should have had better sense. The sheriff was still at the Trails house and I should have turned around the second I saw his car. Instead, I tied Rainbow to a tree and went to look under the front porch for Festal. He wasn't there; at least I didn't see him. I knocked at the front door, then, and Sam opened it.

"Are you crazy?" she hissed. "The sheriff is here and Coy or Pa will break your neck!"

"I thought the sheriff and Coy would be headed for the jail by now."

"Well, they're still here. You light a shuck out of here, Jeff."

I turned to go and paused. "How's Festal?"

Samal closed the door.

I was standing there trying to decide whether to leave or hunt for Festal when the sheriff came outside. I started to walk away and stopped when he yelled.

"Who are you, boy?"

I started to answer, but Old Trails had followed the sheriff and answered for me. "That's Bant's boy. What are you doing here, boy? Don't you know Bant put the law on Coy? What are you doing here, I say?"

"I came to see about Festal."

"You just high tail it out of here. You're not wanted on this place, not now and not ever. I've warned him, sheriff, and you're my witness."

The sheriff waggled a motioning finger at me. I looked him over while I approached and didn't like what I saw. I didn't like his face or his hat or his unborn calf-hide boots or his big belly or his mean eyes.

"Come on in the house," he said. "I want to talk to you."

I thought Old Trails would refuse to let me enter, but he kept his mouth shut. Coy and Sam were sitting near the hearth. Sam smiled and shook her head in a I–told–you so-way and Coy glared.

"Have a seat, son," the sheriff said and dragged a chair close to the fire. "Sit over there. I want to see you when I talk to you."

"Where's Festal?" I asked Sam.

"He's around somewhere." She ducked her head.

"Have you seen Festal?" I asked the sheriff.

"Who's Festal?"

"He's a little boy they beat and make sleep under the house or where he can. They whip him like a dog."

"Who's they?"

"Old Trails and Coy. Sam is good to him."

"I haven't seen a little boy around here."

"He's down at the barn," Coy spoke up. "He plays in the hay down there."

"He's been whipped again and you didn't want the sheriff to see him. Why didn't you speak up, Sam? Now's your chance to stop what's been happening to that poor kid."

Sam just ducked her head and I knew that wasn't like her. I wondered if she was afraid of Coy and the old man, and thought that not likely. Maybe, I thought, blood is thicker than water and she doesn't want her pa and Coy to go to jail.

"You shut your mouth, boy," Coy said. "You're going to get hurt one of these days."

"What would you do? Castrate me?"

Coy made a lunge at me and would have swiped me if the sheriff hadn't stuck out a long leg to stop him. For a second or two I thought Coy would hit the sheriff, but he backed off and sat down again.

"We'll talk about this Festal after a bit," the sheriff said. "Right now I want to talk about Kenty Hooker. You there, boy, whatever your name is. You found Kenty on your front porch. Is that right?"

"Yes, sir. My name is Jeff Carr."

"Well, Jeff Carr. What did Kenty say when you found him?"

"He didn't say anything. He was unconscious and almost frozen stiff. I just dragged him inside."

"What time was all this?"

"I don't know exactly. I didn't notice. But it was probably after midnight."

The sheriff leaned forward in his chair and picked up a kindling stick from beside the hearth. He stared at the stick for a moment and then began to scrape mud off his boots.

"Tell me, boy," he said. "How cold do you reckon it got last night?"

"Down to zero, I'd think."

"At least that."

"It was awfully cold," I said for lack of something else to say.

"It was cold enough to freeze a man to death, Jeff Carr. You're right about that." He looked up at me and then looked at Coy and kept looking at Coy while he asked me the next question.

"How long do you think it would take an unconscious man to freeze to death out in that cold?"

"I don't rightly know. Not long."

"Would you say two or three hours?"

"Yes, sir. Even so, he might catch pneumonia and die. The doctor said that might happen."

The sheriff began to pick at the mud on his boots with the stick. He seemed to have forgotten me. The clock ticked on the mantel almost in tune with the screaking of Old Trails' rocker. He tossed his stick into the fire and stared at Coy.

"Somebody tried to commit a murder," he said. "That's the way I see it. It was bad enough to cut at a man's genitals. I don't see how the job was botched unless it was too dark to see good, but that's not the point. I talked to the doctor about this thing and he said Kenty could have died of the cold and might die of pneumonia. That changes things from assault to attempted murder. Yessiree, bud. That's a serious charge. The trick is to get the man that done it." He turned his stare to me. "What time did Kenty leave your house with Samal?"

"About eight o'clock."

"Where do you think Kenty was from eight o'clock until midnight? It wouldn't have taken long for him to take Samal home."

"I think he was unconscious a great part of that time." He reached over and grabbed my knee. He squeezed and his fingers went deep and then he let go and patted my leg and smiled an evil little smile he probably thought was kindly.

"I'll tell you what I think, Jeff Carr. I think you went to sleep and slept just a little while and then you heard Kenty at the door and you went down to let him in. That's the way the doctor said it. Kenty was scratching at the door. You dragged him inside and covered him and after a while he warmed up and you thought he was fine.

"You went to sleep and when you woke up it was after midnight. You tried to wake Kenty up and then you got scared and called Bant. You didn't tell him Kenty had been in the house nearly all night. You said you'd just dragged him inside."

"That's not true."

Coy laughed nervously. "Pa, the sheriff's trying to build a case against me! Don't you see, Pa? He's got to prove Kenty was at Bant's house before ten o'clock because I was home before ten."

"I wouldn't say that," the sheriff drawled. "I'll admit I can't figure out where Kenty was if he dragged himself to Bant's house after midnight. Samal says she was home well before nine and that leaves three hours I can't account for. Kenty could have died in that time. The truth is, and I hate to admit it, that I don't have a case on Coy right now." He pointed a finger at Coy. "I think you butchered Kenty Hooker, young man. If I had a shred of evidence I'd run you in. Yesiree, bub."

"I didn't do it," Coy said.

"You did," the sheriff said. "I know you did it and you know you did it and everybody in this room knows you did it. If Kenty decides to accuse you, which he probably will, I'll see you behind bars."

"I know how it happened," Samal said.

I saw something at that moment I never expected to see. Coy got out of his chair and sank to his knees before Sam, his hands clasped in supplication.

"I didn't do it, Sam," his voice was hoarse. "You've got to believe me. I wouldn't do a thing like that."

"Sheriff," Samal said, ignoring Coy, "I'll have to admit that I lied when I said Kenty let me out of the car at the road and that I walked the rest of the way by myself. Kenty walked me home. Whatever happened to him must have happened in our barn. I think that after I came into the house Coy must have yelled to Kenty from the barn and somehow got Kenty to go there. That's where it happened. I don't know why Coy didn't finish the job, but Festal must have been sleeping in the hay. Somehow or other Kenty must have dragged himself across country to his car and headed back to Bant's place. He went into the ditch and passed out for a while."

"I didn't do it," Coy said, scrambling to his feet. "I didn't do it. Why does everybody think I did it? Why does it have to be me? It's always me. Somebody could be robbing the bank in town right now and everybody would say it was me."

The sheriff leaned back in his chair. "You think this boy, Festal... your brother?... woke up and Coy didn't finish the cutting job because there was a witness. Is that right? Yes. Well, I'll have to talk with that lad. First, though, I think I just might take Coy to jail on suspicion of battery and assault and attempted murder. By the way, Coy. Let me have a look at your knife."

Coy fished his pocket for a knife and held it out to the sheriff. Samal cracked a pecan and flicked away the broken shell with her thumbnail.

"Coy's knife is on the mantel," she said. "That's Pa's knife he's got there."

Coy moved, but the sheriff was faster. He pushed Coy away with his left hand and felt on the mantel with his right. He stepped over to the window, peered intently, grunted his satisfaction and pocketed the knife.

"There's blood on it," he said.

"I was cutting some hogs yesterday," Coy said. "Ask Pa."

"He was," Old Trails said.

"We'll go now," the sheriff said. "Coy, you get you a change of clothes and a warm coat and we'll be on our way."

Coy started out of the room, but the sheriff changed his mind.

"You stay here with me, Coy. We'll let your sister get your things."

Samal left the room without a word and Old Trails followed her out. Coy went to stand with his back to the fire and the sheriff stood by the door to the hallway. Samal returned, but Old Trails wasn't with her. She had stuffed some of Coy's clothing into a case and handed it to him. Coy went to a hall-tree in the corner of the room and got his woolen jacket.

I cleared my throat. "I still want to know where Festal is."

Neither Coy nor Samal answered me. The sheriff came back across the room to the fireplace for a last warming.

"Sheriff," I said, "I think you ought to see about Festal before you leave."

"Why are you so all fired concerned about that boy?"

"I think he might be hurt. I think he's out in the barn, and I think he's been hurt."

"What would he be doing in the barn if he's hurt?"

"I told you, sir. They beat him and make him sleep under the house or in the barn. They probably won't let him come in here."

Coy was glaring at me, standing stiff, but Sam was watching the sheriff.

"What about it, Coy?" the sheriff asked. "Has your brother been hurt?"

"There's nothing wrong with him that I know of."

"Why isn't he in here by the warm fire?"

"He's a funny kid. He does strange things."

"What about it, young lady? Is this boy Festal hurt in some way?"

"I don't know."

"All right, Sam," I said. "You're lying and I can see it. I'll see about Festal myself."

The sheriff took Coy by the arm and led him outside. Sam and I followed him to the front porch and he turned to Sam.

"I'll be back when I've got Coy locked up, Missy Sam. I want a look at that barn. Meanwhile, you tell your pa that nothing is be disturbed out there."

Sam and I watched the sheriff drive away with Coy. That old boy, Coy, sat tall and straight and didn't look back once.

"Let's go see to Festal," I said.

"I'll see where Pa is first. He's the one nearly killed Festal. He beat the little tyke with a piece of baling wire and put gashes all over his back and legs."

"When?"

"Last night. Festal came in the house and sat in front of the fire. Pa told him to move and he didn't move fast enough. Pa was already mad at me because I'd been rough talking him about his drinking. He doesn't drink often, but when he does I know he'll end up doing something cruel to Festal."

"Where was Coy?"

"He wasn't here. And don't think I didn't try to stop Pa. I picked up a stick of firewood, but he was too fast for me. He clouted me one right under the chin and I went out like a light. See?"

There was a blue-black bruise at the under-edge of her chin that I hadn't seen in the dim light of the living room. I touched it gently and told her I was sorry.

I headed for the barn and Sam went into the house. She was back outside yelling at me before I'd opened the barn door.

"Pa's gone," she called, and headed toward me at a trot. "He's probably inside there trying to cover up anything that would lead to Coy."

I pulled the barn door open and heard Festal call. It was a weak call and I wasn't positive I'd heard it, but he called again and I went inside.

"I'm over here," Festal said, and I found him in a horse stall. He was bedded on straw and I supposed he was warm enough. He looked, though, like a starving varmint.

"Are you hurt bad?" I asked, and he grinned up at me.

"He near about killed me this time, Jeff. He's used baling wire before, but he sure cut me up bad this time."

"Can you walk?"

"I think I can. It'll hurt, but I can stand it."

"We'll get you to the house and doctor you," Sam said from behind me. "The sheriff took Coy to jail and I don't know where Pa is. Anyway, you come on.

I'll shoot the old fool if he tries to bother you again. So help me, I will."

Festal started up and I stooped to put my arm around him. He flinched and moaned when I touched him and I pulled away.

"Can you lean on me?"

"I can make it. I'm strong enough."

He limped to the house, limped like a crooked old man, and Sam and I followed helplessly. He needed help climbing the steps because his wounds were stiff and blood was dried over them. I scrunched down so he could put his arm around my neck and we made it to the porch. We went on in to the kitchen and Samal pulled a zinc tub in from the back porch, put water on to heat, and tried to help Festal out of his shirt and pants. It couldn't be done. When the water was warm, we poured it in the tub and saved enough to soak Festal's clothing. Even after that, it hurt the boy like fire when we stripped him. We opened some wounds and fresh blood flowed. Old Trails had done a job on him. Festal was lashed from his neck to his ankles, and that baling wire had cut like a knife.

Sam brought an evil smelling ointment, the same stuff Old Trails had used on Bant, and we smeared it on as gently as we could. I'll say this for Festal. It hurt him plenty, but he stood in the tub and gritted his teeth and took it. Samal brought a sheet and we ripped it to strips and used it for the bandaging. He looked like an Egyptian mummy when we'd finished and even Festal had to laugh. Sam found a clean pair of overalls and some thick white socks, and then she heated a pan of stew. Festal ate like a starving dog and drank three glasses of buttermilk. I decided then it was time to travel.

"I'm taking him home with me," I told Samal.

"He can't walk and he sure can't ride your horse."

"You'll have to take him, then. In the buggy."

Sam began to cry. "It won't do, Jeff. It would just make things worse than they are now. You go on home. Pa was in the barn, hidden somewhere, all the time we were there. He'll leave Festal alone for a long while. I know him and he'll be ashamed. He wouldn't admit it if his life depended on it, but he'll be ashamed. Until two weeks or two months from now when he gets drunk again. You go on home, Jeff, and tell Kenty and Pearl I'll be there later today."

I turned to go and Sam said, "Jeff."

"Yes?"

"Next to Kenty, I love you best."

CHAPTER SEVEN

We had the coldest October I'd ever seen. It was my job to get up first in the mornings to build a fire in the fireplace. The house would be icy cold and I'd hurry to rake ashes from banked embers, pile kindling on, stack on a big backlog and a pyramid of firewood, and fan the embers into flame with a newspaper. Once the wood was burning, I'd go to the kitchen to start a fire in the cook stove. I'd usually do my chores at the barn and hen-house and bring in wood for the day before Mama and Bant got out of bed. Bant was always the first up in summer, but he was a slug-a-bed in winter.

Kenty stayed at our house for two weeks and Sam came to visit every day. Coy stayed in jail only two nights because Kenty refused to press charges. He wouldn't even discuss the matter. The thing that seemed strangest to me was that Bant was more like his old self with Kenty in the house. We spent most of the days around the fire in the living room and Kenty joined us there when the doctor told him all danger was past.

Kenty went home on a Thursday in mid-month and Sam came to our house late Friday afternoon. She was riding that mean stallion she loved and was wearing a sheepskin coat and heavy boots. Her face was pink from the cold and she stood before the fireplace shivering.

"What in the world are you doing out on a day like this, child?" Mama asked. "It must be close to zero."

"Feels like it, sure," Sam replied. "I ordered a dress from the Sears book and there's twenty-eight cents postage due. I have to go to the post office to get it."

"You're planning to ride a horse to town? In this weather? It's too late in the day, child. You'll spend the night and go with Bant come morning. We need groceries and he had planned to go anyway."

Bant had gone hunting and came in just before sundown, stamping snow off his boots on the front porch, shaking his coat in the breezeway, whewing and puffing and making comments about the weather. Mama had cooked spareribs and sweet potatoes for supper, with apple pie and coffee, and Bant hadn't been so cheerful in weeks. He swapped jokes with Sam about wanting a new dress so bad she was willing to freeze for it and even teased me about Sam. He and Sam played checkers after supper and Mama got out the chess set her father had left her. I suffered through a game to please her, but vowed silently never to become enchanted with something so boresome.

I slept poorly and was up at dawn to start the fires. I was just fanning the embers into flame when Sam came in. She dressed before me as only women can dress. I saw not one inch of bare flesh above her knees. Her undergarments went on under Mama's gown and her dress went on over her head as the gown came down. The gown dropped in a puddle at her feet and all the time she was teasing me with her smile.

I started the fire in the kitchen and Sam put the coffee on. I went to the barn in disgust to feed the animals and, as usual, that wall-eyed sneaky sly mean hearted stallion of hers tried to pin me against a wall of the stall. I fed the chickens and took firewood into the house, the snow crunching beneath my feet and the air like fire in my nostrils. A wild turkey lumbered up from the fencerow between barnlot and field and drummed away. Another followed as I watched the first. The brightest stars were dimming in a lighting sky when I went inside for breakfast.

"I'm not going to try to start the car," Bant announced. "I could pour hot water over the block and get it started here, but the thing would freeze before we start home. We'll take the wagon. Jeff, you fold the tarp good and put it in the wagon. We'll take a robe, too. You'd better bundle up the best you can if you want to go with Sam and me. It'll take us three hours going and three coming."

"I fried a couple of chickens last night," Mama said. "There's another apple pie and I'll fix a jug of coffee. Jeff, be sure to take your gloves. Bant, you take a pillow. I'm tired of your moanings and groanings and limpings every time you sit on that springboard to town and back."

We were on our way an hour later with the sleek fat mules, Josh and Job, in harness. It wasn't snowing, but the leaden gray clouds hung low and threatened. The snow on the ground was crusted and drifts in the road convinced us our car could not have plowed through. The mules, spoiled as children, were accustomed to the barn in such weather and needed constant coaxings and slaps from the reins. The three of us huddled on the springseat, a heavy robe over our laps. The landscape, beautiful to me, would have looked bleak and forbidding to an outsider. The mules breathed smoke, as did we, and the cold became an icy blanket, heavy and penetrating. It was slow going, and boring, the novelty gone in moments. Only the monotony and the thought of long miles ahead, the jangle and screak of harness and the crunch of wheels through snow crust remained. We tried singing and soon gave that up. Bant pointed out a gray fox in the brush and a cold coyote sniffing rabbit tracks in the distance. Samal pressed against me for warmth and I suddenly surrendered to the cold.

"I'm going under the tarp," I said. "Call me when we get to town."

"Who's the big sissy now?" Sam asked.

"I am if it pleases you. Call me, Bant, if you want me to spell you."

Sam followed me off the springseat. "I was afraid you'd be stubborn and never give in," she said. "I would have given up in another five minutes."

We wrapped the robe around Bant and tied it across his shoulders, then crawled under the tarp in the wagon bed. Huddled there, we found warmth and sleepy contentment until the warmth stirred my sluggish blood and caused me to slip my hand inside Sam's dress. She kissed me and fondled me, hissed sharply when I moaned, then pushed me away. In what followed I wished more than once I'd stayed on the wagon.

We ate the cold food Mama had prepared before we reached the still warm coffee, and our spirits lifted. Bant left the wagon at the wagon yard, gave me a dollar, and told Sam and me to meet the wagon at three o'clock. I went with Sam to the post office for a package and we decided to go to the picture show. Al Jolson was in The Jazz Singer, the first picture with sound we had ever seen. We saw it twice. We went to the restaurant for pie and coffee, left with reluctantly and went back to the street to gaze in every shop window. Sam was admiring a watch in a jeweler's window when I heard Bant's voice.

Ten or twelve men were clustered at the curb, pushing and crowding to see something I couldn't see. I started toward them and Sam tried to hold me back. I suppose we both knew Bant was at the center of the crowd. I ran toward them, with Sam following, skirted the cluster and pushed men who stood in my way.

Coy Trails was facing Bant in the space encircled by the crowd of men. He wore no coat and his sleeves were rolled up to his elbows. His arms were big and his hands were big and I still can see the hairs on his arms and hands. I can see their curl and their color. I can see the pores of the skin.

There was blood on Bant's face. It trickled from a cut above his left eye and from his nose. He was pulling off his coat and was calm and smiling. Coy Trails was breathing hard, sucking in air and snorting it out. His chest heaved.

"You've had enough, Bant," he said. "I don't want to hurt you bad."

"You hit me when I wasn't looking, Coy. It isn't as easy to stop as it is to start."

"I'll teach you to sic the sheriff on me, you son of a bitch!"

Bant's coat was still over his left arm and he was using his right to remove it when Coy clubbed him in the face. Bant went to his knees, shook his head, stumbled to his feet and swung a blow that missed. Coy smashed him in the mouth and he dropped.

Sam cried out and ran to Bant, knelt beside him and lifted his head. Coy stood looking down at her and said something, but the murmur of the crowd drowned his words. I slipped my knife from my pocket and was just starting to open the blade when my foot touched something. It was a rock just larger than my fist, smooth and shiny and round. I picked it up and hefted it in my right hand, stepped into the clear and walked up to Coy. He was watching Sam and didn't notice me.

"Coy," I said.

He looked around at me. He saw the knife handle in my left hand and snatched for it. He had to stoop a little and I had a clear shot with the rock. I swung it and caught him just behind his left ear. He fell at my feet, face down, and I kicked his face twice before two men dragged me away.

Bant came to his feet, swaying groggily. By that time there were several men to tell him they'd have waded into Coy if I hadn't acted first. Bant paid them no mind and went to see about Coy. Satisfied I hadn't killed a man, he said we'd better head for home.

Bant walked off up the street and didn't see Samal kneel beside Coy. She lifted his head and used her handkerchief to wipe blood away. Coy opened his eyes and stared up at her, but said never a word. I took her arm and lifted her up and we walked a gauntlet of stares as we followed Bant to the wagon yard. I helped hitch the team to the wagon and told Bant to lie in back under the tarp, but he refused. Sam and I sat on the springseat beside him the first hour, but the cold was unbearable. The robe just wasn't big enough for the three of us, but Bant refused to get in back.

"You kids get under the tarp," he ordered. "I'll be fine under the robe. I couldn't rest and I've thinking to do."

Bant, for three days, treated me as he had in younger days. He didn't mention the fight with Coy or what I did to Coy in my presence, but Mama said he'd told her and that he was proud of me. Then, seemingly without reason, he withdrew more deeply into his shell. I sought Kenty's company more and more often, ducking across the hills and woods every time Bant went to town. Kenty hobbled on a cane to take me hunting, taught me to shoot, and taught me to work with dogs. He was still stiff and in pain, but able to talk me through most of it. When he couldn't bear me making any more mistakes, he would throw his cane aside and show me himself. He had me spend hours breaking in his Appaloosas and worked especially hard with his natural pacers. I know Mama never mentioned my visits to Kenty and I never neglected my chores, but Bant sensed the truth and didn't like it. More than once he mentioned that I spent more time with Kenty than I spent at home, but he never ordered me to stay home. Instead, he found work to pile on me, extra chores after school and on weekends.

Mama cut down one of Bant's suits for me and told Bant I needed a new pair of boots, but Bant said he had a bank payment coming up and that I'd have to wait. Kenty came over on a Saturday night and, leaning against the wall for support, played the fiddle. I sat on the hearth, cracking pecans, and

once I saw him looking at my worn brogans. It shamed me and I was afraid
he'd say something, but he looked away quickly and played another tune.
Bant went off to bed without saying good night and Kenty left soon after.
He came back on Monday night with a pair of boots. I put them on, heard
Bant come into the kitchen, and went to help him strain the milk. He no-
ticed the boots the minute I sat back down on the hearth.

"Where did they come from?"

"They're a present from Kenty."

"Since when have you felt obliged to buy boots for my boy, Kenty?"

Kenty grinned his crooked grin. "The boy's my friend, Bant. You and Pearl
are my friends. I eat food at your table and I thought I'd bring a present.
Friends can do that. I saw the boots in town today and thought Jeff would
like them. They'll go well with his new suit."

"Take them back," Bant said. "Jeff, clean them good and put them in the
box."

"You're being childish, Bant," Mama said.

"Stay out of it, Pearl."

Kenty stood and tucked his fiddle under his arm. "Don't get your dander
up, Bant. I didn't intend to hurt your pride. Let him keep the boots."

"I'll get him what he needs so long as he's under this roof."

Kenty shrugged. I handed him the box and he left, leaning into his cane.

Bant bought boots for me the next day. He left on his bay mare before dawn
and was gone all day. Our early winter was hanging on and the day was cold
and overcast. Dark came early. I had finished the chores and had returned
to the house where Mama was cooking supper. Bant hallooed from the front
yard and Mama told me to go see about him.

"He's been drinking, son. You'd better go take care of the horse."

I had to help Bant out of the saddle and steady his walk to the porch. He
dropped a box and ignored it. I left it there until I'd finished bedding the
mare and then took it inside. Bant was sitting in his rocker and told me to
open my present. The boots looked exactly like those Kenty had given me
and I knew without doubt they were the same. Whether he had retrieved
them from Kenty or bought them I didn't know and didn't ask.

The next day was warmer and by Friday the snow had melted. Bant poured
hot water over the engine block of the Model T on Saturday morning and
got it started. He told Mama he'd be home early and drove out of the yard.
He came home after dark, drunker than I'd ever seen him, and went to bed
without his supper. We went to church on Sunday and in the afternoon I
saddled Raindrop and rode across the foothills to see Johnny and Joe Deacon. We played baseball for an hour and then decided we'd walk the mile
to Black's roadside grocery and service station for a Delaware Punch and
Babe Ruth. We'd finished our drinks and candy when Jim English stopped

for gasoline in his new Model A. Joe asked him if we could hitch a ride and we were told to climb in.

Jim English drove fast until we reached the lane leading to the Deacon place.

"We'd like to get out here," Joe Deacon said.

Jim English seemed not to have heard. His huge, freckled hands gripped the steering wheel and he sat hunched over like a fat toad on a rock.

"Mister English," Joe said, "I live down that lane back there and we'd like to get out here, if you please."

Jim English turned and laughed and the car leaped ahead faster still. Johnny and I were in the back seat and Joe was up front with Jim English. Joe stood and opened the door on his side.

"Don't jump!" I screamed. I stood, leaned forward over the seat back, leaned far forward until more of my body was up front than in back, grabbed the key and switched it off, lifted it from the ignition and threw it to the side of the road. The car coasted a long distance, slowed and stopped.

"You young bastard," Jim English said.

Joe and Johnny were out of the car and I scrambled out. Jim English turned and leaned over the seat, grabbed my leg and pulled, but I jerked free and followed my friends across the ditch and through the fence. Jim English was out of the car and yelling at me.

"You there! You with the black hair! Are you Jeff Carr?"

"Yes, sir."

He shook his head and made a clucking sound. "You're Kenty Hooker's bastard, and that's for sure."

Joe and Johnny were abashed and didn't mention what Jim English said, but I brought it up.

"I'm tired of hearing that," I said. "I've heard it all my life and I'm going to get to the bottom of it."

"It don't mean nothing," Joe said. "Jim English is a bastard himself. He had no right to do what he did and say what he did."

"Yeah," Johnny said. "Forget it."

I rode Rainbow home and saw Kenty and Bant in the front yard. They sat on their heels, whittling, and I knew from their expressions that their talk was serious. Kenty looked up and grinned at me, eyes crinkling, but Bant just glanced at me and didn't bother to nod, smile, or speak. I took Rainbow on to the barn and stabled her and then returned to Kenty and Bant. Kenty was saying something in a low, urgent voice, but stopped speaking when I approached.

"Bant," I said.

"Yeah." An edge of impatience in his voice.

"I want to ask you something. I guess I want to ask you and Kenty something. Jim English gave Joe and Johnny and me a ride and then wouldn't stop to let us out. I grabbed his keys and threw them out of the car and he said I was Kenty's bastard and that's for sure. I've been hearing that word all my life and I have a right to know the truth."

Bant turned red, then white, ducked his head to his whittling. Kenty stood up and snapped his knife closed.

"This is something for me to handle, Bant. Mind if I take Jeff with me?"

Bant went ahead with whittling and didn't bother to look up. He held his stick up and sighted along its length, shaved some parings from it and held it up for another inspection.

"Was Jim English headed toward town?" Kenty asked me.

"If he found his car keys."

"Let's take a little trip. I'll go tell Pearl where we're going. You wait in my car."

I went to the car and sat in the front seat while Kenty headed for the house. He was gone a couple of minutes and then we drove out of the yard. Bant was still intent on his whittling.

We drove down the cut-off to the main road and turned right toward town. Kenty looked stern and mad and drove fast without slowing until we reached the city limits. He slowed and looked closely at cars parked, drove to the center of town, then spotted Jim English's car. He pulled in to the curb and stepped out.

"Come with me, Jeff."

I followed him down the street, Kenty's movements slow but deliberate, past Grant's Drug Store and Brown's Hardware, and we saw Jim English in front of the bank talking to Dick Yoder. He turned his head when Kenty laid a hand on his shoulder.

"I'll have a word with you, English," Kenty said in a quiet voice.

Jim English turned and his lips curled when he saw Kenty. "Whaddaya want?"

"You gave this boy and his friends a ride and wouldn't let them out of the car. Then you said something no decent man would say to a boy."

"What'd the little bastard tell you?"

Kenty dropped his cane and hit him. So fast it was that I could hardly see. One minute Jim English was standing. Then, in an instant, he was on the sidewalk unmoving. Blood trickled from his mouth and nose.

Kenty turned away, rubbing the knuckles of his left hand. "Come along, Jeff."

A sleety rain hit us before we reached home. Kenty was brooding quiet all the way home and my mood matched his and the black, menacing clouds. He let me out in our front yard and told me he wouldn't come in.

"Don't worry about it, Jeff. I know that's easier said than done, but let me tell you a little story that happens to be true.

"I was eating in a restaurant down south a few years ago and I was in a depressed state of mind. I had a corner table and I just wanted to have a drink and a meal in peace and quiet. The restaurant was pretty crowded and I noticed a large, well-dressed man moving from booth to booth. At times he would stand talking to people and at other times he would sit with them for a few minutes and talk. I thought he was the proprietor, but I was wrong. Still, I didn't look at him and hoped he wouldn't bother me.

"Well, bother me he did. He came to my booth and sat down without an invitation. 'Mister,' he said, 'I'd like to tell you a little story. Long ago there was a young man whose mother didn't know who sired him. That kid was called a bastard by everyone, right to his face. He pretended not to be hurt when his schoolmates called him that name, but it scarred him. He attended school and was bright, but he stayed at his desk during recesses and stopped going into the school yard until it was time to go home.

"'One Sunday morning he went to church as usual. He sat in the back row as usual. He ducked out the door and headed home the minute the preacher said his closing prayer, as usual. But this Sunday was different. The preacher didn't say the closing prayer. A deacon did. When the deacon finished, the kid ducked out the door and was starting down the steps when a heavy hand fell on his shoulder. It was the preacher standing there, holding him.

"'Whose boy are you?' the preacher asked. 'I've seen you in church every Sunday, but I don't know who your father is. Wait a minute! Let me look at you! Why, of course I know your father! You're the spitting image of Him! Son, your Father is the Greatest Father of all.'"

"'Jeff, I learned later that man was the three time governor of his state.'"

"Well," I said. "I know who my *Father* is. I just don't —know my pa."

Kenty gave me a knowing sort of nod and told me good night.

Bant and Mama were sitting at the kitchen table. There was a lost look in Mama's eyes, but Bant stared into his cup of coffee. Mama brought me a glass of milk and passed the beans and cornbread. I ate in silence, stealing glances at Bant, feeling Mama's eyes on me. I cleaned my dishes, went to the barn to do my chores, brought in firewood and then went to bed. I could hear Bant pacing in the living room and he was still pacing when sleep slipped up on me. Once during the night I awoke and felt him in my room. I lay still until I heard him slip out. He had wanted to say something, I knew. I'd wanted to say something, too. He hadn't known what to say and neither had I.

CHAPTER EIGHT

I had been riding Rainbow to school all semester. Mama helped me make a covering for the filly that I could strap under her belly, and I was teased by those who let their horses stand in the cold all day. At home, I helped Bant as much as he'd allow. We rebuilt the pasture fence, expanded the corral, sawed wood for the fireplace and stove, but we worked without speaking most of the time. Bant became more and more unpredictable and short-tempered. He began to criticize Mama and that was something he'd never done before. Twice he slapped me in the face and once I lost my temper and swung at him. He parried the blow and didn't hit me again, but acted as if I didn't exist for three days. He was drinking more often. He'd go into town early and come home late at night. Many times I'd lie awake and listen to his angry stampings through the house and angry shouts at Mama. One night I heard the Model T clatter into the yard, heard the front door slam, heard the rattling dishes in the kitchen. After a bit the house was quiet, but I smelled coffee.

"Bant?" Mama called.

There was no answer and I heard the scraping sound of Mama's slippers in the hallway. There was the murmur of voices in the kitchen, more clattering of dishes, and then Bant's shouting anguish.

"I can't stand it, Pearl! I didn't start it and I can't seem to end it! You and Kenty started it long ago! I don't know why he came back, but it's more than I can bear! I've kept it out of my mind the best I could, but now I can't hold my head up! I can't stand the stares and the whisperings and the sniggers I get every time I go to town!"

"I've always been honest with you, Bant," Mama said. "I've never hidden anything from you. You could stay out of town so much and you could stop drinking. You'll go mad if you go on rubbing salt in your wounds."

"We'll move away," Bant said. "That's the only thing I know to do."

"There's no place to move. This is our place and we've fought hard to hold it. It'll be ours, free and clear, and one more good year will put us on easy street."

"I could stand the past, Pearl," Bant said, "but I can't stand the way you feel about Kenty now."

I don't know what Mama said then. Their voices dropped to murmurs again. I drifted off to sleep, finally, with the murmuring still teasing my hearing.

We had another snow before Thanksgiving and for a while Bant stopped drinking and seemed more like the old Bant. He even took me to town with him one Saturday and I began to hope the bad times were past. School let out for the Thanksgiving holidays, a week before Thanksgiving, and we had more snow. Bant puttered about the barn all one morning, but in early afternoon he shaved and dressed. He dilly-dallied around the house for a long while and it was obvious he had something on his mind.

Mama ignored him and went about her kitchen work, humming a little. Bant was nervous as a cat, walked from room to room, went to the fireplace and stirred up the fire, and then went into the kitchen.

"Pearl," he said, "I'm thinking about moving to East Texas. John Denty went out there last week and thinks he'll be moving."

"John Denty," Mama said.

"He's a good farmer and rancher."

"He's a drunkard, Bant, and you know it. There was a time when you wouldn't wipe your feet in his shadow."

"He's convinced there's money to be made out there and I'm going into town to talk to him."

Mama began to hum again, began to clear the table, and Bant came through the living room and opened the front door. He looked at me hard.

"Stay close around the place today, Jeff," he said. "I'll need your help later setting some posts for a lane fence."

"Yes, sir."

Mama entered the room, wiping her hands on her apron. "Bant, John Denty has a scraggly little farm in East Texas. I remember hearing him talk about it. He probably wants to sell it to you, so be careful. Don't make any agreement until we've had a chance to talk."

I walked to the window and watched Bant walk to the car. Mama sighed and walked slowly back to the kitchen. I moped around for a while, tried to read, went to the barn to see about Raindrop, and then decided I had to get away from the place. Mama was sitting before the living room fireplace with her knitting when I came in from the barn.

"I think I'll ride Raindrop over to see Kenty," I said.

She pursed her lips. "You heard what Bant said."

"He won't be back in time to set any fence posts. Besides, I'll be back by mid-afternoon."

"Try to be here when he gets back, Jeff. He's been awfully touchy."

I saddled Raindrop and was off at a gallop, half sure that Kenty would be home and half sure he'd be gone. It was good to be away from the house, away from Bant, and the cold air whipping against my face, stinging it, was welcomed. The filly seemed just as glad to be out of her stall, ran easily and gladly and freely. I took a short-cut, opened a barbed wire gate and headed across rough pasture. Woods began at the fence line and it was colder there, cold in the shade, but the snow wasn't deep and it was easy going. At a shallow creek I stopped for a drink, cracked thin ice and drank from cupped hands, let Raindrop nose the water, then mounted and rode across. Raindrop stepped through the thin ice with dainty hoofs, but didn't shy, and I let her run for warmth once we'd crossed. I reached another fence, found another gate, and re-entered the dirt road that I'd left earlier. I'd saved at least a mile of travel because the road had looped around the pasture I'd crossed.

Kenty's house looked like a mansion, its out-buildings behind it, spread out, and stables forming a T behind them. A long porch ran the length of the house in front, shaded deeply in summer by giant oaks in the front yard. Dogs, six of them, came to meet me, long eared and sad eyed, saddle brown. They knew me, but they still bayed, had their fun and then snuffed around me and turned away without interest.

"Kenty?"

There was a quietness about the place and I called again, finally stepped up on the porch to knock at the door. I had just turned to leave when I heard a noise from somewhere inside the house.

"Kenty?"

There was no answer, but there was someone inside. I could hear his footsteps.

"Kenty," I called again. "It's Jeff. Let's go hunting."

The living room door opened and Bant stood there. The sight of him froze me, sent cold prickles up my spine, caused goose pimples to form, caused the hair on my neck to bristle. I couldn't run. He stood looking down into my face, stood unmoving, and there was naked hatred glaring from his eyes.

"What are you doing here, Jeff?" His voice was quiet.

"I just came over to see Kenty."

He just stood there and stared at me. There was no sound except the sound of wind and the pounding of my own heart. Finally he moved forward and I edged back toward the steps.

"Next time I tell you to stay home you will believe me and mind me."

He walked around me and went out into the yard. I followed and was ready to run, blind with terror.

"Don't run, Jeff. It'll go hard on you if you run."

"What are you doing here, Bant? Where's Kenty? What have you done to Kenty and why were you in his house?"

"Stop your babbling. Kenty's in town."

He walked across the yard and cut a long switch from a hackberry tree. The switch was as long as his arm and big around as his thumb. He cut twigs from it and tested it, flicking it until it whistled as it cut air.

"Don't whip me with that thing, Bant. I think you're drunk and I don't think you're my real pa. You don't have the right."

The switch lashed and cut the backs of my legs like fire, hit the side of my left leg and curled to the back of both legs. I backed away as he raised the switch, hoping to catch it and wrest it from him. The switch came faster than sight and hit me in the side, curled around my ribs and burned like molten fire.

"I'll kill you, Bant!" I screamed, backing away. "So help me, I'll kill you!"

I tried to fight back, swung and flailed at him, but he had me dancing as the switch went thwack, again thwack, and then thwack thwack thwack until it was hard to tell whether the sound was greater and more hurtful than the pain. I screamed and couldn't hear my own screams, cursed myself for screaming and dancing, but I jumped and danced and screamed and could not run to escape the switch. Now it was cutting my back and now cutting my legs and once I caught it in my hands and held only the stinging pain. Alive it seemed, vengeful and alive, fiery hot on my shoulders and buttocks and sides and thighs, coursing from ankles to neck. All I could see was Bant's face, a twisty snarling face. Once, to my shame, I went to my knees to beg, but still the cutting slashing blows rained.

"I'll kill you, Bant," I said, and then everything was soft black nothing.

I awoke on earth colder than death, awoke after how many minutes or hours I do not know. My shirt and pants were stuck to my body and stiff with dried blood. Only the numbness of my wounds made it possible to bear the walk to Raindrop, to mount and ride home. Bant wasn't there when I arrived and Mama bathed me and salved the wounds, her tears stinging, her soft muttered words of hurt and hate and grief stinging more. I lay on my bed, on my stomach, and wondered whether *honor thy father* applied to Bant, to Kenty, neither, or both. I'll kill Bant and go to hell, I thought.

Fever came, and with it delirium. The fever broke before dark and I slept. Bant was sitting at the kitchen table when I went in, his chin resting on his cupped hands. He didn't look up. Mama was at the stove and turned as I entered.

"Sit down, Jeff," she said. "I'll have your supper ready in a minute."

"I'm not hungry, Mama. Maybe a glass of milk."

"In the cooler. No," she turned and hurried to the cooler. "You sit down. I forgot for a moment there that you'd been whipped within an inch of your life."

"The boy will learn to mind," Bant said. "Hurry with supper, Pearl. I don't know when I've been so hungry."

"You'll eat your own cooking tonight," Mama said.

Bant's head came up and his nostrils flared. "What do you mean by that?"

"You whipped Jeff as I wouldn't whip a dog. A man who whips a boy like that is not a man. I told him he could go see Kenty."

"And I told him to stay home."

"You didn't whip him because he didn't obey, Bant. You whipped him because your mind is sick. You whipped him because of some twisted hate you have for Kenty and me."

"I'll be the judge of why I whipped him."

"You be the judge and the Lord will be the jury. Every lick you gave that boy is written in the Book of Life."

"Let's not bicker," Bant said. "Let's eat."

Mama turned to face him. "Why were you in Kenty Hooker's house?"

"Looking for Kenty. What else?"

"You knew he wasn't home. Why did you go inside his house?"

"I knocked and he didn't answer. I thought he might be asleep."

"You knew he was in town. What were you hunting?"

"Put supper on the table, Pearl."

"You'll cook your own food tonight. I'll serve your meals after this, but not tonight. And one thing more, Bant Carr. Don't ever hit this boy again."

I finished my milk, standing, and started from the room. Mama stopped me.

"Jeff, do you feel able to saddle the bay mare and bring her and Raindrop to the front?"

"Yes, ma'am."

"Could you ride as far as Kenty's?"

"Yes, ma'am."

"We'll go see if Kenty is all right."

"You'll *what?*" Bant asked.

"We'll see if Kenty is all right. I think he is, because child beaters don't pick on men who can fight back. They might burn barns, though."

"Don't push me too far, Pearl."

"I'm not pushing. I'm shoving back. I've been pushed to the limit."

"Go to him, then. That's no more than I expect. But the boy can't go."

"Jeff will go. Jeff will go so you can't accuse me of... anything improper. The stove's hot. Cook and eat."

I turned away and Bant gripped my arm, his fingers digging deep.

"Don't leave the house, Jeff. You'll not go to Kenty."

"I'll go," I said. "I'll go because I'm not afraid of you now, Bant. And remember what I said about killing you. I will."

Bant's fingers loosened. "You'll be sorry."

"Don't make threats, Bant," Mama said. "And, Jeff, don't ever say you'll kill anyone."

Bant's breathing was ragged and hoarse. "You'll both be sorry."

"Harm either one of us, Bant, and I swear you'd better watch the food you eat and the coffee you drink."

"You'd threaten me with poison?"

"A mother protects her own." There was a quirky little smile on her face.

It was good dark when we rode into Kenty's yard. One of the hounds bayed, but then a cluster of them came to nuzzle us as we dismounted and tied the horses to a tree. The house was dark, but I heard the front door open.

"What are the two of you doing here at this time of the day?" Kenty asked, approaching. "Where's Bant?"

"He's home," Mama said. "We came to see if you were all right and to get some advice."

"I'm fine. Come in the house." He guided Mama up the steps and went in first to light a lamp.

"Bant was in your house today," Mama told him, taking a chair in front of the fire. Kenty sat on a rocker, bent slightly forward, and I stood behind Mama.

"I knew someone had been inside, Pearl, and figured it must have been Bant. I keep my letters in a shoe box and someone went through them. One letter is missing."

"I shouldn't have written it."

"I shouldn't have kept it. I should have heeded your advice. You warned me to stay away and I came back. I know I should sell out and move now, Pearl, but I think it's too late."

"It is too late."

"Maybe I could talk to him, reason with him. Again."

"Drink has driven him crazy, Kenty. He beat the boy today. He was here when Jeff came over to see you."

Kenty stood. "Let's have a look, Jeff."

I slid out of the shirt, wincing as it raked over my shoulders and back.

Kenty whistled softly and shook his head. "Drop your pants, son. I'll stand between you and Pearl.

"This can't go on," he said, on his knees to examine my lashes. "Old Trails whips like that, but I thought he was the only man in the county who'd do it. Bant could be jailed for this."

"Kenty," Mama said, "I'll have to leave. I'll have to take Jeff away."

"Where would you go?"

"I don't know. San Antonio. Dallas, maybe. Fort Worth. Somewhere. There should be work in the city."

"We'll have to think about it, Pearl. I could take you and you wouldn't have to worry about money. That's not a problem. The problem is that Bant would know that I would know where you were and there'd still be trouble. Still and all... you can't go on like this."

"He was a good man," Mama said. "He is a good man, down deep. It's just his jealousy and his rage that's causing a sickness. That and drink."

Kenty stared into the fire. "Pearl," he said at last, "I could get the sheriff to talk to Bant. I could try to have him placed under a peace bond. I said he could be jailed for whipping Jeff, but I'm not really sure about that. It seems courts don't interfere in family affairs. Try to stick it out a few days. If you can do that, I'll put my mind to thinking about your next step."

"There's just one thing, Kenty. I don't intend he should hurt the boy again. If he does...."

"Don't even think it, Pearl."

The weather cleared and the sun warmed the land, though we knew it wouldn't last. Our winter feed did well and our cattle and horses were sleek and fat. Mama had started with a hundred turkey poults and six had survived. We had chickens for frying and for chicken and dumplings, eggs for selling, meat in the smokehouse, potatoes in the cellar, canned fruits and nuts, and apples in a barrel. Best of all, Bant was off the bottle. He was quiet and sometimes moody, but reasonable. Mama was polite to him, but she slept in the guest room. I answered when spoken to, obeyed orders, and stayed out of his way as much as possible.

There was a box supper at the school before Thanksgiving. Mama cooked pies and cakes and fried chicken. She packed a big box supper, wrapped it with red paper, and tied it with a green ribbon. She tucked it into a brown paper sack so Bant couldn't see it, but I was sure he peeked.

The school yard was crammed with cars and wagons and the largest room was packed. There was a school program and my part was the Gettysburg Address. A piano recital seemed to go on forever, and then the fourth graders did a Thanksgiving skit. Finally, when I was starving, the auctioning of supper boxes began. All the women and girls had wrapped suppers in packages and the top bidder for a box was entitled to sit and eat with the one who prepared it. Everyone seemed to get a kick out of seeing a man eating with the wife of another man, or with a single girl.

I sat at the front of the room, just across the aisle from Mama. Bant sat at the rear and Kenty leaned against the wall across the room from me.

"What am I bid for this box?" Jess Gold, the principal of the school called, his glasses catching the light as he tiptoed and peered around the room. He was holding Mama's red box with the green ribbon.

"I'll bid seventy five cents," Kenty said.

"I'm bid seventy five cents, seventy five cents, seventy five cents, who'll make it a dollar?"

"Seventy six cents," Bant called.

Laughter. Everyone was looking at Samal and I hadn't known she was there.

"I'll bid a dollar," Kenty shouted.

"A dollar and a penny," Bant yelled from the back of the room.

Kenty thought he was bidding on Sam's supper. I knew it and tried to catch his eye, but he was looking toward Bant and there was a puzzled expression on his face. I wished I could go to Bant and tell him what was in Kenty's mind.

"Kenty," Jess Gold said, "I've been offered a dollar and a penny. Would you care to up the bid? What about a dollar and two cents?"

Laughter was thunder and I thought I was the only person in the room not laughing. I looked at Mama and saw she wasn't laughing. There was a stricken look on her face.

"A dollar and a quarter!" Kenty called.

"A dollar and twenty six cents," Bant countered.

The crowd loved it. Men called encouragement to Kenty, then turned to Bant to egg him on.

"I'll bid two dollars," Kenty said. "Bant, stop trying to steal my girl."

Laughter dwindled.

"All right, Kenty," Bant said. "I'll let you eat with your best girl."

Kenty went to the front of the room for the box, turned and started toward Samal, and then saw Mama.

"Wait a minute," he said. "There's been a mix up."

A woman laughed nervously and several men forced coughs. Kenty seemed glued to the floor and the silence was thick enough to feel.

Laugh, I thought. Laugh, you fools. Make a joke of it.

Sam's box was auctioned next and, like Mama's, was wrapped in red paper and tied with green ribbon. I looked back for Bant to be sure he had noticed, but he wasn't in the room.

I ate with Kenty and Mama and the food choked me. All around us people were eating and laughing and joking, teasing, even teasing Kenty and Mama and Samal. Poor Sam had to eat with Irv Dawkins, the fattest man in the county, but she made the best of it. At least she knew Kenty had wanted to buy her supper.

Bant was in the car when we left the school. He didn't speak. We drove home in dead silence. The wind had come up, wild and snappish, and I huddled under a robe in the back seat. Bant went into the house first and I lagged behind with Mama. He was stirring up the fire when we entered, tossed on more logs, and then went into the kitchen. When I went there for a glass of water, he was standing with a brown bottle and a glass. The dark and brooding look was on his face.

Mama joined us. "I'll make a pot of coffee."

Bant seemed not to hear.

"Bant, please. Don't drink that stuff and don't look like that. You know what happened, don't you? Kenty thought he was bidding on Samal's supper."

"Did you notice how still it got in that room when they found out I was bidding against Kenty for my own wife's supper?"

"Kenty didn't know and neither did you. Sam's supper was wrapped just like mine. It was auctioned next, so everyone knew what had happened."

I went to my room and undressed for bed. The wind was shrill and moansome as it whipped around the corners of the house, but still I could hear snatches of talk in the living room.

"...and you can't deny it," Bant said. "Here it is, in black and white."

Mama said something I couldn't understand.

Bant said something and the words were a mumble of sound.

"...just eighteen years old." Mama.

"...confirms what I thought all along." Bant.

The wind quieted for just a moment. "It was so long ago, Bant. I was young and silly. It was before you asked me to marry you. You knew all about Kenty and me. You knew all about Jeff. You said it wouldn't matter."

"I don't know," Bant said. "I just don't know."

"How did you get the letter, Bant?"

"You know. I searched Kenty's house and I found it."

"That was stooping pretty low, Bant."

"I know, I know."

"Look at the date on that letter. Look how long ago it was."

"That's what bothers me," Bant said. "Kenty treasured it."

CHAPTER NINE

I ran into Coy Trails and Forbis Fancher in the woods one day and ran into trouble I hadn't bargained for. The two saw me first. I'd been hunting squirrels with Bant's twenty-two rifle and had just seen a fat one skin up a tree. After a bit it became curious and showed itself. I was taking careful aim when a rifle cracked a shot right behind me. The squirrel fell to the ground at my feet, so I picked it up and stuffed it in my coat pocket with two others I had bagged.

"You've got my dinner there, kid," Coy said. "I've got seven so far, so hand over the one I just shot and any others you've got."

I cradled my gun. "You shot it, Coy, but it was my squirrel. I treed him and it was my shot."

Coy walked toward me and Forbis spat a stream of tobacco juice near my foot.

"You're too young to make trouble with me, kid," Coy said. "You ought to have learned that by this time. Either one of us could break you in half with one hand, so don't make trouble. Just hand over the squirrels and run home. You've got no business in these woods."

"These woods don't belong to you."

Forbis spoke. "You don't want to get hurt, kid. Are you going to hand over the squirrels or make us take them away from you?"

"You'll have to take them."

They moved faster than I expected. I tried to lift my little rifle and didn't have a chance. Forbis jerked it out of my hands and Coy slapped me down. He didn't even bother to hit with his fist; just slapped me down. I saw stars and tasted blood, and before my head cleared they'd taken the three squirrels from my jacket pocket.

"That ought to teach you a lesson," Forbis said. "You can eat salt pork tonight."

"We'll leave your gun down the hill a ways," Coy said. "I wouldn't want you to take a pot shot at us."

"I'll get back at you. Just you wait, I'll bide my time and get back at you."

Forbis grinned, showing yellow teeth. "I don't believe he's learned his lesson, Coy. Why don't we give him a switching?"

"I've got a better idea. Let's take his pants."

I put up a pretty good fight, but I was whipped before I started. They skinned my pants off and left me. They had horses back in the bushes and I heard them riding off. I stood shivering and came as near to cursing as I'd ever come. I would have killed either or both if I'd had the power. I heard their mocking laughter as the clumpety clatter of their horses hooves faded, and then I stood there in cold silence. I was warm enough from the waist up, but colder than a well digger's rear end from the waist down. Alone as I was, I felt as silly as I looked in my red-handled long johns with the flap in back. I fumbled in my coat pocket for matches and found none, huddled up against a tree and imagined myself going home. Even Mama would be forced to laugh, the way I saw it, and Bant would be fit to be tied.

Well, I decided, I wouldn't go home without my pants.

I walked the way Coy and Forbis had gone and, after a hundred yards, found my rifle leaning against a tree. I had been afraid they would smash it. The fools had not left a shell in the gun, but I had a half dozen in my coat pocket. A saucy squirrel flirted his tail at me from a tree, but I was no longer interested in squirrels. I headed for the Trails house and my temper flared hotter with every step, boiled hotter as my shanks became colder. I knew I wasn't using my head, but I didn't care.

Dusk was falling when I neared the Trails house. The lamps had been lighted inside and cast an orange glow to the outside. It looked homey and comfortable.

I shot my gun into the air and yelled, "Hello the house!"

Old Trails was the first out on the porch and Sam was right behind him. Coy came, then, and pushed past Sam, but Forbis didn't appear. Festal came out from under the porch a moment later and stood grinning at me.

"Supper will be ready in an hour, Jeff," Sam said, still on the porch. It was too shaded there for me to see her eyes, but I knew they were twinkling at me.

"I want Coy to step out here in the yard," I said. "Where is Forbis Fancher?"

"He went on home," Festal said.

"Festal, you go inside and get my pants."

"Why, you little Satan," Old Trails said musingly. "Of all the simon pure gall, this takes the cake."

"You just stand hitched," I said, waving my rifle barrel. "Maybe Coy and Forbis can knock me down and take my pants, but you'd better teach them not to fool with me." I didn't feel half as brave as I tried to sound.

"Maybe I ought to take that gun away from you and tan your hide," Coy said.

He came down the steps and I brought my gun to my shoulder, snugged the butt and pointed the barrel straight at his guts. I lowered the barrel slowly until it was pointing at his feet.

"I don't aim to kill you, Coy, but I sure as hell mean to make you a cripple for life."

Sam laughed. "Go ahead, Coy. Show him how brave you are."

"You shut up!"

"Samal," Old Trails said, "he won't harm you. I want you to go down there and take his gun."

"You do it," Sam said.

"Coy," I said, "I'll take your pants."

"You go straight to hell."

"I'll cripple you before you can say your name. I mean it, Coy. I'm not fooling one little bit."

Coy tried to laugh.

"I think you'd better do what the boy says," Old Trails told Coy.

"That little twenty-two won't hurt anybody," Coy said. "Besides, you'd probably miss."

"You can hope I'll miss."

"You've just got one shot in that little toy."

"That's all I need."

"Well, you won't get my pants."

"I'll count to three," I said. "It's getting dark and I can't wait any longer."

Coy turned to look at Old Trails and I could see he was wavering.

"Give him your pants, Coy," Old Trails said.

"Oh, what the hell," Coy said, and let his pants drop. He kicked them toward me.

Festal came out on the porch with my pants, came down the steps, walked around Coy and picked up his pants, handed both to me. I tucked them under my left arm and cradled the rifle under my right elbow with my finger on the trigger.

I started backing away. Coy inched forward, but Old Trails stayed up on the porch with Sam. I waved the gun at Coy until I reached the big rocks beside the trail. "Don't follow me," I warned. "I could be behind any rock or tree and I can wing you good."

I left Coy's pants in the trail and hurried home. I didn't say a word to Mama or Bant about any of what had happened.

Things at home, for several days, became a little more relaxed. Mama still slept in the spare bedroom, but I could see an easing in her relationship with Bant. Not a great deal, but some. I found myself responding to Bant's mood, but still tried to speak only when spoken to. Kenty had not been on our place since the night Mama and I had gone to his house, though, and I missed him.

I did take the twenty-two out near the woods where I'd last seen Festal Trails and shot a few rounds in the air while walking slowly in the general area. After a while, I heard his voice call, "Hallo, Jeff Carr."

He'd brought a lunch spread wrapped in an old cloth and we sat and ate and talked mostly about the paths in the woods, and just a little bit about his family. He said Samal was still looking after him and that he'd been staying out of sight for a while anyway, just to be sure.

We met up a few more times after that and the better I got to know of him, the more he reminded me of Sam. They had a lot of the same personality traits, their temperament, the same good thoughts, and some of the bad ones, too. Every now and then he'd say something that was just too odd to answer. Sam was never like that. We spent time exploring the canyons in the Narrows, sometimes just hiking, sometimes just looking at stuff.

Bant went into town early on a Saturday and I went straight to Kenty's place. He was working with a colt in the barnlot when I arrived, but turned the colt loose and headed to the house with me. We had just stepped up on the porch when Old Trails walked into the yard. He had been crying, from the look of his eyes, and Kenty asked him what was wrong.

"It's my only nephew," Old Trails answered. "Dale Singleterry. He's dead."

"I didn't know you had a nephew," Kenty said.

"Well, I do. Over at Sweet Springs. My sister is a widow there and I've supported her for ten years. Not that you could tell it by the way she treats me. She sleeps under a roof provided, wears clothes I provide, and eats food she wouldn't have it wasn't for me. But she treats me like trash."

"What happened to your nephew?"

"Killed. He was seventeen years old and was shot down like a dog. Priss Fancher was in to Sweet Springs and told me when he got back."

"Who shot him?"

"The town constable. Said Dale was caught while burglarizing the hardware store before daylight. I hate to ask you, Kenty, but I need to get over there. Can you take me?"

"We'll go right now," Kenty said.

I thought I'd be sent home, but Kenty must have seen the look on my face. "Come along," he said. "We can have you home in a couple of hours."

Old Trails sat in the back seat all the way to Sweet Springs. It was cold, but I doubt that he noticed. He sat stiff and straight and said never a word. Sweet Springs is not much of a town. There'd been a boom at one time because a big oil company bought up some leases, but the first well was a duster and the town went back to sleep. There was a general store, a hardware store, three or four grocery stores, a post office and bank, and that was about all. Some of the buildings were brick, but most were frame, sun and wind bleached and ugly.

Old Trails spoke just as we reached the city limits. "Priss said the boy is lying just where he was shot. Lying like a dead dog in the street. Said the constable wanted everybody to see what happens to transgressors."

We had no trouble finding the body. A sizeable knot of people stood clustered, stood still, stood looking at something. Kenty stopped the car in the middle of the street and we got out. Old Trails seemed to walk in his sleep with his eyes open. There was a set, hard look on his face and his eyes were squinted. He moved slowly, deliberately, and the people gathered around the dead boy moved aside to let us pass.

Dale Singleterry was lying on his face and his back was black with encrusted blood. The blood was frozen, slick hard frozen, black and glisteny, and I felt my stomach churn and my legs grow weak. Kenty put his hand on my shoulder and pushed me back several steps.

Old Trails went to his knees and rolled Dale over. The body was stiff as a board and he rolled over as a tree trunk would roll over. His eyes were wide open and there was dirt on his face and in his eyes and on his lips and clogged in his open mouth. Old Trails pulled a red neckerchief from his pocket and wiped the dirt away, wiped it away gently, tenderly, lovingly.

The constable came walking up the street. He was fifty or sixty, I guessed, and he wasn't sorrowful. He was puffed up with his own importance and strutted like a bantam cock. His belly looked like a tub of lard and his pants wouldn't fit up over the protruding keg of fat. He wore a Stetson and his face was round, flabby, red and raw looking. He had an angry mole over his left eyebrow and a triangle of moles on his chin. He walked with his hand on the butt of a holstered revolver. You'd have thought Wyatt Earp was approaching. Men gawked as if Billy the Kid had walked into their midst. They nudged each other and fell back to leave a clear space for the constable. That fearless gentleman stalked up behind Old Trails and stood looking down at him.

"Why'd you shoot him?" Old Trails didn't bother to look up.

"He was askin' fer trouble and picked the wrong town and the wrong man."

"He was shot in the back."

"He pulled on me first. I warned him not to fool with me."

"What did he aim at you? His ass?"

"I warned him."

"What was he using for a gun?"

"He had a pistol."

Old Trails spread his handkerchief on the ground and eased Dale's head down on it. He stood up and faced the constable.

"You didn't need to kill this boy. I've got only your word he was breaking the law. For all I know, he might have been walking across the street."

"I warned him to stay out of town after dark not more than a week ago. I warned him not to start 'ary a thing here."

Old Trails slapped the constable across the face. He was as calm as could be, as cold as ice, and the smack of his open hand across the constable's fat cheek was as sharp and loud as a gunshot. The constable turned red and began to bluster. He cursed a while and threatened to throw Old Trails in jail.

"You're a yellow bellied coward," Old Trails said. "You'd better turn in that badge and gun and find yourself a place to hide that's awful far from here."

"You're crazy with grief," the constable said. "I'm not going to do anything to you this time because you're crazy with grief. I can understand that. Fact is, my heart goes out to you. It breaks my heart to have to shoot a man. I'm going to forget what happened here today. I'll even help you get the boy in your car so you can take him home, or call the undertaker, or whatever you…."

Old Trails slapped him again. This time the constable took a step back and began to tug at his holstered revolver. Old Trails, though, looked like a coiled rattlesnake. He didn't rattle his tail, but he gave plenty of danger sign. He just sort of coiled, allowed his legs to bend at the knees, arched his back, twisted at the waist, and sidled toward the constable.

The crowd became scarce. People scattered, ran across the street and up and down the street, then stopped to watch. I stood my ground and so did Kenty, but the constable started backing away. His eyes bugged and the red flush paled from his cheeks. He licked his lips and tried to speak, babbled, and then said stop where you are you just stop where you are or I'll fill you full of holes you hear me now you'd better just back up there and leave me alone, you hear me, I'm not wanting 'ary bit of trouble and you know it I had no choice, I tell you, I had no choice I thought he was going to shoot and I shot first and I didn't know he didn't even have a gun or else I would not have shot him, hear me, it was sort of accidental and you can't blame a man for that because things like that happen, you hear me, now?

It was pitiful and I felt ashamed for the man, but I didn't blame him for being scared. Old Trails had no pity and I didn't blame him for that. He backed the constable all the way to the sidewalk, crowded him, trying to make him pull that gun, and yet he never said a word and the constable never stopped babbling.

The second the constable started pulling his gun from the holster I knew he would be too slow. Old Trails leaped and a knife flashed in a wicked arc. I didn't see him draw the knife and I didn't see him open it. The knife just appeared. Old Trails cut and slashed so fast my eyes couldn't follow the action, but that constable was bleeding from neck to belly, all across his front, before he broke and ran. Old Trails didn't bother to follow.

"Will he die?" I asked Kenty.

"No. Old Trails was choking his knife blade. He had his fingers covering all the blade except for about a quarter of an inch at the point. A good knife man can slash a person almost to ribbons without killing him."

"I thought he wanted to kill him."

"He does. The constable knows it, too. He'll never know whether Old Trails or Coy will get him. He'll just wake up dead. He'll get out of this country if he's smart."

Old Trails had gone back to the dead boy's body and Kenty brought the car from down the street. He got out and helped lift Dale, and together they laid him in the back seat. Old Trails got in the back with his dead nephew and I sat up front with Kenty.

"Will you take us to Fort Davis? I'll come back tomorrow for my sister."

"We're on our way."

I didn't notice the cold so much. Old Trails sat in the corner of the back seat and Dale's head was in his lap. The old man's hand stroked the boy's hair, stroked it gently. Kenty drove as fast as the car and the road would allow, drove into Fort Davis and stopped at the funeral parlor. Kenty went inside and came out with two men and a stretcher, but Old Trails didn't follow the body inside.

CHAPTER TEN

We went to Dale Singleterry's funeral. We didn't go because we wanted to go. We didn't go for the same reasons most people in the county had for going. It wasn't curiosity on our part. We went because of Sam and because, like him or not, Old Trails was a neighbor. The funeral was held just outside Sweet Springs on a cold, rainy day. The clouds were dark and low, the wind wet and bitter, and the rain was a slow weeping thing. There were more people on the outside of the small church than inside, but we were inside because Bant and Kenty were pallbearers. I knew the preacher, Brother Hornbuckle, and felt sorry for him. He must have known Dale and couldn't find many good things to say. Mostly, he talked about Dale's mother, that good and kindly woman who had taught school so many years and had been such a stern disciplinarian of all students but one, her son. The poor preacher didn't have a word to say about the uncle, Old Trails, or Coy, but I couldn't blame him for that. Old Trails sat unmoving beside his widowed sister, and showed no emotion. Samal didn't cry, either, and Festal wasn't even at the funeral. Only Coy sobbed a little, and that did surprise me. I hadn't known he had feelings.

Coy killed the Sweet Springs constable, Abel Green, that very night. He killed him in the street in full view of ten citizens. It was cold-blooded murder. He used both barrels of a shotgun.

They say the amazed witnesses stood and gawked while Coy used his foot to roll the constable over on his back. They say he looked down at the dead man a moment only before walking over to untie his horse from a barbers' pole. He trotted out of town and that was the last anyone saw of him for a while, except for the Trails family. Festal told me Coy came home in the middle of the night and talked for an hour with Old Trails.

"I was watching from under the house," Festal said. "They went to the barn and stayed nearly an hour. Then they went into the house for a while. Coy came out with a sack over his shoulder and his rifle in his hands. He walked off into the woods."

"Where would he hide?"

"I don't know. Somewhere in the Narrows."

"Well, a sack of food won't last long."

"Heck, all he'd need would be some salt and lard. He can live on squirrels and deer and fish. For that matter, he can get potatoes or side meat or nearly anything for the taking. Nobody locks smokehouses or root cellars."

Kenty came to our house that night and told us the sheriff had passed word that he needed all men to scour the countryside.

"I don't have the stomach for it," Bant said. "I know the boy is rotten mean and sorry, but it's not all his fault. I can't condone the way he killed that constable, either, but the county's a better place now."

"I feel the same way," Kenty said, "but maybe we ought to go so we can calm the hotheads if they find him."

"Could be."

"They're not likely to find him. He knows every warren and hole for twenty miles around."

"He's bound to be in the Narrows, though," Bant said. "I don't think he'd cut and run far from home."

"Well, I hope he's long gone and far away," Kenty said. "He wouldn't have a chance in court."

It was agreed that the search would begin at the Trails place at first light.

Festal came soon after Bant had left. He had a single shot twenty-two rifle and leaned it against the side of the barn. It was warm on that side of the barn. The wind couldn't get to us and early morning sunlight bounced off the wall. Festal sat, cross-legged, while chickens scratched the dust around us.

"What're we going to do?" he asked.

"About Coy?"

"Yep."

"I don't know."

He picked up two pebbles and rattled them like dice. "You think they can find him?"

I thought of all the caves and crevices and ledges and lost places in the Narrows and about Coy growing up exploring those places.

"They won't find him."

"They won't starve him out. He won't hunt or trap for a while, but I'll bet he took some canned goods and coffee and corn meal and stuff like that to live on until things cool down. He'll make little traps for rabbits and shake possums out of trees at night. He'll cook somewhere way back in a cave and he'll get fat and all the men in the county can look for him until hell freezes over. Then he'll light out for parts unknown."

Festal picked up some more pebbles and looked at them, turned them over and over and held them close to his eyes, held them up to catch the sun, breathed on them and polished them with his shirt tail and threw them away.

"Coy ought to be dead."

It sounded right, but the thought of Coy dead didn't seem to sit well with me.

"Coy ought to be dead and we ought to kill him," Festal said it sadly.

"I don't think it would be right for us to kill him."

"After the things he's done?"

"I don't want to kill anybody."

"He ought to be dead, though."

"I think he will be."

"I don't guess I'd kill him," Festal said, "but I ought to. That posse will kill him if they find him."

"They might not. They might give him a trial and send him to the penitentiary."

"I could find him."

"How?"

"Well, I'll be able to feel him."

"If you don't want to kill him, why would you want to find him?"

Festal stood shifting from foot to foot. "I guess I really want to help him. Blood's thicker than water."

"I won't help you," I said, my mind made up.

"I'll do it by myself."

"Do it," I said in a don't care tone, hoping all the time he'd change his mind. "Just leave that little old twenty-two at home. He'll shoot you if he sees you with a gun."

"I'll be seeing you," he said, and walked away.

The warmth went out of the sun and I huddled tight against the barn wall and wondered if I should get Bant's twenty-two and run to catch up with Festal. Maybe by going with him, I thought, I could lead him on a wild goose chase long enough to talk him into giving up. I hadn't quite made my mind up when I heard him yell at me.

"Jeff!"

There was the sound of horror in Festal's voice, in that one call. I jumped and ran, thinking Coy had come to our place.

It wasn't Coy. It was Samal.

Four men brought her in on a litter they'd made of two poles and a couple of heavy coats. They'd covered her with a coat and still the blood had seeped through in a dark stain. Her eyes were closed and she looked blue white, dead, and the men walked with funeral step, two in front and two behind. Mama met them on the porch. She didn't take on like women usually do; just held the door open and stood aside so the men could take Samal into the house.

"We've sent for the doctor," Smoke Smith said. "She's hit bad and I wouldn't want to fool you about that. She's hit bad."

Mama had them lay Samal on the bed in the spare bedroom. She went to work right off. I was sent to heat water while she undressed Sam, and then she washed the wound, washed away crusted blood. Under the blood was a bluish little hole above and to the left of her left breast. It looked like a nail hole that was puckered inward, except that it was bigger than a nail would cause.

"Help me turn her over. Gently now," and I helped. She felt Samal's back with gentle fingers and then she breathed a big sigh and stepped back.

"The bullet almost came through her body. It's just under the skin. I don't think it's as bad as it looks. Unless she dies of the shock."

The four men who'd brought Sam were waiting in the living room. Tom King spoke first.

"Nobody in the posse done it, Miz Carr. It was Coy Trails. He come out of nowhere and he wasn't ten feet from us. He had just a little old twenty-two rifle and it didn't hardly make no sound at all. I didn't even know he'd shot until Samal fell down."

"Did you shoot him?" Festal asked.

"No," Tom King said. "He just disappeared. He was gone before I could lift my gun. The truth is, we had come on Samal out there and we figured she'd gone to help Coy. We made her stay with us and my guess is that Coy just shot first without knowing who he was shooting at."

Fred Cawker and Chet Purdue stood with their backs to the fire and stood aside to let Mama heat a blanket. Mama went to the bedroom to cover Sam and then came back.

"The real danger is the shock and maybe pneumonia. We mustn't let her get sick. Jeff, bring the basin full of warm water. Bring me a little of water in a glass and the whiskey bottle. You know where to find it. You, Tom King, heat some bricks for her feet. Hurry. She'll be awake any time now. If we can ward off the pneumonia, she'll be fine."

She kept me busy until the doctor came. That stooped, tired old man bent over Sam and counted her heartbeats and then found the bullet in the skin where Mama told him it would be.

"Bring my satchel," the doctor ordered, and I found it on a chair by the fireplace. He fiddled around inside and brought out a sharp little scalpel and a bottle of something. He poured liquid over the scalpel and then cut the bullet out, sliced through skin quickly and deftly and the bullet just popped out.

"Whiskey," he ordered then. "All you people clear out of here, too. The girl will be fine. You, Miz Carr, help me turn her over and we'll take care of the entry wound."

Festal and I went outside with the men, but we stayed on the porch while they walked out toward the Narrows.

"Well," Festal said, "I'll be going."

"Wait. I'll get Bant's twenty-two and go with you."

Half the men in the county were spread out in the Narrows. They sat around fires, huddled in gullies and behind rocks and trees, their guns laid aside while they built up reasons for abandoning the search. We passed a half dozen groups, stopped twice to warm ourselves, and knew from what we heard that most of the men would be gone well before nightfall.

"He's clean gone now...."

"...couldn't catch him with bloodhounds."

"The sheriff couldn't find his ass with both hands."

"No use settin' here."

"...didn't tell her where I was goin' and she'll be worried."

"...ain't my job nohow...."

We walked through the cordon and decided Coy could have walked out of there any time he wanted.

"I wouldn't put it past Coy to be wandering around with those people hunting himself," Festal said.

"Maybe he's standing around one of their fires drinking their coffee."

"It'd be just like him."

I knew Festal was hoping Coy had gone and that he hadn't meant a word about shooting his brother. He had pride in Coy, strange as it seemed, and he talked of things Coy had done and things he'd said. Cruel as Coy was, mean as he was, his was a spirit wild and untamed and strong and unchanneled. Festal responded to that spirit and was drawn to a man who went against all patterns.

We passed the last of the searchers, tried to skirt around them unseen, and were hailed.

"Hey, you boys! You come back here! You can't go in there!"

"Why not?" I asked.

"Coy Trails is in there. He'll shoot you, sure as thunder."

The speaker was a small man, skinny and weathered as a prune, a dried-up man who'd left his sap in the furrows of a wornout field. He came toward us, walking with the bent bodied, long-stepping walk of the plowman. He carried a shotgun, set the butt into earth and leaned on the barrel.

"You're Bant's boy, ain't you?"

"Yes, sir."

"Thought I'd seen you with him in town. How is the girl? Hurt real bad?"

"I don't know, but I don't think so. The bullet went through her and the doctor took it out of her back."

The man whistled. "We heard about it. Fact is, we saw them taking her out but they had her covered up and we didn't get a look."

He nodded toward the Narrows. "You hunting Coy?"

"Yes, sir."

"He ain't in there. We figure he made a break for it as soon as he shot the girl."

"We'll take a look."

"Well, now, I don't know as I ought to let you. Who is that boy there?"

"That's Festal Trails."

"Well, you boys better go on back. You might get hurt."

"I've got to talk to Coy if he's in there," Festal said. "He'll listen to me."

"Maybe he would," the man said. "You're his brother, you say?"

"Yessir."

"Well, now," and the man rubbed his chin, "you just wait right there a minute. Hey, boys!" he yelled at the men around the fire. "This here's Coy's brother! He says Coy'll listen to him!"

"Aw, Coy ain't in there," a fat man with a bottle said. "He's high tailin' it for Old Mexico right now. Send them kids packin' and come on to the fire. About an hour more of this and I'm goin' home, sheriff or no sheriff."

"You boys go on home," the man told us, then turned away and ambled back to the fire.

Festal took off running and I followed. We thought the men would yell at us and tell us to come back, but if they saw us they didn't try to stop us. We lost ourselves in the woods and then cut toward the Narrows. We didn't stop until we reached the river.

"Where'll we look first?" I asked Festal as soon as we'd caught our breath. "The Needle's Eye?"

"Naw," Festal said. "Coy wouldn't hide there."

"Well, then, where?"

"The Pipe."

"He couldn't get through the Pipe."

"He could if he wanted to bad enough. Nobody'd try to follow him, either."

"He couldn't have gone through the Pipe," I persisted. "It's too little and nobody knows about it but us."

"That's what you think. Coy was born and raised here the same as us."

We were talking about a tunnel through rock, a tunnel so like a pipe that we named it the Pipe. We had found it by accident. I'd read a book about prospectors who panned for gold, and Festal and I had gold fever bad for more than a week. We had panned for gold and we had mined for gold. We found rock that glittered more than once and Kenty had trouble convincing us that we hadn't hit pay dirt.

There was a cleft in the rocky canyon wall, a fissure that ran from the floor of the canyon to its top, more than a hundred feet. We had entered the cleft and the Pipe's opening was high above us. We climbed to it and the climb was hard and dangerous. The rock was smooth, offering few hand holds, but we managed to get up. But once there we feared to enter the Pipe, so small and round it was and so dark. We headed for it now and we were breathing hard when we reached the canyon. We left our guns and climbed the rock wall. I went first, entered the Pipe, wriggled and squirmed my way inside, and Festal followed. My arms were in front of me and I was forced to inch along like a snake. I could use my hands a little and my fingers a little, but I couldn't bend my arms. I could push a little with my toes, but progress was slow and painful.

"Go back, Festal," I called at him. "This thing seems to be getting tighter."

"I've been trying to go back," Festal said calmly, "but I can't."

"Why not?"

"My coat gets all bunched up and I get stuck."

"Try," I said. "Try again."

"Look, Jeff," he said, and he was near to crying. "There's not any sense in me trying again because that's what I've been doing for the longest time and I can't budge."

"We're trapped, then."

"We could keep going."

I lay there in the dark, my arms outstretched and my face resting on cold, smooth rock, and fear built up inside me. The Pipe seemed to close in on me, seemed to get smaller, and I could feel it squeezing. I wanted to claw and scream and kick and dig, but I knew I didn't have time for panic. I bit my lip and raised my head and peered into the darkness, hoping to see a glimmer of light.

"Maybe we'd better stay where we are," I said. "Maybe we'd better start yelling. Maybe somebody'll hear us."

"Not likely. The sheriff and all those men'll probably go home."

"It's cold."

"You're telling me."

"You're sure you can't back out?"

"Well, you try it," Festal said. "Try backing out yourself."

I pushed with the palms of my hand and wriggled my body back, used my knees and a slight bending of my legs to pull me back, and my body went back one inch and two inches and more and I felt like shouting because I wasn't trapped. And then I felt my coat bunching up on my back and wedging against the top of the Pipe and it was harder to push myself backward and my progress was slower and at last I couldn't wiggle another inch and I stopped and lay panting. It wouldn't have mattered anyway, for Festal was blocking the way behind me.

"We'll have to go forward," I admitted at last. "Maybe we'd better pray first. If this thing gets smaller we're lost."

"We're lost anyway," Festal said. "We'll just starve to death if we stay here."

"Maybe we'll get so skinny we can get out," I said, and we both giggled insanely.

I began to inch forward again. Once my hand touched a bump in the rock and I jerked it away.

"Festal," I said, "this place could be full of rattlesnakes. They hibernate in the winter and this would be a perfect place."

"They couldn't get up here. Snakes couldn't crawl up that rock wall."

"There might be another entrance. Anyway, snakes can go just about anywhere."

"Well, you might as well go ahead. If you get bit it'll probably scare you so bad you'll claw your way out."

"It's easy for you to talk! You're safe and sound behind me!"

"Well, move over and I'll go first!"

It was so silly I had to laugh again. Suddenly, the darkness wasn't so fearsome and the tight squeeze not so fearsome. I squirmed forward and made good progress, though it was impossible to tell how far we'd come. Festal was right behind me I knew, because his hand frequently hit my foot.

"The tunnel's getting bigger," I said. "I feel looser."

"I can't tell any difference."

"I can. There's more room where I am now. We're going faster, too."

"Well, just the same," he said, "we're wasting our time. I guess you had it right in the first place. Coy couldn't possibly get through here."

"Not even if he pulled off all his clothes," I admitted.

"Just keep crawling," Festal said. "The way I figure it, this hole in the rock didn't just happen. Water must have done it a million years ago. It had to start somewhere, so there must be a way out."

"I just hope you're right. I must have been crazy ever to stick my head in this place."

"Don't cry, Jeff."

"Cry?" I was furious. "Who's crying? I'll bet you a hundred dollars you'll be crying before I cry!"

"Where would you get a hundred dollars?"

"Well, just the same. Just you wait and see. Wait'll we're caught so we can't go forward and we can't go backwards. You'll cry plenty then, I'll bet."

"And you'll just die real quiet, I guess?"

"Aw, shut up!"

Festal laughed. "I got news for you, Jeff, I can get out of here anytime I want."

I stopped squirming and rested, bare cheek against cold stone. "What are you talking about?"

"I'm littler than you," Festal said. "I can back up right now."

"What about your coat? Won't it bunch up and stick against the top of the tunnel again and stop you?"

"I think I could back up hard enough to make it slide off over my head."

"Good," I said, and began to breathe easy. "Do it, then. Get on out and get somebody with a rope to help me. Maybe they can pull me out."

"We've come this far," Festal said. "Let's keep going."

"Are you crazy?"

"No crazier than I was when we started in here."

"Well, all right," I said. "I guess if you can get out now you can get out later. But if it gets any tighter I'm going to stop before you get to the tight spot. I can think of a lot of places I'd rather die than here."

I started squirming ahead again, most of my fear gone. I thought the tunnel got tighter at one point and almost stopped, but I got past the tight place without any trouble. After a while I realized I was moving faster and I stopped to explore the pipe with my hands. There was no doubt about it. The pipe was bigger. I began to ooch my way forward, almost had enough room to get on all fours, and I felt like shouting. My hand touched nothingness and I recoiled, inched forward cautiously and felt down and up and to the sides and felt nothing.

"I've come to a hole," I said hoarsely. "We've gone as far as we can."

"Can you see anything?"

"I can't even see nothing. It's darker than the inside of your stomach."

"It must be a cave. Keep going?"

"That's easy for you to say, Festal Trails! For all I know this hole might be a bottomless pit!"

"It's not a bottomless pit, Jeff. It's where Coy's hiding out."

"Then we'll just be falling right into his hands. How do I know he's not about to grab me?"

"Because he'd have grabbed you long before now, that's why!"

"Just the same," I said, "I'm not about to go dropping out into dark nothing head first."

"Go ahead," Festal urged. "It's not deep. It's just a room or something and I'll be right behind you."

"That's just it. You can stay behind me and talk brave enough but you wouldn't go first."

"I'll hold your feet. You go ahead and I'll hold your feet."

"Wait a minute," I said. "I've got a pebble here. Be quiet and we'll see if we can hear it drop."

I held my breath and got ready to drop the pebble, put my head down as far as I could and tuned my ears to listen.

"I heard it!" Festal yelped. "It couldn't have dropped more'n two or three feet!"

"Aw, I haven't even dropped it yet! Now shut your mouth and hold your breath and be still!"

I dropped the pebble and heard it strike stone or gravel. I couldn't judge the distance it fell but I knew it couldn't have fallen far.

"Did you hear it?" Festal asked anxiously. "Have you dropped it yet?"

"I dropped it and I heard it. Hold on to my feet, now, and don't turn loose. You hear me, Festal? Don't you turn loose. You pull, too, if I tell you. Hear me, now?"

"I hear you," he said, and his hands closed over my ankles.

I edged forward, got my chest over the rim and slid my hands down a smooth rock wall. Little by little I bent my body at the waist until finally I was perfectly balanced. I could push myself back into the Pipe with Festal's help, or I could slide forward another few inches and there'd be no turning back.

"Do you feel anything?" Festal grunted.

"I can't touch bottom, if that's what you mean. Maybe you'd better pull me back. If I go too far I won't be able to back up."

"Well, try again, just a little bit," Festal begged. "I can pull you back."

"I don't know about that. I'm bigger than you and you might not be able to pull me."

"Just a couple of inches, Jeff. I've got a good hold on your feet. Go ahead. I'll hold you."

"Well, just an inch or two."

I slid forward, slowly and cautiously, until more than half of my body hung downward from the mouth of The Pipe. I supported my weight on the palms of my hands against the rock wall and I could feel Festal's hands strong and sure around my ankles. I reached down as far as possible with my left hand, stretched my arm, but I felt nothing.

"Pull me back, Festal," I called, and Festal chose that moment to turn me loose.

"Festal!" I roared, more in fright than in anger. "Festal, you fool! Pull me back!"

He caught my legs, but he didn't pull. He pushed me forward and I slid out of the hole and fell head first. I scraped my chin against the rock wall, scraped my hands as I clawed desperately. I screamed.

I landed on my left side, landed in soft sand, and lay quietly, let the terror drain from me, and planned what I'd do to Festal Trails.

"Jeff?"

Let the little devil call.

"Jeff! You all right?"

Well, if I am it's none of your doing, so you can call me from now until doomsday for all I care.

"Jeff!"

His voice seemed magnified a hundred times, but I lay still and didn't answer.

I heard him coming through the Pipe, heard the scratch of his shoes against stone, knew when he reached the lip of the Pipe, could feel him there above me.

I heard his hands scratching around on the stone wall and I could almost hear him thinking, wondering how deep the pit was and whether I'd been smashed or if the pit was so deep I'd still be falling a mile or two below.

It dawned on me then that the little devil would be crazy enough to come in after me. I knew he was like that. The way he'd figure it was that he'd dared me and pushed me and that if I was dead it'd be his fault. He'd have to follow. According to his code, there'd be nothing else to do.

I barely had time enough to roll to the side. He came plumping down, but he didn't scream like I'd done. He landed beside me and lay there panting, and then he began to feel around and I could hear the rustle his body made against the sand.

"Jeff?" he called.

Go to hell, I thought.

"All right, Jeff. So you're mad. Well, you're not hurt. That wasn't much of a fall and it was just like I said."

I didn't answer him and he was still, but I knew when he thought of Coy.

"Coy," he said. "Are you in here, Coy?"

He might be, at that, I thought.

"Coy, don't hurt us. Do you hear?"

"Aw shut up," I said. "Coy's not in here, I reckon. He'd be on us before now."

"Light a match," was all Festal said.

I fumbled in my pockets and found two matches, and then I felt around for a pebble to strike them on. I struck one and held it carefully. The first thing I saw was Festal's face looking as big as a moon.

We were in a room of solid stone no larger than the room in a house. The ceiling was domed and the floor was sand. There didn't seem to be any way out, except through The Pipe.

"There's Coy's bedding," Festal said. "Save that other match and let's see what he's got."

We crawled across the room in darkness, found the bedding and unrolled it in darkness, heard pans clatter and glass tinkle. I lit the other match and we examined Coy's plunder. It wasn't much. A frying pan and a pot and some potatoes and jars of fruit.

"He's been eating light," Festal said. "I'll bet he's hungrier'n a bear."

"Well, he's not here. That's for sure."

"Let's wait for him."

"Outside," I said. "Our guns are outside. He'd have us where he wanted us in here."

"I guess you're right. We'd better hurry, too, or he'll get the guns."

Something clattered above us, clattered and skittered, and even in the darkness I knew someone had thrown a rock through the Pipe. It thudded into the sand and we crawled to the wall under the Pipe for protection.

"He's back," Festal said. "He's found our guns outside and he knows we're in here."

"He won't know who's in here."

"Think he won't know my gun?"

"That's right."

Another rock came clattering, and still another, and Festal let out a banshee wail.

"Why'd you do that?" I asked.

"He'll think he hit me."

"Well, shut up. Let him throw all he wants. We need some rocks in case he tries to come in."

"You don't think he'll come in without a gun?" Festal asked scornfully. "You think we can hold him off with rocks?"

"Well, it's a cinch he can't come in head first. He'll have to take off his clothes, or most of his clothes, and he'll have to come in feet first. That way he can push himself. He's too big to pull himself in like we did because he wouldn't be able to bend his arms at all and he couldn't budge."

"Let's find the rocks."

We hunted on hands and knees, scoured the sand with our hands until we found two rocks.

"This'll do it," I said. "Let him try coming in now."

"He wouldn't have to come in," Festal said. "He can stay out there and starve us out."

"You're both wrong," Coy said. "I'm right here with you and you can throw those rocks down."

I felt the hair stand up on my head, felt hair I didn't have stand up on the ridge of my back, felt the hair on my neck bristle, felt a cold chill tickle my body from my toes to my scalp.

"Where are you?" I asked. "How'd you get in?"

"Never you mind," Coy said. "There's a way, though. Just drop those rocks before I strike a light. Drop them good and hard so I can hear them thump."

I heard Festal's rock drop and I stamped my foot.

"All right," Coy said. "Now we'll have some light on the subject."

He struck a match and it flickered, caught. He held it up and peered at us, but we could see him better than he could see us. He had a rifle under his arm and our rifles were in the sand at his feet.

"You, Jeff," he said. "See that flat rock over there?"

I looked where he was pointing, but just then his match went out and he struck another.

"Lift it," he said.

I went across the cave floor and stooped to lift a stone two feet along and a foot wide. It was thin and light and came up easily. It had covered a hole, but I couldn't see anything until Coy came up behind me with the match. "Rummage around and you'll find a candle," he said.

I felt shotgun shells and rifle shells and a knife and a hatchet, and at last I found a candle and handed it to him. He lighted it and stuck it in a crack in the wall.

"Now, then," he said, "we'll find out what you're doing here."

"We were hunting you," Festal answered him.

"I reckoned that, but how'd you find me?"

"It was just a guess," I said. "At first we didn't figure you could get through the Pipe, and then we figured you could do it if you took off your clothes first. Then we decided you couldn't even do it naked."

"No need for that," Coy said. "I found another way when I was a kid."

"Gosh, I wish you'd show it to us. I don't like that Pipe."

"What're you doing here?"

"Hunting you," Festal said. "We figured you'd need help or something. We figured you'd be getting hungry."

"So where's the food?"

"The men took it away from us," Festal lied. "I told them we were hunting squirrels but they said we couldn't bring food in here because we might give it to you."

Coy thought about that a minute, and I guess he believed it.

"Who'd I shoot?"

I started to answer, but Festal beat me to it.

"Samal."

"She hurt bad?"

"Naw. Just a nick."

"Well, I'm glad," Coy said. "I've got enough trouble as it is."

"What're you going to do?" Festal asked.

"Get out of here. Come night I'm going to get out of here. I've got to have clothes and I've got to have money and I've got to get out of here."

"You want us to get clothes for you?"

"Later. Now, listen, both of you. I want a change of clothes and a razor and some soap and a bottle of water. Festal, you'll have to go for it. You can make it because you know the way better than Jeff does. You can get along better by yourself, too. Jeff can stay here with me."

"I'll need help with all that stuff," Festal said.

"You can wrap it in a blanket or put it in a pillow case."

"What about money?" I asked. "Maybe I could get some money."

"Festal can bring the money. Festal, you go to the smoke house. Start at the door and count five floor boards. Get a crowbar and prize that board out of the floor and you'll find money in a can. Bring it to me."

"All right," Festal. said. "What about something to eat?"

"Go to the hen house and get two pullets and wring their necks. Bring some salt, too. Bring Pa's pipe and some tobacco. I'm about to have a nicotine fit."

"You want me to go now?" Festal asked. "I don't think anybody would see me."

"We'll wait a while. You boys just sit down and make yourselves comfortable."

Coy stacked the guns and lay down on the sand. He turned on his side and I could see the candlelight glinting in his eyes. I knew he didn't trust us, knew he was trying to figure what we'd been up to. I didn't think he figured his own brother had come to kill him, but I didn't think he swallowed that business about us coming to help him, either.

"Douse the light," he said. "No sense wasting the candle."

I went over to the candle and snuffed it and dropped to the sand, leaned back against the rock wall, stretched my legs and set myself to wait. I could hear Festal moving, though, and Coy heard him, too.

"Don't come any closer, Festal," Coy said. "You can drop that rock, too."

"What rock?"

"Don't play sly with me."

I heard something thump, but I couldn't have said for sure whether Festal dropped the rock or stamped his foot.

"Now back up," Coy said. "Go over there by Jeff and sit down. Be quiet and don't come at me. I'm going to nap, but I'll know if you move."

"You don't even trust your own brother," Festal said.

"Why should I? You think I shot Samal on purpose and you'd bash my brains out if you got a chance."

"You did."

"I'm not going to try to make you think any different."

"Well, you did."

"It was an accident, but that's the least of my worries right now. You shut up and let me rest."

"You rest," Festal said. "Go right ahead and sleep."

"See here, now," Coy shouted. "What are you two little devils doing here? You didn't come here to help me! Just what are you up to, anyway?"

"We came to help you," Festal said. "You're my brother."

Coy grunted.

"That's right, Coy? You're my brother. Ain't that right?"

"That's right," Coy said.

"Are you sure that's right?"

"What do you mean by that?"

"Are you really my brother?"

"Now what the devil do you mean by that? What're you talking about?"

"You could be my father," Festal said. "You could be my father and Samal could be my mother. That's what I've heard, anyway. And I've heard that Old Trails was my father and Samal was my mother, so that would make my mother's father my father and that would mean my own father was my grandfather and you're my brother. So, if my own father was my grandfather and you were my brother, why then my grandfather would be your father and you would be my uncle and my brother all at the same time."

"You're crazy," Coy said.

"And if you're my father, then my mother is my father's sister, That is, if Samal is my mother. If my mother's my father's sister, then my own mother is my aunt and her brother would be my uncle. That would mean that my father would be my uncle."

"Get out of here," Coy said. "Both of you get out of here!"

"Could we have our guns back?" Festal asked.

"You can come back for your guns after I'm gone."

"Where you going?"

There was a long silence. "I don't know," Coy said uncertainly. "As far away from here as I can get."

"How do you get out of here?"

"Back through the Pipe."

"Not me," Festal said. "You know another way."

"Come to me and hold my hands," Coy ordered. "Both of you."

We groped our way in darkness and he led us through darkness. I bumped into walls on either side but there seemed to be space above. Coy stopped after a dozen steps and we jammed into him.

"You'll have to climb," he said. "It's easy. Just feel around for hand and foot holds. After about twenty feet you'll reach a ledge and you'll see the opening. I trust you not to tell anybody I'm here."

We climbed slowly and carefully. I reached the ledge first and saw dim light, just as Coy promised, at the end of a shaft that led upward at a thirty degree angle. Five minutes later we were standing on a cliff top in darkness lighter than the darkness of the cave. The embers of the posse's fire gleamed in the canyon below.

"What do we do now?" I asked Festal. "Do we tell on Coy?"

"No."

"You wanted to kill him a while ago."

"Yeah, but that's before I knew he didn't mean to shoot Samal."

"I'm going home."

"Go home," Festal said. "But don't tell anybody about Coy. You promise?"

"I promise. Are you going to bring him food and money?"

"He's my brother," Festal said.

And I kept my promise. I thought my conscience would hurt. It didn't.

Samal stayed at our house a week and Festal came to see her every day. Even Old Trails came once.

Coy disappeared. The posse combed the Narrows for two days and gave up the search. Festal and I went back to the Pipe, climbed to the cliff top from the outside and went in the way we'd come out. Coy was gone and we found our rifles where he'd stacked them.

"I hope I never see him again," Festal said.

CHAPTER ELEVEN

Our valley was blanketed with snow the first week in December and Sam came over to help me hunt a Christmas tree. She had recovered from her wound and was her usual teasing self. Her coat was red with white fur trim and she brought a white toboggan. My heart raced at sight of her. We trudged through the snow in the foothills and began to climb the slopes, but Sam scorned a dozen trees I liked. She seemed to know where she was going and stopped before an eight-foot tree fully formed. I felled it with a hatchet, tied a short length of cord to the trunk, and we skidded it behind us to the house. I built a stand for it and we decorated it after supper. Even Bant became interested and helped thread popcorn for decoration.

Sam spent the night and we left for town in the Model T early next morning, a Saturday. I had six dollars saved and knew exactly what presents to buy. I meant to buy a knife for Bant that cost two dollars, though I had half a mind to get him nothing at all. A purse for Mama was priced at a dollar-and-a-half and I decided to get two, a black one for Mama and a brown one for Samal. A framed print of a hound dog cost a dollar, and that was for Kenty. We all separated to do our shopping and I had had mine finished by mid-morning. The clerks wrapped my presents and I took them to the car. I hadn't been there more than a couple of minutes when Sam came, arms laden with packages.

"Your mother said we should meet at the Elite to eat, Jeff, at twelve o'clock sharp. Here, help me with these packages, guntzel. Careful with that one, now. It's glass. That's for Pearl. This one is for Bant. I got him a new pipe, but don't tell him. I almost decided not to buy him anything because of what he did to you, but maybe he's changing. What did you get? Have you bought my present yet? Don't tell me. Maybe you're not even buying me a present. I got a music box for myself. It holds candy or face powder or sweet smelling herbs. The music is just beautiful. The Old Rugged Cross. Here's my present for Festal. I won't get anything from Pa or Coy, so they won't get anything from me. Here now, put this box on the back seat and let's go look around before we eat. That's your present, so you'll have to buy a present for me. I spent two dollars on you, so don't be chintzy. You hear? I just love Christmas, don't you? It's better to give than receive, don't you think? I hope you think so, because I like to get presents, too. I'm selfish, I suppose."

We strolled the street and stopped to window shop. Most of the windows were decorated with crepe Christmas bells and ribbons. Some had figures of Santa and his sleigh and reindeer, and the bank had a Santa that bobbed his head and dipped his hand into a pack. We were watching that Santa when a real Santa Claus came down the street.

There must have been two hundred kids in the long block that made up our main street. They popped out of stores and off the sidewalks and filled the street, leaving a narrow lane for Santa's topless touring car. Santa was standing up, throwing candy kisses and yelling Ho Ho Ho at the top of his lungs. The driver was dressed like an elf, with mask and tasseled cap, and he inched the car along.

I caught three candy kisses and Samal scrambled among the kids to fight for candy. It was a mess. I finally backed up to the sidewalk and got clear of the melee. Santa went on up the street and, when his car cleared the crowd, gathered speed and turned around. Slowly, then, it came back down the street and Santa finished throwing his candy. The elf stopped the car and Santa climbed out. A few kids followed him to the sidewalk, but he said Ho Ho Ho that's all the candy, kids, and you kids be good and mind your parents and I'll come to see you Christmas Eve.

I followed along. Samal caught up with me and took my hand. We followed Santa to the corner of the bank building, but he ducked inside and closed the door after him. We heard the gunshot from inside within thirty seconds.

Things became confused. The first thing I noticed was Santa's elf in the touring car. He started backing up the street and came close to hitting a woman and a little boy. He stopped in front of the bank and I saw the pistol in his right hand. Samal yelled something, but people were babbling and yelling and I couldn't understand her. Men, women and kids were frozen in their tracks and the babbling stopped. Except for the motor of Santa's car, all was quiet.

Sam and I went over to the door of the bank and peered through the glass. There were eight or ten people inside. They were standing against a wall, face to the wall, and they weren't moving. Santa was at a teller's window with his back to the door. He must have finished getting the money he wanted because he hefted a canvas sack in his left hand and turned toward me.

"That's Coy Trails!" I yelled, and then turned to find I was yelling to myself. The first shock had passed and the sidewalks were cleared for a couple of hundred feet from the bank. Samal was gone. The elf in the touring car was pointing his pistol straight at me and I knew he meant me to get away from that door.

The bank door flew open and Santa came bursting out. He ran into me and knocked me back. I threw my arms wide for balance, but Santa's knee caught me in the abdomen and my breath whooshed out of my lungs. I grabbed him around the waist and held tight. Santa squirmed and dragged me along, then slapped me full in the face. He screamed in my ear and

shoved, but then I fell and he fell with me. We rolled off the curb and old
Santa flailed at me with his money pack. He punched me once in the chest
and then he was clear, and turned to run. I stuck my foot out and tripped
him. He sprawled on his face.

I'll never know why I did what I did next. I crawled to Santa and grabbed
his left foot just as he was getting up again. I dragged him down and somehow managed to get on his back. He bucked like a bronc and tossed me off
just as something exploded and another something stung my ear. I looked
up into the barrel of the elf's pistol. That's when I decided to forget Santa
Claus and let him go. I just flattened myself to the pavement and stayed there
while Santa and the elf got into their car. The car careened down the main
street, crossed the railroad tracks, and went out of sight around the corner
by the funeral parlor.

People came running. They seemed to think I had just fought the James
brothers to a standstill. They pounded me on the back and shoved me around
and hugged me until I was bruised and breathless. It was then that someone came out of the bank and shouted that Sam Pelton had been shot and
killed by jolly Saint Nick. That put a stopper on all the excitement. The doctor finally came and stayed inside about five minutes. He came out and told
everybody to stop gawking and clear a way for the ambulance to come for
the body.

It was almost sundown when Bant decided that we should go home, and
that's when they brought Santa Claus back into town.

Santa had been caught not five miles from the city limits. Farley Orr, the
constable, had a fast car and had given chase. We hadn't seen him while the
robbery was taking place because he'd been getting his car gassed up at Or-
win's Filling Station on the outskirts of town. He'd seen Santa and the Elf
hightailing it down the road and had been trying to decide whether to stop
them for speeding when Fabian Worth drove up with news of the robbery.
Santa's car had run out of gasoline and the robbers had headed for the tall
timber. They crossed a field and reached a grove of pecan trees on Bailey's
farm before they stopped to fight. Constable Orr shot the elf right between
the eyes with his first shot. Santa missed with three shots and then surrendered.

It was a sight to see the constable bring Santa to jail. He'd picked up Lew
Bailey and Frostey Pine on the way in and they had shotguns stuck in Santa's
back while Constable Orr drove. The crowd in town swarmed around the
car and things became ugly in a hurry.

"Who is he?" someone yelled.

"I don't know, folks," Constable Orr said. "I've been too busy to find out.
Listen, now, all you men! Go home to your families! The other man is dead
and I'm going to lock this one up. Somebody go get the sheriff and tell him

what happened. Somebody else go to the funeral parlor and get them to go
back for the dead man. He's in that pecan grove on the Bailey place."

At least half the men in the crowd hurried away, but the others followed
Constable Orr and his prisoner to the jail door.

"Come on, Orr," a big man with a bushy beard called. "Take that killer's
mask off and let's see who he is!"

"You people go on home," the constable said. "I'll take care of the prisoner.
Go on home! Now! Hear me?"

The big man and a half dozen other men I didn't know walked up the steps
and pressed close to the constable and Santa. Constable Orr pushed them
away and fumbled with a key, but the men grabbed Santa and pulled him
off the steps. Santa didn't show any fight. He just stood there, quietly,
while one of the men removed his cap and Santa mask.

It was Coy Trails. He looked at me and winked. "The kid knew who I was
all along."

Constable Orr opened the jail door and hustled Coy inside, locked the door
behind him. I suppose he took Coy to a cell and locked him in, but then he
was back locking the outside door behind him.

"I'm going home," he said. "I'll be back here in half an hour. I don't want
to see a mother's son of you within fifty yards of this jail when I get back.
I'm serious now, men, so you pay heed."

"You can't keep us off the streets, Orr," the big man with the beard said.
"We've got a right to be here."

"I don't aim to argue with you, Haberman. I'm going home. Just don't let
me find you here when I get back."

He went to his car and I went to hunt Sam, Bant and Mama. I found them
on the corner of the bank, ready to go home, and they knew Santa was Coy.
We started across the street to the car when a truck rolled by with three or
four men in the back. They had a big piece of timber on the truck and one
of the men was trailing a rope.

"They're going to hang Coy," I said.

"No," Bant said. "They're just showing off."

The truck parked in front of the jail and was soon surrounded by a mob
of men. The whiskered man, Haberman, stood in the truck bed and began
to talk and flail his arms.

"It looks like trouble," Bant said.

"We should find the sheriff," Mama said.

"We need Kenty," Sam said. "Find Kenty, Jeff. Hurry. He's bound to be in
town."

"I'm going to the jail," Bant said. "Maybe I can talk some sense into them."

"Don't go up there, Bant," Mama begged. "Go find the sheriff."

"They sent someone for the sheriff," Bant said, "and I can't just stand here.

They'll hang that boy if they're not stopped. I want all of you to go to the car and stay there."

He walked off with long strides. I saw him reach the crowd around the truck, push his way through and disappear in the restless, moving, formless mob.

"I'm going," I decided. "I'm going to help Bant."

"You stay here!" Mama snapped, but I was moving away at a run.

I circled the crowd and pushed my way through. Bant was at the jail door, his back to the door, facing the crowd. At least a dozen men had the beam of wood to use as a battering ram, and their leader was the bearded Haberman. The noise was deafening and Bant, though talking, might as well have been whispering to himself. Men were cursing and yelling and threatening.

The constable came out of nowhere, shouldered his way to the jail door and stood beside Bant. He had a sawed-off shotgun and he pointed it at Haberman.

"Listen to me! I won't hesitate for one second! I'll shoot the first man that makes a funny move! I'm going to give you just about a ten count to break it up and get out of here!"

Someone threw a rock, big as a hen's egg, and hit the constable in the belly. He doubled up and lifted the gun barrel as he doubled. He fired both barrels, but it didn't stop the mob. He was flattened and Bant was flattened and the men with the wooden beam rushed the door. They banged the door three times and knocked it off its hinges.

I tried to wangle my way through to Bant, but couldn't make it. I was knocked down and someone stepped on my right hand, scraping the skin off the knuckles. Someone kicked me in the ribs. I made it to my knees and was knocked flat again. When I tried to crawl, I was pushed back down and someone kicked me in the chest. I grabbed a man's leg and held on, climbed him like a tree, held on until I saw an opening and was able to dart into the clear. Bant was sitting up, not much the worse for wear, and I helped him to his feet.

"Where's the constable?" he asked.

"I think he followed the men inside."

"They'll kill that boy and I can't stop them."

"Maybe the sheriff will come."

"He's not about to come. Come on. We'll see what we can do."

We ran across the street and down it to the hardware store. The place was empty of customers and clerks. Bant went behind the counter and came out with a double-barreled shotgun. He rummaged around for shells and then yelled at me to follow him and we went back to the jail. Coy had been brought out and men were hitting him, spitting on him. His Santa Claus suit was in shreds and his face was a bloody mess. The whiskered man had him by the collar and two men were holding his arms.

"You'd better do your praying!" Whiskers Haberman screamed. "You're on your way to eternity!"

"Go to hell," Coy said.

Whiskers cuffed him in the face, hard, once and twice and once and twice again. Coy shut his eyes and didn't make a sound. Whiskers belted him in the stomach, smashed him in the face, caught his hair with his left hand and drove his right fist into his face time after time.

"Shoot him, Bant," I pleaded. "Shoot that man or give me the gun."

"You stand right here," he ordered. "What I'm about to do is going to be touchy. You stay well out of it."

He skirted the crowd and came up behind Coy. I lost sight of him for about a minute, but then he was standing beside Coy and that shotgun was waving at the mob. All the yelling stopped and I could hear Coy groaning.

"Both barrels are loaded," Bant called out. "My first shot is going to blow your guts out, Haberman. My second shot is going at anybody in front of me if just one of you tries something stupid. Somebody can jump me and I wouldn't be able to stop you, but Haberman and somebody else will die. Do you believe me, Haberman? Do you think I'd shoot?"

Whiskers didn't want to answer. He stalled for time, but he couldn't take his eyes off the shotgun.

"Do you believe me, Haberman?" Bant pressed him.

Whiskers nodded.

"Not everybody can see you. I asked you a question and I want an answer. Do you think I'd shoot you if somebody jumps me?"

"Yes, dammit!"

"All right. Now listen. I'm going to start backing up the steps to the jail door. Coy will be backing right beside me. Haberman, you follow me. Go slow and easy. Keep your hands down by your sides and don't come too close. If anybody so much as touches me, I swear, *I will shoot*. I'll shoot you first, Haberman, and then I'll shoot somebody else. Then the rest of you can hang me beside Coy."

No one replied. Some of the men backed away uneasily. Bant took one step backward, up one step, and Coy stepped back with him. Haberman took one step forward, and then Bant and Coy moved up the second step. Slowly, so slowly, a step at a time, they backed up toward the jail door. It seemed to go on forever. Haberman didn't make a false move. Bant seemed calm and cool and Coy seemed completely unconcerned. They reached the door and my breath came more freely.

"All right, Haberman," Bant said, his voice loud and clear. "I want you to follow Coy and me through the door. I don't know much about the law, but I think I have the right to lock you up. If I don't have the right, I'll lock you in a cell anyway. I'll let the shotgun deputize me."

Bant took a backward step through the doorway and Coy backed beside him. Haberman didn't take a step forward, but turned to the crowd and yelled, "Are you going to let him get away with this?"

The tables turned quickly. Bant pitched forward, fell out the door and landed on his face at the feet of Haberman. I didn't see the blow that felled Bant, but a young man, almost a boy, pushed Coy out onto the step landing and swaggered out to look down at Bant. He had a child's baseball bat in his right hand.

The mob went wild, surged forward, and men screamed like animals. They were insane, crazy for blood, and they dragged Coy Trails to the truck. His passage wasn't easy. Men hit him, kicked him, scratched him, spat on him, and he was almost too weak to stand on his feet. They threw him up onto the truck bed, lifted him to his feet, and dropped a noose over his head. They were careful to tuck the knot under his left ear.

Haberman made a speech, or tried to, but gave it up when the noise didn't subside. The constable burst out the jail door, ran down the steps and made his way to the truck. He tried to climb up, but Haberman kicked him in the face and he fell out of sight. The truck moved forward, turned, and made a trip down the main street to the railroad track. There was a tree there, a massive pecan, near the sidewalk. Haberman threw the rope over a limb.

At least twenty men had a hold on the rope and they pulled. Coy went up to his tiptoes, but this time Haberman made himself heard and the men stopped pulling.

"Now," Haberman yelled, "don't pull until I say pull! When I give the word, the truck will move away and all you'll have to do is hold the rope! Coy will be walking on air!"

He got off the truck and stood beside the cab. A dead silence came as he held his arms high. Coy stood with shoulders squared, head up, hands at his sides.

"You got anything to say, Coy?" Haberman asked.

"No."

"You're about to die. You know that, don't you?"

"Yes."

"Don't you want to square things? Don't you want to pray?"

"It's too late for that."

"All right, then! You'll get no mercy from us!"

"Wait," Coy said. "I want to make a statement."

"That's more like it. Bare your soul."

Coy spoke, loudly. "Listen, all you men. Do you remember when Thompson's Hardware was burgled? Well, I helped burgle it. I had help, though. I had help when I broke into King's filling station and when I took the safe from Kemble's Grocery. Do you want to know who helped me? Well, do you?"

The crowd roared.

"Old Whiskers Haberman helped me, that's who! He's a robber and a thief, just like me. The only reason he didn't drive the get-away car today was that he lost his nerve!"

Haberman spoke against dead silence. "He's just saying that to get even. Hang him! Pull this truck from under him!"

The man in the cab drove the truck from under Coy and Coy was left hanging by the neck, kicking, strangling, twisting, and flailing his arms and legs. I lost my head and tried to get to him, found Sam beside me, but men held us back. I cried and screamed and kicked and fought, but was held tightly. Some man had his arms around Sam, his hands clasped to her breasts, and she was screaming and kicking and fighting. We were let go when Coy was dead. The killers tied the rope to the trunk of a tree and Coy hung in the twilight, a lonely and pitiful figure in a tattered Santa Claus suit. I wondered why I cried for a man I didn't even like.

CHAPTER TWELVE

Bant found Sam and me at the hanging tree and stayed with us until the undertaker came for the body. He helped lower Coy, helped load him in the hearse, and then we walked up the street to the café. The street lamps were burning and store lights were burning, but the town seemed empty and quiet. We found Mama sitting at a table by the window and she made me down a hot bowl of soup. Sam refused to eat.

"We tried," Bant said. "We did our best. Those men committed murder and it will rest heavy on their minds and hearts. The sheriff hid like a yellow dog and he'll have to carry some of the blame."

"The constable did his best," Sam said. "Haberman I know. He raises chickens and pigs out at the edge of town. I'd never seen that young man who hit you on the head, Bant. Who was he?"

"Les Weaver. He works at the feed mill."

"Pa and Festal will want to know."

"Old Trails is at the funeral parlor, Bant," Mama said. "I saw him pass not more than ten minutes ago."

"I'll go help him," Bant said. "They say that Coy's driver was a kid named Ralph Simmons from Van Horn. Just a kid, and now he's dead."

"There's going to be bad trouble over this," Mama said. "Old Trails will kill somebody. You did all you could, Bant, and you stay out of it."

"My head hurts," Bant said. "There's a knot on my head as big as a hen's egg."

"Maybe you should see the doctor."

"I'm all right. Well, Old Trails needs me. Wait for me here," and he was gone.

Sam ordered a cup of coffee. "You know, I guess I should be crying, but I just can't. Coy wasn't much, but he was my brother. Is it wrong to feel sort of... relieved?"

"No, child," Mama said.

"I'm going to the funeral home," I decided, and Mama didn't try to stop me.

The streets were deserted and most of the stores had closed their doors. A wind had blown in, advance guard for a fresh Norther, and I shivered as I ran. Bant and Old Trails were standing on the sidewalk in front of the funeral home, half leaning against the brick wall, huddled and hands in pockets. A single electric bulb burned above the doorway.

"I'm sorry about Coy," Bant was saying. "I did my best."

"I heard that, Bant, and I want you to know I appreciate it. I wish I had been there. The Lord couldn't find ten decent men in this town. He should destroy it and all the people in it. They murdered my boy."

"I know they did. They did, and I'm sorry. But Coy killed a man, too. That doesn't make the mob right, but there are a lot of people grieving tonight."

"Well," the old man sighed, "I'd appreciate it if you would take Samal home. I'll do what needs to be done here."

"Is there anything I can do?"

"Just see that Samal gets home," and Old Trails opened the door to the funeral home.

Bant shrugged and walked away, deep in thought, and I didn't speak until we'd reached the door to the café.

"He acted like he blames you," I said.

"He's deep hurt."

"Do you think he'll go after that Whiskers?"

"Well, I'd hate to be in Haberman's shoes."

We didn't go to the funeral because it was all over and done with before we learned what Old Trails had done. He had loaded Coy's body on the midnight train for the trip to East Texas and burial in the old family graveyard. Not even Samal and Festal knew about it until Old Trails came home. By that time, two more funerals had been scheduled. Someone shot Haberman with a twenty-two rifle. Two hours later, the young man who clubbed Bant down was shot with a twenty-two. The shooter was an expert marksman, people said. Both men were shot through the left eye and killed instantly.

I went to see Festal on a cold Saturday and found him in the barn.

"Pa, or Grandpa or Uncle Pa or whatever he is has been treating me like I am almost a human being," he said. "I can go in the house whenever I want and he don't even fuss at me."

"He's your pa."

"Aw, I know that. Anyway, he sure has changed these last few days."

We went on up to the house and stood in the hallway for a moment to get our eyes accustomed to the gloom. We'd just started on down the hall toward the living room when we heard Samal scream. Festal stopped me and we started edging back toward the outside door.

"We'd better go see about Sam," I whispered. "What's wrong with her?"

"That old goat's after her again."

"Why?"

"Don't you know? He's always pestering her. She's stood him off with a shotgun more than once."

"Well, we'll just go stop him."

"We'll get the hell belted out of us if we do."

I pushed him aside and walked toward the living room door, half feeling my way. Sam screamed again just as I started to open the door, and I paused.

"Stand back, you old devil," Samal was saying, and I think she was leaning against the door I was about to open. I could hear the sound of her breathing, the heavy sobbing sound, and her panic added to my fear. "Stand back, you old filth! You're drunk out of your mind! I'll club you with this poker as sure you live!"

Old Trails laughed.

"You'd better back away!" Sam warned. "I'm going to let you have it if you come closer!"

"Put that poker down," Old Trails said.

"You're drunk, Pa. Coy's barely cold in his grave and you're trying to rape your own daughter. Don't you see what you're doing? You lay your filthy hands on me and I'll go to the sheriff."

"He wouldn't believe you."

Old Trails yelled something and Sam screamed and there were scuffling sounds and Festal had me by the arm and I couldn't shake him loose. I heard a thwacking sound, a sound that thwacked with a thwump, and somebody or something fell to the floor and Sam laughed a wild laugh and I scurried after Festal down the hall and out the front door. We ran around the house and stopped at the corner. In just a few seconds Old Trails came staggering out to the front porch. He had blood all over his face and he had his arms up around his head and he stood there on the porch mouthing curses.

"She really let him have it that time," Festal said.

Festal and I came up behind Old Trails. Sam burst out of the house, rolling the raised poker like a batter with a bat, and followed the old man into the yard. Old Trails seemed determined to take it away from her. They circled like dancers, circled in a slow and deadly dance, and then Old Trails jumped at her.

He wasn't fast enough.

Sam caught him in mid-air with a blow that laid part of his scalp back. He fell sideways, hit the ground and rolled over and over, got to his knees and held his arms up over his head to ward off blows. Sam hit him again and he fell flat on his face.

Festal wasn't trying to hold me and I dashed at Sam.

I didn't try to grab the poker but did the next best thing. I hit her with the full force of my body right in the small of her back and bowled her over, knocked her tail-gate over breakfast, and she lost the poker. I grabbed it and threw it as far as I could. When Sam came at me I slugged her in the face. That seemed to jar her to her senses.

The old colored woman was sitting in the rocker on the front porch and

Sam went up there and dragged a straight chair to the edge of the porch. She sat for a minute and then went inside and came out with a little old single-shot twenty-two rifle. She sat in her chair and stared at Old Trails. Festal went under the house and I went up to talk some sense into Sam. She seemed to listen to me, but I'm not really sure she heard what I was saying.

"You had a right to do what you did," I said. "I can be your witness to that. He was trying to hurt you and you had a right to protect yourself. I heard his threats, too. But they'll get you if you let him lie out there and die. They'll send you to jail."

The old colored woman rocked and crooned, rocked and crooned, and Old Trails moaned and muttered in the yard.

"Let me go for the sheriff, Sam. Just let me take a pillow and a blanket and cover Old Trails and then let me go for the sheriff. You and the old woman can bandage his head and wash him up and maybe give him some whiskey or something and then they won't do anything to you even if he dies."

"You mind your own business, Jeff. This has been building for years and it's time it's finished."

I stood beside her and wondered what chance I'd have of getting the gun away from her. She was pale as death. Her hair was tumbled about her shoulders and her dress was torn, but she was the prettiest girl I'd ever seen. She gripped the stock of the gun until her hands were blue-white with strain and she sat without moving.

"Let me help him, Sam."

"I'm sorry, Jeff."

I saw that arguing wasn't going to do any good. She wasn't thinking straight. She just stared at Old Trails. She didn't seemed to notice when I went into the house for a blanket and pillow and I thought I could cover Old Trails without any trouble. I thought wrong. I was just about to spread the blanket over the old man when the gun crraaacked a bullet into the ground not more than a yard from me.

"Don't make me hurt you, Jeff."

"You wouldn't shoot me." She slipped another bullet into the chamber.

She shot again and this time I thought I could feel the breath of the bullet as it passed. I dropped the blanket and pillow and went back to the porch. Festal stuck his head out from beneath.

"She'd shoot you."

"I believe it. I think she's out of her mind."

"Don't blame her. She puts up with a lot."

"But that's her father!"

"So?"

"He's bad hurt out there."

"It's his fault."

"We could slip away and go for the doctor. Some help."

"It's a long way."

Old Trails moaned loudly. "Whiskey," he said, and rolled over on his back.

"I'll get it," I said.

"Sam won't let you," Festal replied.

I went across the porch and Sam didn't say anything, didn't even look at me. The old woman just went on rocking and crooning. I went through the hallway to the kitchen and rummaged around in cupboards until I found a bottle of whiskey. Sam paid me no mind when I crossed the porch again and walked down the steps.

"Drop it, Jeff," Sam said, not even raising her voice. "Don't try to help him."

"Go ahead and shoot me. I'm not going to stand around and let him die."

"I'm warning you."

I knelt beside Old Trails, slid my left hand under his bloody head and touched the bottle neck to his lips. He drank some, but most of the whiskey dribbled over his chin. Something nudged me in the small of the back.

"Stand away," Sam said, and prodded me hard with the gun.

"Go ahead and shoot."

She lifted the gun barrel and tapped me on the side of the head. It didn't hurt much and it didn't scare me. It did make me mad.

"I'm going to get the doctor, Sam."

"You stay here. I don't want you sending the sheriff out here."

I walked with her to the edge of the porch. "He'll die, Sam. Festal can help me get him into the house."

"Leave him where he is."

"We're going to take him inside, Sam. He'll die out here."

I walked back to Old Trails and leaned down to see if he was still breathing. He moaned and said, "Whiskey, more whiskey." I called Festal and he came to me. I took the old man under the arms and Festal took his legs. The old man's rear end dragged the ground but we managed to get him as far as the steps. That's as far as we were able to go because Sam sent a bullet to the ground close to my feet.

"Leave him where he is," Sam said. "I mean business."

Festal went back under the porch and I stayed on the porch with Sam and the old woman. Old Trails groaned almost continuously. Now and then he'd call Coy and now and then he'd call his dead wife. It made me sick, but didn't seem to bother Sam. We sat on that porch and watched the old man for an hour, and that's when Festal came out from under the porch again. He walked over to the old man and looked at him, then went over and picked up the blanket and pillow I'd brought from the house. He spread the blanket over his pa, went down to his knees and tucked the blanket under, then lifted his pa's head and slipped the pillow under. He came to the porch for the whiskey bottle, went back to his pa and poured some dribbles into his mouth, then motioned for me. I went over and knelt beside him to help give the old man a swig.

"I might as well put him out of his misery," Sam said from right behind us.

"You wouldn't," I told her.

"After what you've seen, you still don't think I would?"

"Yeah, I guess you would."

She took a step forward and pointed the gun at her pa's head, but I grabbed the barrel and pointed it straight into the ground.

"Here, Festal," I said. "Take hold of this gun barrel and don't let her lift it."

Festal took a good hold on the barrel and I let go. I stood up and brought my right fist up with all the weight of my body behind it. I caught Samal on the point of the chin and she flew back to land on her butt. The gun fired; the bullet went into the ground, and she lost her grip on it.

"Thanks a lot, Jeff," she said.

"You had it coming, Sam."

"Yeah, I guess I did. But that old goat deserved what he got. Maybe he'll think twice before he decides to pester me again. Well, come on. Let's get him in the house."

Sam and the old woman took Old Trails' arms and Festal and I took his legs. His butt still dragged, but we took him down the hallway, through the living room, down another hallway and into a room I'd never seen. It was a bedroom, but it was more than that. The furniture was massive. The old man's bed had a canopy. There were bookshelves along all four walls, all filled, and a massive fireplace. We got him in his bed and Sam sent Festal for warm water. Sam went for a needle and sheep-gut thread while the old woman took off Old Trails' boots and pants. She covered him up good and placed two pillows under his head. She left then and I stood looking around at all the books.

"I didn't even think he could read," I muttered.

I looked down at the old man. He grinned at me, showing teeth, opened his eyes, gave me a wink, closed them and began to moan.

The old he devil.

Sam and Festal came back into the room and Sam cleaned Old Trails' wounds. She did it with gentle care while the old man moaned and called out for Coy and his dead wife.

"It's a good thing he's unconscious," Sam said. "It'll hurt when I sew that scalp back."

She did twenty stitches and the old devil didn't quiver a muscle.

"Do you think I should get the doctor?" I asked.

"He'll be fine," Sam said.

I went on home and didn't see any of the Trails family for five days. Old Trails was up and about the day after his clubbing. He spent the second day out in an icy rain hunting a beef steer that had wandered into the Narrows. He was sick with a cold by evening and had pneumonia before morning. He died on the fifth day.

The undertaker must have reported Old Trails' wounds to the sheriff, because he came out and arrested Sam. Kenty happened to be there at the time and, luckily, had seen Old Trails the day he went out to hunt his steer. Kenty posted a thousand dollar bond for Sam and took her home. Old Trails was taken to East Texas and buried beside Coy.

CHAPTER THIRTEEN

December was a bad month for the Trails family. Year's end was making an end of them all, it seemed. I didn't tell Mama and Bant the whole story and they didn't question me. The sheriff came out to the house the Sunday before Christmas and said there'd be an inquest the next day and I had to be at the courthouse at ten o'clock the next morning. The way I saw it, they'd send Samal to the electric chair or to the penitentiary at Huntsville if I told the whole truth.

I couldn't sleep that night and thought of waking Bant, but he'd been in one of his dark brown moods and I feared to disturb him. I thought of Kenty and crawled out of bed, dressed in the dark and tiptoed out of the house. The moon was glinting off the snow and the night was almost as light as day. There was a snow crust that crunched underfoot and, though the temperature must have been near zero, there was no wind. I saddled Raindrop and we float-skimmed our way to Kenty's place. His living room window was aglow with lamplight and I found him sitting before the fire reading *Oliver Twist*.

"I guess I've read this a hundred times," he told me, "and I never tire of it. Pull up a chair and take the load off your feet and tell me what brings you here. Bant acting up again?"

"No, it's the inquest tomorrow and the sheriff said I'll have to testify."

"I know. He was by here and asked me to go tell Samal and Festal. They're to be at your house bright and early to ride in with you."

"I'm afraid for Samal."

"Do you want to tell me about it?"

So I told him, told him all of it, and he sat brooding before the fire for a long while after I finished.

"Well," he said finally, sighing as he spoke, "you don't have any choice. You'll be sworn to tell the truth and you'll have to tell it without leaving anything out."

"But what'll they do to Samal?"

"The inquest is not a trial. Only one thing will be decided, and that is whether the case should go before the grand jury."

"What do you think they'll do?"

"I can't guess. Now, Jeff, listen to me. You can't lie and you can't hold anything back. If you do, they'll ask questions and trap you. I'll explain all that to Samal and Festal. For right now you'd best hightail it home and get in bed lest Bant finds you're gone."

Samal and Festal were at our house before breakfast and Festal gobbled pancakes and eggs like a starving man. Samal sipped coffee and stared out the window. Kenty came at eight o'clock and was surprised Bant hadn't dressed for town.

"I've decided not to go," Bant said. "You drive them in and I'll restring barbed wire back of the woods lot."

"The boy may need you to lean on."

"He can lean on you."

I noticed then that Mama was red-eyed and I figured she and Bant had argued before breakfast. She inspected me after I'd dressed and told me not to worry and not be afraid and just tell the truth as I saw it and everything would be all right.

I was the first witness called and I told it all, just as it happened. When I'd finished I was told I should leave the room.

"You go over to the Blue Bonnet Café and wait until we've finished," the coroner said. "There're things going to be asked and said here that young boys don't need to be exposed to. Now, then, we'll hear Festal Trails."

I sat in a booth in the café for thirty minutes before Festal joined me.

"We'll have a cup of coffee," I said. "I've got a dime. Did they make you leave?"

"Yeah. I wonder what'n hell that old geezer thought we'd hear we ain't heard or seen with our own eyes."

We drank our coffee and watched the clock. At eleven we went outside and looked in shop windows until we were chilled and then went back to the café. It was twelve-thirty when we saw Kenty and Samal coming across the street.

"It's all over," Kenty told us. "They had a deposition from old Emma and her story decided it."

That was the first time I'd thought of the old Negro woman.

"Why wasn't she here?" I asked.

"Well," Kenty said, "she's old and colored and they decided to take her deposition."

"And they won't do anything to Samal."

"That's right. No jury in the world would convict her and they know it. That old man was in love with his own daughter and he's well off dead, the way people around here feel about it."

A new snow fell and the earth was blanketed on Christmas Eve Day. Kenty came past the house early in the morning, riding his Appaloosa.

"Hi, Jeff. Where's Bant?"

"Gone to town, Kenty."

He rode into the yard and sat his horse, leaned down. "You bought a present for your mother, Jeff?" he asked.

"Not much of one."

"Run ask Pearl if you can go over to my house for a while."

"She won't let me, Kenty. Bant wouldn't like it."

Mama came out on the porch. She must have heard.

"Go ahead, Jeff," she called. "Hello, Kenty. It's a beautiful snow."

"You're looking well, Pearl. How's Bant?"

"As usual."

Kenty gave me a hand up and I sat behind him, my arms around his waist.

"I'll have him back home in a couple of hours," he said. "Hope you have a Merry Christmas."

"Same to you."

I can't describe their voices or what their words did to me. At the time I didn't understand. But I heard tenderness and love in how they said what they said, that and a great deal of sadness, and it made me feel sad for all the things unspoken between them.

We rode off, Kenty and I through the deep fall of snow, the only sound the creaking of saddle leather and the soft plop-plop of the horse's hooves in the snow. Kenty served as a windbreak for me and I leaned tightly against him, my face buried in the folds of his heavy coat. I felt at peace because of his nearness, almost happy, and it wasn't necessary for us to talk.

The sun came out briefly just as we rode into the yard, shining the whiteness into brilliances that hurt the eyes. Smoke came from the chimney and the place looked peaceful and homey and secluded. I dismounted and Kenty rode on to the barn.

I went into the living room. There was a good fire in the fireplace and the room was warm. The shades were drawn and the natural pine walls reflected the warm glow of the flames. I knelt on the bearskin rug in front of the bookcase and began to browse, soon found the *Complete Works of Sherlock Holmes* that hadn't been there when last I'd visited. I took a heavy volume from the shelf and moved over to the fire for better light.

"Jeff?"

"Yeah, Kenty?"

"Want to help me clean out the cow lot?"

"Sure."

I went outside. Kenty had two shovels. He tossed me one and we waded through the snow to the lot. Manure was deep under the shed and we set to work shoveling it into a wagon he'd backed up to the fence. We worked hard and began to sweat. Kenty relaxed then and began to talk. He told me about Christmas Days when he was a kid, told me about the food his mother cooked, how he tried to stay awake to see Santa Claus, about the time his father gave him a pump shotgun.

"I doubt I'll ever have a real gun until I'm grown."

"Maybe Santa'll bring you one this Christmas."

I leaned on my shovel. "I doubt it. Bant's acting real strange again."

"Maybe Bant will change."

"He won't. I keep telling myself he'll stop drinking and that things will be like they used to be, but I know it'll always be like this. I don't know how to explain it, but sometimes he gets a look in his eyes that makes me think he doesn't know what he's doing."

"What do you feel for him, Jeff?"

"I try to remember him like he used to be."

"Do you know why he started acting like he does?"

"I think I do."

Kenty tossed his shovel under the shed and began rolling a cigarette.

"Tell me what you think, Jeff." He sounded embarrassed, uneasy, and he wouldn't look at me.

"Well, sometimes I think... aw, Kenty, it's silly what I think."

"Tell me," Kenty said, and his voice was gentle.

I sat down on a feed bucket and Kenty squatted beside me, sitting on his heels. He finished rolling his cigarette and flicked a match on his thumbnail. His face was on a level with mine and there was the hurt look in his eyes that I felt inside. Tears stung my eyes and I got all choked up.

"Sometimes I think Bant thinks you're my papa."

Kenty ducked his head and bit his lip. He took a long drag from his cigarette and let smoke trickle lazily from his nostrils.

"That's a funny thing to think," he said after a while. "Just the same, I wish you were my boy."

He ground his cigarette under his heel and we finished shoveling the manure into the wagon. It didn't take long. Not long enough. We walked to the house and Kenty led the way to the kitchen. It was a large room, paneled in smoky oak, with plates and brass plaques and copper pots and pans on the wall. The stove was fat and black and it kept the room warm as toast. There was a circular table, large enough for ten or fifteen people, and captain's chairs with plump red cushions.

Kenty made coffee and we sat at the table next to the stove. After a bit Kenty finished his coffee and stood up, laid his hand on my shoulder.

"I'm not going to pay you in money, Jeff," he said. "I knew you'd want to buy a present for your mother, so I spent your pay on a present for her."

I followed him into the living room and he took a box from the mantel, handed it to me.

"Open it."

It was a purse, a genuine leather purse with a gold buckle, a beautiful purse.

"This cost a lot of money, Kenty."

"You earned it."

"Mama'll know you gave it to me."

"She'll know you earned the money for it."

"There's Bant."

Kenty frowned. "It's Christmas, Jeff. If Bant...."

"Thanks a lot, Kenty," I said. And then the tears came. It shamed me but I couldn't stop crying. I buried my face in my arms, but Kenty threw his arms across my shoulders, patted my back awkwardly and shook me gently. After a while I felt better. Some of the grief and blackness in me seemed to dissolve.

"You deserved that cry," Kenty said.

"I don't know what came over me."

"Don't be ashamed of it. More men cry than you'd think."

"Well, anyway, I thank you for the purse. Mama'll be real pleased."

"I'd better get you home."

"No need for you to saddle up. I'll cut across country and be there in no time."

"It's awfully cold."

"I'll trot."

"Well, all right. But don't shilly-shally around."

I was out in the yard and Kenty was on the porch before I thought of how he'd spend Christmas all alone in that big old house.

"Kenty," I said, "why don't you come over tonight and bring your fiddle?"

"Well, I don't know," he said.

"It's Christmas."

Kenty frowned a little and thought on it. "I might do it. I'll think about it. Expect me when you see me coming."

"I'll tell Mama to set an extra plate."

"Jeff, listen. Tell your mother to think about it after Bant comes home. If he's sober and in good humor, I'll come. If he's been drinking, you slip outside just at dusk and meet me at the barn. That way he'll never know I've been around and no harm will come of it."

"All right," I called over my shoulder, anxious to be gone.

It hurt to breathe. The cold air stung my lips and burned my throat and chest and I had to stop trotting. The crunching of my footsteps was the only sound. The whole world was quiet, hushed, and being in the woods was like being in church. It would have been a perfect hunting day.

In the old days, Bant would have had a dog or would have used Kenty's dogs. He'd have been out the night before, or up early today, and we'd have gone on a hunt. By this time we'd have had some rabbits and squirrels. Maybe a turkey. I shrugged and tried not to think of the old days.

Bant wasn't home. I went straight to the kitchen, and it was warm and fragrant with cooking smells. Mama had a hen in the oven and pies baking. She was all smiles, humming a tune as she moved from cabinet to table to stove.

"Mama, I told Kenty to come eat with us tonight and bring his fiddle."

She frowned. "You shouldn't have, Jeff. I'm afraid...."

"We thought maybe Bant would be in good temper because it's Christmas Eve. Maybe if Kenty plays a few tunes and can talk to Bant everything'll be all right."

Her eyes saw something far off. After a while she brought herself back and sighed.

"Maybe you're right," she said.

"I told Kenty I'd meet him at the barn if Bant comes home in a bad mood."

"We'll see."

She was looking at the package under my arm. "It's some books Kenty let me have," I lied.

I hid Mama's package in my room and hunted some paper to wrap it. There was tissue paper in her bureau drawer but I couldn't find ribbon. I finally tied the package with string and slid it under my bed.

Bant came home an hour before dusk. I peeked out the window to see if he had packages, but all he brought into the house was a sack of sugar. I heard him stamping his feet on the porch, heard him enter the kitchen.

"It's getting colder," he said.

"Supper'll be ready in a little while," Mama said. "You and Jeff better do the chores."

I stepped into the kitchen, slipping into my coat. Bant looked over his shoulder at me and I thought I saw the hint of a smile.

"You get the wood in," he said. "I'll milk and feed the chickens."

He followed me out the door and across the yard. At the woodpile I stooped to gather wood and he stood beside me. "What've you been wanting for Christmas, Jeff?" he asked.

"A shotgun," I said, not really thinking.

His words seemed to sing in my ears while he trudged away through the snow.

I almost ran with my load of wood to the kitchen.

"He asked me what I wanted for Christmas," I told Mama. "I said I wanted a gun."

"Don't count on it, Jeff. Even if he got you a present he wouldn't have known you wanted a gun. Don't count on it."

"He asked me what I wanted and didn't say a thing when I said I wanted a gun."

"Don't count on it," Mama said again.

I fed the stock and threw out grain for the chickens. Bant was whistling in the barn and I thought things were shaping up for a good evening. I took another load of wood to the house and Mama opened the door for me.

"He's not drinking," I said. "Do you think he'll be mad if Kenty comes?"

"I don't know. He may be mad at us afterward, but I doubt he'll act mad while Kenty's here."

"Why don't you find his bottle and break it, Mama?"

"He hides it outside. I've hunted and I can't find it." We heard footsteps on the back porch.

Bant came into the room with two pails of milk.

"It's cold," he said. "But it's sure pretty."

He sounded happy and even whistled a little as he strained the milk and put it away in the cooler. Mama was setting the table and making a clatter but the worry was gone from her face. Papa poured warm water from the kettle and washed.

"Better use this water, Jeff," he said. "I wasn't very dirty."

His words made the whole room bright, made me want to say something or do something to make him stay as he was. Still, I half expected to see the friendly look disappear from his face, half expected him to turn silent and sullen.

"When do we eat?" he asked. "I'm starved."

"In a minute," Mama said.

"Smells good."

Mama smiled. "The good smells are for tomorrow. Tonight we'll have ham and beans and apple pie."

"That's good enough, eh, Jeff?"

"Yes, sir," I mumbled.

"Bant?" Mama said, a question in her voice.

"Yeah."

"Jeff saw Kenty today and asked him to eat with us."

For only a moment the hard look was there on Bant's face. His fingers curled up into his palms. And then the hard look was gone and his fingers uncurled and I could breathe again.

Mama stood stark still, frozen, and happy relief was plain on her face and in her eyes and in the way she breathed deeply when the hard look passed from Bant's face.

"I hope he brings his fiddle," he said.

"He will," I promised.

Bant took his seat at the head of the table and I took my place at the foot. Mama brought the hot biscuits, poured milk into the glasses, brought a platter of ham steaming hot from the oven.

"Sit down, Pearl," Bant said.

"Well, I...."

"Kenty won't mind if we go ahead."

"It's a little early," Mama protested. Her hands were clasped and she clenched and unclenched them, the fingers entwining.

Bant folded his hands and bowed his head. I closed my eyes and waited for the blessing.

Footsteps on the porch.

Kenty.

Bant began to mumble his blessing, the words I could never understand.

Kenty knocked on the door.

Bant continued to mumble his blessing. I opened my eyes and looked up to see Mama with eyes tightly closed, her lower lip caught between her teeth.

Kenty knocked again.

Bant said Amen. And then, "Come in, Kenty!"

The door opened and there stood Kenty. "I knew you'd be in the kitchen," he said. "I could smell that ham from my place."

"You're just in time. Have a seat."

Kenty had his violin under his arm. I got up and took it. He winked at me and caught my arm, squeezed it. I took the violin to the living room and put it on the table.

Kenty talked about hunting, about his dogs, about the snow. Bant grunted his answers, nodded his head, helped his plate to more ham. Even his eating was different, for he usually ate sparingly. Mama wasn't eating. She pushed her food around on her plate, dabbled at it, darted quick, nervous glances at Kenty, at Bant, at me. I smiled at her and she smiled back, fleetingly. She brought hot coffee from the stove, cut wedges of pie and served it on her best china.

For some reason I wasn't hungry.

"Well," Bant said at last, pushing his chair back. "Don't know when I've enjoyed a meal more."

"Nor me," Kenty said.

Kenty smoked a cigarette, Bant his pipe. Mama washed the dishes and I dried. We finished and Mama led the way to the living room, sat before the fire while Kenty played his fiddle. Bant didn't say much, but it wasn't a bad time.

I went straight to bed after Kenty had gone, straight to sleep. Once in the night I heard Bant walking around the house, but I wasn't afraid. It was full daylight when Mama called me. She came to my room and kissed my cheek.

"Merry Christmas, Jeff."

"Merry Christmas, Mama."

I dressed and got her package from under the bed. She called me from the living room.

Bant was there, a cup of coffee in his hand. On the floor, near the hearth, were two packages.

"They're for you, Jeff," Mama said.

I handed her the package. "Open yours first, Mama." She opened it and gasped when she saw the purse, turned white, stooped and kissed me, said nothing.

Bant stood beside the fireplace, a small smile frozen on his face.

"Now open yours, Jeff," he said.

One package was long, one square. I opened the square one first. It was a jacket. The card said, "From Bant and Mama." But it was Mama's handwriting.

"Open your other package, Jeff," Bant said.

I wanted to grab the package and run. His eyes seemed to be boring into me. Somehow I knew what it was and who had sent it. The cord was strong and I couldn't break it, had to untie the knot, working with stiff fingers.

It was a shotgun. There was no card, but I knew it was from Kenty.

"He hid it outside and came back with it after you went to bed," Mama said.

There was no joy in it because of the way Bant looked. "Where'd you get the money for the purse, Jeff?" he asked.

"Aw, I just...."

"Where'd you get it?"

"I helped Kenty clean his cow lot."

"That purse cost at least ten dollars."

"Bant," Mama pleaded. "It's Christmas."

"Let me see the purse."

She handed him the purse and stepped back, white of face and lips trembling. Bant ran his fingers over the leather. And then he walked over to the fireplace, stopped, pitched the purse into the flames.

Mama turned and left the room, walking slowly.

I stood facing Bant, as angry as I'd ever been in my life.

I handed him the gun. He turned on his heel and walked out through the kitchen, out the door, into the yard. I followed and watched him. My lips were twisted into a smile, so tight a smile it hurt my face, and I was still smiling when he smashed the gun against the oak tree, was still smiling when he walked back across the yard, up on the porch to the door. He handed me the gun and I took it. The stock was shattered.

"It's a good thing you broke it, Bant," I said.

He hit me full in the face with his fist. I saw it coming and could have ducked. It seemed to come slowly, the blow, and the fist looked as big as a plate. I seemed to float through the air for a long time, landed on my back and slid across the linoleum floor until my body hit the wall. Mama's scream was a thin and haunting thing. I rolled over, suddenly sick to my stomach, made it to hands and knees and rested there until the dizziness passed. Then, with great effort, I stood.

Mama stood by the stove, her mouth open, the scream frozen in her throat, her eyes dull with shock.

"I'm all right, Mama," I said.

"Your nose," Mama moaned. "Your poor face."

Bant stood staring at his fist, flexing and unflexing the fingers.

"I'm leaving," I said.

Bant looked up. "Go ahead."

Mama followed me to my room and helped me pack my clothing in a box. Once she threw her arms around me and held me close, kissed me and cried a little.

"Go to Kenty, Jeff, and I won't worry. While you're gone I'll do some thinking. We'll go away. Maybe we'll go to the city. I can get a job waiting tables or keeping house or something. We'll get by."

"I'm not afraid of him any more."

"Oh, I was proud of you!" Mama said. "When you get a little bigger...."

"He's not to hit you," I said, and meant it. "He can hit me if he wants, but he's not to hit you."

"I'll let you know when I've decided what to do. Keep an eye on the place, and when you see him leave for town you come see me. It's best I don't come see you."

"You don't think he'll stop me from going?" I asked.

"No, he'll see it through. He's gone too far and he knows it, so he'll let you go for a while, anyway."

"I'll be all right," I told her. "You're not to worry."

"He's made you grow up too fast!"

Bant was drinking coffee in the kitchen when I walked through. He didn't look up until I reached the doorway to the porch. I turned at the doorway, ready to run if he made a move.

"You're not to hit Mama," I said, looking him square in the eyes.

"I'm sorry I hit you, Jeff," he said. "It was wrong and I'm sorry."

"Merry Christmas, Bant."

It hurt. I could tell it. As soon as I knew it hurt I turned on my heel and walked out across the porch, into the yard, and crunch-crunched my way toward Kenty's place. It was cold, but the prickles at the back of my neck were colder than the wind, Not once did I look back. Whether Bant walked to the doorway and watched I don't know, but I seemed to feel his eyes on me until the house was out of sight.

CHAPTER FOURTEEN

The hounds bayed me long before I broke out of the woods into the clearing. Smoke was coming out of the chimney and I knew Kenty was home. As I crossed the yard, he came out onto the porch.

"I caused it," he said. "I should never have given you the gun."

"It was the purse, I think."

He ran his hands over my face and felt my nose. "It's not broken, but he must have given you a pretty good lick. You'll have a couple of black eyes. Did he hurt Pearl?"

"He hadn't when I left."

I stood before the fire and Kenty washed the crusted blood from my face. He made a cup of steaming chocolate and had me take off my boots. The drink made me sleepy.

"Tell me about it, Jeff."

"I gave Mama the purse and opened the package you gave me. Bant threw the purse in the fire and took my gun outside and smashed it against the oak. He hit me after that. I wasn't afraid, but I left."

"Maybe it's just as well. This thing had to come to a head sometime."

"Mama says we'll leave. She thinks she can get a job in the city."

"Bant won't stand for it. He'd follow."

"We can't go on like this."

"No."

"Maybe he couldn't find us."

"That's the way it'll have to be. We'll have to slip off one day while he's in town and go somewhere he can't find you."

"Fort Worth, maybe," I said.

"He'd think of Fort Worth first. So we'll go to Houston or Shreveport. I'll take you and stay until I get you settled. We'll go through Fort Worth and Pearl can mail him a letter from there. We can make it seem she has a job keeping house there and that'll throw him off the trail."

"When, Kenty?"

"When Pearl decides to go. I don't want to rush her. She's going to have to make up her own mind."

I wanted to sleep. My eyelids were heavy, my eyes gritty. "Kenty, does Bant think I'm your son?"

Kenty stared at the flames a long time.

"Yes."

It snowed again during the night and Kenty and I were housebound all the next day. There was a hush over all the world, a hush that seemed to soothe me. We were up early to do the chores and then settled down in front of the fireplace to read. In the afternoon we popped corn and Kenty played his fiddle some, talked of hunting, but not once did we mention Bant.

Kenty went out before dusk to milk and feed the stock. I brought in wood and swept the living room floor, heated water and washed dishes. Kenty fried potatoes and made cornbread and we ate before full dark.

Bant came just as we finished eating.

I heard his halloo in the yard and peeped out the window.

He was standing under a giant oak at the edge of the clearing with his shotgun cradled. He wore his old army coat and had a scarf around his neck, his hat pulled low.

"He's come for me," I said.

"Well," Kenty said, "he can just go home empty handed."

"He's got his gun."

"Maybe he's thinking of bagging a rabbit."

"Don't go out there, Kenty," I begged as he left his chair by the fire. "Let me talk to him."

"You sit still and don't worry," Kenty said, slipping into his coat. "Bant Carr's got more sense than to use that gun, and he'd only wear his fists out against my hard head. We won't have any trouble."

He opened the door and stepped outside, closed the door behind him. I stayed at the window, not able to see Kenty on the porch. Bant stayed where he was, shifted the gun only slightly.

"Is Jeff in there, Kenty?"

"He's here."

"Tell him to get his things and come with me."

"I'll not tell him, Bant."

"Don't cause any trouble, Kenty. You're treading shaky ground when you get mixed up in family trouble."

"You didn't try to stop the boy when he left your place, Bant. What's more you hit him with your fist. That's pretty rough treatment."

"What's your interest?" Bant took three short steps and let his left hand slide up and down the barrel of the gun.

"I've known you a long time, Bant. You and Pearl have been my best friends. But I'm not going to have Jeff mistreated any more. Go on home, Bant, and think it over. Go home and think about a man that uses fists on a boy. Think about a man who hardened his heart against his son and learned to hate his wife. Think about a man who poisoned his own mind with hate and whiskey."

"Send Jeff out here, Kenty," Bant said. "I'm within my rights and I'll go in and get him if I have to."

"The boy is free to go with you if he wants, Bant. But he's free to stay here, too."

"Jeff?" Bant called. "Come out on the porch!"

"Stay where you are, Jeff," Kenty said.

The way I figured it, I might as well go out and face Bant and get it over with. He wouldn't leave until I did. All along I'd known he'd show up.

Kenty didn't try to stop me. I walked to the edge of the porch and faced Bant, took a few steps forward.

"Come on down from there," he said.

I shook my head, the courage draining out of me. "Don't argue with me! Come on out here!"

"Not until Mama sends for me." My voice trembled. It was hard to face him and it seemed senseless. I wished I'd listened to Kenty and stayed inside.

"Are you going to mind me, Jeff?"

It was then Kenty touched my shoulder and then I made up my mind. For a moment I had wavered, but Kenty's touch helped me spin around and run back inside the house.

"There's your answer, Bant," Kenty said.

"Then it's on your head. I'm within my rights."

"Bant!" Kenty shouted. "Don't be a fool!"

He came diving through the doorway to land rolling on the floor. "Down, Jeff!" he yelled. Bant's gun roared and glass shattered. I ran to the door and slammed it shut, and in an instant's time before the door slammed I saw Bant standing with gun raised. Kenty pulled me down then and held me down. Bant shot again and buckshot rattled around the room.

"Send the boy out, Kenty!"

"Go home, Bant! You must be crazy drunk!"

"I'll give you one minute! That door better open in one minute!"

"You'd be a good target out there, Bant," Kenty shouted. "I'd be within my rights to shoot you down!"

"You wouldn't do it, though," Bant said, laughing. "You know I'm not trying to hurt you and I'm not trying to hurt the boy. But you'd better not crowd your luck too far."

"Tell you what," Kenty said. "You go on home. Tomorrow you meet me in town in front of the bank and we'll talk this whole thing out."

"You've got about ten seconds!"

I counted to ten but I must have counted too fast. I started counting again and was at six when Bant's gun roared again.

A dog yelped once.

"That does it!" Kenty said, jumping up.

Kenty was like a mad thing. He ran to the fireplace and took his gun from its deer-prong resting place above the mantel. I yelled at him to stop, but he opened the door and raged outside. In panic I followed, but Bant was gone.

One of Kenty's dogs was dead in the snow. The other dogs stood around it, sniffing, and then crouched and whined as Kenty knelt.

"The man's crazy!" Kenty raged. "We've got to get Pearl away from there, Jeff! The man's really crazy!"

"It's my fault," I said, miserable. "I shouldn't have come here."

Kenty shook his head. "It's not your fault, son. This trouble started without your help. I'm more to blame than anybody."

I helped Kenty bury his dog. He didn't have much to say and I felt guilty. The dog was valuable. I knew that, but I knew, too, that Kenty wasn't thinking of the dog's value. There was nothing I could say or do to help him.

We went to bed early. Kenty banked the fires and saw me to my bed.

"Get some sleep, Jeff. Try not to worry. We'll figure things out tomorrow. This thing had to come to a head sooner or later and it's time for a showdown... even if I have to talk to the sheriff."

"I'm sorry about everything, Kenty."

"It's not your fault. Above all things, it's not your fault."

I heard him moving around the house, then heard the springs of his bed creak in the next room. My bed had been his mother's bed, a four-poster stuffed with feathers. I was warm and tired, even sleepy, but I knew I couldn't sleep.

Why, I asked myself, don't you admit Kenty is your father and just tell him you want to live with him? Wouldn't that solve everything? Yet, wouldn't that shame Bant more than he's been shamed? And why do you cling to Bant? You do. You do. After all that's happened, you do. You can't bring yourself to believe, really believe, that Kenty is your father and Bant is not. You dodge around it like a child.

It was too much for me to solve. Plans went around and around in my head, but most were fanciful things that wouldn't work or couldn't work until years had passed. All I knew was that I'd cause more trouble, maybe a killing, if I stayed under Kenty's roof. In my mind's eye I could see myself going to the city and making a fortune. I could see myself returning in a big car, could see Bant old and gray, with tears in his eyes, telling me how sorry he was.

Common sense pushed the thoughts aside.

The clock in the living room struck twelve and even while it was striking I thought of the Narrows. Something told me it was silly to think I could live in a cave, but I made myself believe I could go there and hide until Mama made up her mind to go away. I couldn't stay with Kenty. That I knew. Bant would be back and bring trouble with him.

I threw the covers aside and dressed in the darkness, shivering in the cold,

crept on tiptoe down the hall and into the living room and to the door. The
wind mourned around the corners of the house and the house groaned and
creaked. I stopped with my hand on the doorknob, wondering if I could really live in the Narrows, thinking for the first time of what I'd eat there. I
even thought of going to stay with Samal and Festal and then decided that
would be the first place Kenty or Bant would look.

Kenty's shotgun was over the mantel but I didn't know where he kept his
shells. His .22 was leaning against the wall near the fireplace and I'd seen
a box of shells on the mantel the night before. I didn't think Kenty would
mind if I borrowed the gun and shells. I even thought of returning to the
bedroom for a blanket but decided against it for fear of waking Kenty.

"Jeff?" Kenty's voice came to me faintly and I froze with my hand on his
gun. I heard bedsprings creak and then it was quiet except for the sound of
wind outside and the groaning creak of rafters. I fumbled for the shells on
the mantel, found them and put them in my pocket. Then, on tiptoes, I went
to the door and eased it open. The wind was an icy blast. I eased the door
shut behind me and walked cautiously to the edge of the porch. Snowflakes
stung my face and I was glad it was snowing again, hoped it would snow
enough to cover my tracks.

The snow was knee-deep and I floundered. I had no gloves and the gun
was cold to my hand. My coat was heavy but in no time at all I was shaking with cold, walked with face down and chin buried in my collar, tired before I'd gone a hundred yards.

It was a nightmare trip, never ending. I ran into trees, stumbled into brush,
struggled through the woods half-crying. More than once I was tempted to
go back, but the thought of Kenty's dead dog kept me going. I did wish I'd
left a note.

A low-hanging limb hit my face, raked across my swollen nose, and stab-
bing pain made me sick. Ten minutes later I ran into a fence. The barbs raked
my chest and arms, but I knew where I was and felt my way down the fence-
line until I sensed an intersecting fence ahead of me. Beyond was the road
running north and south and the Narrows lay three miles to the north. I
crawled under the fence and waded through the ditch, chest deep in drifted
snow. After that the walking was easier and I stepped out briskly, spirits rising. Still it took another hour to walk the three miles and I was exhausted
when I saw the first hills at the edge of the Narrows.

A chill of fear touched me for the first time. I remembered the stories about
lost boys, of the girl who'd drowned in a pool and whose ghost had been seen
by hunters. I was hungry, too, and couldn't help but think of Kenty's flap-
jacks with maple syrup, of Mama's scrambled eggs and biscuits with butter.
Maybe at first light, I thought, I can pot a rabbit or find a possum or maybe
a squirrel. And then I thought of fire, and fire made me think of matches. I

felt frantically in my pockets, breathed a little easier when I found three matches. But my stupidity scared me and shook me and I wondered if I could keep a fire going and if I could really get along on my own. I thought of Mama, too, and what she'd think when she learned I'd left Kenty. I began to wonder if I shouldn't have stayed at home, because now I wouldn't know if Bant mistreated Mama. Still, thinking back, I remembered all the trouble started with me and that my presence always started the trouble with Bant. Maybe with me gone there'd be no trouble.

The road dipped downhill and snowbanks piled dimly white on each side. It had stopped snowing and the quiet was eerie, unnatural, a smothered quiet that made me think I could hear my own blood coursing through my body. My breathing was labored, the crunch of my footsteps loud, and I walked hesitantly, poised for flight, every sense alert, my body one immense tingling prickle. I stumbled over a boulder and fell full-length in the snow, came up to my knees with a scream choking in my throat. I was off the road.

Tears of fright rolled down my cheeks and turned to ice.

I shuddered as though with ague. But for some inner voice that attempted to calm me I would have bolted back up the hill and straight to Kenty's house. But the voice of reason cajoled and threatened, said: Listen, Jeff, you've come this far and if you go back now you're licked and Kenty will think you a fool, and besides he'll know you came back in fright and he's never been afraid in his life and won't understand what scared you.

It helped. After a while the shaking fear left me, though I still shook with cold. The darkness couldn't last forever and I had little chance to find a cave in the dark. I crawled around until my hand touched the bole of a tree and then I sat on a rock and scrunched up to wait out the night. Cold as it was, I slept for minutes at a time, roused myself to run in place and flail my arms. It was gray light when I awoke the last time, and with the night went my fear. Again I was confident I could fend for myself.

In the dawn the Narrows stood revealed in soft light.

Trees were weighted with snow, their branches drooping. Hillocks and rocks were indistinguishable from snowdrifts and I realized it would be no easy task to find the cave I remembered.

I was stiff with cold, sluggish, slow moving, and knew I had to have a fire. Food I must have, too, but how to get it was another problem. I scolded myself for not getting meat and bread from Kenty's kitchen.

I gathered up my gun and stumbled along, hesitant and worried, trying to think what Kenty would do in my place. I'd not gone more than a dozen steps before a cottontail jumped from its nest at the base of a snow-covered bush to crouch, nose quivering, in my path. It startled me. I dropped the gun and shouted in dismay as soon as I realized what I'd done. The rabbit scurried while I fumbled in the snow for the gun.

The rabbit bounded away, kicking up snow with its hind feet, and I fell to my knees and tried for a sighting. Once I fired and the bullet went wide of its mark. The sound of the little gun, a sharp crack, bounded off the hills and bounced again, echoing now near and now far. The rabbit stopped, half-buried in the snow, and I sighted carefully. My stomach was queasy, my breathing fast, and my hand trembled. I forced myself to breathe deeply, breathed in and exhaled, squeezed the trigger slowly, squeezed slowly. The rabbit jumped with the cr-rr-aaack of the gun, leaped high and kicked its feet convulsively, and there was my breakfast in the snow.

My spirits soared. I shouted in triumph and ran to the rabbit. It was fat, warm and soft and fat, and I could almost taste it, so hungry was I.

The drifts were deep and more than once I stumbled into snowbanks deeper than I stood. How far I walked I had no way of telling. Nor could I determine in which direction I traveled. Canyons intersected canyons and I had little choice but to follow, all the while searching for shelter. The sun came out, cheering me with its promise of warmth, and then disappeared. It began to snow again, slowly at first and then harder, the flakes as large as my fingernails, so thick I felt they'd smother me. At last weariness forced me to rest. My hands were numb and my face throbbed and hurt. I knew my nose was swollen, knew my eyes were puffed. I felt feverish, light-headed and sleepy.

Crouching there in the snow it was easy to feel sorry for myself. I even imagined myself dead, cold and dead and lost there in the canyon of the Nar-rows. I imagined how it would be when they found me, the neighbors led by Kenty and his dogs. They'd find me there, half-buried in the snow, and stand silently around me while Bant stooped to pick me up. Tears would stream down his cheeks and he'd hold me close and sob aloud, but never a word of sympathy would the others give him.

But it was too cold to sit there and die. I wanted to be warm, wanted to fill my stomach with rabbit, wanted to curl up on the leaves before a fire and sleep.

My eyes must have seen the two holes a dozen times and hadn't registered the information in my brain. One hole in the cliff above me was ten feet up, with another to the right and five feet higher. The cliff face was filmed with snow, but I saw, or imagined I saw, a ledge just beneath the lower hole.

I raked snow from the cliff wall and studied the cracks and outcroppings. Desperation more than anything else helped me make up my mind. I took off my belt and slung the rifle on my back, stuffed the rabbit under my jacket, and began to climb.

It was easy at first. I scrabbled at the snow above me and cleared it from the face of the cliff, wedged fingers into cracks and found footholds on knobs of stone or small outcroppings. Once I missed a handhold, slipped a little and scratched my hands, found fingers suddenly numb, strained to hold myself, looked down for a place to land if I fell. I realized then how foolish I'd been, for surely there were stones beneath the snow below. If I should fall and turn an ankle or break a leg, I'd freeze or starve before Kenty could find me.

There was nothing for it but to go on up the cliff and I gritted my teeth and took chances I had to take. Twice more I slipped. Once I hung free without foothold, hanging by my fingers, and was saved only when my foot scraped an outcropping far to my left. And then, when I least expected it, I reached the ledge, found a good handhold and pulled myself up.

The ledge was no more than twelve inches wide, not more than four or five feet long, tapering to nothing at both ends. The hole was not more than four feet above the ledge, perfectly round, a chimneylike hole more than two feet in diameter. Standing, I peered inside. It was dark in there, black dark, but the first thing I noticed was the warm air that touched my face even though I barely poked my head inside.

My eyes became accustomed to the darkness and I saw a nest of grass and leaves. At first I feared some animal might be lurking inside, but finally decided an owl nested there. Still, to be on the safe side, I shoved the gun ahead of me as I crawled in, using it for a shield. I was forced to slide along and found the tube not so dark as I thought. It was a queer feeling to slide along through solid rock, a shut-in feeling, but the discomfort was more than discounted by the warmth.

Still, I thought, I can't stay here. The place will do for one night's sleeping, but there is too much danger in the climbing to risk coming out. Sheer luck was with me. Or the Lord. The tube curved sharply to the right and widened, and there below me was the cave I'd visited on the possum hunt with Kenty and Bant. It had been dark then, but light came through the second hole I'd seen. Drifting snow had covered the opening at ground level and I would never have found it from the outside. I became convinced the Lord had guided me and that everything would be all right in the end. I was more convinced of it still when I saw the wood and leaves on the cave floor, some of the wood charred and blackened by hunters' fires.

When you have three matches only, you take care in building a fire. I gathered leaves and wood, shielded my match carefully until the leaves were blazing. Then, carefully, I fed twigs to the fire, nursed the flame, coaxed it and took no chances. In no time my hands were warm and soon my shivering stopped. I explored, then, found a battered coffee pot and a fruit jar half-filled with coffee. I filled it with snow from the opening and set it over the fire.

The rabbit was cold and stiff, hard to skin and clean. It didn't look so large and fat after I'd cleaned it, but my mouth watered as I spitted it on a stick and held it over the flames.

I added more snow to the pot and poured coffee in. In the end I ate the rabbit half raw, tearing at the meat, half chewing, crunching the bones for the marrow. And when I'd swallowed the last morsel, I drank coffee from a tomato can and then I slept until late afternoon.

I tunneled through the snow at the opening, took my gun and stepped outside. It seemed colder. I walked down the canyon and searched for tracks, hoping to follow a bunny to its lair. Tracks there were aplenty, tracks running helter-skelter, but though I hunted until it was too dark to see I didn't find a rabbit.

There was plenty of wood in the cave for the night, but for lack of something else to do I burrowed in the snow under a dead oak to look for more. In the cave, warm and snug, I found I wasn't sleepy.

Somewhere a coyote mourned and somewhere an owl hooted.

Try as I would I couldn't sleep. The fire cast flickering light and shadows moved on the walls. It would have been easy to make out figures of monsters in those shadows.

Once I dozed, but the sound of a hunter's horn brought me wide awake. Finally, after long hours, I fell into a shallow sleep. Dawn was breaking when I awoke coughing, a pain in my chest.

At first, half-asleep, I was only half-conscious of the pain. My throat was raw with coughing. It hurt to breathe, but sleep was a coveted thing. I pushed pain back, held on to sleep, and came awake only when a spasm of coughing racked my body.

I knew at once what it was, knew at once it wasn't flu because I'd had flu and knew the musty taste that went with it. This was pneumonia and I knew it, for already the fever was high and already the pain in my chest seared with each breath, with each cough.

The fire had burned out, but embers still glowed. One match of three had lighted that fire. Two left. In sudden panic I crawled to my supply of wood and fed the fire, blew until it flamed, then lay back down. I shivered and yet I wasn't cold. I realized it must have been cold in the night, with the fire burned out, and that the fever must have made me unaware of the cold.

A fit of shaking hit me, doubled me, made my teeth chatter. Sweat poured, wet my face. I coughed raspingly, fighting for breath. I realized I was thirsty and had to crawl to the entrance for snow to melt. I washed my face in the snow and let huge mouthfuls melt in my mouth.

Back at the fire I tried to think what to do. There were two choices: stay where I was and die, or risk walking to Kenty's house. There was a possibility, though slim, that Kenty would find me in the cave or that hunters would use the cave for shelter and find me. Whether I had the strength to walk I didn't know.

Mercifully, the choice wasn't mine. Sleep, or perhaps a light delirium, made a choice unnecessary. I remember hearing voices, remember being lifted, and remember being cold for a short time only. And then someone lifted me and held a cup to my lips, held it there until I swallowed a warm liquid. I opened my eyes and saw a fire in Kenty's fireplace. Samal's face seemed to be floating pretty near.

"Go to sleep," Kenty's voice came from afar. "Go to sleep and don't worry about a thing. Your mother's on the way."

CHAPTER FIFTEEN

I was sick three weeks, and in all that time Bant didn't come into my room. Mama told me it was Bant who wrapped me in a blanket and brought me home from Kenty's house, but not once did he come into my room.

When I was able to walk I looked for the gun Kenty had given me. I figured it was smashed beyond repair, but I wanted it because Kenty had given it to me.

Mama saw me looking. "It's under the house, Jeff, on a beam by the chimney. Don't let Bant know you've found it."

The stock was splintered, but the gun was unharmed. I left it under the house and went to the barn for some baling wire and pliers. Under the house again I wrapped the stock with the wire, wound it tight, and the gun was as good as new except for looks. I cleaned it good and wrapped it in rags, left it on a crossbeam under the house. Two weeks later I was strong enough to go to school.

Bant ignored me and I ignored him. I did my chores, studied my lessons, ate at the same table with Bant and shared the same fire. My teacher helped me at school and I made up my grades, but life at home settled back into a dread routine. Mama let me slip over to see Kenty on Saturdays and told Bant I was in the woods if he came home early. Twice I visited Festal and Samal. Festal helped me carve a new stock for the gun.

"Where's that gun Kenty gave Jeff?" Bant once asked Mama.

"You smashed it, Bant," she said.

"Where'd you throw it?"

"In the ditch down the road a piece. More than likely some kid picked it up."

Bant scowled and looked a hole through me.

Spring came at last and Bant began breaking the ground for planting. It had been a wet winter and looked to be a wet spring.

There were times that spring when I thought Bant was losing his mind, times when I thought he was just plain mean, and times when I thought liquor was driving him mad. One thing I knew for sure. He couldn't stand the sight of me. Looking back on it, I can see that he fought himself hard, reasoned with himself, tried to quit liquor. I didn't have many chances to slip off to Kenty's house or roam the woods with Festal or visit with Samal.

Summer came on and we had a good stand of cotton and corn, but we had little rain and the sun dried the earth, baked it until veinlike cracks opened in the fields. The cotton drooped and the corn was stunted. Even the weeds wilted and the Johnson grass turned yellow and sick.

I worked harder than I'd ever worked before. Bant gave me no directions, no orders, and I hoed and plowed from sunup to sundown in an effort to please him. Sometimes I worked at his side, but never a word did he have for me. He was a stranger. Even his physical appearance changed. Once he had been wide shouldered and straight and strong. Now he was stooped. His face was lined and his hands trembled. His eyes seemed vacant, dull, and once they had been wide and clear, laughing alive.

July came and I knew we must have rain. We had plowed constantly in an effort to bring up the moisture, but now only rain could save the crops. We watched the skies and prayed for rain, but day after day the sun came up in a cloudless sky.

Bant didn't spare himself and rarely went to town. At night he went early to bed. He was always in the fields ahead of me in the mornings.

Festal had a few acres of corn and potatoes, but no cash crop. I wondered how he and Samal would live, but they didn't seem to worry. I found out later that Old Trails had hidden money in fruit jars and Festal knew their hiding places.

One day after lunchtime Sam and Festal appeared on the porch and Mama brought out some cookies she'd baked. Bant was working on the engine of the Model T. We talked about the drought and though I'd never seen him look as fit, Festal looked tired, but it was tired from working the farm, not from having to hide under houses or in barns.

Bant never came to the house. Samal took me aside while Festal helped Mama clean up after our snack. The first thing she did was pull me around the side of the house and kiss me full on the lips. It reminded me of our times past but there seemed something else in it as well.

"We're leaving, Jeff. Festal and me. That money Festal dug up isn't going to last forever and the two of us can't work the farm unless we give up to it, just like Pa. I'm not going to do that, Jeff, and I won't let Festal. Do you understand?"

I didn't want to let go of her. "But why, Sam? You know Kenty will look after you if the crops don't come in."

She pulled away. "It's not that, Jeff Carr. We can't live on that old place forever and Festal needs something he's never had before. I still have a hard time making him sleep in the house some nights."

"But Sam...." I really didn't know what else to say, I just didn't want her to leave.

"Hush now, Jeff. You helped make me who I am, and a woman doesn't just forget her first." She stepped closer and kissed once more. "You'll see me again." And just like that the spark was back in her eyes and she bounced back around the porch, calling for Festal.

He came out of the house and we shook hands. He knew what Sam was telling me. "Goodbye, Jeff. You've been the only friend I've ever had."

I knew it was true but I just kept thinking about losing Sam. "Take care of her, Festal. Like she'll take care of you."

"I will," he promised.

I slept late one morning and Bant had been in the field an hour when Mama called me. She fixed my breakfast and I ate hurriedly.

"Take a jug of water when you go," Mama said.

"Where's he working?"

"In the east forty." She went to the door and peered through the screen. "He's plowing the peanuts today... I see a cloud bank in the west. Maybe it'll rain." She turned to me and I saw how tired she looked, saw the circles under her eyes like bruises. "If it would only rain," she said. "If we could make a good crop...."

I filled the water jug and walked across the field. It was not yet nine and already the heat was a living and hating thing. There were clouds in the sky, far distant, and even as I watched they scudded away before the wind, leaving the sun to glow and parch and bake.

The jug I left in the shade of a tree at the fencerow. The peanuts didn't need hoeing, but there was nothing else to be done and I meant to hoe. My hoe was leaning against the fence. I sharpened it and went to work.

A wind came up at noon and low-flying clouds sent shadow patches across the earth. I saw Bant unhitch and throw the trace chains over the backs of the horses, heard the chains jangling as he led out toward the barn. I shouldered my hoe and followed, helped unharness, ran after Bant to the porch.

We stood there, faces uplifted, watched the sun disappear behind the clouds.

Long before the rain fell I could smell it, moist and clean and cool. First there was the smell of rain on the breeze and then the breeze stiffened and dust came skirling. At last came drops of rain, big splattering drops that plopped in the dry dust to skid and roll wet dust balls. The rain came at last, a torrent. Water ran into cracks with sucking sounds. I never see rain now that I don't think of that rain. And in my mind's eye I can still see those first drops falling in the dry dust, can see them balling up and rolling along, covered balls of water.

Bant lifted his arms and shouted, laughed and shouted, and Mama drove the chickens into the henhouse. I ran to help her, was drenched, and ran with her to the porch to watch the rain. Mama's lips moved and I knew she was praying her thankfulness, knew she was praying that Bant would stop drinking, that he'd make his peace with me, with her, with himself.

"This cinches a good crop," Bant exulted. "It's all we needed."

"I hope the tank fills up," Mama said.

"It's full by now."

The rain continued for another hour, slackened, and the skies began to clear. Soon the sun peeped from behind a cloud and steamed against the wet earth.

"It's over," Bant said. "It's over, but it's enough for now."

Mama sent me to let the chickens out of the henhouse. Bant was shaving on the front porch when I returned. He had hung a mirror on the wall.

Drops of rain still dribbled from the porch roof. I sat on the steps and looked at the new-green world.

Bant lathered his face, using the brush that was his father's before him. He began to shave, sweeping the long, straight razor through the heavy bristles on his face. The razor made a dry scraping sound and left small neat rows of brown skin behind. Finished shaving, he went into the bedroom and dressed. He put on his blue suit, combed his hair and got his white Stetson.

"Bant," Mama said, "let the boy go with you. He's worked hard all summer."

Bant glanced at me. "All right," he said.

I wanted to go and didn't want to go, wanted to go to town but didn't want to ride alone with Bant. Just the same I changed clothes, put on a white shirt and clean overalls, slicked my hair down with water.

Bant waited in the car. He'd had a drink. I could tell that first off, could smell it on his breath. I wished I could think of a reason for not going and was afraid to say I didn't want to go. He cranked the motor, adjusted the spark, and we drove out of the yard. Mama stood on the front porch and watched us go. I huddled into my corner of the seat and didn't speak all the way to town. Bant was engrossed in his own thoughts and paid me no mind.

We parked in front of the drugstore across the street from the courthouse. Bant got out of the car and stepped up on the sidewalk. After a minute he went into Berry's Clothing Store and I followed him.

"This boy needs a cap," Bant told the man behind the counter.

I didn't know what to say, didn't know what to think.

"He sure does," the clerk said, pleased to make a sale. "How about this one?"

The clerk took down a Baker Boy with a brown, herringbone pattern.

"Looks good to me," Bant said.

"I'll take that one." I said it before I even had a chance to think about it. The cap I pointed to was rounder, Brooklyn style like the baseball players wear. And red.

"A little flashy," Bant said.

"I like it."

Bant nodded and carefully counted out his money.

We walked out, and it seemed the temperature had dropped a good ten degrees. No rain now, but the clouds had thickened enough to make it feel like dusk.

"Where's that music comin' from?" Bant asked.

I hadn't noticed. Then I caught it, flutes and strings, drifting on wind.

"That must be the circus," I said.

"They in town already?"

"Didn't you see the posters?"

I could feel the excitement building up in me now. I felt ready and smart in my new cap. We crossed town, and headed to the fields past the rail line. A good half-dozen canvas tents rolled and flapped in the wind.

I hurried ahead of Bant a little, the scent of dung not strong enough to overpower the sweet odor of cotton candy, popcorn and other treats.

"Hold on there," Bant said.

He smiled at me, reached into his pocket, and gave me four quarters and a nickel.

"Really?"

"Meet me in front of the bank in two hours," Bant said.

That's when I knew. Bant wasn't happy to get me to the circus. He just wanted more to drink.

The circus only had some mangy llamas from somewhere in South America that looked sort of like that camel Sam and I had seen so long ago. There were a few cages with sad-eyed monkeys begging in their cages. In truth, the circus was more of a traveling show with a few wore-out animals.

I jumbled the coins in my pocket, trying to decide between the geek shows and Luxor, Magician and Mindreader of the Nile. The whipping wind made the canvas painting of his assistant, Isis, seem to belly dance.

It cost me twenty cents.

The inside of the tent was dark and cool. I strained to look over the crowd of big farm boys and men in front of me, the stench of their sweat almost overpowering.

Luxor performed some magic tricks, mostly sleight-of-hand, and let loose a dove that seemed to fly out of his sleeve. Isis wasn't as pretty as the picture outside, though she did have a good figure. I stared at her breasts and bare stomach.

Luxor said something about the spectral powers of the mind. He sat down, and Isis blindfolded him. She walked around among the people. Now and then she would stop and touch some article of clothing or ring worn by a man or woman and immediately the magician would name the article and color.

Isis reached me, smiled, and touched my cap.

"What am I touching?" she asked.

The magician laughed, started to speak, then doubled over with laughter. "You're touching a cap!" he gasped.

"What color is it?"

"It's red! It's a red cap!" And he bellowed with laughter and the room was alive with laughter, resounding with laughter.

I fled.

I ran through the crowd until the laughter was behind me and then I took off the cap and threw it on the ground.

It took a long time to find Bant.

He wasn't at the bank. He was at the monkey show. I saw him go in. Tickets were only fifteen cents, so I went inside, too.

Bant was drunk.

He reeked of liquor. His shirt collar was open, the tie askew, and even his Stetson was rumpled. His eyes were bleary and his mouth slack. It made me sick to look at him, made me sick and ashamed inside.

"Where's your cap?" he asked, thickly.

"I... lost it."

He grunted.

"I'm sorry, Bant."

"Waste of good money," he muttered. "Such a pretty cap, too."

"I'm sorry."

We watched the monkeys walk on stilts, skate, jump off poles into the arms of their master.

"Let's get out of here," Bant said. "Get some air."

He drove back to town, not fast, and parked in front of the lumberyard. "Stay here if you want," he said. "I'll be ready to go home in a little while."

"All right."

He walked off up the street, weaving a little, and I waited in the car. It was hot. I slept a little, walked up and down the sidewalk. Two hours passed and it was five o'clock. I waited until six and then decided to go find Bant.

He wasn't hard to find. He was on the street corner by the bank, his back against a lamppost, encircled by men.

Kenty Hooker was there.

"How's my boy?" Kenty asked, tousling my hair. "You haven't been over lately. I've got a new calf. Thought if you'd come over I'd let you name it. You're about the best when it comes to naming animals."

Papa scowled. "Thought I told you to wait in the car."

"He's had a long wait," Kenty said. "You've been here a while."

"None of your business," Bant growled. "Go on back to the car," he ordered.

"Mama'll be worried," I said. "Let's go home, Bant."

He motioned with his thumb. "In the car. Now."

"I'm hungry," I said. "Why'nt we go on home, Bant?"

His slap was as fast and unexpected as the striking of a snake. It caught me on the cheek and sent me spinning, burned like fire and made me see stars. I almost fell.

Kenty slapped Bant.

It was the wrong thing to do. I knew that as soon as it happened. Kenty should have known better, too.

Bant went at Kenty like a wild man, clawing and kicking and hitting out with his fists. I doubt if he knew where he was or why he was fighting or if he even cared whether he fought fair or foul.

Kenty backed away and protected himself the best he could. The crowd of men made a big circle and it was hard for me to break through.

Bant went down, got back up. Kenty struck out suddenly, like a cat, and Bant went down. He didn't stay down. He shook his head like a mad bull and swarmed right up and into Kenty. I screamed at the top of my lungs for them to stop, but neither heard me.

Kenty swung a left at Bant, slipped and almost fell. Bant wasn't too drunk to take advantage of the slip. He went in fast, pumping both fists, and I could hear the crunch as his blows landed against Kenty's face. Kenty fell back against the bank wall. His knees sagged.

Bant had the liquor bottle in his hand. I hadn't seen him get it from his hip pocket.

"Don't!" I screamed. "Look out, Kenty!"

Maybe Kenty heard me, maybe not. It didn't matter; he couldn't dodge. The bottle glinted as Bant swung it, shattered into a hundred shining pieces as it landed. Blood spurted on Kenty's forehead, ran into his eyes and down his cheeks. Bant still had the neck of the bottle in his hand, the jagged glass a wicked weapon.

I dived. My shoulders hit Bant at the knees and he fell heavily. He hit me just the same, hit me with his left fist. I felt myself falling and rolling, came to my knees beside Kenty.

"Stay back, kid," Kenty said thickly. "Stay out of the way. The man's crazy drunk."

There was a sudden hush. You could have heard a pin drop if it hadn't been for Bant's sobbing breathing. I stayed where I was, on my knees, and Kenty was on his knees beside me.

"He sure looks like his daddy," I heard a man say.

"That's not his daddy," someone answered. "That's Kenty Hooker."

Bant was staring at me with wide eyes. He looked like he'd just seen a ghost.

"My Lord," Bant moaned. "Oh, my Lord."

He put both hands over his face and walked away.

It was crazy, a nightmare, a crazy nightmare. Bant disappeared after the fight. I looked high and low and so did Kenty, but we couldn't find him. It was good and dark when Kenty decided to take me home.

"He'll cool off," Kenty reasoned. "Tomorrow he'll apologize to both of us."

"He looked so funny," I said. "He looked at me so funny."

"Dog drunk on corn," Kenty said. "Probably couldn't see you from where he was standing."

"No," I decided. "That's not right. He could see. It was what the man said about me looking like my papa. Only he thought you were my papa."

"Don't worry about it. Come on. Your mother'll be worried."

"She'll worry more if I don't find Bant."

"He's a grown man and ought to know better. Let him be and come with me," Kenty said. "I think it'll be better if we let him be. Right now he won't be in the mood to see me. Besides, my head hurts. That wasn't exactly a love tap he gave me with that bottle."

Kenty took me home and it was after nine when we arrived. Mama was up, worried almost sick. The minute she saw Kenty she knew something was wrong.

"Where is he?" she asked. "Is he... drunk?"

"Drunk as a hoot owl and feeling fine the last we saw of him," Kenty said. "He'll be along later, so don't you fret yourself."

"You're hurt."

"A scratch," Kenty said. "Why, when I was in the Navy I wouldn't have noticed a thing like this! Guess I'm getting soft."

"You fought?"

"I didn't do much fighting," Kenty grinned. "Didn't have much of a chance."

Mama bit her lower lip, half turned away. "I'll get some warm water."

Kenty put his arm across my shoulder. "She's all fretted, Jeff, so we'll have to make it sound like nothing much happened."

"You can't fool her."

"I guess you're right."

"He looked so funny, Kenty," I said. "I felt sorry for him."

"He's a broody man," Kenty said. "Always has been broody. Even liquor won't make him happy for long. Sometimes the blackness inside him just gets the best of him, that's all."

"I thought the rain would cheer him up. I thought he wouldn't drink any more if it would rain."

Mama came in with a pan of water and a bottle of iodine. She washed the cut on Kenty's head and swabbed it with the iodine. Kenty winced and grinned.

"Now tell me what happened," Mama said.

"Aw," Kenty shrugged. "Nothing much happened. It was getting late and he was drunked up some. The kid came hunting him and wanted to go home. He slapped the kid and it made me mad, so I slapped him. I shouldn't have done it, but I did. We fought and he clipped me over the head with a bottle and that ended it."

"Mama," I said. "Mama, I tried to help Kenty instead of Bant, but Bant knocked me winding and I landed beside Kenty. Some man said I looked a lot like my daddy, only he was thinking Kenty was my daddy. And all at once Bant stared at me and Kenty like we were a couple of ghosts. He went away and we never did find him."

Mama covered her face with her hands. "I don't think I can stand it," she moaned.

Kenty patted her shoulder awkwardly. "Don't fret yourself. He was drunk and won't remember a thing about it when he sobers up."

Mama said again, "Kenty, I don't think I can stand it."

"I should have stayed away," Kenty said. "I shouldn't have come home."

"You couldn't stay away forever."

"Get that pan of water and pour it out, Jeff," Kenty suggested. "And don't let Bant know I was here."

"Kenty?" I called.

"Yeah, kid." He stopped at the door.

"I don't care if I do look like you," I said.

He grinned, shook his head, and stepped out into the darkness.

I went to bed and to sleep, but once during the night I heard Mama crying. Bant came home before daylight.

The footsteps sounded hollow and lonesome and it took me a long time to understand why they sounded so eerie and out of place. Bant was walking around with his shoes on and there was no light burning.

I heard Mama say, "Go to bed, Bant." He growled something I couldn't understand and I knew he was still drunk.

The footsteps were louder and I knew he was in the kitchen. And then the door to my room opened and the footsteps were there, just inside my doorway.

"Just a little bastard," Bant whispered.

The footsteps came into my room and waited there at the foot of my bed.

"When I was a boy," Bant said, "my old man got in a fight over a cow that got in his corn patch. The other man was bigger and stronger and was getting all the best of the fight. So do you know what I did?"

I didn't answer, couldn't answer.

"I picked up a hoe handle and laid that man out cold as a fish! That's what I did!"

But how could I hit Kenty? I wanted to ask. How could I hit Kenty?

"I guess blood is thicker than water," Bant said.

He stood there and I couldn't see him. I could hear his breathing and I could smell the whiskey on him, but though I strained my eyes I couldn't see.

And then there were footsteps outside my door, light whispering footsteps, and I knew Mama was coming into the room and I wanted to warn her to go back to bed and still I couldn't speak.

"Come to bed," she whispered. "Leave the boy alone."

There was a smack, a loud and sharp smack, and Mama cried out.

"Go to bed!" Bant screamed. "This is all your doing and you'd best stay out of my reach!"

I sat up, rage-filled and heartsick.

"Leave her alone, Bant!"

His weight was on me and his hands were on me cruel hard and he slapped me and bright streaks of light filled the room, and then his fist crashed into my face and I heard a fragment of Mama's scream and tasted blood and then I slept.

My mind came awake before my body and I lay there listening to familiar sounds, but for the life of me I couldn't remember what had happened. I knew it was late because I could feel the lateness. Birds chirruped outside. A calf bawled. I heard the contented clucking of chickens. And none of the sounds had the sound of early morning.

The house was still and quiet.

I tiptoed through the kitchen and into the other bedroom.

Bant was on the bed, sound asleep, mouth open and breath rasping. There was a heavy stubble of whiskers on his face, a dark bruise on his cheek.

Mama was on the floor. Her face was bruised. She lay on her back with her long black hair outspread like a net over the floor.

Something came over me, something dark and twisted and ugly. I screamed, turned, still screaming, and ran from the room. Without thinking, without really realizing what my actions meant, I ran to the living room fireplace and grabbed the iron poker from its nail. When I entered that room again and saw Mama on the floor I knew what was in my mind.

Bant opened his eyes and saw me standing there with the poker in my hands.

"What...?"

He moved as I struck, rolled aside, and the poker thudded against the mattress. That was my only chance to strike, for he jerked the weapon from my hands and hurled it across the room.

"Wait up," he said. There was wonder in his voice.

"You've killed her," I said.

He saw Mama for the first time, saw her and drew back with a stricken look. Almost in fear he walked around the bed, and in fear he knelt.

"She's just asleep," he said after a moment. "She'll be all right."

He picked her up and carried her to the bed, knelt there beside her briefly, his head buried in a pillow.

And for the first time I saw Bant cry.

CHAPTER SIXTEEN

Bant left the house and I got a pan of cold water and a towel, bathed Mama's face until she opened her eyes.

She smiled and her hand came to rest on my hand.

"You're my strength," she said. "I don't know what I'd do without you."

"Lie still."

"Your face is swollen."

"It doesn't hurt."

"We'll leave today." She sat up, grimaced. "We should have gone long ago. Now we'll have to leave. He hasn't left us any choice."

"I'll bring you some coffee."

"Where is he?"

"He went out."

She got out of bed and I followed her into the kitchen. She put water on to boil and went to the back porch, pulled the rocker into the shade and sat down.

We could see Bant in the cotton, hoeing like mad, chopping with fury, walking along in ankle-deep mud and chopping as if his life depended on it. It was sheer insanity. No farmer tills or hoes wet earth. Mama sat watching him, rocking and watching him. After a while I made coffee and she sat sipping it, rocking and sipping coffee and watching Bant. I sat on the steps and waited, but after an hour I went to my room. The morning passed and Mama stayed on the porch. Bant went right on chopping in the cotton patch. At noon I made some egg sandwiches but Mama didn't eat. My face was swollen and my head hurt. Mama must have been in pain, too. Her face was puffed and bruised, her left eye blacked. I bathed my face in cold water and asked Mama to let me bathe her face. She seemed not to hear me, just rocked and watched Bant hoeing in the field. I went to my room, lay across the bed, and fell asleep. The sun was scarcely two hours high when she called me.

"Jeff," she said, "go to Kenty's house and ask him to come here. Tell him I want to leave today."

I ran as fast as I could across the field, crossed the fence and ran through the woods, waded through the stream, ran faster than I'd ever run before.

Kenty was sitting in his rocker on the front porch. He saw me coming and walked down the steps.

"What is it, Jeff?"

"It's Bant. He beat Mama last night."

"Is she hurt?"

"She's all right now. She said for you to come quick because we're going to leave today."

He touched my cheek with a finger. "He hit you, too. Where is he now?"

"Hoeing cotton. He's wading in mud out in the cotton patch and flailing away like mad."

"All right," Kenty said, turning. "I'll cut across the field and talk to Bant first. Let me get my gun."

I waited in the yard and in a minute Kenty came out with his twelve-gauge cradled. He walked across the woods so fast I had to trot to keep up. We crossed the fence and headed across the cotton, slogging in mud. Bant was still flailing away with the hoe. We'd covered half the field when the rabbit jumped, a big jack. Kenty raised the gun, without thinking, and shot it before it made a half dozen leaps.

We were within fifty yards of Bant when Kenty stopped. Bant was leaning on the hoe handle.

"Jeff," Kenty said, "you go on to the house. Tell Pearl to start packing. I'll take the two of you to Fort Worth, or wherever Pearl wants to go, and get you a place to stay until we can get this thing worked out."

He walked toward Bant and I stood where I was, rooted to the spot.

Bant began to hoe. Kenty fell in step beside him and I couldn't hear what was being said.

I walked a few steps forward.

Kenty was saying something. He held his gun in his left hand and I was glad it wasn't loaded.

Bant just went on hoeing, head down, went striding along. Kenty walked beside him, still talking. They were almost to the end of the row and I walked along after them. I knew I should go to the house and tell Mama to start packing, but I couldn't leave the field.

Bant threw the hoe from him, threw it with both hands, lifted it high above his head and threw it far from him.

"Why didn't you stay away?" he yelled at Kenty. "Why didn't you leave well enough alone? You've ruined my life and shamed my home! Why did you come back?"

Kenty stepped back, half stumbled, took a quick step backward.

Bant lunged and grabbed Kenty around the waist, held him close in a bear hug, and for a long while they swayed and struggled, bending this way and that, slow and graceful with the sun low behind them, two silhouettes locked in a terrible dance.

I ran, mouthing pleas, begging them to stop, yelling for Mama.

They were down, rolling over and over in the mud. First one of them was on top and then the other. They were covered with mud, slippery smeared with mud. I stood back and yelled at them, but they didn't know I was within a hundred miles. Their breathing was raspy and labored. Once I heard Kenty say, "Bant, you crazy fool, what in hell's got into you? Why don't you stop this foolishness and act like a grown man? Don't you know you're going crazy? Why don't you calm down and think?" And Bant cursed him with bitter curses I'd never before heard pass his lips.

Kenty worked an arm out of Bant's bear hug and used his muddy hand to force Bant's chin backwards as far as he could push. Bant broke his grip and reared back on his knees, still sitting atop Kenty. He brought his right fist up behind his shoulder and I was scared to see the look on his face.

"Bant, stop!" I screamed but it didn't make any difference.

Bant slammed his fist downward at Kenty's head but he half-rolled on his side as Bant's giant hand pounded a hole deep into the mud. Kenty gave another shove as he rolled again and got to his knees before Bant could come square around. They stood up, wiping mud from their faces with their forearms. Quick as anything Kenty started hitting Bant with those fast jabs of his, dodging the wild, more powerful swings of Bant's.

All the wet hoeing had taken its toll on Bant, and he tired quickly. Kenty kept at him until Bant finally fell to his hands and knees, then slowly collapsed into the mud, going down like a circus tent after the stakes had been pulled.

I went to Kenty and stopped short of touching him. He tried to give me a smile through all the mud on his face but I could hear the difference in his breathing after being in the force of Bant's grip. "Guess maybe I should have tried to talk to the old fool from a greater distance."

"You okay, Kenty?"

He looked down at Bant, using his foot to clear some of the mud away from Bant's face. "I'm okay, Jeff. Let's go see about Pearl."

I put my arm around Kenty's waist because it felt right and he did lean a little of his weight against me as we walked. Mama met us halfway out in the yard. "How is he?"

"Bant's all right, Pearl," Kenty said. "But it's past time we took care of what we both knew was coming."

Mama looked into the field at the still figure of her husband, then looked away. "Jeff," she said, "could you see to the chickens and cows while Kenty and I talk about some things?"

"Yes, Mama."

"Thank you, Jeff," said Kenty.

I went to the barn and fed the chickens but I didn't do any milking. I kept thinking about Bant laying out there in the mud and wondered if this time Mama and me were really going to leave. When Kenty finally called me outside, I ran all the way to the porch.

"Bant okay?" he asked.

I looked over at the still figure in the mud. "Doesn't seem to have moved much. You sure licked him pretty good."

Kenty scratched at his cheek. "Well, he was good enough to have already started in on himself before I got here."

"How's Mama?"

He knelt down and put his arm on my shoulder. "Jeff, I promised you both I wouldn't let Bant hurt you any more. And I won't. She's in there packing. I want you to make sure the chores are done in the barn while I go get my car. When I get back, I'll take you both out of here."

I just looked at him.

"You understand me?"

"Yes, Kenty."

"Go on, then. Bant should be well enough where he is for now. A hang-over and a beating would keep most men quiet for a time."

I didn't want Kenty to go. I was still too afraid of Bant. Kenty looked like some kind of creature that had just crawled his way up out of the field. I put my arm around his waist again and helped him make his way back toward the road.

By the time we got there, Kenty's breathing was close to normal. "I'm all right now." He tousled my hair with a dirty hand. "I appreciate your support, though. Go on now, look after Pearl. I'm counting on you."

"I will, Kenty." I watched as he made his way through the fence, walking straighter and faster as he went. After he disappeared into the trees I thought about his twelve gauge and wondered if I should look for it. I started to head back to the muddy field where the fight had been.

Then I saw Bant.

He was staggering toward the house.

I yelled at Mama, yelled as loudly as I could, then ran to the fence and yelled for Kenty. I knew he couldn't hear me, but I yelled just the same. Mama came to the door and watched Bant for a moment only.

"Stop yelling, Jeff," she said calmly. "Don't be scared. I'm not going to let him hurt us this time." She turned back into the house and I heard her say, "You can depend on that, Jeff! He won't hurt us this time!"

I stood at the edge of the yard and watched Bant. His chin was on his chest and he didn't move his arms as he walked, just staggered along looking at the ground. He reminded me of an ape I'd seen in the movies, a monstrous ape that ambled along with head down, hands almost dragging the ground.

"He's nearly here, Mama," I called.

"Don't get in his way," Mama answered. "I'm nearly packed. Kenty will be back for us and we must be ready to go."

Bant stopped not a hundred yards from the house. Slowly his head came up. It was too far for me to see his mud-smeared face clearly, but I felt his eyes on me just the same. He stood there for an eternity and I was power-less to move. He dropped his head again and ambled toward me. At the fence he stooped painfully and crawled through, stood straight and looked at me. He came walking on, then, and came into the yard.

I heard the door open, heard the screen slam shut, heard Mama's footsteps on the porch, saw her shadow lengthen before me.

"Jeff," Bant said, "go to the barn and wait for me."

Terror gave me courage. "I won't go, Bant."

I was poised for flight. He was ten feet from me, facing Mama, and I fig-ured I could make it to the house ahead of him. He could outrun me, that I knew, but I knew where I was going and he didn't.

"You're making it hard on yourself, Jeff," Bant said. He took a step toward Mama. "Go to the barn and wait for me, Jeff. Get the plowline out of the sta-ble and wait for me."

"I'm not going, Bant." Terror was gone, quite suddenly gone, and I felt light as a feather, free as a bird, so suddenly happy I felt like laughing.

Bant took another step toward Mama, another, and Mama backed away, eyes wide and frightened.

"I'll tend to you later, Jeff," Bant promised.

"Don't touch Mama! If you promise not to touch Mama I'll go on to the barn like you said!"

"It's too late now. I'll tend to you when I'm ready."

He was going to hit Mama and I knew it. He was crazy and I knew it, crazy with hate. He was going to hit Mama and I was powerless to stop him.

"You hate me, Bant," I said. "You hate me, don't you?" He looked at me and laughed, baring his teeth.

"You like to whip me," I said. "Don't you? You like to hit Mama too. It makes you feel good to hurt us."

He stood still, looked at Mama, looked at me.

"I know why you hate me," I said.

Mama turned and ran into the house. Bant watched her go and laughed.

"Let's go to the barn," he said. "You went for Kenty Hooker and put him on me. You stood there and laughed because he got the best of me."

"You think Kenty's my father."

He started for me, hands outstretched, and I darted away. I made a half cir-cle, running hard, hearing his pounding steps behind me, gaining on me, and I ran, ran fast toward the house, toward the porch, but swerved just be-fore I reached the porch. I ran around the house, gaining on him because he had been sure I was going inside the house. I passed the chimney, stopped and stooped, crawled fast under the house, halfway under the house, knowing I could crawl out before he could crawl under because my size was with me and his size against him.

I crouched and peered, saw Bant crouching and peering.

"Bant," I called.

"What?"

"You know you're crazy, don't you?"

I couldn't see his face clearly, but was sure he winced. "You're crazy, Bant! You think Kenty's my father! Do you know something? I hope Kenty is my father!"

He stuck his head under the house, peered around, and I was sure he couldn't see me in the gloom.

"You're crazy, Bant!" I yelled.

I heard Mama's footsteps on the front porch, on the steps. "Don't come outside, Mama!" I yelled.

"I have Bant's gun, Jeff," she said. "It's loaded."

My gun was on the crossbeams near the chimney and I wanted it. I wanted to feel it in my hands, but Bant still crouched beside the house and was too near the chimney, too near the gun.

He stood up and I could see his legs only.

"Mama!" I yelled. "He's coming."

But Bant went the other way. I saw his legs moving away toward the fence, saw more of his legs, his hips, his body up to the waist, and then all of him as he stooped to climb through the yard fence. I crawled to my gun then, found a shell Kenty had given me, loaded the gun and crawled out from under the house. Bant was standing in the field, in cotton up to his waist, looking at me.

I couldn't think of anything to say.

"You, Jeff!" he bawled at me. "Is that a gun you've got?"

"Yessir."

"That the one Kenty gave you for Christmas?"

"Yessir."

"You'd take a gun after me, Jeff?"

"Not unless you tried to hurt Mama."

He laughed, snorting and gasping. "And she's got a gun in case I try to hurt you!"

"Yessir."

Mama came around the corner of the house. She held Bant's shotgun awkwardly.

"Jeff," she said. "Put your gun away."

"No, ma'am," I said. "You wouldn't use yours."

"Jeff has his gun to protect you, Pearl!" Bant shouted. "You have your gun to protect him! I wonder if Kenty has a gun to protect both of you!"

"Bant!" Mama called. "You come on in the house and behave yourself! It won't do for anybody to see us like this, and somebody might drive by any minute!"

"You two put those guns away and I'll come in."

"We won't bother you, Bant," Mama promised. "We'll hold on to the guns, but we won't bother you if you don't bother us. I meant it when I say you'd given the boy his last beating, Bant! And I'm serving notice you're not to cuff me around any more, either!"

Bant walked up to the fence and I held my breath for fear he'd come into the yard. He stood there staring at us, and then he began to laugh. He laughed silently, shaking all over, pointed a finger at us and slapped his thigh.

"You two make a mighty funny sight!" he said. "I tell you the truth! I wish the neighbors could see you now!"

Mama was looking at him as if she'd seen a ghost. She walked closer to the fence and leaned forward, peered closely into his face. Bant stopped laughing and the dark look came back. He scowled.

"Bant," Mama said.

"What is it'?"

"Your eyes," Mama said. "There's an awful glassy look in your eyes."

Bant backed away and held his hands out as if to push her back.

"You're out of your mind," Mama breathed. "Bant, you're out of your mind!"

Bant turned and stumbled across the field, running awkwardly through the tall cotton, weaving drunkenly.

"He's headed for Kenty's house," I said.

"You'll have to beat him there, Jeff! Run fast and circle around him! Go over to the corn patch and run down a row so he can't see you! Find Kenty and bring him here as fast as you can!"

I climbed through the fence and started running, but Mama called after me.

"Jeff! Tell Kenty to hurry! And you come back with Kenty! And leave that gun! Drop it where you are!"

But I was running fast across the cotton, the gun held slantwise across my chest, running in mud through the high cotton to the tune of swish-swish, swish-swish, brushing through the cotton with fear for Kenty urging me on.

Bant was halfway across the field by the time I reached the woods. He had veered to his right, drunkenly weaving, and I had made a beeline for the fence. I was barefooted, but still the mud sucked at my feet. Bant, I knew, would have more trouble because of his sodden work brogans. In the woods, trees formed walls on either side and branches made a roof. Except for the noise of my passage, the world was silent. I ran easily, untired, sure I could beat Bant to Kenty's house. And, strangely, I found that fear of Bant had been supplanted by fear for him. I feared Kenty would hurt him in fear.

I ran a hundred miles, a hundred yards, a mile, a yard, through a forest never ending. With each step I seemed to run faster and go slower, but I tapped some energy yet untapped and seemed to float. I thought of nothing except taking a step and a faster step and a faster longer step faster still.

Something nudged at my mind, warned my mind, and I tried to think. I remembered how Bant had veered to his right as he crossed the field. Yes, something told my mind, he was to your right and you had to turn right after you reached the woods. So he could be ahead of you or even with you, out of sight, waiting to pounce.

Fear returned and my scalp prickled.

My breath came short.

I wanted to turn around, run back.

The gun I clutched tighter, hugged it tight as if to hide behind it, suddenly cold in the knowledge I could never use it except in flaming anger.

I stood still and listened.

The leaves rustled, danced and rustled.

I'd have to leave the woods and look across the field. You're wasting time, Jeff, the voice inside me said. You're wasting time. He could be slipping up on you.

Look behind you, Jeff.

See if he's behind you.

I jumped in sudden fright and looked behind me. Then, in a panic of hurry, I ran out of the woods and looked across the field.

Bant wasn't there.

He's in the woods, I thought. I'll hide in the corn. I climbed through the fence and ran across the rows of cotton toward the corn, the stalks whipping my legs.

"Here I am, Jeff," Bant said.

I whirled around. He had stepped out of the corn and was crouched not two steps away, a crazy smile on his face, that glaring staring wild look in his eyes. I couldn't move, stood rooted, and a scream burned my throat.

He leaped at me.

I turned to run and felt his hand scrape my back. Cotton stalks seemed to clutch at my feet, fought me, seemed determined to hold me back. I turned to the right, heard cotton stalks swishing behind me, turned right again and knew I'd gained a step, maybe two. The gun was in my way and I decided to drop it, pushed it from me, saw it whirl lazily through the air, saw it land butt first and heard and almost didn't hear the sharp splatting crack and thought it odd that the gun should fire.

Bant cried out.

I looked back over my shoulder. Bant was standing quite still and straight with both hands clasped to his chest. He made a gurgling sound and blood trickled from his mouth, crimsoned his chin. He fell on his face and disappeared from my sight.

Perhaps I ran ten paces before I stopped. It was a long moment before I realized Bant had fallen because I'd thrown the gun and the gun had gone off. It took another long moment to add the cracking sound of the gun's report to Bant's cry of pain and the gurgling sound and the blood on his chin. I walked back the way I had come, afraid not to hurry and afraid to hurry.

"Jeff," Bant said, his voice muffled.

"I'm here, Bant."

"Come help me, son."

He was crawling, reaching ahead and pulling himself along, crawling and sliding and fighting his way. I reached him and walked beside him, afraid to touch him, walked slowly beside him while he wallowed his way down a cotton row. He pulled himself along a foot at a time and then lay still, face in the mud, and reached out and pulled himself forward a foot and two feet and three feet, fell flat again and rolled over.

"Bant," I said. "Be still, Bant. Be still so I can help you."

He groaned, lay still, and rolled over. There was blood on his chest, a lot of blood, and I didn't know what to do. I used my sleeve to wipe the blood from his face, wiped blood from his lips, and he smiled at me.

"I didn't do it on purpose, Bant," I said.

"You didn't do it, son," he said, his voice thin and weak. "I saw you throw the gun away. Always remember I said that. You didn't do it. I did it myself. Except that it was an accident more than anything else. It wouldn't have happened if I'd...."

A spurt of blood stained his chin.

"You oughtn't to talk, Bant. I'll run and get Kenty and he'll know what to do."

"Don't go, Jeff." I could barely hear him. "You stay with me until it's ended."

He closed his eyes and I held his hand. There was deep sorrow within me, but what had happened seemed a natural thing and a right thing and the only thing that could have happened to end the nightmare that had been building.

"I must have been crazy, like you and Pearl said," Bant whispered. "It's a funny thing. I remember everything that happened and it seemed I was doing the right thing and still something told me I was acting crazy."

"Let me go for Kenty," I said. "He'd know what to do."

"I don't want to die alone, Jeff." And then, "Jeff... listen, son. Go to your Uncle Lafe. Hear me? Go to him if you need someone. Look by the corral gate post. There's some money buried there. In a fruit jar. It's yours. Leave it until you need it and then dig for it."

I was crying and my tears fell on his face and then Mama was kneeling beside me. I hadn't heard her come, hadn't seen her, wasn't startled when she appeared from nowhere to kneel beside me.

"Bant," she said.

"I'm sorry, Pearl. Like you said, I must have been crazy."

"It's all right," Mama said. "Don't try to talk. I'll send Jeff for Kenty and he'll get the doctor."

Bant groaned and sweat beaded his face. "There won't be time. I'm a goner, sure. Take my other hand and hold it tight, Pearl, because I'm going and I'm scared. But I'm glad, too, because I was crazy and getting crazier. I'm going and I'm not ready to go and, oh, Pearl, it hurts."

"Don't talk, Bant. Don't talk. I'll send Jeff for Kenty and he'll get a doctor. We don't want you to die, Bant. We don't want you to die. Jeff wouldn't have done it if he hadn't been afraid. You know that, Bant, don't you?"

"Don't blame the boy. Don't blame the boy. Say you don't know how it happened. Hide the gun so they can't find it."

He gasped, shuddered, and died.

Mama didn't have to tell me to bow my head and fold my hands. She prayed, long and earnestly, but not once did she raise her voice and not once did her voice falter.

She prayed for herself.

How odd, I thought. Bant's dead and she should be praying for him and, instead, she's praying for herself and asking forgiveness for her sins.

I prayed silently. I asked God to forgive me. Not just for throwing the gun away and causing Bant's death, but for the things I'd thought and the bad feeling there'd been between us.

If there was salt in my tears there was alum, too, bitter alum, and I cried the bitterness and lostness out of me. Mama cried, cried quietly, the tears streaming. I think often of how we must have looked.

We cried ourselves out. It was quiet, the noise of violence gone and dead gone from our lives. We were alone, alone with our dead, alone and scared alone, bewildered and empty and sorrying.

"We'll go now," Mama said. "He's dead and there's nothing we can do but leave."

She looked at me with empty eyes, looked down at Bant, picked up his right hand and laid it gently on his chest. She stroked the hair back from his forehead.

"We must go now, Jeff," she said. "We'll take the gun to the house. You get it and hide it under the house. Bury it. It'll be dark soon and we must hurry."

"Mama, we shouldn't move the gun," I said. "They'll want to know just how it happened and they wouldn't want us to move anything."

Mama half heard me. "I hate to leave him," she said. "Get your gun, Jeff.

We'll hide it."

"But what'll we tell the sheriff?"

"Nothing."

I went to the gun and picked it up.

"It's my fault," Mama said. "Now you'll go through life with this on your mind."

"Mama, I didn't do it!"

Her look was an awful burning thing. She didn't believe me.

"You're not ever to worry about it," she said. "You couldn't help what you did. Bant knew you couldn't help what you did and he didn't blame you for it. Don't blame yourself, Jeff! Don't ever blame yourself!"

"Mama," I cried, the tears streaming fast. "Mama, you've got to believe me! I started to run and he was chasing me and...."

She took one step and her hand fell as gently as a falling leaf over my mouth.

"Let's not talk about it," she said. "We've much to do. Run get Kenty. It's getting late."

"Let's go, Mama," I said, dead inside as Bant was dead, stone cold dead with my mother's unbelief.

"I hate to leave him," Mama said.

She cried as we trudged toward the house. Not once did she look back. Nor did I. It was too late for looking back.

CHAPTER SEVENTEEN

Bant was fated to die. That's the way it had been from the beginning. The tensions he'd built, Kenty's return, and the very role he'd played pointed to the way it ended. Somehow, Bant had known. He had smashed my gun. He had squirmed and twisted, but he hadn't altered the pattern. The train of fate stayed right on track.

John Parl, too, was fated to play a role.

John Parl was our neighbor. He was a funny little man, a timid man who minded his own business and let other people mind their own. He hadn't been on our place three times that I could remember, but he found Bant's body.

We had left Bant's body in the muddy field. Mama had placed Bant's gun on its rack and I had hidden mine under the house. I had just returned to the porch when I heard Kenty call. He was at the barn and leaned his gun against the wall and then came on to the house. Mama came out, walked down the steps and walked into his arms. They walked out of earshot, stood talking, and Kenty turned to look at me.

"No," I said. "I didn't do it, Kenty! He was chasing me and I dropped the gun and it went off!"

"Let's not worry about that now," was all he said.

"You don't believe me, though. I wouldn't shoot him like you think. I would have hit him, maybe, but I wouldn't have killed him on purpose."

"We don't know who killed him," Kenty said. "Remember that, Jeff. He's out there dead, but we don't know who did it. Do you understand, Jeff?"

I nodded, opened my mouth to speak, and it was then John Parl came running into the yard. There was a wild look on his face and his mouth opened and closed, opened and closed. He moaned, gurgled and moaned.

"Bant!" he croaked. "Bant's dead!" He pointed toward the field, ran a few steps toward the road and then whirled around to point again at the field.

Mama buried her face in her hands.

John Parl was wringing his hands. "He's been shot, Kenty!" he wailed. "I was walking along looking for my cow and I crossed Bant's cotton patch and just started into the corn when all at once I looked down and there he was at my feet! Right at my feet! Blood all over his chest, dead as he could be! Somebody shot him!"

"We'll go look," Kenty said. His voice trembled. He looked at Mama, looked away, looked at me straight in the eyes and looked away quickly. "We'll go take a look, John."

John Parl started across the yard at a trot. He reached the fence and Kenty called after him.

"Wait, John," Kenty called. "We might as well get something fixed up so we can bring him to the house."

John Parl stopped, parted the wires, thrust a leg through the fence, paused, backed out and turned to face Kenty.

"We've got to do something, Kenty!" he said. "We ought to get the sheriff or tell the neighbors or do something!"

"Come along," Kenty said. "We'll do what we can as fast as we can."

Kenty went straight to the woodpile, picked up the axe and held it in his left hand while he rummaged around in the pile, stooping and lifting lengths of wood, scattering the pile. He dragged two slender branches to one side and trimmed the limbs and knots from them. John Parl went to the woodpile and stood behind Kenty, dry-washing his hands. He came back to the porch and started to say something, said nothing, and turned to look at Kenty.

"What's he doing?" Mama. asked. "What's Kenty doing?"

"Somebody ought to get the sheriff," John Parl said.

"Yes," Mama said. "Or the doctor."

"It's too late for a doctor, Missus Carr," John Parl said.

"Poor Bant," Mama said. "Poor, sick man."

"Who done it, you reckon?" John Parl asked. "That's what bothers me. Who could have done it?"

Kenty finished trimming the slender branches from the saplings and came toward the house dragging them behind him.

"Pearl," he said, "get me two of Bant's coats. Maybe you'd better bring three."

"Why?" Mama asked. "What are you doing, Kenty?" And then her words came in a rush, tumbling out. "Somebody ought to get the doctor, Kenty. Or the sheriff. What'll we do, Kenty? The poor thing is still lying out there and there's nobody with him and here we are at the house...." She began crying again, soundlessly at first, and then began to sob.

"Stop it, Pearl," Kenty said in a low voice. "You've got to get hold of yourself. Go get me three of Bant's coats."

Mama got up, raised her apron and wiped her eyes. "The poor, sick thing," she said.

"Go on, Pearl," Kenty said. "Bring me the coats. We'll bring Bant to the house."

Mama went inside and Kenty dropped the poles, caught hold of my chin and lifted my head until my eyes met his.

"Come out of it, Jeff," he said. "Snap out of it."

"I can't think who could have done a thing like that," John Parl repeated.

"I think we ought to go get the sheriff or the doctor or somebody."

"You take Bant's car and go into town, John," Kenty directed. "Go straight to the sheriff's office and tell him what's happened."

"It's nigh onto milking time," John Parl murmured. "My old woman will be wondering what happened to me."

"You'll have to let that pass. You take Bant's car and go after the sheriff."

John Parl sighed. "To think a thing like this would happen," he said. "There I was looking for my cow and then I looked down and there he was at my feet. I tell you, it was a shock. At first I couldn't believe my own eyes."

"Take the car and go into town," Kenty said.

John Parl started walking toward the car. Half way there he turned around and retraced his steps.

"Kenty," he said, "I've been wondering what you're going to do with those tree limbs and Bant's coats."

"You'd never make it to town," Kenty said. "I can't leave Pearl right now. I'll tell you what, John. You stay here until we've moved Bant's body to the house and I'll go get the sheriff."

"That might be best," John Parl said. "I've got my milking to do, anyway."

Mama opened the screen door and stood holding it open with her right hand, three of Papa's coats draped over her left arm.

"Kenty," she said. "I've been thinking. Maybe you shouldn't move the... maybe you'd best not move Bant until after the sheriff comes."

"We can't leave him lie there, Pearl; it wouldn't be decent."

"I know," Mama said, stepping out on the porch. The screen door slammed shut behind her, snapped shut by the coiled spring. "It's not right he should lie there. But maybe the sheriff will want to look around."

"We'll take a look around first," Kenty said. "If there's anything to see I'll be a better judge of it than the sheriff."

He frowned and nodded at John Parl as if to warn Mama to be careful, to keep quiet.

"Maybe you're right." Mama walked across the porch and handed Kenty the coats.

Kenty laid the poles side by side on the ground and slid the ends through the sleeves of Papa's coats, fashioning a crude stretcher. When he'd finished he picked up one end and John Parl picked up the other.

"We'll be back directly," Kenty said. "Pearl, you and Jeff stay here."

"I guess we'll go," Mama said.

We walked out of the yard, in a file, Kenty and John Parl first, Mama next. I brought up the rear.

It must have been a strange procession. The cotton was almost waist high. Kenty and John Parl brushed it aside but it swayed straight before Mama could get through. She, in turn, brushed it aside, and it sprang back straight and I had to wade through, swishingly through. We all seemed to be wading in water that curled deep around us.

We neared the corn patch and I slowed my steps, only then realizing what Kenty had done. He had followed the footprints Mama and I had left when we came out of the field.

"I'm glad we decided to come," I heard John Parl say. "You're right, Kenty. It wouldn't be right to leave him here until the sheriff comes."

"We'll have a look around," Kenty said.

"I don't need to look around," John Parl answered. "I can shut my eyes and see it just like it is. It's a sight I'm not likely to forget in a hurry."

"There must be clues," Kenty said, "but footprints in this mud won't help. One print looks like any other. Maybe we'll find the shell, though. That ought to tell us whose gun fired the shot."

"It was a shotgun," John Parl said. "The shell will still be in the gun. Besides, a shell won't prove anything."

"You and Pearl stand back," Kenty said. "We don't want to track up the ground any more than we have to."

"My tracks'll be there, all right," John Parl said. "I walked right up to him before I saw him. There he was, right at my feet. I hardly was able to believe my eyes."

Kenty walked in a circle, a half circle in the corn and the other half in the cotton. He walked slowly, stepped carefully, stopped and peered at the ground. Now and then he squatted to look at a sign.

"Did you see my tracks, Kenty?" John Parl asked.

"Yeah," Kenty said. "I saw where you came up and where you took off across the cotton. I couldn't say they were your tracks if you hadn't told me."

"It startled me," John Parl said. "I can't think who'd do a thing like that."

Mama stood all the while with her back to me, stood like a statue with drooping shoulders. Not once did she move until Kenty called her.

"Come here, Pearl," he said. "You, too, Jeff."

Mama turned then. "Come, son," she said.

I walked up beside her and she took my hand. Together we waded through the cotton.

Bant was as I knew he would be, all twisted on the ground. The position of his body was tortured but his face was serene. One hand clutched a corn stalk. The other was palm down on his chest.

Mama didn't break. She moaned a low moan and clutched my hand tighter, but not once did she flinch.

"God bless him," she said. "He was sick in his mind."

"Walk around a little," Kenty said. "See what you can find."

I followed Kenty in an aimless circle. Mama followed me and John Parl followed Mama. It seemed foolish, but I figured Kenty knew what he was doing.

"All right," Kenty said. "We'll take Bant to the house now. I'm going to go get the sheriff."

Kenty and John Parl lifted Bant's body to the stretcher and each lifted an end. Poor John Parl staggered beneath the weight, but Kenty carried his end easily. He stepped out strongly, half dragging John Parl behind him.

"Jeff," Kenty called as we neared the house. "Run ahead and hold the door open."

I did as I was told, glad to leave the procession. I held the backdoor open and stared into space as Kenty and John Parl brought Bant inside.

Mama walked as one in a trance, walked right past me and didn't see me. I followed her into my bedroom and waited in the doorway as she stood by my bed and looked down at Bant.

"Cover him with a sheet, Kenty," she said.

Kenty stood at the foot of the bed, tossed the sheet high and let it settle.

John Parl went home. "Don't worry about your chores," he told me before he left. "I'll go home and do the milking and then I'll come back and tend to your things." He was still shaking his head in doleful puzzlement as he left.

Kenty took our car and went for the sheriff. I wanted to go with him, but he bade me stay with Mama. "She needs you now, Jeff," he said. "You're all she has now."

"She has you."

"Yes, for what that's worth."

I sat on the front porch and watched him drive away. After a bit Mama came out and sat beside me. For long we sat, thinking our own thoughts, and at last my mind hit on something I'd been wondering about.

"Why'd Kenty have us mill around out there, Mama?" I asked.

"What do you mean?" she asked absently.

"Why'd he have us mill around in a circle out there where it happened?"

"He doesn't want them to find your tracks," she said. "They'd send you away, Jeff, if they knew."

"I couldn't help it, Mama," I said. "He chased me and I threw the gun down and it went off."

I couldn't see her face clearly in the gathering darkness.

"You don't believe me," I said. "You think I killed him on purpose."

"Don't say that, Jeff," she said. "Don't ever say that again. The sheriff will be out here asking questions." She reached for my hand, held it tight between both of her hands. "We'll tell them nothing, Jeff!" she cried. "It wasn't your fault! I'm to blame and Kenty's to blame and Bant was to blame! You'll not be punished for something you couldn't help! I'll not have you sent away!"

"What'll we tell the sheriff?"

"Nothing," she said. "We'll let Kenty do the talking and we'll say what he tells us to say."

Panic was a thing alive inside me. For the first time I realized that nobody would ever believe I'd dropped the gun.

Kenty was gone a long time. Mama sent me to the cow lot to turn the calves in with the cows, though John Parl had said he'd return to do the chores.

"I just don't feel up to milking," she said, twisting her hands. "You go along and turn the calves in and throw some feed to the stock. Give the chickens some grain, too."

I went on down and let the calves in, kicked some hay out of the loft, took a bucket of maize to the chickens, pumped some water into the trough. I went to the back porch and got the chip bucket and filled it at the wood-pile, took it to the back porch and left it. The house was dark and lonesome and I didn't want to go inside. I went back to the woodpile, scrabbled around for stove-sized sticks of wood, and these I dumped on the back porch.

Mama was still on the front porch, sitting all huddled up.

"Are you hungry?" she asked.

"No," I said, though my stomach was rumbling with emptiness.

"It's strange," she said, and her voice was soft and fuzzy. "I'm as hungry as I can be. I'm hungry and Bant is lying in there dead. I didn't know I could be hungry with him dead. I always thought a death in the family would stop everything else. Like being hungry or sleepy or tired. Things like that."

"I'm hungry, too," I said. "I'm hungry, but I don't want to eat."

"That's the way it is with me, I guess," Mama said. "It just wouldn't seem right to go in there and cook."

"What'll we do, Mama?"

She didn't understand. "We'll have to go ahead and eat, just to keep up our strength. I know it doesn't seem right, but we'll have to go in there and eat. And Bant lying in there dead."

"I mean, Mama, what will we do now? For a living, I mean."

Mama sighed, the most wearisome sigh I ever heard. "We'll manage, son. Some way we'll manage. Bant had a little insurance. He nearly dropped it last year, but I kept up the premiums out of egg money until things got better. We can farm some. It'll be hard on you, Jeff, but we'll get by."

"Mama?"

"Yes."

"Why'd he hate me so?"

"His mind was sick, Jeff. He didn't really hate you. It was me he was striking out at. You took the punishment, but it was me he wanted to hurt."

"Why?" I was pressing her, wanting to hurt her, asking questions I didn't need to ask.

"I can't tell you now, Jeff," she said. "Don't ask me to tell you now. When you get older you'll understand a lot of things you don't understand now."

"Did he think Kenty was my real father?"

"It's true," she murmured. "That's what he thought."

"Why'd he think that, Mama?"

She sighed deeply. "Kenty and Bant were friends," Mama said. "Kenty was over here a lot. Then you were born and Kenty went off to the Navy. There was a little talk around the neighborhood, nasty talk, but Bant didn't pay much attention to it. Later, though, he'd get mad at me about something and mention it. At first he didn't mean it. But it was like a slow poison. He got mad more and more often and after a while he began to believe what people said about Kenty and me. The talk died down, but then Kenty came home and talk started again. It sickened Bant's mind and soul. I reasoned with him and begged him and it did no good."

"They say I favor Kenty."

"So you do! Kenty has two legs and so have you! His hair is black and so is yours!"

"Mama?"

"Yes."

"Kenty and the sheriff ought to be back."

"I know."

"Maybe we'd best eat."

"Maybe we had. Come on in. I'll fry some eggs and ham."

We walked through the dark house, our footsteps loud, and the presence of Bant was a heavy thing. Mama fumbled in the cabinet for matches and lighted the lamp. I was careful not to look at the door leading to my room. Mama got out the pan and eggs and meat and I brought chips and wood from the back porch, started the fire with kerosene, and sat at the table. It didn't take long. We ate cold bread and drank milk, but I couldn't taste the ham, couldn't taste the eggs, and the food was like rocks in my stomach.

Kenty and the sheriff came while we were still in the kitchen. Kenty drove our car around the house and parked it under the oak in the back yard. The sheriff parked in front and walked around to the back. I took the lamp out on the porch and lighted them inside.

"Evening, ma'am," the sheriff said, his eyes on the table.

"Good evening," Mama whispered, her hands twisted in her apron.

"Go ahead with your meal," the sheriff said. There was accusation in his voice, suspicion, and I could see that Mama felt it and was afraid.

"We weren't hungry," Mama said. "We couldn't eat."

"Kenty tells me you all moved the body."

"Yes."

"You shouldn't have done that. The body shouldn't have been touched until I'd come and said the word."

"We couldn't leave him lay," Kenty spoke up. "I told you that, sheriff. Even if you'd been in your office where I could have found you, it still would have been an hour before we got back. As it was...."

"Makes no difference," Sheriff Johnson said. "You had no right to move the body. Where is he, anyway?"

"In there," Kenty said, nodding his head at the door.

"Let's take a look."

Kenty took the lamp from me and led the way. I stayed in the kitchen with Mama, but the sheriff turned at the door and stared at both of us.

"You two come along," he said.

"Stay where you are, Pearl," Kenty said. "There's no need for you and Jeff to see."

"Please do as I say," the sheriff said, his voice seemingly tinged with boredom. "Kenty, you let me give the orders. If you please!"

Mama straightened her shoulders and marched toward the door. I followed. Kenty went first, the sheriff after him, and the sheriff almost blocked out the light Kenty carried.

Bant's body, sheet covered, looked lost and lonely.

The sheriff threw back the covers and I turned my head. Mama turned her head, too, but once I peeked around and saw the sheriff's eyes on Mama.

"Where's the gun?" he asked.

Kenty shrugged. "There was no gun around. I looked."

"Did Bant have a gun?"

"Yes," Kenty said.

"Where is it?"

"In the living room where he always kept it."

"Let's take a look."

Kenty again led the way, carrying the lamp. He walked across the living room to the fireplace and held the lamp high.

"There it is," Kenty said. "Just where Bant left it."

The sheriff lifted the gun from the rack. For an instant he stared at it. Then, deliberately, he lifted the gun and sniffed. His eyes lifted to Kenty's face, but he kept his nose to the gun, sniffing.

"This gun's been fired," he said.

"I don't doubt," Kenty murmured.

"It's been fired right recently."

Kenty took the gun and sniffed. "Stop the crap, sheriff. Bant used this gun every day and this powder smell could be two days old. You cut the crap and do your job. Don't hint that you suspect some of us of killing Bant! You're barking up the wrong tree and you're making it hard on this woman and the kid! There's a man dead here, sheriff! Now, do what you're going to do and leave these people alone!"

Sheriff Johnson cradled the gun and let his eyes shift from Kenty, to Mama, to me. "Don't rush me, Kenty. The undertaker'll be along. I've got my duty to do and I intend to do it."

"You want to see where we found him?"

"That's right."

"I'll get a lantern."

Kenty left the room. I wanted to follow, but the sheriff's eyes were on me and I couldn't move. There was a knock on the front door and Mama went to open it. John Parl and his wife, Bertha, stood there. When they came inside I saw Ellen, their daughter, carrying a cloth-covered dish. As always the sight of her stirred me, and I thought it odd that even with Bant dead in the other room the sight of Ellen could bother me. Her hair, blonde golden, hung in curls to her shoulders. Her eyes were wide and blue, her skin cream clear, her breasts already swelling tight against her dress. Bertha Parl went straight to Mama and hugged her, but I saw Mama stiffen and stand in politeness until Bertha released her and stepped away.

"It was good of you to come," Mama said.

"We'd have been here earlier," John Parl mumbled, "only the cows didn't come up and I had to search the pasture out. Never did find the brown cow." He turned to the sheriff. "I was hunting the brown when I found Bant Carr dead in the field. It was a sight fit to startle a man, I'll tell you that. I was walking along thinking about that cow when I came up on Bant. There he was, dead at my feet. It upset me, I'll tell you that."

"When was that?" the sheriff asked.

"An hour by sun, I'd judge."

"What'd you do?"

"Lit out for the house," John Parl said.

"This house?"

"Sure enough. Figured Pearl and the boy had a right to know first of all."

"Was Kenty Hooker here?"

"Yep," John Parl said, nodding.

"Did he have a gun?"

John Parl scratched his head. "It seems to me he did. And then it seems to me he didn't. To tell the truth, I'm so used to seeing Kenty with a gun under his arm and a hound dog at his heels that I can't rightly say whether he had a gun or not."

The sheriff turned to Mama. "Did Kenty Hooker have a gun, Missus Carr?"

"I didn't notice," Mama said. "I guess not."

Those cold eyes were on me. "What about it, boy?"

I didn't answer, just traded him stare for stare.

"What's the matter?" he asked. "Cat got your tongue?"

Bertha Parl cleared her throat. "Pearl, I brought a dish of vittles. Thought you and Jeff might be hungry."

"Jeff will take the dish," Mama said.

Ellen Parl took one step forward and lifted the dish. I took it to the kitchen, tiptoeing, set it on the table and hurried back to the living room. Kenty had a lantern.

"You ready to go, sheriff?" he asked.

"I reckon."

"Let's go."

They went out the front door and I followed. Neither noticed me and neither spoke. We walked through the cotton patch, fighting the tall stalks, the lantern shedding a puddle of yellow light around us. It was a lonesome trip, broken only by the sound of our breathing and the swishing sound of our passage through the thick-leafed cotton.

Kenty held out his free arm and the sheriff stopped. I almost ran into him.

"Right over there," Kenty said. "Right at the edge of the corn patch."

The sheriff took the lantern and walked forward. I stepped up beside Kenty and placed my hand on his arm. He slid his arm around me and pulled me close.

"Looks like you had a parade or something here," the sheriff called.

"Guess we did that when we moved the body," Kenty said.

"You did a good job."

Kenty cleared his throat. "We looked all around, sheriff. There was nothing to see. Take a look for yourself. This plowed ground is still too wet to show footprints. We're just seeing holes in mud."

"I'll bet," the sheriff said.

"You can see John Parl's tracks leading up if you step off to your left."

"I can see four sets of tracks," the sheriff said. "Five, counting Bant's tracks. That gives me four suspects."

"You're crazy," Kenty said, his voice gone dead. "You can see where four people walked, maybe, but you can't identify four tracks."

"I'm not crazy," the sheriff said. "You're crazy for messing up this place to where I can't make heads nor tails of anything! You find a shell?"

Kenty hesitated a split second only. "No shell."

The sheriff grunted.

"Let's go back," Kenty said. "We ought to be there when the undertaker comes. Pearl won't know how to handle things."

"You're mighty considerate of Pearl Carr," Sheriff Johnson said. "Mighty considerate."

"She's a neighbor."

"Was you always so considerate of your neighbor?"

"I don't like the way you're saying that," Kenty said.

"It's not for you to like or dislike," the sheriff said. "I've heard tell you and Bant Carr didn't strike it off so good."

"We had our differences."

"They tell me you and Bant locked horns a time or two."

"Bant liked to fight when he got likkered up."

"I hear tell he always wanted to fight with you and that you obliged him."

"He had other fights."

"Name one."

"Look," Kenty said. "You've got a murder on your hands and I guess it's natural for you to want a scapegoat. Well, I'm not hankering to be the goat. You're going to have to do more than talk, Johnson!"

"Things'll add up, I reckon," Sheriff Johnson said. "Let's get back to the house. I'll be wanting to ask some questions. Like, for instance, how the woman and boy got their faces all bruised up."

"Bant got drunked up last night," Kenty said. "He smacked them around some. But it seems to me all this could wait until morning." He stepped out leading the way. "It would only be decent to wait."

"I do a lot of things I don't like," the sheriff said. "But I'm elected to do a job and I do it."

Kenty stepped out faster. The sheriff stayed at his heels, but I dropped behind. I was tired, so tired my legs trembled and I was sick, sleepy and dizzy. Kenty and the sheriff were in the house before I climbed through the yard fence. Lights were burning in every room and I could hear a babel of voices. A dark shape loomed ahead of me and I stopped in horror as I recognized a hearse backed up to the porch.

"Open the door," someone said, and footsteps clumped, slid, scraped. Someone said, "Take it easy! I'm about to drop my end! Why don't you watch where you're going?" The screen door creaked open and shuffling footsteps walked out on the porch and a man said, "Gosh, ain't he heavy? I didn't know he was such a solid man. He always looked well built, but I would have said he wouldn't have weighed more than a hundred and seventy or eighty."

"Is the hearse door open?" someone asked.

"I think so, but I don't know for sure," the other man answered. Both breathed heavily. I could see them against the light coming through the door, but I couldn't make out their faces.

They carried a stretcher, white sheeted. I wanted to scream, wanted to run forward and put my arms around the still figure under the sheet and say Listen! Bant, listen to me! I forgive you for all the licks you hit and all the hard and mean things you did and said and maybe if you'd lived a little longer you'd have changed back to the Bant you used to be before you turned into the Bant you turned out to be.

The two men pushed the stretcher into the hearse. The door slammed and the starter hummed. The motor purred, the lights switched on, and the hearse rolled around the house, out of sight, out of sound.

I wanted to run after it and knew it was useless. Voices gabbled inside the house. I walked out into the yard and lay down on the ground, buried my face in my arms and cried until the knot in my heart uncoiled. Kenty found me there.

"Come inside," he said. "Come on in and go to bed."

"I can't sleep in there, Kenty," I said. "They had him on my bed."

"We can change the sheets."

"I don't care. I just can't sleep in there."

He patted my shoulder. "Well, the house is full of people anyway. They'll leave after a while. Suppose I bring a pillow and quilt out on the porch?"

"Is the sheriff still here?"

"Yeah," Kenty said. "Yeah, he's still here."

"Does he think you did it?"

Kenty grunted. "He doesn't think anything, kid, but he'll pin it on one of us if he can. But don't you worry. You just keep your lip buttoned, Jeff. Don't say anything."

"Kenty," I said. "What would they do to me if they thought I shot Bant on purpose?"

"Send you to reform school," Kenty said. "But I won't let them do that. You can depend on that, Jeff. Just don't tell them anything. You hear?"

"I'll go to bed," I said.

"You do that, Jeff. I'll be over bright and early in the morning to tend to things."

I sneaked inside and got a quilt from Mama's bed, went outside and made my bed beside the chimney.

Footsteps on the porch, voices low-pitched, scraping sound of footsteps in the yard. The sheriff's voice getting louder.

"...but that's just your word, Kenty, and I'll have to see for myself. Tell you what we'll do. We'll just take a little run over to your house and I'll take a look. If your gun is there, like you say, I'll head in to town."

"Suit yourself," Kenty said.

Kenty's gun was leaning against our barn. I remembered seeing him leave it there. The sheriff and Kenty walked toward the sheriff's car. I skirted the house and ran to the barn, found the gun, crossed the fence, and ran as fast as my legs would carry me across the field. I reached the pasture fence, crawled under it, and ran hard through the woods. More than once I bounced off a tree or caught a tree limb in the face. Still, I knew I would make it because it was twice as far by car.

Kenty's dogs surged around me as I entered the yard. I stumbled, fought them off, scrambled up the steps and across the porch, opened the door and entered the dark living room. I didn't dare make a light and fumbled on the mantel until my fingers touched Kenty's gun rack above it. I was laughing inside as I stood on tiptoe and placed the gun on its pronged mounts, then tiptoed out of the room into Kenty's bedroom.

The living-room door screaked open.

"Look all you please," I heard Kenty say. "Gun or no gun, you're not going to pin this on me."

"Strike a light," the sheriff growled.

A long minute passed.

"Well," the sheriff said, "the gun's where you said it'd be. It don't prove nothing. Just how do I know this is the only shotgun you own?"

"Ask the neighbors," Kenty said. "Everybody around here knows everything about everybody."

"I'll ask them," Sheriff Johnson said. "But I'm not so sure they'd tell the truth. I'll talk to you some more tomorrow."

"Good night," Kenty called from the porch. "Watch those rocks in the lane or you'll ruin a tire."

The car motor roared in the yard, rumbled away.

"Come on out, Jeff!" Kenty called. "We'll make some hot chocolate!"

CHAPTER EIGHTEEN

I walked home alone through the night, taking the long way round to avoid the field where Bant died. Mama was still up and knelt with me to pray. I took a quilt and pillow to the front porch to sleep, but didn't sleep until shortly before dawn. Kenty was shaking me before good daylight, rousing me out, shushing me so Mama could sleep.

"Let's get the chores done," he whispered. "There'll be a million things to do. I'll have to go into town and buy a suit for Bant to be buried in and pick out the casket and arrange for a cemetery lot. Where are your folks buried, Jeff? Piper's Creek?"

"I don't know," I said. "I think I've got a grandpa and a grandma buried in East Texas. But I don't know where."

"You hear Pearl say anything about where she wants Bant laid to rest?"

"No. She didn't mention it."

"We'll have to ask her, but we'll wait and have some coffee."

We took our buckets and walked to the cow lot, fed the animals, let the calves suck just enough to bring the milk down, and eared the calves out of the lot. Kenty milked the brown and I milked the white.

By the time we'd finished, Mama had coffee on the stove and eggs frying. She smiled wanly and motioned us to the table.

"Get any sleep, Pearl?" Kenty asked.

"A little," Mama said.

Kenty picked up a fork and drummed on the table. "Pearl, I hate to bring this up so early. But where do you want to bury Bant? Piper's Creek?"

Mama took the eggs off the stove and dished them onto a platter. She brought the platter to the table and returned to the stove, opened the oven, tucked up her apron and used it as a pad to slide out the pan of biscuits.

"I guess so, Kenty," she said at last. "All of Bant's folks are buried in East Texas. We'll send a telegram to my brother Lafe in Victoria, but I know he can't come. I had a letter from Bonnie last week and she said Lafe has pneumonia."

"Piper's Creek would be best. I didn't want to mention it, but a long time ago at a graveyard working I heard Bant say it was the most peaceful place he'd ever seen."

"I'm glad to know that. The poor thing needs a peaceful place."

"We'll have to remember him like he used to be," Kenty said, and his eyes met mine. "You think you can do that, Jeff? Think you can forget the bad things and remember the good?"

"I guess."

Mama came to stand behind me. "Kenty, what are we going to do? What are we going to tell the sheriff? He wasn't satisfied and he'll be after us."

Kenty stared at his plate. "We'll do nothing. We'll tell the sheriff nothing. He'll suspect us all and in the end he won't be able to prove anything."

"Maybe if I told how it really happened," I said, hesitantly. "Maybe they'd believe me."

Mama's fingers tightened on my shoulders.

Kenty shook his head. "You wouldn't have a chance, Jeff. Everybody in the community knows how Bant beat you. Why, I even talked to John Parl about having Bant arrested. Both you and Pearl have bruised faces. Nobody'd believe you dropped a gun and that the gun went off."

I swallowed. "You and Mama don't believe me, either. And I'm telling the truth."

Kenty traced a pattern on the plate with his finger.

"I couldn't stand it," Mama said, tears behind her voice. "Kenty, they'd send him away and I couldn't stand it. He's a good boy and it wasn't his fault."

Kenty stared at his plate. "It's our fault. We're to blame." He looked up, then, looked down again, stroked his chin, and looked up into Mama's eyes. "They'll blame me. They'll say I killed him."

Mama began to cry.

They were fighting a battle I couldn't understand.

"They can think what they want!" Kenty said savagely. "Jeff won't suffer for it!" He slammed the table with his fist.

"Thank you," Mama said.

"Listen!" Kenty said. "This won't be easy. The sheriff will hound us all. He knows something happened out here. All he had to do was look at your faces to know Bant beat you both. He'll do his best to pin it on one of us, so we'll have to keep our mouths shut."

"What if they arrest you?" I asked. "Or Mama?"

"They won't arrest Pearl. More than likely they'll try to pin it on me. Maybe that's a good thing. Let the sheriff waste his time trying to prove I did it."

"But what if it goes that far?" Mama asked. "What if they arrest you and you go to trial. What then, Kenty?"

"They'd need something to go on before they can arrest me. They'd have to have some concrete evidence to take before a grand jury before they could try me."

"Suppose it goes that far? What about circumstantial evidence?"

"Well," Kenty said thoughtfully. "Suppose they arrest me and get an indictment. They'd still have to convince twelve people I did it."

"Think ahead, Kenty," Mama said, a warning in her voice. "Think ahead and tell me what you'd do and what I'd do if it did go that far."

"We'd have to ride it out. It was our fault more than Jeff's."

"So be it," Mama said.

She brought the biscuits to the table, poured coffee, brought me milk. She sat down and bowed her head and I knew what she wanted of me. I said the blessing, said it haltingly.

"Thank you, Jeff," Mama whispered when I finished.

I went outside while Kenty and Mama made plans for the funeral, and then he took the car and left for town. Mama got out the scissors and trimmed my hair. She heated water and brought out my best clothes, made me shine my shoes and slick down my hair. We sat on the porch until noon, not talking, just sat on the porch and waited.

The hearse came down the road slowly, turned into our yard, circled slowly and backed up to the front porch. Even before the two men got out of the cab I could see the neighbors coming, could see their cars churning up dust. The yard was full of cars by the time the men had opened the back doors of the hearse.

Mama walked down the steps, stood straight and stiff and faced the porch.

Men and women and children came to stand beside her, a sea of faces. I recognized Jack Medford and his fat wife and three flat-faced children, Josh Singletree and his wife, Ripple Dawkins and Onion Brown, the Widow Cloud and Jerry Lawrence, the Stern family, all twelve, Penn Garfield and so many others I lost count.

Six men stepped forward at the undertaker's call, helped slide the casket out of the hearse and carried it inside.

A blonde youth wearing a solemn expression like a mask pulled a wheeled thing from the hearse and unfolded it, forming a stand. This he rolled into the house. Later, when I had pushed my way through the crowd to the living room, I found the casket had been placed on the wheeled stand. People stood around the room, all their faces alike, sad and solemn.

Women began to leave the room, to return later with dishes of food. The kitchen table was heavy laden. Immediately, people began to eat. There was a smell of death in the house, but still the people ate. Mama made coffee and served, made another pot. When the second pot was gone a strange woman made coffee. There were meats on the table, puddings and pies and cakes, bowls of vegetables and fruit. Men would eat and leave the room, only to return a few minutes later for coffee and cake or second helpings of meat and vegetables. It made me sick and I went outside.

Kenty drove into the yard and came to me. "Go on in and see him, Jeff." I walked toward the barn. Kenty followed, walked beside me. "Jeff," he said, "I bought him a new black suit and I think it would do you good to see his face because he looks so peaceful, as though he'd never had a worry and never got mad or upset at anybody in his life. He looks just like he used to look before his mind got sick and before he started drinking. That's why I want you to see him. That's the way you ought to remember him."

I followed Kenty into the house and people stood aside to let us pass. Some-one said, "The poor thing, isn't he taking it like a little man?" And someone else said, "Have you noticed how Missus Carr is bearing up? I'll bet she breaks before the funeral because that's what happens when people keep their grief all bottled up inside them. I don't know how many times I've seen women hold up right until the very last and then go all to pieces."

Bant's suit was nice. He was cleanly shaven and his face was smooth and unlined. But, though I heard people murmur time and again that he looked so natural, I couldn't understand how they thought his face could look nat-ural. He was like a statue I'd seen, made of wax, and though he looked like Bant and his expression was peaceful, I couldn't see why people could say he looked natural.

Tears stung my eyes and I rushed from the room.

A group of kids stood around, giggling and laughing, the boys teasing the girls. I went out to the woodpile and sat on a log. Joe and Johnny Deacon came over and sat down, too embarrassed to speak, and I pretended I did-n't see them. Marie Dabney and her cousin, Martha, left the group and joined us on the log. We sat there like bumps, not speaking, staring into space, un-comfortable. After a while I couldn't stand it any longer. Afraid I was going to cry, I trotted out to the near pasture and sat beneath a tree until the sun sank behind the western mountains.

I straggled home, then, to do the chores. With all the men about the place, only Kenty had a mind to help. The others clustered in the kitchen, eating and talking. I went in for the milk buckets and Mama gave me a wan smile. It was easy to see she was near the breaking point.

At the cow lot I asked Kenty if the sheriff had come. He took his time an-swering, just milked away, the squirts steady and long and strong.

"He hasn't been around all day, Jeff," he said. "That's got me a little bit wor-ried."

"Maybe he won't bother us any more."

"Oh, he'll be around, right enough. I'm surprised he didn't show today. Maybe he's thinking to make me worried, hoping I'll up and confess."

"Maybe he'll give it up."

"Maybe he didn't show up for fear he'd offend somebody," Kenty said. "He's a vote getter and probably knows to wait until after the funeral to come out again."

"I don't like that man," I said. "His eyes give me the cold shivers."

"Neither do I like him. He's got his hooks in me because Bant and I fought. That's enough for him. If I judge him right, he'll try to cook up… something…

between Pearl and me. That'd make it real nasty."

"John Parl was around," I said. "Why didn't the sheriff suspect him?"

"You can look at John Parl and tell he wouldn't hurt a flea."

It was almost dark when we walked to the house. We passed Jude Murray and Blinky Green in the yard. They were drinking from a bottle.

"A funeral is like a circus to some people," Kenty said loudly.

"Sorry, Kenty," Jude Murray muttered.

Five men sat around the kitchen table, drinking coffee. We had heard the murmur of their voices from outside, but they stopped talking the minute we walked through the door. I recognized Buford Hamilton, but the others I didn't know. There was a guilty look on Buford's face, a hog-stealing look. Kenty didn't speak. The men just sat there and looked at us while we strained the milk and put it in the cooler. They started talking again when we went out, the murmur of their voices fading out as we went to the woodpile.

Kenty dumped an arm load of wood in the box behind the stove and stood aside while I dumped mine. He dusted wood shavings from his shirt and scowled at the men around the table.

"You men have been Bant's neighbors a long time," he said. "Now he's dead and his wife and kid are alone in the world. There's a lot to do, but you sit around swilling coffee and stuffing your guts while the kid goes out to milk and tote wood. Why don't you go home, anyway? You're not helping around here."

Buford Hamilton wiped his thick lips with the back of a hairy hand.

"Maybe we ain't as close to the family as some, Kenty."

Kenty's voice trembled. "I'll skip that crack, Buford, if you tell me you didn't mean anything by it."

Buford Hamilton shoved his chair back and stood, moving swiftly and lightly for a big man. His shoulders swelled under the shirt, bulged and swelled, and his chest heaved with his breathing. He had big, pop eyes, light blue, and no eyelashes at all. His face was pitted, the nose fleshy, but his hair was raven black and made his face look washed out and sallow.

"You're the busy little helper around here, Kenty. They tell us the sheriff noticed it right away."

"I'd say you're treading mighty dangerous water, Buford," Kenty said, his face gone flushed and dark. "Careful you can swim your way out all right."

"We've been doing some talking," Buford Hamilton said heavily. "Bant was our friend and we don't aim to sit by while his killer is running around loose."

"You've been sitting idly by, all right!" Kenty said. "The least you could have done was chop some wood and help around the place!"

"There's more important things to do," Buford Hamilton said.

"Such as?"

"Finding out who killed Bant!"

"What're you driving at, Buford?"

"I think you know."

Kenty stepped out into the middle of the room and spoke to the men at the table.

"Anybody else feel like Buford does?" he asked.

The men shifted uneasily and ducked their heads. Kenty turned to Buford.

"Maybe we'd better step outside, Buford."

It was what Buford wanted, but I was powerless to stop it. Kenty couldn't overlook what Buford had implied because it would have been an admission of guilt. Yet, to fight about it would serve to throw a spotlight on Buford's accusation. Kenty had been forced into a corner.

Kenty went first, Buford second. Somebody brought the lamp out to the porch. Not a word was spoken, yet the word spread quickly. The lamp cast a puddle of light into the yard and the puddle was soon surrounded by men, women and children.

Buford slipped out of his shirt and his shoulders were massive, the chest thick, the neck bull-like. He stood with his arms outspread, the fingers flexing. Kenty tossed his shirt to me and stood expressionless, a slight figure, yet a tight figure, finely muscled. I could hear the sound of his breathing and he scraped his feet in the still-damp dirt exactly as a game rooster claws the dirt before charging. For one brief instant I saw Mama's face, and then she stepped back out of the light and I saw a score of faces, open mouthed, eager, intent.

Kenty said no word, but took short steps forward, mincing little steps, shoulders slightly drooped and chin tucked low. Buford stood wide-legged, solidly braced, left shoulder forward, posed in old-fashioned stance with arms hooked, fists up. Kenty jabbed with his left and landed a blow with a sharp splat, another, then splat, splat, splat. Buford's head jerked with the blows, but he refused to give ground. Kenty danced lightly back, forward again, and the snakelike left flicked out once and twice and yet again. Buford lowered his head and waded in slowly, swinging wildly, grunting with the effort of each blow, fanning air. Kenty retreated, danced away to return again with punishing jabs to Buford's bloody face. Once Kenty braced himself and threw a mighty right, snapping Buford's head back, but the big man plodded toward him, still swinging. Kenty retreated a full circle, remaining always in the lighted area. He maneuvered his back to the light and shifted his attack to Buford's middle. In a sudden spurt of rage he stepped in and swung toe to toe with the big man. Their fists landed with booming thuds and both grunted, but the weight of Buford's blows sent Kenty reeling back. And then, suddenly light and graceful afoot, Buford sprang and brought a swinging right to Kenty's face. Kenty flew backward, arms outflung and heels dragging, hit the porch hard and slid slowly to the ground. Buford dived at him, but Kenty rolled aside and scrambled to his feet.

"Stop it!" Mama called. "My husband's dead in the house and you fight in the yard like animals!"

Buford regained his feet and went in on Kenty, fists cocked, head ducked. He was breathing hard, snorting a little. Kenty wavered, stepped back, tried to dance a little, tossed hair out of his eyes and stepped back again. Buford lumbered forward, swung and missed. Kenty came in like a cat and threw his full weight behind his blows. His fists landed with sharp cracking sounds, again and yet again, and he drove Buford back. A right staggered Buford, and his guard dropped. Kenty stood flat-footed and brought up a left, a right, the left again and again the right. Buford crumpled, fell slowly, fell to lie face down. Kenty stood over him, breathing hard.

"Now, that was a right good fight." The sheriff's voice came from the darkness.

He came into the light, elbowing his way through the crowd, stepped over to Buford and knelt down, rolled him over.

"Guess he's all right," he said. "Somebody ought to bring some water and douse him good." He stood and faced Kenty. "Guess I'll be taking you in."

"For what?" Kenty gasped.

"I'm arresting you for the murder of Bant Carr," the sheriff said. "John Parl is willing to testify he saw you carrying a shotgun."

"You saw my gun in my own house," Kenty said. "John Parl said he couldn't remember whether I had a gun or not!"

"He remembers now, though," the sheriff said. His eyes came to rest on me. He grinned crookedly. "And I've got some ideas, Kenty. Yessir, I've got some ideas. I think when the time comes I'll be able to find out how that gun got put back in your living room."

CHAPTER NINETEEN

The sheriff handcuffed Kenty and took him away. I took a quilt and pillow to the far end of the porch and bedded down. Onion Brown and the Widow Cloud sat up with the body. I could hear them as they moved around and could hear the murmur of their voices, but I couldn't hear what they said. It rained near midnight and the air grew chill. I didn't sleep until just before daybreak, and then I slept until the sun came up. The yard filled with cars and there were people on the porch, in the yard and in the house. Nobody paid me any mind and I had to rummage around the kitchen to get a bite to eat. After I'd finished I went to the cow pen, but somebody had done the milking. Mama met me in the yard and spoke in a whisper.

"Bear up, Jeff," she said. "I wouldn't wish for all these people, but I can't ask them to leave. Did you sleep any last night?"

"A little, Mama. When will the... when's the funeral?"

"This afternoon, child."

"What'll they do to Kenty?"

She tried to smile. "Nothing. The sheriff had to arrest somebody. They'll hold him a day or two and let him go."

"I won't let them do anything to him," I warned. Our eyes met, locked, and she looked away.

"You've got to promise me something, Jeff," she said. "Promise me to keep quiet about this whole thing. It'll all work out in the end. Everything will be all right."

I tried to pull free and her hands tightened on my shoulders.

"Promise me, Jeff! I don't think I'm able to bear any more right now!"

"I promise," I muttered. She let me go.

"Why don't you come sit with me?" she asked.

"No, ma'am."

"It'd be the thing to do, Jeff."

"I can't, Mama."

"Not even for me?"

"No, ma'am."

"It's all right." She tried to smile. "But stick to the house so I can get you if I need you."

"Yes, ma'am."

She kissed my cheek and let me go, turned and went into the house. I turned and walked across the yard, climbed under the fence, followed a cotton row to the cornfield and sat down close to the place where Bant died.

There I stayed until the sun was overhead. I stuck a stick into the ground, waited until it's shadow shortened to nothingness and knew it was noon, and then I returned to the house. I scraped the mud from my shoes with a stick and as much as I could from the seat of my pants.

There must have been a hundred people in the house and yard, strangers to me, most of them. They milled around, gabbled and laughed. I went into the kitchen and wriggled through to the table, grabbed a slab of meat and a slice of bread and went back into the yard to eat.

Mama called me. I knew it was time. She told me to get myself ready for the funeral. By the time I'd finished, most of the crowd had left the house and sat in their cars to wait. The hearse pulled into the yard, backed up to the front porch, and the same mournful man opened the back doors and marched into the living room. Six men carried the casket out, three to a side, walking slowly, eyes straight ahead. They lowered one end to the bottom of the hearse and the sad-faced man slid it inside. Mama took my arm and we descended the steps to march slowly across the yard to Kenty's car.

"We ought to get somebody to drive for us," Mama said.

"I can drive. It's my place to drive."

She consented with her silence. I felt all eyes on me as I opened the door and helped Mama inside, then went around the car and climbed over the door on the steering-wheel side. I stamped on the starter and the motor caught. I adjusted the gas and spark and waited for the hearse to move. When it rolled out, I followed.

The hearse rolled slowly and slowly I followed. Cars strung out behind. Once we met a stranger in a car and he pulled over to the side of the road and stopped, removed his hat and waited until we passed. We crossed the highway at the intersection and drove down Piper's Creek road, crossed the wooden bridge, drove in the shadows of giant oaks and pecans, and finally turned through the gate of the cemetery.

It was a pretty spot, a quiet place, a clearing in the midst of bottom-land forest. Birds called from nearby treetops and insects buzzed in the tall grass. Roses bloomed and shrubs flourished.

The hearse stopped and I braked the car, killed the motor, climbed out and walked around to open the door for Mama. The cars following us stopped in line. People dismounted and walked toward a fresh mound of earth, gathered around it and stood waiting. The six pallbearers went over to the hearse and the sad-faced men opened the doors.

I walked with Mama to the graveside. The crowd parted and we walked through. Brother Perkins waited on the opposite side of the grave, his Bible in his hand, a withered and stooped old figure in a worn frock coat. He nodded at us and I saw tears ooze from the corners of his eyes, watched them roll down his withered cheeks, heard him sniff and sigh. I took Mama's hand

and stood waiting. Two of the sad-faced men brought some shiny rods to the grave, fitted them in place over the hole and connected them with straps. The pallbearers came marching with the casket, gently lowering it to rest on the straps.

Brother Perkins lifted his face to the sky and began to pray, his voice shrill and shaky, but for some reason I could make no sense of what he said. He prayed a long while, and when he had finished four men and a woman walked around the grave and stood behind him. They sang "Nearer My God to Thee." An old woman behind me began to sing in a cracked voice, but someone said, "Shush, Mama, this is a special song and we're not supposed to sing yet." The old woman spoke aloud. "I don't care," she said. "That's my favorite song and I like to sing it." I wanted to tell them to be quiet. But as I turned, Mama nudged me in the ribs. I turned back around and stood quietly until the song was finished.

Brother Perkins preached to the sky, arms uplifted. He preached long and furiously, his voice rising to a high pitch at times, sinking to a whisper, playing on our emotions as finely as bow ever played fiddle. I did not cry. I felt tears well, but fought them back. Once I looked up at Mama and saw tears on her cheeks, but never did she lift hand to brush them away and never did she cry openly. Women I didn't even know cried and wailed, and tears were shed by some of the men. After a long while, the four men and the woman began to sing again and one of the sad-faced undertakers turned a knob and the casket began to sink into the grave.

No cars followed us home. The house was dark when we arrived. I had the milking and feeding to do, the wood to bring in, and for supper we had cold meat and bread.

We sat at the table a long time, reluctant to go to bed. Mama made a pot of coffee and sat sipping it, staring into space. I tried to think about the future, about the crop to be made and harvested, about next winter's schooling. The cotton needed plowing and the corn needed one last plowing with a middle buster.

"Let's go to bed," Mama said. "There's much to do tomorrow."

"I'll plow the cotton, Mama."

"We'll have to go into town," Mama said. "We'll have to go Kenty's bail. Besides, it's too wet to plow."

"Will they let him out of jail?"

"If we go his bail."

"Kenty has plenty of money for his bail."

"They won't take it. They know he won't run if a friend is at risk."

"I can't let him stay in jail," I said.

"Let's go to bed," she repeated.

"I can't sleep in there," I said, nodding toward my room.

"I've changed the bedding, Jeff. It's all right."

In the night, long after Mama slept, I slipped out of my room and made a pallet in the kitchen. Lying there, I listened to the old house creaking and groaning. Almost it was as if I could hear Bant walking back and forth, back and forth.

I came awake soft and easy, mind free and rested. I went into the yard to stand in the gray cool dawn, walked out to the fence and looked at the leaf-wet cotton, thought of Bant as he stood out there with that crazy look in his eyes and saw him again as he ran across the field. The sun came up and I turned away and went into the kitchen. Mama was drinking coffee.

"You slept on the floor," she said.

"It didn't feel right in my room."

"The fear will go away, Jeff."

I took the milk pails from the shelf and started out the door.

"We're going into town, Jeff," Mama said.

"I'll hurry."

The cows were nervous and didn't want to give down their milk. Twice I had to let the calves suckle, had to ear them out of the lot, but still I didn't get full pails. I took the milk to the house, went back to the lot and threw hay to the horses, turned the calves into the pasture, fed the chickens and gathered the eggs. I drew a pail of water from the well and took in an arm load of wood. The sun was an hour high.

"We can do it, Mama. I can tend things and make a crop."

"We'll manage, son. We'll have to manage and we will. I'll help with the crop and we'll buy more chickens, maybe two hundred, and we'll keep the heifers and sell milk and butter. I've always wanted more chickens, but Bant.... Our egg money kept us going more than one winter. We'll manage, son."

I ate my breakfast and changed into a clean shirt and overalls, combed my hair, went to the living room and took Bant's car keys from the nail where he always hung them. I tossed them from one hand to the other and remembered how Bant always tossed them, remembered how he always hung them on the nail, remembered just the way he did it, just the way he looked.

I drove slowly, seeing nothing but the road ahead, grateful because Mama didn't caution me. I tightened up when we reached the city limits, but Mama patted my shoulder and I steered the car into the middle of town. I pulled in at the curb beside the courthouse, switched off the motor and pocketed the keys.

"You did good," Mama said.

We went into the courthouse, down a hallway, up some stairs and down another hallway to an office with the words COUNTY ATTORNEY on the door.

Mama knocked.

No answer.

Mama knocked again.

"Maybe there's no one here," I said. "Maybe it's too early."

Mama raised her hand to knock again, tapped at air, let the hand drop to the door handle, pulled it away, again grasped the handle and turned the knob. The door wasn't locked. She pushed it open and stepped into the room.

A man sat behind a gray steel desk. He wore glasses. His head was bald. His eyes were as large as walnuts, blue eyes that bulged, blue eyes that stared unblinkingly. There were pouches under his eyes, fatty wrinkled pouches. His nose looked as big as my fist and a thousand blue veins crossed the nose. The man's cheeks were fleshy and loose, drooped like a hound's cheeks, and his chin was buried in rolls of fat.

"Come in," the man said, and his high thin voice startled me.

"I beg your pardon," Mama said. "I'm looking for the county attorney."

"You've found him, ma'am."

"I'm Pearl Carr," Mama said. "My husband was killed and they've arrested Kenty Hooker."

The man nodded.

"Kenty Hooker didn't kill Bant," Mama said. "I want to get him out of jail."

The man toyed with a fountain pen, not looking at it. "That's unusual," he said. "It's not often that the widow of a murdered man wants to get the killer out of jail."

Mama shook her head. "I told you," she said. "I told you Kenty Hooker did-n't kill Bant."

"That's not what the sheriff tells me, ma'am. The sheriff seems to think Kenty Hooker did kill Bant."

Mama bit her lip. "Kenty wouldn't do it. Couldn't do it."

"Can you prove that, ma'am?"

Mama's head went up and her eyes flashed. "The burden of proof lies with you!"

The fat man nodded his head and smiled grotesquely. "That's true, ma'am. You understand, of course, that the district attorney will prosecute in the case. It may be that he will feel as you do that proof does not exist. I have studied the facts supplied me by the sheriff, however, and feel that Kenty Hooker is guilty beyond the shadow of a doubt. I think the grand jury will indict him."

"I want to get him out of jail," Mama said. "I want to make bond for him."

The fat man twirled the pen. "That can be arranged, of course. I will be happy to assist you in making the arrangements."

"Has bond been set?"

"Not as yet. That can be taken care of, though, if you're prepared to make bond."

"How much will it be?"

The fat man pursed his lips. "At a guess... ten thousand dollars."

"Bant was offered more than that for the farm a few years ago."

"Ma'am, I'm afraid the farm's value won't be the, ah, factor. In the first place, even if there are no liens against the farm, you wouldn't have clear title until your husband's will is probated. Did he leave a will, ma'am?"

"I don't know," Mama said.

The fat man touched the tips of his fingers together and stared at them. "Land prices have dropped."

"What are you trying to say?" Mama asked. "Are you saying you intend to hold Kenty in jail? Are you saying you don't want him out on bond?"

"Lady," the fat man said, "I'm not trying to say anything. The decision won't be mine. The judge will set bond. But I am trying to warn you that Kenty Hooker was away for years. He seems to have plenty of money and he might skip the country."

"When will the trial be held?"

The fat man shrugged. "Maybe a month. Two or three at most. The man hasn't even been indicted yet."

"Thank you," Mama said. She turned away from the desk. I followed her out the door.

They set Kenty's bond at twenty thousand dollars. Mama cried the night she heard the news. The next day we went to see Kenty.

The jail was on the top floor of the courthouse. The stairway was narrow and dark. Mose Swift, the jailer, led us up those stairs with his big ring of keys jangling in his hand. He was creaky old, stiff with rheumatism, toothless and dirty, without pity. We stopped before a massive iron door and Mose fumbled for the key, tried key after key in the lock, finally found the right one and pushed the door open. We stepped into the jail proper, stepped into a wide hallway formed by barred cells. It was a damp and gloomy place, ill lighted by a single naked bulb. Catcalls greeted us. Feet stamped and someone whistled.

"He's in the first cell on your left," Mose said. "You can stay ten minutes."

We stepped up to the cell and Kenty appeared before us, his hands grasping the bars. It took a minute for my eyes to become accustomed to the darkness. He needed a shave. His clothing was wrinkled.

"I'm glad you came," he said. He was looking straight at Mama when he said it, but his right hand came through the bars to rest on my shoulder for an instant. "I'm darned glad you came."

"We tried to raise the bail," Mama said.

"They set it too high," Kenty said. "I'm good for it and they know it, but they're afraid I'd skip the country."

"Kenty," Mama said. "What are we going to do?"

"They don't have a case," Kenty said. "Remember that. They can try me but they can't convict me. So... keep quiet and let them try me. We mustn't give them anything else to work on."

"We'll get your stock over to our place, Kenty," I said. "We'll take the dogs, too."

"I knew you would," he said.

He asked the news and Mama told him all she knew. They made small talk for a while, but when they heard Mose at the door they put their heads close together and talked in whispers. Mose opened the door and Mama stepped quickly back.

"We'll come again, Kenty," she said.

"Do that. And, Pearl... remember what I said. Let them try me, just me. Don't give them anything else to work on."

"I'll try it your way, but if things go against you...."

"Don't let them work on you and the boy!"

"Time's up," Mose said.

The cotton was chest-high and the corn flourished. I laid it by with a Georgia stock, using a scoop to throw the dirt high around the base of the stalks. We had a rain, a slow-soaking rain, and the weeds came thick. The crop was too far along for hurt and I didn't hoe, couldn't hoe because of the press of work. Mama helped me in the fields and wore herself thin. We were up early and late, had the chores done before day and did them again after dark.

Six weeks passed slowly, dragged by. We went to see Kenty every Sunday, and with each passing week he became thinner and paler, became stooped and haggard. The freedom was gone from him, the sense of freedom gone, and what was gone left him a man only.

The sheriff came to the house on a Saturday. He brought Mama a paper and Mama's face paled as she took it.

"Monday?" she asked.

The sheriff nodded.

"What time?"

"Nine o'clock," the sheriff said. "Bring the boy."

He drove away and Mama stood in the yard holding the paper.

"The trial starts Monday," she said. "It's a funny thing, but I'm glad it's starting. I dread it. But I'm glad, too. I want to have it over and done with."

We went to the cemetery to visit Bant's grave on Sunday. I didn't want to go and Mama insisted. But why? I wanted to know. Why, after all this time and we hadn't been there a single time since the funeral? Why go now? Mama didn't answer, only looked at me, and I didn't ask again. I took the bucket to the well and filled it with water for the car radiator.

It was four miles to the cemetery. Bant's grave was in a corner, the far corner, and already grass was growing there. A rosebush grew just behind the tombstone and was in full bloom. A cluster of roses formed a cap of red that seemed from a distance to sit lightly atop the stone.

Mama knelt by the grave and said a prayer. I stood afar, filled with an unease I felt was sinful, unpraying and unfeeling, moved by the feel of the place and by its beauty, sad a little but sorrowing not.

I drove Mama home in the cool of the evening and neither of us spoke. The day had been queer and we needed time to add it up in our minds. Only one thing I knew, and it was that Mama's adding wouldn't equal mine. Her two and two wouldn't add up to four, and neither would mine. The whole thing, the sums to be added, would have to be multiplied by what we knew and subtracted from what we felt. And neither of us knew what the other felt, nor felt what the other knew. Too many feelings and happenings shaded the problem, and we couldn't talk it out. We didn't even try.

Mama's long Indian hair had fallen in the back. A half smile crinkled the corners of her mouth. At the cemetery, not long ago, her lips were set and thin and her hair was braided in a bun on the top of her head. But the pins came loose and her hair fell. Her body seemed suddenly to loosen and relax.

It was almost sundown when we left the cemetery. It was dark when we got home. Mama told me to turn the calves in with the cows and we'd skip milking. "But feed Kenty's dogs," she said. "Feed them well for he loves them and can't care for them. I'll cook supper. We must eat and keep up our strength."

The cow lot was mucky, dung littered and dark as pitch. The calves, when I opened the gate, jostled me and stepped on my feet. I tugged a bale of hay from the barn and untied the wire, kicked it into the open and went back to the house. I couldn't see and didn't need to see, knew when to turn and when to pick up my feet, skirted the woodpile and stepped over plow points and boxes and the chopping block.

Mama was in the kitchen. She had changed her dress and looked like a girl in the gingham, her hair loose and swinging free to her waist. I washed, stealing glances at her, sniffing the ham and biscuits. I wasn't hungry. She set the table and centered the lamp on the oilcloth-covered table.

"Why don't you let me tell them the truth, Mama?" I asked.

Her eyes were sad brown on me with an expression I couldn't fathom. She didn't speak, not for a long while, but got up and filled her cup with coffee.

"I can't let you," she said.

"You don't believe me."

"It's not a question of believing or not believing, Jeff."

"They'll hang Kenty."

"No," she said. "They don't have any proof."

"We shouldn't have moved Bant. We should have told the truth at the beginning."

"Hush, Jeff! You're just a child!"

I pushed my chair back and stood, felt myself trembling and couldn't stop trembling.

"You think I killed a man," I said. "You think I killed my own father and you call me a child!"

Her face was like chalk. "You'd better go to bed, son," she said. But when I'd reached the door she called, "It's gone too far, Jeff! We can't tell the truth now! They wouldn't believe us!"

I closed the door behind me, closed it gently.

All night long I rolled and tossed, slept fitfully just before dawn, was up at first cock's crow and built a fire in the old black stove. Mama must have been up before me. She came into the kitchen wearing the black dress, her hair up in a bun.

She'd used a little powder, a little rouge, and her eyes were fresh and clear.

"I'll cook breakfast," she said. "You see about the chores."

The sun was coming up by the time I'd finished milking and feeding. Mama had breakfast on the table.

"They might ask you questions," she told me. "You're not to be afraid. Just say Bant hit both of us the night before... it happened. Tell them he went into the field the next day and we didn't know he was dead until John Parl told us."

"How about you, Mama? Will they ask you questions?"

"Yes."

"Will you be afraid?"

She hesitated. "Yes."

She drank her coffee quickly and left the room. I dabbled with my food, cleared the plates and stacked them. Mama was back in a few minutes, her hat on, the veil down.

"We'd best be going," she said.

CHAPTER TWENTY

The streets of the town were filled. Wagons and buggies were parked around the square, in the middle of the broad street in front of the courthouse. They overflowed into side streets. The sidewalks were jammed and people clustered like flowers, ebbed into the street, and forced the walkers to flow around them.

I drove slowly, hunting a place to park. Men, women and children stared at us, their curiosity an ugly thing. Their stares licked us like serpent tongues, but Mama seemed not to notice. The red crept up my neck. I could feel it. But Mama sat straight and still beside me.

"Park beside the lumberyard," she told me. "That's where Bant parked on the Fourth of July."

I drove down a side street and parked in front of the lumberyard. We had to walk back up the street and through the town, running a gauntlet of eyes. People stood aside to let us pass, nodded at us and talked in low voices within our hearing. A hundred people, maybe more, clustered around the courthouse door, on the steps and on the walk and on the lawn, but stepped aside and formed a narrow aisle for us to tread.

The hallway was sprinkled with people. They, too, stepped aside to let us pass. I followed Mama down the long hall, the stale stench of it strong in my nostrils, up the stairs and down another dark hallway to a pair of massive oaken doors.

Mama stopped dead still and lifted her veil. Her eyes caressed me.

"It'll be strange to you," she said, "and they'll say a lot of things to get you rattled."

"I went to court once with Bant."

"This will be different because it'll be about us. Keep your chin up. Keep your head high."

Lon Bibby, the deputy sheriff, opened the doors. Every seat was taken, every bench filled. Three hundred people sighed as one and leaned forward, the rustle of their clothing like wind through leaves. I felt their eyes on me and wanted to run. Lon Bibby led us up front to an empty bench. Several men sat at tables beyond a railing.

A man told us to stand.

The judge came in. He wore a black robe and his face was red, flushed with heat. His hair was white, snow white, and his eyes were bright and shiny blue, the kind of blue you can see from far off. A man started talking the minute the judge stepped through the door, started talking in a sort of singsong, "Hear ye, hear ye, the mumble mumble court of mumble mumble is now in session the Right Honorable James Jeff Fenton presiding you may be seated."

There was a lot of talk and I got restless. Once I turned and peeped a look at all the people behind me, but they seemed to be looking right at me and I turned around fast. Mama nudged me.

All at once the crowd sighed again, sighed for all the world like wind sighing through the trees. At first I didn't understand, and then I saw why: Kenty Hooker had stepped through a small door just behind the jury box. Sheriff Johnson was right behind him, a hand on Kenty's arm. I wanted to stand up so Kenty could see me, wanted to speak to him, wanted to go to him. I tensed my body to leave my seat and felt Mama's hand fall gently on my knee.

Kenty looked pale and drawn. The spring was gone from his step, the gladness gone from his face.

Kenty Hooker, my friend.

He walked straight to a table, sat down and pulled back a chair for the sheriff. A little man, a stooped little man with the face of a gnome and a body to match, took a chair on Kenty's left.

"Tumblin Green!" someone behind me said. "Tumblin Green from Calonok! If anybody can get Kenty off, it'll be Tumblin Green!"

The big clock on the wall said ten o'clock.

"Feeling is running high," someone whispered. "They ought to hang him, that's what they ought to do! Hang him high! Why, I heard the whole thing started years ago before he went away. I wouldn't be surprised if all they say about the boy being Kenty's flesh and blood ain't true after all!"

Mama seemed not to hear.

I turned and looked behind me. The whisperer was a woman, a wrinkle-faced woman, a woman old and ugly and mean through and through, slack mouthed and long toothed, yellow toothed, with snuff dripping at the corner of her mouth.

"Shut up!" I gritted.

Mama nudged me.

Things began to happen. Papers were read and men whispered together, shuffled papers, walked hurriedly out of the courtroom and hurriedly back, approached the bench to whisper to the judge, mentioned points of law and read from thick books, sought rulings on this and that.

Prospective jurors, all men, were questioned and only two were not seated because of challenges. Those two didn't believe in capital punishment.

Court was recessed until one o'clock. Most of the people kept their seats. They took Kenty away, but not before he smiled at me and winked.

Mama was pale and her hand shook on my arm as we walked down the hall, down the stairs and out the front door. The crowd still clustered at the door and on the lawn, and again we had to run the gauntlet of their eyes. We stopped at Conway's Grocery and bought sandwich meat and bread. Mama took change from her purse to pay, though Bant had always charged. Mister Conway, fat and red and perspiring, seemed embarrassed. We ate in the car and then crossed the street to a filling station and had a cold drink. By that time it was nearly one, and again we braved the eyes of the curious and entered the courthouse, walked again up the stairs and down the hall and again followed Lon Bibby to our seats.

John Parl was first on the stand.

Ellis Type was our district attorney. He looked like a turkey buzzard. I don't think I'd ever seen him smile and doubted that he could smile. He was all bones and elbows, a mournful man with a mop of black hair that fell over his eyes, over his ears, down his neck. His face was like a hatchet.

His nose was hooked like a beak and he had but a small knob for a chin. His Adam's apple bobbed with every word he spoke. As always, he wore black. He paced back and forth, back and forth, hands clasped behind his back, long body stooped.

"Mister Parl, I believe you are, or were, a neighbor of the deceased?"

"Yes, sir."

"How long had you known the deceased?"

"Twenty years... maybe more.... He moved to the place the year of the drought, or the year after, I forget which."

"You've also known Kenty Hooker for many years, have you not?"

"All his life."

"His farm is adjacent to yours?"

"His farm joins mine, if that's what you mean."

"And what kind of neighbor has Kenty Hooker been?"

John Parl rubbed his chin, pulled at his ear, his nervousness showing plain.

"Well," he said. "Well, and admitting that I don't know a thing about the rights or wrongs of this case...."

"Just answer my question as briefly as possible," Ellis Type said, grinning at Tumblin Green who was already on his feet. "What kind of neighbor was Kenty Hooker?"

"Fairly good," John Parl said.

"What do you mean by fairly good?"

"Well, he was a mite quick tempered and too ready with his fists. He improved that place of his, but he don't seem out to make it pay. Kenty Hooker has always liked a good time, not that liking a good time is bad, mind you. Well, I remember the time...."

Tumblin Green was on his feet again, but the judge waved at him before he had time to open his mouth.

"Mister Type," the judge said. "Please confine your questions to the development of this case. Your witness is apt to go around Robin Hood's barn with his answers."

Ellis Type bowed mockingly to the judge, turned and bowed to Tumblin Green. Old Tumblin Green bowed right back, as courtly as you please, and even the jury tittered.

"Was Kenty Hooker quarrelsome?" Ellis Type asked.

"Not exactly," John Parl said. "No, you couldn't exactly say he was quarrelsome."

"Was the deceased, Bant Carr, a good neighbor?"

John Parl scratched his head. "Well, I never had any trouble with him."

"You knew him intimately... saw him quite often?"

"Well, being neighbors and all, we saw each other now and then."

"Would you say Bant Carr was of sound mind?" Ellis Type asked.

John Parl chewed his lower lip and thought a moment. "Well, I couldn't rightly say. He acted peculiar sometimes."

"But he wasn't hard to get along with?"

"Not for me. We always got along just fine."

"Tell me, Mister Parl. Did you notice a change in Bant Carr after Kenty Hooker came back to his home place to live?"

John Parl stroked the chair arms, forgot them and allowed his hands to flutter together again. He looked at the judge, looked at the jury, moved his lips without speaking.

"Mister Parl?" Ellis Type prompted.

"Well," John Parl said, "I'd have to say he did change some. Seems to me he started drinking more."

Tumblin Green was on his feet, chest outthrust and head back, his shrunken little body taut with rage, his long white hair tousled. "I object!" he bellowed. "Your Honor, the witness has no way of knowing whether the deceased changed for the better or worse just because Kenty Hooker came home after many years! It was a leading question and the answer is based on assumption!"

"Objection sustained," the judge rumbled.

Ellis Type turned his back on John Parl, and I thought he looked at me.

"Mister Parl," he said, drawing out the Mister, slurring it. "Mis-ter Parl, I want to know if you've ever seen Bant Carr abuse his son."

"Well," John Parl said, "I've heard tell that...."

Ellis Type whirled around and pointed a bony finger at John Parl. "I didn't ask you what you'd heard! I asked you a direct question and I want a yes or no answer."

Old Tumblin Green was on his feet, laughing aloud. "Your Honor," he said, "I'd like to point out that the district attorney did not ask the witness a direct question. He said he wanted to know if the witness had seen Bant Carr abuse his son."

"Do you have an objection, Mister Green?" the judge asked.

"No objection, Your Honor," Tumblin Green said. "I merely establish a point in the interest of proper procedure."

"I remind the district attorney to phrase his questions properly," the judge droned. "Please proceed."

Ellis Type bowed low to the judge. "Mister Parl, have you ever seen the deceased abuse his son?"

"I've seen bruises on the boy's face."

"Have you ever seen the deceased abuse his son?" Ellis Type asked, his words fairly crackling with anger.

"I can't say that I have," John Parl said. "I'd have to know exactly what you mean by the word abuse."

"Did you ever see Bant Carr whip his son unmercifully and unjustly?"

John Parl scratched his head. "Well, they tell me...."

"Yes or no, Mister Parl," Ellis Type drawled. "Did you ever see Bant Carr beat his son unmercifully or unjustly?"

"You ain't giving me a chance," John Parl whined, spreading his hands palms up. "I was Bant Carr's neighbor for years! You get to know a neighbor and what he does and what goes on inside his home without seeing everything! You get to where you can put two and two together with what you see and what you hear and what you guess! And you get to where you know exactly what's going on."

"I'm waiting for an answer to my question," Ellis Type said. "Did you ever actually *see* Bant Carr abuse his son?"

"NO!" John Parl shouted, his face red. "If you put it that way, no!"

Ellis Type turned to the judge and spread his hands, his turkey head cocked to one side.

"I'll remind the witness that he is under oath to tell the truth the whole truth and nothing but the truth and he must do so in a courteous and respectful manner," the judge said. "There will be no more outbursts such as the one we have just witnessed. Proceed, Mister Type."

"Thank you, Your Honor," Ellis Type said, smirking. "Now, Mister Parl, I want to know if you ever saw Bant Carr hit his wife?"

"No," John Parl said sullenly. And then his head came up and he pushed himself out of the chair. "But I saw her with her eye blacked and I saw bruises on her face and I've heard that Bant Carr...."

"Confine your answers to the questions put you," Ellis Type screeched, hopping up and down in rage.

Tumblin Green laughed aloud, laughed a booming laugh with head thrown back and hands clasped to his middle. The laughter spread and deepened until the room was filled with the sound. The judge banged his gavel, banged again, and the laughter dwindled and faded out. Ellis Type stood with hands folded behind his back. John Parl sat with head up, puzzlement on his face.

"Mister Type," the judge said, "I'm afraid I'm going to have to ask you what this line of questioning has to do with the case."

"A great deal, Your Honor," Ellis Type said. "I wish to establish that Bant Carr was the decent citizen I know him to be. The defense will attempt to gain the sympathy of this court by a line of questioning designed to show that Bant Carr was cruel to his wife and child."

"Then I suggest you wait for a more fitting time to establish your point. For the time being, I must ask you to develop your case. At this rate we'll be here until fall."

"As you wish, Your Honor," Ellis Type said.

Tumblin Green laughed again, but this time the judge hammered with his gavel before the laughter could spread.

Ellis Type pinched his nose and cocked an eyebrow at the jury. He swung around and walked a few paces, retraced his steps, pinched his nose again and lowered his head, lifted himself to his toes.

"Mister Parl, did you see Kenty Hooker and Bant Carr fight on the streets of this town?"

"No."

"They did fight?"

Tumblin Green started to stand, thought better of it and slumped back in his seat.

"I heard they fought," John Parl said.

"Did you ever see them fight? At any time or any place?"

"Yes, sir. I saw them fight the day Bant Carr was killed!"

I knew then that Kenty was as good as dead. I felt Mama stiffen beside me, felt her hand on my arm, felt her fingers clutching into my flesh. The room was still. Ellis Type threw back his head, stood still and quiet. I saw Kenty sit up straight and stiff and lean forward.

"Tell us about it, Mister Parl," Ellis Type said at last. "Tell us about the fight."

"Well, sir," John Parl said. "I was in the woods by the creek when it happened. I was looking for my cow, you see. She's a bad one to go through a fence. Well, I saw Kenty and the boy come out of the woods and cross the field. Bant saw them coming and leaned on his hoe. The boy stopped and Kenty kept going. He walked right up to Bant and walked along beside him while he hoed. I just stood there and watched, you see, not wanting to get involved. But I could see right off there was going to be trouble."

"They fought?" Ellis Type asked.

"Yes, sir. They fought. It was a pretty rough fight from what I could see.

The cotton was pretty high and I couldn't see too good. But after a while Kenty got up and Bant stayed on the ground. Kenty and the boy went on to the house, so I judged Bant was knocked out cold."

"I see," Ellis Type said. He ducked his head and seemed to be looking at his feet. "Tell me," he said, then. "Tell me whether or not Kenty Hooker carried a gun at that time?"

John Parl took a deep breath. "That's what puzzles me," he said. "I seem to remember that he carried a gun when he first walked up to Bant Carr." He shook his head. "But I can't say for sure. It seemed to me like the boy was carrying something, too, but I can't quite remember."

"Very well," Ellis Type said. "We'll come back to the fight a bit later. Right now I want you to tell me whether or not you ever heard Kenty Hooker threaten Bant Carr."

John Parl shook his head. "Not exactly," he said. "No, sir, I can't say I ever heard him really threaten Bant."

"Did you ever hear him say anything against Bant Carr?"

"Well, sir, once he knocked at my door early of a morning. I was eating breakfast at the time. He came inside and had some coffee and told me something had to be done about Bant. He said Bant was beating the kid something awful and knocking Pearl Carr around with his fists. He said he wasn't going to stand around and let it go on much longer. He said if it happened again he had half a notion to sign a complaint against Bant and have him arrested. He wanted me to go with him to talk to Bant, but I told him I didn't want to get mixed up in any family troubles."

"But he made no threats, Mister Parl?"

John Parl shook his head slowly. "No. Not unless what he said about not standing by and letting Bant beat up on the boy and Pearl Carr was a threat. Said it was going to be stopped one way or another. Said a man couldn't stand aside and let a man beat a boy like Bant beat his boy. Said no man could stand aside knowing a man was beating up on his wife."

Ellis Type walked over to the jury box and leaned on the railing. He stood there a long while with head bowed, letting John Parl's words settle, letting the silence add emphasis to the words, the heavy words, and I felt like screaming. Mama shifted uneasily beside me. People moved uneasily. Ellis Type turned at last, turned slowly as if tired. His body sagged as if with great sorrow.

"Mister Parl, how did you happen to find Bant Carr's body?"

John Parl's eyes were frightened. "My cow," he said. "My cow was...."

"Go ahead, Mister Parl," Ellis Type said.

"My cow was in heat," John Parl said, the red flooding his face. "She got out of the pasture and I followed the fence and found where she'd broke through. She's a bad cow about a fence. Gets out of the pasture at least once a month."

"The fence adjoined the Carr property?"

"It separated Bant Carr's cotton patch from my pasture, down there where the creek makes the bend."

"And the cow was in Bant Carr's cotton patch?"

"No, sir."

"But you found the break in the fence and thought the cow had crossed over?"

"She had crossed over. She was in Bant's corn. Wasn't anything to eat in the cotton, so she crossed on over to the corn."

"And you found Bant Carr's body in the cotton patch?"

"Yes, sir, just where the cotton meets the corn."

"How far over in the cotton was the body, Mister Parl?"

"About three rows."

"Were there signs of a struggle?"

"Well, sir," John Parl leaned back and puffed out his chest, all fear gone, "it looked like Bant was shot closer to the corn patch and crawled a ways. You could see plain as day where the cotton was pushed down. Some stalks laid on the ground, just broke down. Blood was all around."

"Bant Carr was dead when you found him, Mister Parl?"

"Dead as a doornail."

"You are sure of that?"

"Sure as I'm settin' here! I know a dead man when I see one! Many's the body I've helped lay out!"

"What was the position of the body when you found it, Mister Parl?"

"He was flat on his back."

"And you did see signs of a struggle?"

"Well, sir, you could see plain as day how Bant pulled his way through the cotton. Cotton stalks was matted down, the blood thick. Like I said, the stalks was pushed everwhich way, broken and mashed down like as if Bant had been trying to pull hisself along."

"But were there signs of a struggle? Did you see any other tracks there?"

John Parl shot a glance at Kenty Hooker, a furtive glance full of fear.

"I saw other tracks," he admitted.

"Could you identify those tracks?"

And all at once Tumblin Green was on his feet, blood dark in his face, eyes flashing. "I object! This witness is not qualified to identify footprints!"

"Objection sustained," the judge said.

A buzz filled the courtroom. Tumblin Green sat down, breathing hard, but the district attorney only smiled and waited for the noise to subside. He was cool as a cucumber, full of confidence, and his coolness made me afraid for Kenty Hooker.

"You said you saw Bant Carr and Kenty Hooker fight the day Bant Carr was killed. This fight took place in Bant Carr's field?"

"Yes, sir."

"Where were you?"

"At the edge of my pasture, at the fencerow."

"What did Kenty Hooker do after the fight?"

"He went to Bant's house with the boy. Left Bant in the field."

"And what did you do?"

"I was hunting my cow, you see, so I went back into the woods. She wasn't in the woods and I finally found the break in the fence and decided to look in Bant's field."

"After you found the body," Ellis Type said, "you went to tell Pearl Carr her husband was dead. You found Kenty Hooker at the house. Is that right?"

"That's right, yessir."

"Did Kenty Hooker have a gun?"

"Well, sir, I'm not sure. Seems to me he had a gun or that I saw his gun. I seem to remember he had a gun when he fought Bant, but I'm not sure."

"At Bant Carr's house, after you found the body, did you see a gun?"

"I don't know. But I do know I saw a dead rabbit somewhere, either in the field or by the woodpile. I was a mite upset and don't remember exactly."

"What happened after you reached the house, Mister Parl?"

"Well, sir, I told the bad news and then we discussed back and forth what we should do. I was all for going right into town to get the sheriff, but Kenty Hooker said we couldn't leave Bant laying out there in the field."

"Did Kenty specifically say the cotton field?"

John Parl hesitated. "I think he did."

"And you say the body was found just inside the cotton field, at the edge of the corn patch?"

"Yessir."

"But Kenty Hooker specifically said he couldn't leave Bant Carr lying out there in the cotton field?"

"Yessir."

"All right," Ellis Type said. "Tell us what happened next."

"Well, sir, we finally rigged up a sort of stretcher. We cut some poles and got some of Bant's old coats and stuck the poles through the sleeves for a stretcher. Then we went for the body."

"Pearl Carr and the boy, Jeff, went with you?"

"Yessir."

"Did you find anything near the body?" Ellis Type asked.

"I didn't," John Parl said. "Kenty Hooker found something."

"Tell the jury what Kenty Hooker found, Mister Parl."

John Parl looked at the jurors. "He found a shell."

The words excited the crowd, brought a low humming sound of whispers.
Ellis Type waited until the room was quiet.

"Did Kenty Hooker walk around the body?"

"He did."

"And did he ask you and Pearl Carr and the boy to walk around to look
for clues?"

"Yessir," John Parl said, nodding his head emphatically.

"And you saw tracks?"

"Yessir."

"Did it occur to you that in walking around you might be stepping over
tracks already there?"

"Yessir, but Kenty said it was important to look for clues."

"All right," Ellis Type said. "So you all walked around the body looking for
clues and marked out what tracks were already there. It's possible, isn't it,
that Kenty Hooker's tracks were already there? Isn't it possible he made those
tracks look innocent and easily explained by walking around the scene?"

"I object," Tumblin Green said mildly. "The district attorney is surmising
and asking the witness for an opinion."

"Question withdrawn," Ellis Type said.

Three hundred people drew deep breaths.

"Mister Parl," Ellis Type said, speaking slowly and distinctly. "Tell me
what Kenty Hooker did with the shell he found near Bant Carr's body."

"He put it in his pocket," John Parl said.

"Thank you," Ellis Type said.

CHAPTER TWENTY-ONE

"Old Tumblin Green can go to town now!" a man in front of me whispered. "Yessir, you just watch Old Tumblin go to work. He'll mix old John Parl up something awful! Not that John's so goshawful bright to begin with, but Old Tumblin has saved more necks from stretchin' than Ellis Type has had cases! Just you watch! Just you wait!"

Tumblin Green from Calanok. Many's the long winter evening I'd heard Bant tell about Tumblin Green. He didn't look like much, being so humped and wizened, but he walked with authority and confidence and I half expected to see him perform a miracle.

"Mister Parl," he said, his voice old and rusty and cracked. "You told the district attorney you saw Kenty Hooker and Bant Carr have a fight. Is that true?"

"Yessir!"

"You say you saw Kenty Hooker leave the field and go to the house?"

"Yes, sir."

"Bant Carr stayed in the field?"

"Yes, sir, I figured he was out cold."

"But you went back into the woods to hunt your cow. You didn't go see if Bant was hurt?"

"I didn't want to get mixed up in it."

Tumblin Green took a pair of horn-rimmed glasses from his inside coat pocket and hooked them over his nose. He studied a piece of paper for a long moment, crumpled the paper and held it in his hand.

"Tell me, Mister Parl, if you know any reason why there should have been bad blood between Kenty Hooker and Bant Carr."

The room was in sudden uproar. Some men actually stood. The judge banged his gavel, but men and women turned around in their seats to talk to people behind them.

"Order in the court," the judge monotoned. "Order in the court! If there's one more outburst like this I will clear this court! Order in the court!"

John Parl was fidgeting in his seat, white as a sheet, his hands fluttering.

Tumblin Green was calm. He turned his back to the nearest window for light and held the crumpled paper high, smoothed it, held it close to his nose and peered at it.

"Two to one there's nothing written on that paper," a man behind me whispered to his neighbor. "I know Tumblin Green and his slick ways! He'll do anything to make the jury think he knows something he's not letting them in on! Just you wait and see!"

"Now, then, Mister Parl," Tumblin Green said. "Tell me if you know why there should have been bad blood between Kenty Hooker and Bant Carr."

"Why, as for that," John Parl said, "I've heard it said that Kenty...."

"Whoa up, now!" Tumblin Green said, waving both hands in the air. "Let's be sure you understand the question put you. Do you *know* why there should have been bad blood between Kenty Hooker and Bant Carr?"

John Parl looked around the room, looked wildly, as if seeking some escape. He looked at the judge questioningly, besought Tumblin Green with the very expression in his eyes. His lips trembled.

"I've always heard Kenty Hook...."

Tumblin Green was waving his hands in John Parl's face. "Whoa up, now!" he said. "I didn't ask what you'd heard, Mister Parl!"

"Well, they say...."

Tumblin Green cut him off. "And I don't care to know what they say, Mister Parl! Now if you want to identify the persons you mean when you say *they*, Mister Parl, why I'll call them to the stand."

John Parl closed his lips tight.

"Can you tell me from your own knowledge why there should have been bad blood between Kenty Hooker and Bant Carr?" Tumblin Green badgered.

"No," John Parl said.

"Then, for all you know there was no bad blood between them? No hard feelings?"

"They fought."

"Why, I had a fight with one of my neighbors once," Tumblin Green said. "Of course, that was a long time ago. Have you never had a fight, Mister Parl?"

John Parl was desperate. Sweat beaded his forehead, formed droplets on his cheeks.

"I've always been told that the boy is really...."

Tumblin Green stepped forward and pointed a finger at John Parl. Ellis Type bounded out of his chair and hopped across the room.

"I object!" he screeched. "I object to the line of questioning! I object to the badgering this witness has undergone! The defense is asking a question to which the only answer must be based on hearsay!"

"Objection sustained," the judge droned.

Ellis Type returned to his seat. John Parl took a red bandana, from his hip pocket and mopped his face.

"Very well, Mister Parl," Tumblin Green said. "Let us talk about the day you discovered Bant Carr's body. I believe you went immediately to the Carr home to tell the family about Bant. Is that correct?"

"Yessir."

"Kenty Hooker was at the house when you arrived?"

"Yessir."

Tumblin Green pointed a finger at John Parl. "Did Kenty have a gun?"

"I think so, but I'm not sure."

"When he fought with Bant Carr in the field, did he have a gun then?"

"I'm not sure, but I think he carried a gun when he went to the house."

"But you're not sure?"

"No, sir."

"You're not sure Kenty had a gun, but you saw a dead rabbit by the wood-pile?"

"Yessir. Either there or in the field. I remember seeing one, but not just where I saw it."

"Had the rabbit been killed by gunshot?"

"Well, there was blood on it."

Laughter.

Tumblin Green held his hand, his right hand, in the air. He walked to the jury box, walked along the railing with his hand held out, then walked to the witness stand and held his hand close to John Parl's face.

"What do you see?" Tumblin Green asked.

"Your hand," John Parl said.

Laughter.

"Do you see blood on my hand?" Tumblin Green asked.

"Yes, sir."

"Do you think I might have been shot in the hand?"

"I wouldn't think so. No, sir."

"But you think the rabbit died of gunshot wounds?"

"Well, that's what I figured."

"Did you figure he was killed with a shotgun or a rifle?"

"A shotgun, I guess."

"Could a boy have killed him with a nigger shooter?"

"If he was a good shot."

"So you don't know for sure whether Kenty Hooker killed that rabbit or whether Jeff Carr killed it?"

"No, sir."

"You can't swear the rabbit was shot?"

"No, sir."

"Maybe that rabbit committed suicide," Tumblin Green said.

Laughter.

John Parl hung his head, abashed.

"You didn't see Kenty Hooker with a gun?" Tumblin Green asked.

"I'm not sure," John Parl said.

"You didn't see the gun anywhere about the Carr place?"

"I may have. I was excited."

"You saw a dead rabbit?"

"Yessir."

"All right, Mister Parl. When you and Kenty went for the body and looked around for clues, you say Kenty found a shell and put it in his pocket. Now tell me this. Was the shell a shotgun shell?"

John Parl licked his lips. "I think so."

"You think so? Didn't you see it?"

"Well, no. You see, Kenty picked something up and put it right in his pocket. I never saw it."

"Maybe it was a seashell, Mister Parl."

Laughter.

Tumblin Green shook a trembling finger at John Parl. "You told the district attorney that Kenty Hooker said he couldn't leave Bant Carr's body in the cotton fields! Now I want you to think hard, Mister Parl! Did Kenty say he couldn't leave the body in the cotton field? Or did he just say he couldn't leave the body in the field?"

John Parl rubbed his face. "Well, I seem to remember he said the cotton field. And then again...." His voice trailed off.

"You're not sure, are you?"

John Parl shook his head. "No, sir," he said.

Court recessed at five o'clock and the spectators bolted like animals, crowded at the doorway, pushed and jostled. Mama hung back and I waited with her, saw Kenty Hooker led from the room, felt his eyes on me and saw his quick smile. I waved at him.

Mama was worried and had little to say on the way home. We did the chores and ate a cold supper.

"What do you think, Mama?"

"It's not going good, Jeff. Tumblin Green is a good lawyer and all that. But it's not going good."

"He sure tore into old John Parl," I said. "He made John Parl back down about the gun and the rabbit and the shell."

"Making John Parl back down and making people laugh at his cleverness is all right, Jeff. But Ellis Type planted doubts in the minds of the jurors, and that's another thing. John Parl saw Bant and Kenty fight in the field, and that's bad for Kenty."

"I'll have to tell the truth, then," I said. "Tomorrow I'll tell them how it happened."

"It's too late."

"Maybe not, Mama. Maybe if I tell them now they'll believe me."

Mama cried. Her tears splashed on the oilcloth. "They'd tear you up, Jeff. They'd tear your story up in a minute!"

"Why can't you believe me?" I was shouting.

"It's too late, Jeff! They're sure Kenty did it and we can't change their minds! Even if you told it now, son, they wouldn't believe you! Can't you see that?"

I could see it.

I buried my face in my hands and cried.

Mama cried and couldn't stop, cried and cried and couldn't stop, and I cried with her but not for her, cried for myself and for Kenty and for Bant.

The second day of the trial is blurred in my memory. It seemed unreal at the time. I hardly knew what was going on. Ellis Type had men on the stand I'd never seen, men who said Bant talked about Kenty Hooker a lot. John Dabney took the stand in the late afternoon and said Bant came to him a month before he died and told him he was thinking of putting Kenty under a peace bond. Jim English told about the time Kenty Hooker knocked him unconscious because he'd called me Kenty's little bastard.

Kenty sat that day with head down. I didn't see him look up a single time. He still needed a haircut, needed a shave.

I sat there all day wondering how I could save Kenty Hooker.

The way I figured it, they wouldn't pay much attention to me. I wasn't even sure they'd listen to my story. Still, I made up my mind to stand up and shout the truth if they convicted Kenty.

That night I couldn't sleep. Mama was restless, too, because I could hear the springs of her bed as she rolled and tossed the night out.

Next day's crowd was the largest I'd ever seen. I couldn't drive to the square and had to circle around it to reach my parking place at the lumberyard. The press at the door held us back, and we didn't get in until the sheriff came to clear a path. People really buzzed then, pointed at us as if we were strange animals, pointed and talked aloud, as if we couldn't hear. They said, "That's her, the woman in black with the little boy! That's her! They say she was carrying on with Kenty Hooker and that boy is Kenty Hooker's boy!"

The sheriff was first on the stand.

Ellis Type was in fine form. He fairly bounced on the balls of his feet while the sheriff was being sworn in. He nodded at people, waved at people, smiled big.

"Sheriff Johnson," Ellis Type purred, honey fairly dripping. "I understand you've been sheriff of this county for twenty-one years."

"That's right."

"As sheriff, you have investigated many cases of murder?"

"I have."

"On the evening of July twenty-ninth you were called to investigate the murder of Bant Carr?"

"I was."

"Who notified you that Carr had been killed?"

"Kenty Hooker."

The sheriff leaned back in his chair and folded his hands over the buckle of his big belt. He crossed his right leg over the left and jiggled his foot.

"Was Kenty Hooker unduly excited, sheriff? Did he seem to be agitated?"

"He was very excited."

"What were Kenty Hooker's first words to you?"

"He said he wanted me to come with him quick because Bant Carr had committed suicide!"

I shouted aloud at the lie and immediately covered my mouth with my hand. Six hundred eyes fell on me and looked through me.

Ellis Type must have waited a full minute to ask his next question. He was always doing that, always pausing after establishing a point.

"Sheriff Johnson," Ellis Type said, "tell us in your own words what happened on the way to the Carr farm that night."

The sheriff leaned forward, hands resting on his thighs. "Well, to begin with, we didn't make the trip together. I followed Kenty out. But before we left town we went by my office so's I could tell my deputy where I was going. While we were in the office I asked Kenty a few questions. He didn't seem to want to answer. Just sort of grunted and evaded the issue, so to speak. But he did say he'd made a mistake when he told me Bant committed suicide. Said he guessed he was excited."

"What occurred after you reached the farm, sheriff?" Ellis Type asked. His questions didn't seem like the same sort of questions he'd asked John Parl. Something was different, and for a while I couldn't think what it was. Then I had it. The questions he asked the sheriff were mechanical. They sounded memorized. When he had questioned the other witnesses, he had leaned forward, had listened as eagerly as any of the spectators in the room. He didn't seem to be listening to the sheriff, though. It seemed he knew the answers.

"Well," the sheriff said, "I asked a few questions and then I examined Bant Carr's shotgun. It hadn't been shot. Leastways, it didn't have a powder smell to it. I can usually tell just by sniffing if a gun's been shot."

I wanted to yell again.

"Continue, please," Ellis Type said.

"Well, I took a lantern and...."

The sheriff stiffened. He screwed up his face and chewed his lower lip.

"What is it, sheriff?" Ellis Type asked.

"I just thought of something I'd forgot," Sheriff Johnson said. "Kenty Hooker said he'd get a light so we could go out to the field to see where Bant was shot. I was talking to Bant's widow and the boy, and I remember Kenty was gone a long time."

"How long, sheriff?" Ellis Type purred.

"Well, maybe a half-hour. Yeah, at least a half-hour."

I could have screamed my rage.

"He returned with the light?"

"Yes."

"Did he say where he'd been?"

"No. I figured he'd been hunting a lantern at the barn or someplace, so I didn't think to ask him."

Ellis Type paced to and fro in front of the witness chair. Sheriff Johnson's head turned from side to side as he watched Ellis Type walk. There wasn't a sound in the room, not a sound.

"Sheriff Johnson," Ellis Type said, "how far would you judge a man like Kenty Hooker could walk or run in thirty minutes?"

"Why, I don't know for sure," the sheriff said thoughtfully.

"Let's see. I reckon a man could walk a good eight miles in a couple of hours. That'd make him able to walk two or three miles in a half-hour. If he was running, though…."

"And how far is it from the Carr house to the Hooker house, sheriff?"

"Not more than two miles, I'd say, across country."

Before I knew it I was out in the aisle. I remember how hard it was to squeeze my way out. I remember the feel of knees against my thighs, but I don't remember seeing anything or hearing anything or thinking anything until I got clear.

"It's not true!" I shouted. "It's a lie! Kenty wasn't gone more than ten minutes! Not even that long!"

The room was a sea of movement. I saw Ellis Type saying something to the judge, saw the sheriff leaning back in the witness chair as relaxed as could be, saw the gnomelike figure of Tumblin Green bobbing toward Ellis Type, saw the wavelike motion of people as they twisted in their seats, saw Mama staring at me and saw her lips moving and knew she was saying my name.

Nobody touched me.

Everything went quiet.

"Bring that boy down here," the judge said.

"Your Honor," Tumblin Green said, "I'd like to ask this boy a few questions."

"I haven't finished with my witness, Your Honor," Ellis Type said.

"Have the boy seated," the judge said. "We will hear him in due time."

Tumblin Green took my arm and steered me to a seat in the front row. I looked up, straight into the cold eyes of the sheriff, felt the chill in those eyes and shivered.

"Sheriff Johnson," Ellis Type began, "I'd like for you to tell us how you found the scene of the crime."

"You mean how I knew where to look? Kenty Hooker showed me the way."

"Will you describe what you saw, sheriff?"

"Well, sir," the sheriff said, "I wasn't able to do much by lantern light. But I could see enough to know the place had been walked over. Kenty Hooker and John Parl and Pearl Carr and her boy had trooped around that place looking for clues... so they said... until you couldn't make heads nor tails of anything."

"Did you visit the scene again?"

"I slipped out there early the next morning," the sheriff said. "I went over that place with a fine tooth comb. The only tracks around there belonged to Bant and John Parl and Kenty and Pearl Carr and the boy. And myself, too, of course. I'd been there the night before."

"What about a weapon, sheriff? Did you find a gun?"

"I did not. There was no gun there."

"All right then. We'll come back to that point later. On the night you were called out there, sheriff, you say you asked some questions and that Kenty Hooker left the house to look for a lantern. He was gone for thirty minutes. When he returned with the lantern, you visited the spot where Bant Carr was killed. Now, what else did you do?"

"I went to Kenty Hooker's house."

"Alone?"

"No. Kenty Hooker went with me."

"And what did you find?"

"His gun."

A buzz in the courtroom, the beginning of babble, and then the judge rapped for order.

"And did you examine this gun?" Ellis Type asked.

"I did."

"Will you tell us what you determined?"

"The gun had been fired not many hours before," the sheriff said, nodding his head for emphasis.

Tumblin Green stood and hobbled forward.

"Your Honor," he said, "I object. I doubt that the witness is qualified to tell whether or not a gun has been fired within a matter of hours."

"We have not yet heard the witness tell how he formed his opinion," the judge said. "Objection overruled."

Ellis Type smirked. "Tell us, sheriff, how you determined the gun had been fired."

"I smelled it," the sheriff said.

A man somewhere in the room laughed aloud.

"That gun had been fired not too long before," the sheriff said stubbornly, his eyes searching the room for the man who had laughed. "I can tell every time."

"Are you prepared to demonstrate your ability?" Ellis Type asked.

"I am."

Ellis Type turned to the judge. "Your Honor, a man in the hallway has two guns. I ask the Court to appoint any person of its choice to leave this building and fire one of those guns. The witness will then smell both guns and tell the Court which has been fired."

Again a man laughed.

Tumblin Green stood, both hands on the tabletop before him.

"Your Honor," he drawled, "on my way to court this morning I saw a rock sprout wings and fly. If anybody in this room doesn't believe me, why, I'll be glad to produce the rock!"

Laughter, loud laughter, thundered in the room.

If looks could kill.

Ellis Type was white, so white he was tinged with green, but Sheriff Johnson was red, not the scarlet red of embarrassment but the flushed red of anger. He came out of the chair in one lithe movement, stepped down from the stand and stood shaking with anger. Ellis Type had enough presence of mind to motion him back.

Tumblin Green turned his back on the two and hobbled to his chair. His face was the face of an imp. He was enjoying himself hugely, reveling in the rocking gales of laughter.

What was it Mama had said?

It's one thing for Tumblin Green to make them laugh, but Ellis Type is putting seeds of doubt in the minds of the jurors.

The room was quiet.

"All right, Sheriff Johnson," Ellis Type said. His words were tight, clipped. "Tell me whether or not you searched Kenty Hooker."

"I did," the sheriff said. "I searched his pockets."

"What did you find?"

"A shell," the sheriff said. "I found a shotgun shell."

Three hundred people sighed.

"What gauge?"

"Twelve," the sheriff said. "It was a twelve-gauge shell."

"What kind of shotgun did Kenty Hooker have?"

"Twelve gauge."

"Thank you," Ellis Type said.

The sheriff was lying. My shotgun was a .410.

I sat there, all keyed up, sorting the pieces and forming them in my mind. This time I knew what I was doing, knew all the time, planned it all and staged 'it all.

"It's a lie!" I shrieked, jumping up. "Kenty didn't have a shell! He's lying! I can tell you the...."

A hand was clapped over my mouth. All I could see was the hand, the wrist, my head held stiff and straight so I couldn't turn it or lower it. I could see hairs on a wrist, could see fingers, dirty fingernails. I tried to bite and couldn't. The fingers pinched cruelly into my cheeks.

"Take that boy out," the judge said. "Explain to him that he must stay quiet if he wishes to remain in the room."

Somebody turkey-trotted me down the aisle and out the door. I could hear the gibbling laughter long after we'd left the room.

"All right," a voice said. "Now, behave yourself."

I was free. The man was a deputy, for he wore a badge, but I'd never seen him before. His face wasn't unkind. He was a tall man, a thin man, neatly dressed in khakis. He wore a straw hat, rancher style, and his eyes were blue and wide, the face deeply browned, the eyebrows thick and heavy, the nose long and thin, the mouth wide and chin square. He was grinning.

"Looks like you don't put much faith in the sheriff, partner," the man said.

"He lies!" I said. "Kenty didn't pick up any twelve-gauge shell like the sheriff said!"

"How do you know?"

"I was there!"

"Did you see the shell he picked up?"

"No. He just stooped to study sign."

"We'll go back in if you promise to keep quiet."

"I promise."

"We'll go in, then. I want to hear the rest of it. But, mind me. First peep out of you and out you go."

"I'll keep quiet."

CHAPTER TWENTY-TWO

Tumblin Green from Calanok.

The little man shuffled across the room toward the witness, brushed elbows with Ellis Type in passing, stood before the sheriff like a gaunt question mark, head bowed.

"Sheriff," Tumblin Green said in a voice low pitched, "Where is that twelve-gauge shotgun shell you found on Kenty Hooker?"

"On that table over there," Sheriff Johnson said, pointing. "I think it's marked Exhibit B."

"Can you prove it came from Kenty Hooker's gun? Can you prove it was fired in Kenty Hooker's gun?"

"I don't mean to prove it," Sheriff Johnson said. "I'm the sheriff of this county and my word ought to be enough."

"A man's life is at stake here!" Tumblin Green said. "I'm not prepared to accept your word or anybody's word on a matter like this! I want proof!"

"That shell was fired in Kenty Hooker's gun!" the sheriff said.

"Sheriff," Tumblin Green said, "John Parl testified on this stand that he didn't actually see a shell picked up by Kenty Hooker. Are you prepared to swear that the shell on that table over there once contained the shot that was fired into the body of Bant Carr?"

Sheriff Johnson stared hard and straight at Tumblin Green. The seconds ticked by, ticked by, ticked by. Stillness was a thick and heavy thing.

"I can't swear to that," the sheriff muttered. "One buckshot is like any other. But I can swear I found that shell at the scene of the killing."

"Are you prepared to swear that shell on yonder table was fired by Kenty Hooker's gun?"

"I am!"

Tumblin Green turned to face the jury. A smile softened his face. He stood so for a moment only, then whirled to face the sheriff.

"Who fired that shot?"

Sheriff Johnson gasped like a fish out of water. Speech stuck in his throat. He opened his mouth to speak, but Tumblin Green was too fast for him.

"That's all!" Tumblin Green said.

Ellis Type threw his chair back, sent it skittering over backward to the floor. "Just a minute! I object! Your Honor, I object! Just a minute there!"

He charged forward, waving his arms, fairly dancing in anger.

"I object to the tactics of the defense, Your Honor!" he shrilled. "He didn't give the witness time to answer!"

"The witness wasn't prepared to answer, Your Honor," Tumblin Green drawled. "He's had time to think now, and I wouldn't want to accept his answer."

"We will hear the answer," the judge said.

"Kenty Hooker fired that shot," the sheriff said.

"Who fired that shot?" Tumblin Green asked.

Laughter at the old joke, laughter unrestrained, laughter gay.

"Kenty Hooker fired that shot!" Sheriff Johnson shouted against the laughter.

"Did you see him fire it?" Tumblin Green asked.

"No."

"Are you sure he didn't fire it at a rabbit?"

The sheriff's eyes flicked right, left, right, left. He looked at Ellis Type and hesitated.

"Are you sure the shot wasn't fired at a rabbit?" Tumblin Green repeated.

"No," Sheriff Johnson said.

"How do you know that shell was fired by Kenty Hooker's gun?"

"Well," the sheriff said, "there are some little dents at the butt of the shell. They're just exactly like the dents on the butt of that other shell over there, the one marked Exhibit C."

"Where'd you get the shell marked Exhibit C?" Tumblin Green asked.

"Well, I fired the gun and then I took the shell and compared it to the other one."

"You fired Kenty Hooker's gun?"

Sheriff Johnson pinched his nose. "Yes."

"When did you fire the gun? After you arrested Kenty Hooker?"

"Yes," the sheriff nodded assent.

"How many times did you fire the gun?"

"Oh, I don't know. Two or three times."

"Where are the other shells?"

"Well, I only kept one."

"Maybe you kept two," Tumblin Green said. "Are you sure you didn't keep two? Isn't one marked B and the other C?"

The sheriff gritted his teeth and remained silent.

Tumblin Green laughed in his face.

"Sheriff, you want us to believe you allowed Kenty Hooker to leave the Carr house and go look for a lantern. You say he was gone thirty minutes, but you didn't think anything about it at the time. Now, in an obvious attempt to make us believe Kenty Hooker had time to take his gun home and return, you attach some significance to his long absence. I want you to remember that you're under oath! Do you still contend Kenty Hooker was gone from the house for a full thirty minutes?"

"About that long."

"How long have you been in the witness chair, sheriff?"

Sheriff Johnson fidgeted uneasily. "About an hour. Maybe a little more."

"You've missed it a full thirty minutes," Tumblin Green said. "You've not been on the stand a half-hour."

It is possible at times to feel ahead and know whether things will be good or bad. I knew a bad day was ahead the minute I opened my eyes. All the days had been bad, but I knew at once this day would be worse than all the days before. Mama drank her coffee in silence, her face troubled.

We did our chores as in a ritual, each doing the work to be done in silence, the milking and feeding and egg gathering. I brought water and wood to the house, washed in the warm pan of water Mama poured for me, and waited on the front porch until she was ready. The sun was barely up when we drove out of the yard.

The crowd in town was different, somehow, a silent and brooding mass, no longer driven by curiosity. This crowd seemed to have a purpose, seemed to have the same sense of foreboding I'd had all morning.

As we entered the courthouse I heard one man say Kenty Hooker would take the stand.

Tumblin Green was walking back and forth in front of the jury box. His mouth was tight drawn and twisted. Now and then his lips moved.

The jurors filed in, took seats. They looked tired. There was worry in their eyes, plain as day, sick worry. I felt sorry for them.

Kenty Hooker came in, his right wrist cuffed to the left wrist of Sheriff Johnson. I felt a sob knot in my throat and choked it down. There was no fight in him. The fire was gone from him, the fire bedded down in ashes somewhere deep inside him. I wanted to cry aloud, wanted to tell him to lift his chin, wanted to tell him I cared what happened to him and that nothing would happen to him because I wouldn't let it happen.

We stood when the judge entered, stood automatically, and I could feel the resentment flowing from the bodies of all the people who stood. For the first time I felt resentment, wondered why I should stand for the judge, and knew for the first time that he was a man like any other man and disliked standing for him.

They called Kenty to the stand, and he stated his name, age, and place of birth.

Tumblin Green clasped his hands behind him and faced the jury.

He talked in a low tone of voice, his eyes on the jury. "Mister Hooker," he said. "I want to know if you considered Bant Carr a friend?"

"I did."

"Did you kill Bant Carr?" Tumblin Green asked.

"I did not," Kenty said.

"Do you know who killed Bant Carr?"

Kenty hesitated, for a moment hesitated. "I do not."

Tumblin Green's body seemed to sag. His shoulders drooped.

"Mister Hooker," he said, "you're on trial here for your very life. If you know any person who had reason to kill Bant Carr, I beg you now to speak."

"I don't know who killed Bant," Kenty said.

"A witness has testified that you fought with Bant Carr a short while before Bant was killed. Is that true?"

"It is."

"Why did you fight?"

"Bant beat up on Pearl and the boy the night before. Pearl sent the boy for me. She wanted me to take her away somewhere. I went across the field and tried to talk to Bant because I thought I could reason with him." Kenty spread his hands. "Bant wouldn't listen. He jumped me."

"You knocked him unconscious?"

"Yes, sir."

"You then went to Bant's house, did you?"

"Yes, sir."

"You talked to Pearl Carr and she asked you to take her away?"

"Yes, sir."

"What was your next action?"

"I had to go back to my house to get some money and my car. I told Pearl and the boy to get packed. I got back to Bant's house just about the time John Parl got there. He told us Bant was dead."

"You fought with Bant in town," Tumblin Green said. "Why did you fight?"

"Bant slapped his kid and I slapped him. It was wrong of me and I was sorry the minute I did it. But he had no right to slap the kid and I lost my temper."

"Mister Hooker, you heard Sheriff Johnson say you left the room the night he was at Bant Carr's home. He said you left the room for half an hour. Is that true?"

"That was a lie!" Kenty said. "I wasn't out of the sheriff's sight ten minutes!"

"Did you pick up a shell near the spot Bant Carr died?"

"I did not," Kenty said. "The sheriff lied about that, too."

"Tell me," Tumblin Green said. "Do you think Bant Carr was sane the day he died?"

"I think he was crazy," Kenty said. "I think he'd been crazy a long time."

Tumblin Green turned to Ellis Type. "Your witness, Mister Type."

Ellis Type's smile was an ugly thing. He bowed to the jury, bowed to the judge, stood in front of Kenty and looked him over.

"Mister Hooker," he drawled, "you would have us believe that Bant Carr was your friend."

"Yes, sir. He was my closest friend."

Ellis Type swung around and faced us, all of us there in the audience, his back to the jurors. He spread his hands as if in hopeless appeal, as if to say, "What can you do with a man like this?" And then he whirled around so fast his coattails cut an arc through the air. He pointed his finger at Kenty.

"You mean to tell us you killed your closest friend?" His words popped like whipcracks, sharp and clear.

"I never killed anybody," Kenty drawled. "Least of all my friend."

"You had fights with your... friend," Ellis Type said. "You fought with him the day before he was killed and you fought again the day he died. Do you deny that?"

"Friends fight sometimes."

"Do you deny fighting with the deceased?"

"I fought with him."

"And still he was your friend?"

"When he was sober he was my friend. When he was drunk he was still my friend... but I wasn't his friend. Most times he loved everybody, drunk or sober. But when he got drunk he hated three people. Me, the boy... and his wife."

Ellis Type pulled a sheet of paper from his pocket.

"I want you to tell the jury why you fought with Bant Carr!" he said. "I want the truth!"

"You heard me say. He beat up on his wife and kid and they wanted me to take them away. I went to the field to reason with him, but we ended up fighting."

"And yet you claim he was your friend?"

"It's hard to explain," Kenty said. "He was my friend, but he went all haywire. I couldn't reason with him. I couldn't make him see he was wrong."

Ellis Type twirled his watch chain around his finger, twirled it up tightly and untwirled it, the chain forming a golden circle in the dim light of the room.

"Was Bant Carr jealous of you?"

"No!" Kenty said. "He had nothing to be jealous about!"

"Didn't he suspect you of... carrying on with his wife? Didn't he?" Ellis Type pointed his finger. "Didn't he?"

Kenty shook his head helplessly.

"Isn't it true," Ellis Type said, his voice rolling as a preacher's voice rolls, "that Bant Carr believed his son to be, in reality, your flesh and blood?"

Kenty lowered his head and didn't speak.

Ellis Type twirled his watch chain.

"Were you carrying a gun that day, Mister Hooker?"

Kenty hesitated a second too long. "Yes."

"You had a gun and you shot a rabbit!" Ellis Type accused.

"Yes."

"You left the gun in Bant's yard and forgot it! When the sheriff came that night you went to the barn to hunt a lantern. But you grabbed up that gun and ran with it all the way to your house! You were gone a full half-hour!"

"No!" Kenty shouted.

"You'd been trying to break up Bant Carr's home!" Ellis Type thundered. "You had been after Pearl Carr to leave Bant, hadn't you? You begged her to go to the city and get a job! You told her you'd join her there later!"

"It's not true," Kenty said quietly.

"Bant was in his field that day and you met him there! He remonstrated with you for trying to break up his home and you shot him! Isn't that true?" That finger, Ellis Type's terrible shaking finger, not an inch from Kenty's nose. "Isn't that true, Kenty Hooker? Isn't it? ISN'T IT?"

Kenty took a deep breath and shook his head slowly.

"Don't take on so, Ellis," he drawled. "I'm telling you here and now you'll never get another vote of mine."

Laughter.

Ellis Type stooped and began to weave, for all the world like an old land turtle.

"You asked Pearl Carr to leave her husband. Isn't that true, Kenty Hooker?"

"Yes, I asked her to leave Bant. I figured that Bant would kill her sooner or later, or at least that he'd kill the boy."

"You asked her to go to the city?"

"That's the only place she could go! She doesn't have any folks!"

"And didn't you promise to meet her there?"

"Not MEET her there! I promised to look in on her and see that she had a roof over her head and food to eat!"

"You were showing an uncommon interest in the wife of another man," Ellis Type sneered.

"Bant Carr was my friend!" Kenty said. "His wife was my friend and so was his son! But I couldn't stand aside and see Bant beat the boy within an inch of his life and slap Pearl around the way he did!" He took a deep breath and spoke quietly. "Once I thought about swearing out a complaint against Bant, but I figured that'd just make matters worse."

"Other witnesses don't seem to share your belief that Bant Carr beat his wife and son," Ellis Type said.

"It's true, just the same. Listen!" Kenty gestured, palms up. "The sheriff saw their faces right after Bant was killed! Ask him about it! Listen! I talked to

Bant time after time! I begged him to treat his family decent! Listen! I don't deny there were rumors around that I fathered the boy! I knew it and Bant knew it and that's what was eating Bant up! It was like a poison eating on him! That's why he drank!"

Kenty let his hands fall, let his chin fall on his chest. Ellis Type started to speak, but Kenty's head snapped up and he held his fists shoulder high and shook them.

"Bant never accused me of fathering the boy!"

Ellis Type whispered, but I could hear him in the back of the room.

"Are you in love with Pearl Carr?"

Kenty's eyes found Mama. "I was once. Long ago."

"I demand an answer!" Ellis Type screeched. "Are you in love with Pearl Carr?"

Tumblin Green stood to protest. Kenty saw him, shook his head at him, and Tumblin Green sat down.

"I love her, but not in the old way. Not in the way you think." Kenty Hooker spoke quietly against the quietness of the room, but his words were as loud as thunder, tinged with despair. "I feel responsible for the situation she was in."

"He's a cooked goose now," the man beside me breathed.

The room was in uproar and the judge banged his gavel unseen and unheard. Kenty slumped down in the chair and rested his head on his hand.

The judge said something that I couldn't hear, but then he called a recess. Sheriff Johnson beckoned to Kenty, and a moment later led him from the room. The aisles filled and the uproar swelled to an hysterical pitch. I lost Mama in the crowd, stood aside to let the people ebb past me, found her and caught her arm, entered the tide and with her, was pushed out the door, down the hallway, down the stairs and into the open.

A solid wall of humanity blocked our way, opened up as we advanced and closed behind us. They followed us and it seemed to me we were pushed along by the sound of their voices.

Mama took my hand and led me across the street. "We'll have some coffee."

We entered a café. All the stools at the counter were filled, but we found an empty booth and slid into it, out of sight and grateful for the shelter.

Men were talking in the booth behind us…

…and that's all there is to it, see, because he's the only one that had the motive and the only one that could have done it.

…sure, I'll agree Tumblin Green is smart and that he had the sheriff on the run. But when Kenty Hooker said he loved Pearl Carr, he just the same as tied the noose himself.

…but have you seen the kid?

...spittin' image of old Kenty.

...always wondered why Kenty went away, what with that good farm and his folks gettin' old and him the only one to take care of them.

...she's still a handsome woman.

...don't be getting any ideas, Zave!

...maybe Tumblin's got something up his sleeve.

...only thing he's got up his sleeve now is his elbow!

A girl in a white dress brought Mama her coffee. She sipped it. There was a soft look on her face, a far look in her eyes. If she heard the men in the other booth she didn't let on it bothered her.

CHAPTER TWENTY-THREE

Mama led me to the lumber yard and pulled me behind a stack of lumber to pray. I can't remember all she prayed, but part of it had to do with lies she would have to tell, for which she begged forgiveness. While she prayed she held me close, and I felt tears on my face.

"Jeff," she said after she'd finished, "I want you to promise you'll act right while I'm on the stand. Promise to keep still and quiet, no matter what you hear me say."

"Mama, I'm going to ask one more time. Let me tell the truth."

Her eyes misted over. "We've been over it time and again, Jeff, and it's too late. They've made something nasty of this, Jeff, just as Kenty knew they'd do. All I can do is try to save Kenty by telling how Bant treated you."

"They'll hang him, Mama! Unless I tell them what really happened, they'll hang him!"

"Jeff, listen to me." She took both my hands in hers and cradled them to her breast. "You're big enough now to know the facts of life. If you try to shoulder the blame, they'll say you hated Bant and killed him because of it. They'll send you away, Jeff, and I couldn't stand that! Kenty knows I couldn't stand it!"

"Mama! Listen to me! They're going to hang Kenty! Once the trial's over we won't have another chance to save him! He didn't do it, Mama, and we can't let him take the blame!"

She covered her face with her hands and turned away. She spoke with her back to me.

"Jeff?"

"What is it, Mama?"

"Will you... whatever happens, will you love me always?"

"Yes."

"I want to be strong, Jeff. I wish we'd told the truth at the start."

I couldn't think of anything to say.

"Jeff?"

"What, Mama?"

"Do you want to tell me what happened that day?"

I sat up. "I told you the truth, Mama," I said. "Mama, I told you the truth!"

"Did you, son?"

"I wouldn't lie to you," I said. "I couldn't."

We walked back to the courthouse without speaking.

Ellis Type walked from his table to the jury box and stood staring into the faces of the tired men and women behind the railing. He turned and placed his hands behind his back, twitched at his coattails and walked across the room to the seats occupied by the newspaper people. Then, turning slowly, he looked straight at Mama.

"I call Pearl Carr to the stand," he said.

A man stood up and said, "Pearl Carr to the stand," in a nasal singsong voice.

In all that courtroom there was only one sound, the sound of Mama's skirts rustling as she edged past me into the aisle. She marched toward the witness stand with her head high and her back stiff and straight as a poker. She took her seat and raised her right hand, repeated the oath after the little man with the book.

Ellis Type bowed to Mama.

"Missus Carr," he said. "I regret the necessity of calling you to this stand. Believe me, I know how painful this must be for you."

Mama nodded her head, her expression never changing.

Ellis Type plucked at his lower lip. "Missus Carr," he began, "I'm going to ask you first if your husband was a drinking man."

"You know he was," Mama said.

"Why did he drink, Missus Carr?"

"I don't know." Mama framed the words with her lips.

"Was it out of jealousy?"

"He had no cause."

"All right!" Ellis Type snapped. "Let's talk about the day your husband was killed, madam. You first learned of your husband's death when your neighbor, John Parl, came into your yard and told you. Is that right?"

Mama seemed undecided. She searched the room for me, found me and looked into my eyes, looked away and back again, and then looked straight at Kenty Hooker.

"No," she said. "That isn't true."

My heart went thump thump loud inside me and my blood tingled in my veins, actually tingled and burned, throbbed like a drum in my ears so loudly I thought for a moment there was sound in the room. But the room was hushed as a church. Ellis Type had been taken by surprise. He took a step back, quickly, as if he had been slapped, even raised his hand to his cheek as though to feel the burning there.

"I... understand you to say it is not true that John Parl was the first to tell you of your husband's death?"

"I knew he was dead before John Parl came," Mama said.

"Did Kenty Hooker tell you?"

"He did not," Mama said. Her voice faltered and almost broke.

"May I ask how you knew?"

"I saw him," Mama said.

It was then I died inside, cried at my own funeral, died and mourned my death and lived to die again and cry again so long as I should live.

Ellis Type began to tremble. His very coattails shook with his trembling. He raised his arm and pointed that awful wavering finger at Mama.

"Madam, did you kill your husband?"

Mama's lips parted and her face went pinched white. She flicked her lips with her tongue and tried to speak. And all the while I sat waiting, buried in an awful quiet, a heavy choking stillness.

"No," Mama said.

Ellis Type's voice shook. "Tell us what happened." He mopped his brow with his sleeve and took yet another step backward.

Mama began to speak in a low voice. "Bant was mad at Jeff. He'd had the fight with Kenty in town and Jeff took Kenty's side. When Bant came home he was drunk. He started hitting Jeff and when I tried to stop him... he hit me."

Her voice trailed away and her eyes sought mine. I slipped down into my seat, way down so she couldn't find me. It wasn't that I was scared because she was telling the truth. It wasn't that at all. It was that she'd warned me to keep quiet, had warned me that I'd be sent away if they learned the truth. And she'd told me she couldn't stand it if they sent me away. Now she was telling the truth. Kenty was in danger and she was telling her truth, but she didn't know the truth, didn't believe the truth, wouldn't believe the truth. I wanted to cry out... Mama, don't tell it... let me tell it in my own way... you said you couldn't stand for them to send me away, so why are you telling it when you said you wouldn't and couldn't tell it, Mama, stop.

"Please continue," Ellis Type croaked.

"The next morning Bant went to the field."

She stopped talking.

"Yes," Ellis Type prompted.

I sat up. Mama was looking straight at me and never have I seen a look so sad.

Kenty Hooker stood then, stood straight and tall. Tumblin Green tugged at his sleeve and pulled him down.

"Don't, Pearl!" Kenty called. "Don't do it!"

Mama glanced at him and shook her head slightly.

"Bant went to the field and worked like crazy in the cotton. He was ankle deep in mud. I sat on the porch and thought it out. It seemed to me I had no choice. Either I could stay and let him beat the boy or I could leave and earn a living for the boy and myself. So I sent Jeff after Kenty. I'd made up my mind to leave."

Kenty Hooker covered his face with his hands.

"Kenty and Jeff went across the field," Mama said. "I could see them. Kenty talked with Bant and... they fought. Kenty knocked Bant down and came on to the house. Jeff followed him."

Ellis Type waited for her to speak. He had a panther by the tail and couldn't turn loose. Even I could see he didn't know what to do.

Mama spoke, finally. "I told Kenty I had to leave and he said he'd take me somewhere. He said he'd have to go home after some money and his car. While he was gone... Bant came. He started for Jeff and Jeff went under the house for his gun. I ran into the house and got Bant's gun. Bant said some crazy things and then ran across the field. He was weaving and staggering like a drunk man, only I know he hadn't had a thing to drink all day. I kept thinking he'd fall. But he didn't fall and I was afraid he'd go to Kenty Hooker's house."

All the time she was talking I knew I should stand and stop her, knew I should stand and demand that I be allowed to tell the truth the whole truth and nothing but the truth. My mind worked it out, all the things I should do, but somehow it didn't matter and I let Mama tell it in her own way. She stopped talking and Ellis Type didn't say anything, didn't ask anything, just stood there and waited.

Mama looked at me again. Her lips softened and she smiled. I wondered when she'd made up her mind to tell it. And then I remembered how she'd asked if I wanted to tell her how it really happened.

I wondered how she'd end it.

Maybe she'd say Bant shot himself with my gun.

Maybe she'd say it happened as it really happened.

She found her voice again.

"I told Jeff to run warn Kenty. I asked him to leave his gun, but he ran off through the field. I could see he hoped to beat Bant to the fencerow. But Bant kept staggering and weaving. He went into the corn, but I knew he'd seen Jeff and would try to stop him. I thought of our car, then. For the first time I thought of the car. Jeff can drive and we could have taken the car to warn Kenty."

Mama lowered her head, closed her eyes tightly, fought back the tears.

Not a sound, not one single sound in that big room.

Mama lifted her head.

"I went around the house, thinking I could drive the car to Kenty's house. But the keys weren't in the car and I decided it was more important to see that Bant didn't hurt Jeff. So I went back around the house, and by that time Bant was almost to the corn. I started across the field. I was running and I fell down."

She pinched her lips hard, still fighting the tears.

I hadn't meant to cry, hadn't thought of it, but the tears came streaming.

"I fell down and I heard a shot," Mama said.

So heavy was the silence I thought I could hear my own tears fall.

"You are saying that your son killed his father," Ellis Type said.

Mama bowed her head and cried.

I couldn't see for the tears.

In the silence that followed I blundered my way to the aisle. People seemed to shrink away from me, pulled back their legs to let me pass. I walked toward the front of the room, brushed away the tears, pushed open the little gate in the railing and went to stand before the judge. Ellis Type started toward me, stopped, half raised his hand and let it fall. The judge raised his gavel and then let it sink down.

"I killed him," I said. "I'd do it again."

Quite slowly I unbuttoned the buttons of my shirt and took the shirt off. I turned to show my scarred back to the jury.

"Put on your shirt, son," the judge said.

Tumblin Green hobbled across the room to me, took my arm and led me to his table. He seated me beside Kenty. I looked up at Kenty and saw tears in his eyes. He took my right hand in both of his.

"You mustn't think badly..." he began, and then he choked up.

"I wasn't going to let you hang," I said.

Ellis Type cleared his throat.

"Where is the gun?" he asked.

"Under the house," Mama whispered.

"Do you expect the court to believe the story you've just told?"

"It's the truth."

"You're trying to protect Kenty Hooker!" Ellis Type said. "You'd befoul the name of your own son to protect your lover!"

Tumblin Green objected. "Your Honor," he said. "It has been interesting to watch and listen to the district attorney during this trial. From time to time he has insinuated that Kenty Hooker and Pearl Carr were lovers. However, each time he skirts the issue. I believe he should either attempt to prove his point or avoid referring to it."

"Objection sustained." the judge said. "The district attorney must either make the accusation a point to be developed, or he must refrain from its mention. There is nothing to bar him from making the accusation, but in my court he must at least make an attempt at proof."

"Very well, Your Honor," Ellis Type said graciously. And, to Mama, "Do you deny that Kenty Hooker was your lover?"

"I do."

"You heard Kenty Hooker admit that he loved you. Do you, in turn, love

Kenty Hooker?"

Mama was starch white. "I've never allowed myself to think about it."

"Is Kenty Hooker the father of your son?"

Mama shook her head wildly. "No! It's not true!"

"Why did Bant Carr hate his son, then? Why did he hate Kenty Hooker? Why was he afraid of Kenty Hooker?"

"I don't know," Mama moaned. "I truly don't know!"

"Kenty Hooker shot and killed Bant Carr, didn't he? He was in the field and met Bant and shot him! You saw it! You went back to the house with him and waited for someone to find the body!"

"No!" Mama said. "I've told you the truth!"

"Your own son hated Bant Carr and knew Kenty Hooker was his real father! Now, to save Kenty, you've talked your own son into accepting the blame!"

"No!" Mama shook her head hopelessly. "No, it happened like I told you!"

"If the boy killed Bant Carr, then, why did you allow Kenty Hooker to be arrested?"

Mama looked at Kenty, but Kenty was staring at the polished table top.

"I was afraid they'd send Jeff away!" she said. "I couldn't stand that! He's a good boy and I couldn't stand that!"

"And why did you change your mind?" Ellis Type asked.

"I knew I'd have to tell the truth if things went bad for Kenty," Mama whispered. "I couldn't let him hang for something he didn't do."

Ellis Type turned to the judge. "Your Honor, I do not care to question this witness further. I rest my case."

Tumblin Green stood. "I will not cross-examine, Your Honor. Instead, I call Jeff Carr to the stand."

Kenty squeezed my hand and I left my chair, walked across the room on trembling legs, waited for Mama to leave the witness chair. She whispered my name and held out her hand as though to touch me. I shrank from her touch, waited until she had passed, and then went up the steps to the chair.

The clerk finished his singsong mumbling and I answered, "I do."

Tumblin Green hobbled to a place below and before me. He stood there, bent and shriveled, his head cocked to one side. I noticed his eyes were clear despite his age, and I saw pity in those eyes.

He asked me my name and my age.

"Jeff, your mother says you shot Bant Carr and killed him. Is that true?"

"It was an accident."

"How did it happen, Jeff?"

"I was running to Kenty's house to warn him Bant was coming, but Bant circled over to the corn and waited for me and tried to grab me. I started running and he was chasing me. I threw the gun down and it went off."

He didn't believe me. His face didn't believe me. Not a single face in that room believed me. I looked out over that room in search of just one believing face and in the deathly quiet the room began to spin in slow circles and all faces became one big unbelieving face. The room spun faster and the face with it, and then darkness came. When I could see again, I was lying on my back with my head resting on Tumblin Green's folded coat and the judge was sitting beside me with a handkerchief he had soaked in the water of his own jug. He bathed my face and asked me if I was feeling better.

"Yes, sir," I said, sitting up. "I don't know what happened."

"You fainted, son," Tumblin Green said. "The judge is going to have ice brought in in tubs at recess and he'll have fans running over the ice."

"Jeff," the judge said, "I can recess court right now and let you come back tomorrow. Would that be better for you?"

"No, sir, Your Honor. I want to tell it all right now and I'd rather do it before somebody tries to talk me out of it."

Tumblin Green helped me to the witness chair and the judge told a deputy to bring fresh water. He poured a glass for me and waited until I had finished. He offered to call just a short recess, but I told him I was feeling fine.

"Very well. Mister Green, you may proceed."

Tumblin Green's face was no longer an unbelieving face, if it ever had been. "If you get dizzy or feel faint, Jeff, you just tell me. Now, then. Did Bant Carr hit you or whip you very often?"

"He never used to hit me at all. Just these last few months, when he was drinking or in one of his brown moods. He used to be real good to me. We were friends. He didn't talk much, but I liked being with him."

"Did you love Bant Carr?"

"Yes, sir, I did. Lately, though, I guess I didn't. But I still did. I guess that doesn't make much sense."

"It makes a great deal of sense, son. Did you drop your gun or did you throw it down?"

"I threw it, Mister Green. Bant stepped out of the corn and I turned to run. The gun was slowing me down."

"Was that the four-ten shotgun Kenty Hooker gave you?"

"Yes, sir. Bant had busted the stock, but Festal Trails helped me carve a new one."

"Was it your idea to hide the gun under the house?"

"No, sir. Bant told Mama it wasn't my fault and that we should hide the gun."

"You know that was wrong, don't you?"

"Yes, sir, I do."

"Did Bant die instantly?"

"No, sir. The gun fired and I kept running until I figured out what might have happened. I realized Bant had yelled out, or groaned, or something, and then I heard him call me. He said he needed help and he was crawling. I told him to lie still."

"What else did he say, Jeff?"

"He said I didn't do it. He said it was an accident. I told him I'd go for help and he told me to stay with him. He said I should go live with my Uncle Lafe in Victoria."

"Did you go for help?"

"No, sir. I stayed with him until Mama came. That was right away. He told her he was going to die and that he was scared. But he said he was glad, too, because he'd been crazy and was getting crazier. He asked Mama to hold his hand tight and she did."

"John Parl testified that Kenty picked up a shotgun shell near the place where Bant died. Is that true?"

"No, sir. I was watching Kenty. He stooped to study sign, but he didn't pick anything up and put it in his pocket like John Parl said."

"Very well, Jeff. Just one more question. When Sheriff Johnson and Kenty Hooker started for Kenty's place, did you take Kenty's gun and run across country to beat them there?"

"Yes, sir, I did."

"Did you place Kenty's gun in its rack?"

"Yes, sir. I did it just in time and then I hid in Kenty's bedroom until the sheriff left."

"All right. You took the gun, ran across the field and woods, beat the sheriff and Kenty to Kenty's house and then you placed the gun in its accustomed place. Tell me, though, Jeff. Where was the gun when you left your house? Was it inside your house?"

"No, sir. Kenty had leaned it against a wall of the barn."

"When did he lean it against the wall of the barn?"

"Before Bant was dead. You see, after he and Bant had their fight, he came back to the house with me. He leaned the gun against the wall before we went on up to the house."

"Let's get everything clear, son. You had gone to get Kenty while Bant was out hoeing in the muddy field. Why did Kenty take his gun?"

"I truly don't know, sir, but I do know he didn't want to kill Bant. I think he loved Bant like a brother. He couldn't have meant to hurt anybody because he shot a rabbit before we got to Bant and he didn't reload the gun."

"What about the shell? Bant's gun is a twelve-gauge. Did he take the empty shell out of the gun?"

"No, sir. When I picked the gun up from where it was leaning against the barn, the first thing I did was take the shell out and throw it as far as I could behind the barn."

"What about the rabbit? Did you bring it out of the field?"

"Yes, sir. I threw it down by the woodpile. That's where Mister Parl saw it. I don't know why I hung on to it as long as I did."

"Thank you, Jeff. You are a brave young man. You tried to tell the truth earlier and we wouldn't let you. I think that goes a long way toward making up for the silence you maintained in the first place." Tumblin Green turned to the judge. "Your Honor, the defense has no further questions of this witness."

"Thank you, Mister Green. The prosecution may cross-examine."

Ellis Type approached the bench, turned to peer at me and then said, "Your Honor, I have no wish to cross-examine this boy."

"You may step down, Jeff," the judge said.

"Your Honor," Tumblin Green said, "does the prosecution agree to a recess?"

"It does, if it pleases the Court," Ellis Type said.

"In that case," Tumblin Green said, "I request a recess until two o'clock this afternoon. I wish to confer with my client. I also request that the Court order Deputy Sheriff Macklin to visit the Carr home to search for the four-ten shotgun that belonged to this boy."

"Both requests are granted," the judge said. "Deputy Macklin, you will go to the Carr home and look under the house for that gun. If you find it, bring it directly to the courtroom and hand it over to the bailiff. Court recessed until two o'clock this afternoon."

CHAPTER TWENTY-FOUR

Mama stood waiting for me, but I pretended not to notice. I pressed into the crowd in the aisle and pushed my way to the door, pushed past people in the hall and ran down the steps.

There stood Samal.

"You were wonderful, Jeff."

"Were you there?"

"I've been there every day. You just didn't see me."

"Where's Festal?"

"He's in the Navy now, can you believe it?"

It didn't seem like Festal somehow but there were other things on my mind.

"Why didn't I see you at recesses?"

"You were always with Pearl and I didn't want to bother you. I'm sorry I didn't."

We hurried down the street and around the corner. I had no money, but Samal had a dollar and we had hamburgers and cold drinks. She was beautiful, even with dark smudges under her eyes, and I knew I'd been wrong about all the faces in the courthouse being unbelieving faces. We sat there until almost two and then went back to the courtroom. Samal found seats for us midway back and Mama's eyes found us when she came in. She smiled and waved. She's not mad, I thought, and wondered if she'd go to jail for suppressing evidence. I voiced the thought to Samal and she was reassuring.

"Old Ellis Type and everybody else will be glad to see this thing ended," she said. "Kenty is going to go free and there'll be a lot of red faces around this town."

The room was cooler. Big fans blew over tubs of ice and it was almost comfortable. The judge entered and the bailiff mumbled his words about this honorable court now being in session Judge mumble mumble Fenton presiding.

The judge banged his gavel for order. "Is the defense ready to present its case?"

"If it please the court," Tumblin Green said, "the defense will present just one witness. Deputy Sheriff Macklin. After that, Your Honor, the defense will rest its case and rely on its closing argument to the jury. If it please the Court."

"Just one witness, Mister Green?"

"Yes, Your Honor."

"Have you conferred with your client, the accused? Does Kenty Hooker agree to your strategy?"

"He does, Your Honor."

"I will hear it from him. It is his life at stake. Mister Hooker, do you agree with your attorney for the calling of just one witness?"

Kenty stood. "I do, Your Honor."

"So be it," the judge said, frowning. "You may proceed, Mister Green."

Deputy Macklin was sworn and testified that he had found my four-ten shotgun under the house.

"Were you alone when you found it?"

"No, sir. Before I left the courtroom, Judge Fenton told me to take Deputy Hugh Edom and Deputy Bert Sands with me."

"Did you or any one of you examine the gun at that time?"

"No, sir. We did not. We brought it back to the courtroom and handed it over to the bailiff. He gave it an exhibit number and placed it on the table there."

"Has it been out of your sight since that time?"

"It has not. The bailiff was with me the entire time and so were the deputies I named. Judge Fenton came in about a quarter of two and sent for Mister Type and the court reporter. The judge then had me examine the gun in the presence of all. He asked me to see if there was a shell in the chamber."

"Was there a shell?"

"There was an empty shell in the chamber."

"Thank you, Deputy Macklin."

"Sir," the deputy said, "I'd like to make a statement."

"You may do so if it please the court."

"Are there any objections?" the judge asked.

Ellis Type stood. "I object, Your Honor."

"Objection overruled."

"Mister Green," Deputy Macklin said, "I saw Carr's body at the funeral home when he was brought in. I stayed and watched Mister Vinton undress him and I saw the wounds. I think you ought to have Mister Vinton describe the wounds, but I'd like to say this. Bant was hit at close range. The shots were in a tight pattern, but a few had spread. Mister Vinton probed for three and got them out. They were birdshot, Mister Green. They didn't come from buckshot in a twelve-gauge shell."

Tumblin Green actually recoiled. He was flabbergasted, mortified, embarrassed and rattled. "Deputy Macklin," he choked, "did Sheriff Johnson know about the birdshot?"

"I handed them over to Sheriff Johnson."

"Was the grand jury given the information?"

"I don't know. The sheriff should have turned the shot over to the district attorney for evidence before the grand jury."

"Did you appear before the grand jury?"

"I was not called, Mister Green. Sheriff Johnson was called."

"Do you realize the grand jury might not have been given that information?"

"I do, sir. That's why I made my mind up that I would manage to get it before this court one way or another before the trial ended."

"Thank you, Deputy Macklin," Tumblin Green said, and addressed the Court. "Your Honor, I realize I stated that I would call only one witness for the defense, and that I have done. If it please the Court, however, I should like to call Mr. Cletus Vinton, county coroner, to the stand."

Judge Fenton cleared his throat. "Are there objections?"

Ellis Type stood, face ashen. "No objections, Your Honor."

Cletus Vinton was the sad-faced leader of the sad-faced men who'd come for Bant's body.

Cletus Vinton raised his right hand and answered "I do" to the mumble mumble of the bailiff. Tumblin Green, all confidence gone, approached him and stood with head down for a full minute.

"Mister Vinton, you are coroner of the county?"

"I am."

"As such, did you perform an autopsy on the body of Bant Carr?"

"No, sir. I did not."

"You did not? Deputy Macklin said you.... Well, I beg your pardon. You did not perform an autopsy, but you did remove some shot. Is that correct?"

"That is correct."

"Well, Mister Vinton, is it not regular procedure to perform an autopsy on a body when there is suspicion of foul play?"

"In most counties, yes. In fact, it is a state law. But you know as well as I do, Mister Green, that autopsies are not done in this county unless ordered by the county attorney or the district attorney. There was no order. You must have known that, Mister Green. If you hadn't known it, you would have asked for the report the first jump out of the box."

"You are absolutely right, Mister Vinton, and it is a thing that will haunt me the rest of my life. It was a dereliction of duty and I confess it. But now, did you probe and remove three shot from Bant Carr's body?"

"I did, sir. One from the right forearm, one from the left, and one from the upper abdomen."

"They were birdshot not buckshot?"

"They were birdshot and they came from a four-ten shell."

"Is that necessarily true? Couldn't a twelve-gauge shell be loaded with birdshot?"

"Not likely in this case, Mister Green. A twelve-gauge that close would have caused a much more massive wound."

"But how do you know the shot was fired at close range?"

"Because of the tight pattern."

"Deputy Macklin testified the wound was in a tight pattern except for a few scattered shot. Can you describe that wound?"

"I would say the shot was fired within five feet of Bant Carr. Now, Bant Carr was five feet and eleven inches tall, but the shot didn't hit him straight on. It came from beneath and hit the upper abdomen and went ranging up into the chest area. The wound went upward, you see. It was consistent with the boy's description of the gun firing when it hit the ground."

"Thank you, Mister Vinton."

"Does the prosecution wish to cross-examine?" the judge asked.

An ashen-faced Ellis Type said, "The prosecution has no questions."

"In that case, you may step down, Mister Vinton. Now Mister Green, does the defense still not wish to call other witnesses?"

"The defense rests, Your Honor, and will make its case in closing statement."

"Court will recess until ten o'clock tomorrow morning. Closing arguments will begin at that time."

Samal and I went out well ahead of Mama and I asked if she wanted me to take her home.

"I have my own car now, Jeff. A Star. You should see it climb a hill. Festal and I paid cash."

"What do you think about Kenty's chances?"

"Oh, there's no way they can convict him now. He'll be free and I'm going to marry him."

"What if he decides to marry Mama?"

"You don't understand, Jeff. Kenty was in love with your mother once, before he went away, and that's when you were conceived. He loves her like a sister now. I just hope the jury understands that."

Mama came out and went to our car in silence. Just once she spoke on the way home.

"You were very brave, Jeff. I'm proud of you."

"Do you think they believed me?"

"They believed you. After the things Deputy Macklin and Mister Vinton said, they believe you."

"They believe I did it," I said. "They might not believe it was an accident."

There was no response.

Ellis Type was like a thing unclean, like an old turkey buzzard feeding on filth. He hopped around in front of the jury box, waved his arms, walked to and fro, shook his fists at the ceiling and made his voice throb and sob.

"I'm going to tell you a story, gentlemen of the jury," he said. "Oh, it's not a pretty story and you may feel sick at your stomach after I've told it! And it's not a new story, either! It's as old as sin and you've heard it time and time again and will hear it time and time again as time goes by. It's a human story and you may feel sorry for the characters. Just as I feel sorry for them. But you must never let pity stand in the way of justice!

"You represent justice, gentlemen of the jury. Right now the twelve of you represent the figure of Justice, a figure holding a pair of scales, and in those scales you must weigh the evidence that has been presented to you in this court.

"A man is on trial here. And on trial with him is a woman who has not been accused. Oh, you've heard her get up in that chair and tell you that her son, that child, killed the man who was her husband! You heard her make a feeble attempt to save her lover! You heard the boy, too! You heard him tell his story, a story carefully rehearsed, a story memorized word for word, like the "Gettysburg Address" or "The Boy Stood on the Burning Deck"!

"Don't believe a word of that foolishness about a four-ten shotgun. An empty shell in that gun could have been there for weeks. As for a wound that came from a low point and ranged upward, Bant Carr could have knocked Kenty Hooker to the ground and Kenty could have fired from his knees. No, gentlemen of the jury! A red herring has been introduced into this case. That young boy was coached to say what he said! There's no doubt he loved Kenty Hooker and despised Bant Carr! He doesn't realize how his mother played on his emotions and tender years to save the life of the man who shot down Bant Carr!"

Ellis Type lowered his voice and held out his arms as if asking for silence. "Kenty Hooker is a handsome man. He is a charming man. You've heard of his drinking and his fighting and his lovemaking and his fiddling. The man has no morals, no conscience. He left Pearl Carr pregnant and she had no choice but to marry Bant Carr. Before that child was born, even before Bant Carr married Pearl, Kenty Hooker abandoned his aging father and mother and Pearl to roam the world. He came back a rich man and began again where he left off."

Ellis Type told the whole thing as a story. He repeated rumors, said Mama begged Kenty not to go away, said Kenty left because he was afraid of Bant. He said Mama wrote to Kenty regularly and that Kenty wrote back. He told about Kenty coming home and how Bant started drinking. He told about the fights Bant and Kenty had and said Mama met Kenty in the woods. He said Bant had to let Kenty come into his own home, and he said it was plain to see I was Kenty's son.

"And then came the day!" Ellis Type said. "Bant Carr had given Kenty

Hooker a final warning! Stay away from my wife! He must have said. It was then Kenty knew the time had come. He begged Pearl Carr to leave her husband. He wanted her to go to the city so he could join her there, so he could see her when he wanted.

"I can imagine how it must have been that day. Kenty must have asked Bant to talk things over with him.

"Gentlemen of the jury! Bant Carr must have asked Kenty to walk into the field with him! Maybe he didn't want Pearl Carr and the boy to see what he sensed was going to happen! Because Kenty Hooker had a gun! Bant Carr must have known his last day on earth had come. And like the brave man he was, he met the challenge of destiny with head high!

"Maybe he asked Kenty not to kill him in his own yard in front of his own family! Or maybe Kenty said he wanted to shoot a rabbit, and asked Bant to go along and talk with him while he hunted. The fact remains, gentlemen of the jury, that Kenty Hooker shot Bant Carr down in cold blood."

Ellis Type was a spellbinder. He paced the floor and the jurors turned their heads from side to side as they followed his every movement. His voice was a flute and they swayed to his music. He talked and talked, talked on and on, formed a web of words to entrap Kenty Hooker. He told how Kenty could have slipped out of the house to hunt a lantern while the sheriff talked to Mama and me. He told how Kenty could have trotted home to place his gun in its resting place. Most of all, he talked about the love between Kenty and Mama, about Kenty being my father, about the fights Bant had with Kenty. Once he pointed me out and asked the jurors to look at me.

"That boy is the spitting image of his father!" he shouted. "And his father is Kenty Hooker!"

At last he finished.

Tumblin Green made no effort to defend Kenty in his summation.

"There is no need for me to defend Kenty Hooker," Tumblin Green said. "Kenty Hooker is not on trial here. Oh, he sits in judgment and his life is in your hands! But, in justice, he is not on trial here! Instead, gentlemen of the jury, you are sitting in judgment on a dead man. Bant Carr is on trial here!"

Tumblin Green turned his back to the jury and looked long at Kenty Hooker. Slowly he turned about, slowly turned until he faced the jurors. He raised his right arm and pointed his finger at the jurors, turned slowly to allow the finger to sweep the length of the jury box.

"There has been dereliction of duty here. Sheriff Johnson must be held accountable. The county attorney and the district attorney must be held accountable. The county coroner must be held accountable for failure to perform his legal duty. I must be held accountable because I assumed the fatal shot had been fired from a twelve-gauge shotgun.

"I care not who was the father of Jeff Carr. Perhaps all the rumors are false.

Perhaps Kenty Hooker and Pearl Carr loved apart and sinned not. Perhaps they loved in sin in their early years and now pay the wages for that sin. Be that as it may, for it is not ours to judge. Bant Carr was killed when young Jeff Carr, just a child, turned in fright and threw his gun down. He is innocent of any crime, of course, even though he had reason to protect himself.

"Kenty Hooker is not guilty of murder. Whatever guilt is his is known to himself and Pearl Carr. They have the rest of their lives to wonder if their sin caused Bant Carr to die.

"But Kenty Hooker did not kill Bant Carr, because Bant Carr died of a shot fired accidentally. You have no choice, gentlemen of the jury. Your duty is plain. I ask... no, I demand... a verdict of *not guilty!*"

CHAPTER TWENTY-FIVE

The judge called a recess until one o'clock. I sat with Tumblin Green at the defense table and he told me the judge was going to his office to prepare his charge to the jury. Sheriff Johnson took Kenty away and the jurors filed out of the room. Only a few people remained in their seats. I hadn't seen Mama leave, but she was not in the room.

Tumblin Green studied some notes.

"Will they send me away?" I asked.

He looked at me, seemed to be thinking of something else.

"You let me worry about that," he said absently.

"I didn't do it on purpose," I said.

"I know you didn't son. Don't worry for a minute."

After a bit he finished reading the paper he held in his hand. He patted my shoulder and stood, stuffed the papers in a leather case, and without a word walked across the room and through a doorway. I looked around the room, didn't recognize anyone, didn't know whether to remain in my seat or go outside.

A man left his seat in the rear of the room and walked down the aisle. He wore overall and a duck hunting shirt. His face was red and his neck long, his hair almost colorless and plastered close to his head. He pushed the gate open, hesitated, walked a couple of steps toward me. His eyes were narrow and dark and watery, and he licked his lips nervously.

"Did you really shoot your pa?" he asked.

He made me feel sick to my stomach.

I ducked my head and didn't answer. He stood still for a moment and then turned away. I listened to his footsteps and wished I had spat in his face.

One thirty-five.

I took a quick look over my shoulder. A few people were standing at the doorway, peering in. A man and woman were seated near the front. They were eating bologna and bread, their jaws moving, their eyes bright on me as their jaws moved, their cheeks puffed with food.

That did it. I couldn't stand any more. I ran from the room blindly, and people stepped aside to let me pass. I went down the stairs. Everything was out of focus. People were too big or too small, the hallway too long and the walls too high, the outer doorway downstairs was far away and never reached and soon reached and behind me. And I was outside, pushing and elbowing my way through a press of bodies and a press of sound that said, "That's him.... That's the boy that did it.... That's the boy that shot his Pa.... Did you see his back.... It was cut to ribbons where his pa beat him...."

I ran across the street, the wide street. In the morning the street had been filled with parked cars and wagons, the sidewalks thick with people, but now the walks were empty and only a few cars remained at the curb.

I walked the street, and the few men I met seemed ten feet high, the women ten feet broad. The sunshine was too bright. Show windows were glittery things filled with insane objects of queer shape and violent color. Across the street the courthouse was out-of-sight high, twisted and out of shape. A car rolled down the street and its motor was a whirring crazy thing of sound and I felt I should scream and run and tear my hair.

All at once and without warning things returned to normal. It was a startling thing and I was almost disappointed at the dullness of the change.

Without thinking, I had headed for the café. I opened the door and stepped inside. Mama was seated in a booth near the wall. Her back was to me and she didn't look around. She was drinking coffee.

I went outside, walked around the square, saw the same buildings and the same signs and the same dirty cracked sidewalks I'd seen a hundred times. There was still a crowd at the courthouse steps. I crossed the street and climbed the steps, opened the doorway, walked through the cool hallway and up the stairs and down the upstairs hallway and through the gateway to the chair at Tumblin Green's table.

Two o'clock.

I couldn't see the hands move. It was a big clock, just above the jury box. I stared at it until my eyes hurt. The big hand moved and I couldn't see it move, just knew it moved because the time changed from two to fifteen after. People drifted in, chatting and laughing in groups. Two-thirty and two-forty-five, and the room was filled.

The jurors filed in and took seats. The judge entered. Deputy Macklin brought Kenty to the seat beside me and stood just behind. Kenty tried to smile at me and his smile was almost a grimace. Tumblin Green came in and took his seat to my left.

The judge began to read. He seemed to be telling the jurors what they could and couldn't decide for themselves. His voice droned on and on and the time was four o'clock and five after, ten after, and the judge finished reading and the jurors filed out. The judge left the room. Tumblin Green stayed and the people stayed. I turned to look, couldn't see Mama at first, finally saw her seated next to the wall, midway between front and back of the room. She saw me looking and smiled fleetingly, hugged me with her eyes, and I turned away.

A rustle of sound in the room, a mumbling of voices. Kenty stirred in his seat beside me, leaned over.

"You've got to take care of your mother, Jeff," he said.

I was starving.

Five o'clock. People were leaving, at first singly and then in groups.

Six o'clock and the room was half-filled only.

Kenty leaned across me and spoke to Tumblin Green. "What does it mean if they're out a long time?"

"They're not in agreement," Tumblin Green said. "That could be good or bad."

Tumblin Green gathered up his papers, whispered something to Kenty and left the room. Sheriff Johnson came in from the hallway, sauntered down the aisle, king of all he surveyed. His hat sat far back on his head and he was picking his teeth, walking slowly, looking to right and left, nodding now and then at an acquaintance. He pushed open the little gate, stood for a moment looking around. His eyes met mine and I quailed, looked away. He walked over, stood for a moment looking down at Kenty, then walked across the room and sat down, legs straight out before him. He stared at Kenty, still picking his teeth, leaned back against the wall and stared at Kenty.

"You're holding it against your mother," Kenty said to me. "You think she threw you to the wolves."

"She said she couldn't stand for them to send me away," I said.

"So she couldn't."

"We should have told the truth to begin with, Kenty."

"I can see that now," he admitted. "I can see it and Pearl can see it! To tell the truth, I realized it long ago! But it had gone too far! I'm not even sure they'd have believed us if we'd told the truth."

"It was an accident," I said. "Bant jumped at me and chased me and I dropped the gun and it went off. We should have told them that."

Kenty sighed deeply.

"I can't understand why you won't believe me, Kenty."

"I believe you wouldn't shoot him except in self-defense," Kenty said. "I don't believe you really know what happened, Jeff. It's not that I don't believe you and it's not that Pearl doesn't believe you. It's just that it all happened so fast that we think you got rattled and, well, it happened. You don't know what happened any more than I know."

I leaned back and stared at the clock. It was quiet in the room. Kenty propped his head on his hands and closed his eyes.

Six o'clock.

The judge entered the room. He looked tired, moved slowly, took his seat and studied some papers. Sheriff Johnson went across to him and whispered something. The clerk appeared, joined the sheriff and the judge, listened, nodded his head.

"We'll know in a minute, Kenty," Tumblin Green said.

The door behind the jury box opened and the first of the jurors filed in.

He sidled his way between the railing and front seats, took his seat, and then the second juror walked through the doorway. He took the seat nearest the door, forcing four others to push their way past him. The other jurors took seats in the second row.

The judge banged his gavel.

Quiet was the room. And yet there was thunder in my head, filling my head. The clerk stood, mumbled something, and then the judge's lips moved and a juror stood and answered the judge and I couldn't hear. Kenty tensed beside me, dropped his hand to my knee, gripped my knee until I thought I would cry out. And then Kenty's full weight was on my knee and then gone, and he was standing.

"We have, Your Honor," the standing juror was saying.

"State your verdict."

"We find the defendant not guilty, Your Honor."

Kenty fell into the chair beside me, dropped his head and closed his eyes. He shuddered.

Sheriff Johnson walked across the room and only the sound of his footsteps broke the silence. Even the judge watched him. Eleven jurors stayed in their seats. The foreman still stood, stood motionless as though hypnotized.

The sheriff stood before Kenty Hooker.

"You had it all planned, Kenty," he said.

Kenty didn't seem to hear.

"Leave him alone," Tumblin Green said.

The sheriff looked at me and this time I couldn't look away. He chewed his lower lip and looked at me, narrowed his eyes and looked at me.

Tumblin Green stood and the silence was broken. An excited buzzing swelled in the room. The sheriff turned on his heel and walked away.

Judge Fenton banged his gavel.

"Gentlemen of the jury," he said, "I will tell you now that I was sorely tempted to throw this case out of my courtroom without letting it go to the jury. Only my faith in the intelligence and integrity of twelve men of this county persuaded me to continue to the end.

"I have reason to suspect deliberate obstruction of justice in the case of the State of Texas versus Kenty Hooker. For that reason I will ask the foreman of the grand jury, which is still sitting, to call before it the county attorney, the district attorney, the county coroner, and Sheriff Johnson.

"There are questions that must be answered. Did Sheriff Johnson know about the birdshot taken from Bant Carr? Deputy Sheriff Macklin says he turned the shot over to Sheriff Johnson. Did Sheriff Johnson reveal that information to the grand jury?

"Did the county attorney and district attorney know about the birdshot?

Was the coroner called before that jury? Also, why did he not step forward in this court at the outset?

"Did John Parl lie when he said he saw Kenty pick up a shotgun shell? What he said might not have been true, but he didn't lie about the dead rabbit. He might not know he was untruthful about the shell, but assumed he saw what he later expected he saw.

"Did Pearl Carr lie deliberately when she said her son killed Bant Carr? It seems to me she really thought Jeff Carr's story about the gun going off accidentally was both an effort to save Kenty Hooker and an act the child could not even acknowledge to his own mind.

"Now, Ellis Type said the boy had rehearsed his story about throwing the gun down. Any person in this courtroom who saw that boy's outrage and frustration... who saw his efforts to tell his story... who saw his obvious honesty... must believe him. A judge is only a frail human being, as jurors are frail human beings. In many cases, proof is not clear-cut. A judge and a juror must rely on their instinctive feel for the honesty and integrity of a witness, but that feel is based on past experience often not even remembered. I believe Jeff Carr.

"This Court rules that Bant Carr died of a gunshot fired by accidental discharge.

"Thank you, gentlemen of the jury. Your deliberations and verdict are examples of the highest ideals of justice. Court dismissed."

We walked up the aisle and people stood aside to let us pass. Unspeaking and unsmiling they stared at us, stood aside and stared as we passed. We walked slowly and the stillness of the room seemed to gather as a force behind us, seemed to push us along.

The hallway was dark. We walked through the gloom, Kenty's arm on my shoulder, down the stairs and into the light of the lower hall.

Mama and Samal waited by the door. Mama's eyes were red from weeping. Still, she smiled.... She held out her hand and Kenty took it in one of his, held it for a moment, pushed open the door and stood aside to let us pass.

"Let's go home," he said.

Kenty walked Samal to her car up the street and they stood talking while Mama and I walked down the street. I turned back just as we turned a corner and Kenty had Samal in his arms. He caught up with us before we reached our car at the lumberyard and drove us home. I sat in the back, leaned back and closed my eyes, too tired to think. The air was cool and I slept, but awakened when Kenty pulled into our yard. I lay still, feigning sleep.

"We were wrong," Kenty was saying. "If we had believed Jeff we would have told it in the beginning."

"I should have taken the blame," Mama said. "I pushed it off on him because I didn't believe they'd believe Jeff's story. I was afraid you'd hang, Kenty."

Kenty struck a match and lighted a cigarette.

"He's holding it against you, Pearl," he said. "I believe he thinks you weighed him with me in the balance of your love and that he lost."

"I didn't have a choice!" Mama cried. "Surely he can see that, Kenty! I didn't have a choice!"

"Don't you think I know that?" Kenty asked gently. "I was a gone goose, Pearl! They'd have hanged me! I think I'd have told the truth as we saw it if you hadn't!"

"You wouldn't have," Mama said.

"Don't think I wouldn't have. Only they wouldn't have believed me. It had to come from one of you."

Kenty smoked, his face dimly outlined in the dim glow of the cigarette ember each time he took a puff.

"Kenty," Mama said.

"Yes."

"Maybe we should have told it the way Jeff told it."

"They wouldn't have believed it."

"Do you believe it?"

"Well, Jeff doesn't lie. I think he believes it. I think Bant jumped him and that he doesn't know what happened after that. He really thinks he dropped the gun and that it went off just the way he said."

"I think that, too," Mama said. "But I know he didn't intend to kill Bant. Whatever he did was done in fright. So we could have told him we believed him! We could have listened! We could have told the sheriff it happened as Jeff said it happened!"

"It's too late now, Pearl."

"I know."

"We'll have to make it up to him."

Kenty threw his cigarette away, the fire forming an arc through the darkness.

"Jeff," he called.

I stirred.

"Jeff," he called again.

"We home?" I asked.

"Home again."

"I'll have to tend the stock," I said.

"You go on to bed," Kenty told me. "I'll turn the calves in with the cows and pitch down some hay. You can worry about the chores tomorrow."

"Jeff," Mama said, "go on in and I'll be in after a bit. I'll fix some supper."

"I'm not hungry."

"You'll have to eat something. I'd like to talk to you before you go to bed. I'd like to... explain some things to you."

I left them in the car and went into the house, found a lamp, lighted it. I found kindling, started a fire in the kitchen stove, and put water on to boil.

I walked through the living room, walked through darkness, stood at the door and peered out.

The moon was out, a half moon, and I saw at once that Mama and Kenty had left the car.

They were standing at the end of the porch. At first I thought Kenty was standing alone, and then I saw that Mama was in his arms, her head on his chest, her arms around him, long hair flowing loose in back.

I wondered, as I stood there watching, if my mother and father were standing before me in the moonlight, wondered who lay sleeping in Piper's Creek cemetery and why he slept there, wondered what kin was I to the man I'd called Bant.

I turned back into the house, groped my way to my own room, fumbled in my dresser drawer for a shirt and overalls, socks and underwear, shook a pillow from the pillowcase and stuffed the clothing in the case.

The front screen slammed shut as I slipped out the back. I ran across the yard, crawled through the fence, ran across the cotton for a hundred yards, stopped and looked back.

Mama was standing at the kitchen door.

"Jeff?"

She was a shadow framed in lamplight, a lamplit shadow, from that time on a shadow. I went to the corral fence and dug for the money jar Bant had mentioned, found it and sat it on a fence post for Mama to find. Goodbye, Mama.

I stumbled across the cottonfield, turned down a row and followed it to the road fence, crawled through and walked fast away. Once I turned for a last look at home, felt my heart ache at sight of the lonely far-distant pinpoint of yellow window light, walked on a way and looked back over my shoulder to find the light gone, snuffed out, too dim and weak to penetrate the distance of darkness.

Nor did I think at that time of where I should go or what I should do, of where I should sleep, but walked away because I had to walk away, had no choice but to walk away. Time passed, time without measure, and I had no remembrance of place or knowledge of distance.

Something seen or something felt, or some remembrance of an odor or presence, brought me out of the daze into which I had fallen and told me where I was.

Piper's Creek cemetery was off to my right, down the little lane to my right, not far away.

I turned from the road into the lane and walked slowly, hesitantly, toward the cemetery.

The gate creaked open at my touch.

I groped my way among the stones, placed my hands on cool marble, brushed against a rosebush and felt the sting of thorns, sniffed dimly the fragrance of roses, found Bant's grave and fell full length upon it, opened the floodgate of my heart and cried out the bitterness and lostness. How long I lay there I do not know. When at last I stopped crying there was no pain in my heart. An ache remained, but I felt a closeness to Bant I had not felt for a long while.

Darkness was thinning when I stood and took up my bundle. I stood at Bant's grave and said a silent prayer, turned away, paused at a rosebush and plucked a rose, saw not the color but knew it was red. I remembered then the red cap Bant had given me, the cap I had thrown away. I placed the rose in my pocket, left the cemetery, and let the gate squeak closed behind me. For one last moment I stood there. It seemed to me I could hear the song of a mockingbird, knew I heard it not, listened and marveled that I could hear plain a sound I was yet to hear.

EPILOGUE

Today I saw Kenty Hooker. His hair was as black and his eyes as bright as when first I saw him long ago. He took me to my mother's grave at Piper's Creek and there I saw Bant's grave the second time.

BANTRIM WESLEY CARR
Born June 2, 1894
Died August 3, 1930

My mother lies beside Bant and there is no room for me. Nor would I want to sleep where now they rest. Mama's tombstone is new, fashioned of marble. But Bant's stone is small and made of granite. It is crudely chiseled, rain-washed and weather-worn. Kenty had wanted a finer one and I knew he would have paid for it, but Mama would not agree.

The cemetery was old when Kenty and Bant were boys. Some of the gravestones have fallen and some are chipped beyond repair. Some of the graves are sunken. It is a still place and there are lilacs and roses and oak trees. I am one year past thirty and never thought to see the place again, never thought I'd ever again see Kenty or Samal, or the valley I once called home.

Kenty had known my troop ship landed in San Francisco and had tried to reach me there, but was too late. His telegram reached me in St. Louis five days later and I had driven night and day, two nights and days, to reach Fort Davis. The town was deserted at dawn, but the café where Mama had taken her coffee during the trial was just opening its doors. It was across the street from the courthouse and I could see the old stone building from my table through a fly-specked window. I imagined I could still smell the mouldering walls and tobacco juice. I went to the hotel after I had eaten, and slept until noon before driving out to the home place.

I found the house was a shell, the yard weed-filled, the barns and corrals gone. The old elm and oak still stood in the yard, but were not half so big as I had remembered. I went into the house and walked on floors thick with dust. The wallpaper was stained and torn. I stood by the massive fireplace and stared at ashes, remembered the glow and warmth of fires long dead. It was quiet in the house, too quiet, and I walked out across the valley floor. The trees by the spring stream, far distant, were lush and green and the distant mountains still beckoned.

Kenty was at the house when I returned.

"Jeff," he took my hand in both of his and searched my eyes. "You made a big man, a handsome man. I'm sorry you couldn't come in time."

"Your telegram said she died easy."

"Just went to sleep. Samal was sitting with her and holding her hand. She missed you, Jeff. We all did. She treasured your letters and kept them all. And the pictures especially. It wasn't the same as seeing you."

"I wanted to come back, Kenty, but I couldn't. I was wrong and I realized that way out in the Pacific. I don't know how to thank you and Sam for taking her into your home."

"She was special. To me and to Samal. Don't be taken with guilt, son. You were right to leave. Your life wouldn't have been much around here. There's talk even now, after all these years. You could live with it now, but you couldn't have stood it then."

"I'd like to see her grave."

We drove in Kenty's car to the cemetery and I asked him to leave me there for an hour. He walked with me to the gate and stopped.

"The valley is yours, Jeff. Pearl willed it to you. I hope you'll come home. We can make things flourish, I promise. Something else, too. You'll get a son's share of all I have, and I'm not a poor man. That's the way Samal and I want it."

"I'll think about it, Kenty."

"Do that. One thing more. Why did you decide to go?"

"Bant told me to go to Uncle Lafe. Just before he died."

"Yes... but why did you decide to leave when you did?"

"Well, we were on the way home from court and it was dark. You and Mama thought I was asleep in the back seat, but I wasn't I heard what was said. When we got home I just went inside and out the back door."

"We figured that was it."

"I walked that first night. I stopped at the cemetery and told Bant good-bye. I walked a good part of the next day, too, but a man gave me a ride to San Antonio. I was tired and hungry and a policeman found me and fed me. He took me to the bus station and bought my ticket to Victoria."

"Lafe was good to you."

"He treated me like a son. Sent me through the rest of high school and then through college."

Kenty walked back to his car and I called to him. "Do you and Sam have children?"

"Three. One girl and two boys."

"Do they look like you?"

"Spitting images. Of you and of me."

He drove away and I stood outside the sagging gate. The roses were in bloom, deep red, and I cut one for Mama, one for Bant. Then, with my hand

1-933586-01-x **Benjamin Appel** Brain Guy / Plunder $19.95

1-933586-26-5 **Benjamin Appel** Sweet Money Girl / Life and Death of a Tough Guy $21.95

1-933586-03-6 **Malcolm Braly** Shake Him Till He Rattles / It's Cold Out There $19.95

1-933586-10-9 **Gil Brewer** Wild to Possess / A Taste for Sin $19.95

1-933586-20-6 **Gil Brewer** A Devil for O'Shaugnessy / The Three-Way Split $14.95

1-933586-24-9 **W. R. Burnett** It's Always Four O'Clock / Iron Man $19.95

1-933586-31-1 **Catherine Butzen** Thief of Midnight $15.95

1-933586-38-9 **James Hadley Chase** Come Easy–Go Easy / In a Vain Shadow $19.95

1-933586-30-3 **Jada M. Davis** One for Hell $19.95

1-933586-43-5 **Bruce Elliot** One is a Lonely Number / **Elliott Chaze** Black Wings Has My Angel $19.95

1-933586-34-6 **Don Elliott** Gang Girl / Sex Bum $19.95

1-933586-46-5 **Gene Feldman & Max Gartenberg** (eds) The Beat Generation & the Angry Young Men $19.95

1-933586-12-5 **A. S. Fleischman** Look Behind You Lady / The Venetian Blonde $19.95

1-933568-28-1 **A. S. Fleischman** Danger in Paradise / Malay Woman $19.95

1-933586-40-0 **A. S. Fleischman** The Sun Worshippers / Yellowleg $19.95

1-933586-50-2 **Arnold Hano** 3 Steps to Hell $23.95

1-933586-35-4 **Orrie Hitt** The Cheaters / Dial "M" for Man $19.95

0-9667848-7-1 **Elisabeth Sanxay Holding** Lady Killer / Miasma $19.95

0-9667848-9-8 **Elisabeth Sanxay Holding** The Death Wish / Net of Cobwebs $19.95

0-9749438-5-1 **Elisabeth Sanxay Holding** Strange Crime in Bermuda / Too Many Bottles $19.95

1-933586-16-8 **Elisabeth Sanxay Holding** The Old Battle Ax / Dark Power $19.95

1-933586-41-0 **Elisabeth Sanxay Holding** The Unfinished Crime/The Girl Who Had to Die $19.95

1-933586-17-6 **Russell James** Underground / Collected Stories $14.95

0-9749438-8-6 **Day Keene** Framed in Guilt / My Flesh is Sweet $19.95

1-933586-33-8 **Day Keene** Dead Dolls Don't Talk / Hunt the Killer / Too Hot to Hold $23.95

1-933586-21-4 **Mercedes Lambert** Dogtown / Soultown $14.95

1-933586-44-1 **Dan J. Marlowe** The Name of the Game is Death / One Endless Hour $19.95

1-933586-14-1 **Dan Marlowe/Fletcher Flora/Charles Runyon** Trio of Gold Medals $15.95

1-933586-02-8 **Stephen Marlowe** Violence is My Business / Turn Left for Murder $19.95

1-933586-07-9 **Ed by McCarthy & Gorman** Invasion of the Body Snatchers: A Tribute $19.95

1-933586-09-5 **Margaret Millar** An Air That Kills / Do Evil in Return $19.95

1-933586-23-0 **Wade Miller** The Killer / Devil on Two Sticks $19.95

1-933586-51-6 **Wade Miller** Kitten With a Whip / Kiss Her Goodbye $19.95

1-933586-27-3 **E. Phillips Oppenheim** The Amazing Judgment / Mr. Laxworthy's Adventures $19.95

0-9749438-0-0 **E. Phillips Oppenheim** Secrets & Sovereigns: Uncollected Stories $19.95

0-9749438-6-x **Vin Packer** The Damnation of Adam Blessing / Alone at Night $19.95

0-9749438-3-5 **Vin Packer** Something in the Shadows / Intimate Victims $19.95

1-933586-05-2 **Vin Packer** Whisper His Sin / The Evil Friendship $19.95

1-933586-18-4 **Richard Powell** A Shot in the Dark / Shell Game $14.95

1-933586-19-2 **Bill Pronzini** Snowbound / Games $14.95

0-9667848-8-x **Peter Rabe** The Box / Journey Into Terror $21.95

0-9749438-4-3 **Peter Rabe** Murder Me for Nickels / Benny Muscles In $19.95

1-933586-00-1 **Peter Rabe** Blood on the Desert / A House in Naples $19.95

1-933586-11-7 **Peter Rabe** My Lovely Executioner / Agreement to Kill $19.95

1-933586-22-2 **Peter Rabe** Anatomy of a Killer / A Shroud for Jesso $14.95

1-933586-32-x **Peter Rabe** The Silent Wall / The Return of Marvin Palaver $19.95

1-933586-42-7 **Peter Rabe** Kill the Boss Good-by / Mission for Vengeance $19.95

1-933586-61-3 **Brian Ritt** Paperback Confidential: Crime Writers $19.95

0-9749438-2-7 **Douglas Sanderson** Pure Sweet Hell / Catch a Fallen Starlet $19.95

1-933586-06-0 **Douglas Sanderson** The Deadly Dames / A Dum-Dum for the President $19.95

1-933586-29-X **Charlie Stella** Johnny Porno $15.95

1-933586-39-7 **Charlie Stella** Rough Riders $15.95

1-933586-08-7 **Harry Whittington** A Night for Screaming / Any Woman He Wanted $19.95

1-933586-25-7 **Harry Whittington** To Find Cora / Like Mink Like Murder / Body and Passion $23.95

1-933586-36-2 **Harry Whittington** Rapture Alley / Winter Girl / Strictly for the Boys $23.95

Stark House Press
1315 H Street, Eureka, CA 95501
707-498-3135
www.StarkHousePress.com

on the gate latch, I heard the song of a mockingbird. It sang and flew away, but the fading trills carried me back to a long-gone time when I walked a road at midnight to this place. I had heard a mockingbird then, though no bird had sung. Even then, as I heard bird-song in my mind, I had known it was but an echo of song that had yet to sound.

THE END